The Witch of Wootton Marsh

By
Don Falgrim

The Witch of Wootton Marsh
First Edition
Published by DreamStar Books, December 2007
ISBN: 978-1-904166-30-6

Drovers House
Craven Arms
Shropshire
SY7 9BZ
Tel: 0870 777 3339
e-mail: dreamstar@jakarna.co.uk

Set in 'Garamond'

The events and opinions in this book are fictional and originate from the author.

Printed and bound in Great Britain by RPM Reprographics Ltd

About the Author

Born in Norfolk and educated at King Edward VII Grammar School, Don has settled in a small Hampshire village after a varied career as a soldier, salesman, musician and writer. He has written extensively for radio and TV in Australia, having had two, 3-act stage plays produced in Perth, Australia. He also has experience as a copywriter. He has written over 100 novels, principally thrillers and has also written several novels about aerial combat over French skies during the Great War. He is currently completing a historical novel about the Third Reich.

Dedication

To Richard Rowe,
A good friend and critic

1.

March 1st 1983.
Lewin's Farm, Babingley Marsh,
near King's Lynn, Norfolk.

Jim Lewin stomped into the kitchen, his oilskins dripping rainwater, gleaming in the morning light.

"Take them off Jim, for God's Sake, and get those wellies off. I don't want to have to clean this floor again, I only did it yesterday."

Betty left the frying pan sizzling on the Aga, the ripe smell of bacon permeating the whole kitchen, to assist her husband off with the yellow slicker.

"Bastard thing's done it again."

"You mean Freda?"

"Every bloody time on the Hump, it seems."

"You haven't had her serviced for yonks, saving money you said," Betty hung the dripping oilskins on a peg in the old conservatory as Jim eased off his boots with the remover, shaped like a beetle, concreted into the doorstep.

"Don't rub it in, love, it's wet, cold and I'm hungry."

"God, the bacon!" Betty rushed back into the huge kitchen to pull the pan from the stove, "Blast, look at that, burnt to a frazzle. Why don't we flog that wretched thing, buy a new one, we can afford it."

She up-ended the pan into the swillbin, lay fresh rashers in the pan.

"There's nothing wrong with Freda. She goes like a good-un. I don't know what it is. Every time I take her over the Hump it seems to happen."

Betty jiggled the frying pan, the bacon sizzled fiercely, looked at her husband pityingly, "Sounds like witchcraft love."

Jim sat down gingerly, scowling with pain, "It's true," he protested, "Started in the shed first time. I take it along the track to start on the field and then she just dies on me just as I cross the Hump."

Betty deftly threw the crisp rashers onto a dinner plate, broke two eggs into the pan, using her left hand only. "You say that every time I say Freda needs a good servicing, get Wally out to look at it. Your back's bad, have a rest, Bobby can do Slades for you. He's got nothing better to do, let him earn his keep."

"Wally'll love coming out in this." Jim waved his hand to indicate the rain pouring in slanting rods past the windows.

Betty sliced the eggs onto the plate, threw a slice of bread into the pan, dunked it in the bacon fat until it was golden brown took it over to her husband, "You want a Neurofen?"

He nodded, "Betty it hurts like buggery!"

"Lifting those bales yesterday. You aren't a young bloke any longer you know."

"Yeah, he is getting geriatric Mumsy."

Robert Lewin entered the kitchen from the old servant's stairs.

"Shut the door," cried Betty, "If you're as fit as your Dad when you get to his age you can think yourself lucky."

Robert mimed playing a violin, poured himself a mug of tea from the outsize teapot. "What's for breakfast? What's up Pop? Old age galloping on." Robert sat down at the long refectory table, next to his Father.

"Freda's packed up again," Betty selected four more rashers of bacon and tossed them into the pan.

"Don't tell me," Robert held up a hand, "I've been shanghaied again, plough Slade while he sits in the lounge studying form."

"Bout time you earned your keep young feller-me-lad," reproved Betty, "Instead of swanning around strumming that guitar polluting the countryside in that banger!"

Robert sang, "Tell me the old old story, you're speaking disrespectfully about the woman I love Mumsy."

"You can make love to Freda for a change today," Betty was tart, she jiggled the pan.

"Jesus, look at the weather, why can't we leave it until tomorrow? One day isn't going to make any difference, I'll get soaked and cold."

"Because it won't get done, you'll think of another excuse in the morning. Your Father's back's playing up, now do your duty and help out."

"I was going to Norwich this morning."

"Come on son, it won't take long, four hours should see you through."

Jim's face creased with pain as he forked bacon and egg. "That'll make it midday, I promised to meet Tracy in Norwich for lunch, I'd never make it."

"Phone her, tell her she can come here instead."

Betty did another left hand job on two eggs.

"If Freda's packed up it'll take Wally two hours to fix it, it'll be four o'clock before I'm through. I can't expect Tracy to sit around here all that time, listening to Dad tell her all about his war experiences, bore her out of her skull."

"Put her off, if she's anything like, she'll understand." Betty fried another slice of bread.

"Tracy doesn't understand farms, she's been genteelly brought up, nurtured in a cultivated environment of stocks, shares and money."

"If she marries you she'll soon have to learn, won't she?"

Betty handed him the plate, "Eat that, I'll phone Wally." She went to the medicine cabinet, took two tablets from a packet, "Get those down you love, ease it a bit!"

"Better tell Wally to bring the tow truck," Jim swallowed the pills and washed them down with tea.

"Oh no, not the Hump again?" Robert mopped his egg with dry bread.

"Fraid so son," Jim massaged his lumber region, "Kevin reckons that's an old tumulus, bung full of mystic powers."

"He's worse than a bloody witchdoctor, I bet he has chicken bones hanging behind his bed."

Ellen Lewin was titian-haired, lithe, full breasted, and resembled her Father, bare footed and clad in just a towelling robe.

"How'd you know that?" Robert placed two rounds in the toaster, "You been there?"

"I wouldn't have anything to do with that shit, he's creepy. Hair like black treacle, a little mouth and a face full of acne scars. He drinks mint-tea, no dairy products, always whingeing about pollution and telling us all about ley-lines, at long, boring length."

Ellen poured herself some tea, then watered it down under the tap. "What's a… one of those you said just now?"

Jim arose careful to keep his back straight. "An ancient burial ground, usually located where ley-lines cross."

Ellen sat down at the table as Jim eased himself into the armchair adjacent to the Aga, "You have been with him."

Robert was triumphant. "Do me a favour, brother."

"How'd you know about ley-lines then?"

"I'm not your Tracy Middleton, beautiful and brainless, I can read."

"She's highly intelligent."

"She's fooled me, the only intellect she possesses is between her legs." Ellen sipped her tea.

Betty returned from the phone in time to hear this, "That's enough of that talk young lady, I thought University education was supposed to elevate your mind?"

"The only elevation Uni teaches you is how to keep your legs crossed against all the randy males Mumsy. Education is confined to a study of the Karma Sutra."

"God help us!" Betty lifted the bread from the toaster, tossed it front of Robert, "Marmalade's in there!" She indicated the cupboard and inserted two more slices into the toaster.

"What did Wally say?"

Jim lay back, closed his eyes. "Be down in half an hour, get togged up Bobby, he'll need you to steer Freda, you can give him a hand."

"Bout time the lazy bastard did something, apart from shagging that moon-faced cow Tracy. She pregnant yet? Don't suppose she's heard of the Pill… too plebian for her."

"Ellen, I won't have that kind of talk in my house, do you hear me?"

Betty waited for the toast to pop up, the smell of toast and fried bacon permeated the kitchen.

"You're a dinosaur, Mumsy, this is the end of the twentieth century."

"What's all this about these ley-lines got to do with the Hump?"

Ellen spelled it out for Jim, "Roughly speaking, it is reckoned they're like a printed circuit that covers the entire planet, act like a conductor for energy flowing all over the earth."

"Take no notice of that crap, Dad. Kev's a weirdo, like that Fanny Legge. They'd get on well together."

"There's nothing wrong with Fanny, just a little odd that's all, all those cats she keeps, looking for herbs all the time."

Betty began clearing the soiled crocks from the table, then loaded the dishwasher, "She's made some pretty good predictions in the past."

"Do us a favour Mumsy, she's as bent as a corkscrew, a fruit and nut case."

"What kind of power goes along these lines?" Jim sat still trying not to move unnecessarily.

"Nobody has been able to prove anything." Ellen put more bread in the toaster.

"It's all a load of crap, that's why," Robert chomped away at his toast.

"Kevin reckons that ley-lines cross over the Hump. This force disrupts anything alien, like electrical discharges that interferes with the flow of this energy, like the body rejecting transplants."

"For someone who thinks Kev Wilson is a nutter along with Miss Legge, you've certainly swallowed a lot of his brand of crap, "said Robert, "Spent a lot of time with him, have you?"

"No, I haven't, you asshole. Just because you're too thick to embrace new ideas." Ellen removed the toasted bread.

"Never mind arguing, get your Dad's oilskins on ready for Wally when he gets here," rasped Betty. "We don't want any more fairy tales."

"Why is it Freda always breaks down when you drive her over the Hump then?" demanded Ellen. "Happened last time, a couple of months back and then just before Christmas, and if I recall correctly Wally couldn't find anything wrong with Freda, she started again as soon as he'd towed it off the Hump."

"How come his truck didn't break down then?" Robert pulled on his Father's oilskin trousers.

"He didn't drive onto the Hump, you had to get a longer tow rope," Ellen crunched dry toast.

"Sounds a little weird to me love," said Jim, "It is true though, Wally couldn't find anything wrong with Freda on both those occasions."

"Dad, the only reason that crate breaks down is because you don't have it serviced properly." Robert pulled on his Wellingtons.

"We don't have trouble starting Freda, she's as good as gold, all that rubbish about servicing just to milk more cash out of us." Jim handed Betty his mug and nodded towards the teapot.

"Well, we'll soon find out won't we?" Ellen pointed out the window, "Wally's just arrived and he doesn't look too happy."

"Who'd be happy in this bloody weather? It's pissing down."

"Don't use that kind of language in my house young man," rapped Betty, pouring more tea for Jim.

"Ploughing Slade in this weather, stupid. Should have been done last autumn like all the other fields. It'll be waterlogged with all this rain."

There was an imperative hammering at the door to the house inside the conservatory. Wally Thompson was lean, balding, swarthy, tall. His close-set eyes were black, his cheeks hollow and he always looked in need of a shave. Ellen swore he hadn't washed his engineer's overalls in all the time he'd been handling the Lewin's farm machinery. Apart from the fact he rolled his own, which added pungency to a compote of oil, diesel, grease and dirt, he suffered from body odour and chronic halitosis.

Betty and Jim had long learned to tolerate the miasma, which accompanied Wally. He was a genius with machinery and his charges were reasonable. Robert could endure it for a reasonable period. Ellen's oral toleration threshold was fragile so she kept her distance. Like most halitosis sufferers Wally was blithely unaware of his problem, always insisted on speaking with his face thrust into that of his correspondent.

"Freda again, is it?"

Wally advanced into the kitchen and went over to the teapot, he poured himself a mug full. There were oily finger marks on the mug, "Where is she?"

"The Hump," offered Robert, bravely unflinching when Wally gave a guffaw at close range.

"Good job I brought the long tow-rope!"

****

2.

Monday, March 1st, 1983.
Lewin's Farm, Babingley
Marsh, near King's Lynn.

"Why do you say that?" Jim tried to ease himself from the arm chair, wincing with pain.

"Fanny Legge was gathering those weeds along the lane yesterday on the marsh, said the spirits were strong. Said that you had a bad back."

Wally brought out the pouch containing the makings, and began rolling a cylinder, he licked the paper with his green tongue.

"You're kidding us, of course?" Robert's oilskins crinkled as he moved.

Wally scratched a match on the leg of his overall, lit the evil spindle, puffed out a cloud of choking smoke, "No, why? Have you got a bad back, Jimbo?"

"Lifting bales yesterday."

"She reckons she could cure it for you if you let her," Wally sucked smoke in, his cheeks denting like a crushed can of Coke.

"Incanting over the chicken bones?" jeered Robert, grinning, wafting away the poison cloud enveloping Wally.

"Seen Bill Watson lately?" Wally quaffed tea from the oil stained mug.

"Not since Christmas, the party at the village hall, remember? Betty tried to ignore the noxious cloud that rolled round the kitchen. He'd just been to the chiropractor for his slipped disk, didn't look at all well"

"Don't tell us, Fanny gave him the treatment and he's cured?"scoffed Ellen.

Wally nodded, exhaling twin columns of di-phosgene in dragon tails.

"Hasn't had any pain since she laid hands on him last month. Bill reckons it's a miracle. I'd give it a whirl, Jimbo, wotcha got to lose?"

"You're making this up, of course?"

"Cross my heart, Betty."

Wally was serious, "Ring Bill up, ask him."

"Fluke" declared Robert," Bill was probably getting over it anyway."

"He was on the verge of having surgery, BUPA."

Wally drained the mug, then refilled it. Betty hastily added milk from the bottle before Wally touched it.

"Cancelled the appointment."

"Witchcraft comes to Babingley" Robert headlined, "Our reporter told us that Funny Fanny is now raising the dead in this remote Norfolk village. Bring your granny's corpse to Babingley for a full resuscitation."

Wally shrugged, blew ash from the end of his cigarette without removing it from his mouth. "If I had your problem Jimbo, I'd sooner go to Fanny Legge than I would to old Lassiter, I tell you. He'd tell you to take an aspirin and a hot bath and rest up for a week."

"I find it hard to believe," Betty looked longingly at the canister of air freshener on the shelf over the sink, "Bill's suffered from that disk for years."

"Come on Wally, let's get on with it. I've got to do Slade today, instead of snogging with my girlfriend. I'll be sexually frustrated," said Robert, "I don't suppose Fanny Legge could cure that."

Wally grinned, showing his yellow fangs, advanced pyorhea "Willy's just bought the old Priory, going to have it done up, going to cost half a mil. I'd marry her son. You'll be laughing all the way to the bank. He's a multi-millionaire. That should cure your problems."

"How about that, Bobby? You can have it off in the Bahamas if you play your cards right, won't matter if she's pregnant, just like 'Room at the Top,'" Ellen tried to avoid the gas clouds threatening to engulf her, "I've got to wash my hair. See you again, Wally." She exited up the stairs.

"Sorry to bring you out in this weather Wally," said Jim grimacing.

"It'll start as soon as we move her off the Hump, Jimbo"

"The spirits are strong today," intoned Robert" Let's get with it. I'll have to get Tracy pregnant now in view of the news. I'd buy you a brand new tractor Dad, repair the cowshed, and the fencing."

"Just get on with it, never mind the dreams of love, "warned Betty, "I don't suppose Willy Middleton wants you to marry Tracy, pregnant or otherwise. You're a commoner, no pedigree."

"Do the Middleton stock a world of good, inject some backbone into centuries of in-breeding. Come on Wally, let's go!"

Wally nipped out the cigarette, stuck it behind his ear, 'Think about Fanny havin' a gander at your back, Jimbo. Ring Bill up ask him!"

Jim finished his breakfast, eased his back against the chair, "Have to get Lassiter in, love. I'll be stuck here all week if I don't."

"Perhaps we should do as Wally said, let Funny Fanny have a look? She can't do any harm just incanting over you." Betty began clearing away the debris from the table.

"Oh come on love, you don't believe all that rubbish do you? Faith healing, laying-on of hands?"

"We haven't seen Billy down the Club for the past few weeks have we? Give him a bell, see what he says?"

Betty loaded the powder into the dishwasher, "He's not one to mince words, he'll soon tell you whether Wally's romancing or not."

"You're kidding of course? Billy would just give a belly laugh, tell you about chicken bones or Taro cards."

Betty shut the door to the washer and turned it on. The machine began to pump like an asthmatic donkey. "Ring him," she urged, "Can't do any harm."

"Give us the phone then. He's gonna believe I've flipped. He's always rubbishing Fanny and her cats, herb gathering, thinks she's a bloody witch."

Betty handed him the mobile and read out the number from a phone address book.

"He's gonna love me this time of the morning," groused Jim as he stabbed at numbers.

Betty began clearing the table as Ellen came down the stairs a towel around her head, "Where's the dryer? I suppose that half-arsed bastard's buggered it up again?" She began searching for the drier on the shelving.

"You're coming this liberal stuff too much, my girl. God alone knows what goes on up there in Nottingham, apart from being a seat of learning, Your language is atrocious."

"You're old fashioned Mumsy, language is language if the meaning is clear."

"I prefer to remain stuffy, if that's the case young woman, so less of the gutter stuff, understand?"

"Yes, ma'am!" Ellen gave an American salute, "Now where has he put that bloody drier? Always washing his golden locks, thinks Tracy likes him smelling of underarm and shampoo, gets her all fruity"

"Ellen!" snapped Betty.

"OK, OK, sorry, offending the old working class mores, am I?"

She rummaged amongst the books and piles of newspapers, "Wait til we're invited to the Priory for the wedding, old Middleton looking like an oyster with sulphuric acid poured all over him, sourpuss giving Bobby the evil eye over Tracy's swelling stomach, praying that the local press aren't around to speculate on when the bastard's likely to be dropped. That should be well worth recording on celluloid, and have you seen Mrs? .. Christ! Talk about Beelzeebub... she's like Tutenkhamun's wife, just exhumed her from a casket, tarted up like a corpse in one of those American funeral parlours. She smells of formaldehyde."

"That you, Billy? Sorry to get you out of kip, who? Jim Lewin, Who'd you think it was, The Lottery manager. How're you doing? How's the old disc these days?"

Ellen stopped rummaging to listen, "He phoning Billy Watson?"she mimed. Betty nodded,finger to her lips.

"You're joking?" Jim looked over at Betty, and pointed at the phone with his free forefinger. "No kidding? Yeah, Ive got back trouble, can't move mate, lifting bales yesterday, think I've done it in. You did? When? get away? she came to you? charged you a bomb, of course, nothing? Wouldn't take any money, donation to the cat refuge, is that all? sounds too good to be true. I guess you're right, yeah, I will, if she was able to do that for you, can't afford not to, can I? You're not kidding me are you? OK, sorry but slipped disks aren't easily cured and just Funny Fanny giving you the treatment seems a bit like a miracle, yeah, whenever you're in the Club next I'll stand you one. Thanks mate, be seeing you."

Jim telescoped the aerial and handed it back to Betty

"Well?"

Betty put the phone on the mantelpiece, "What did he say?

"Fanny did what Wally said, cured him, hasn't had any pain, trouble since she did it last month."

Jim plainly found it hard to believe. Betty began shrugging into her plastic raincoat.

"What're you doing, love?" Jim looked alarmed.

"I'm going to get Funny Fanny over here," she announced.

****

3.

Monday,1st March,1983.
Fanny Legge's Cottage
North Wootton Marsh,
King's Lynn, Norfolk.

Myfanwy Legge, or Funny Fanny as everybody in Lynn knew her, lived in a cottage in North Wootton. It was isolated, virtually on the edge of the marsh. The thatched roof suffered from chronic allopoetia, the once white painted walls werepeeling and the woodwork around the windows were thirsty for paint. The last time anybody had seriously tended the garden had been twenty years. Weeds were prolific, a yard high. A flock of geese wandered aimlessly round the house, an ageing donkey grazed in the yard, chickens picked amongst the pile of animal dung. Interspersed were cats of every size, colour and shape. An old Dutch barn leaned dangerously at the foot of the garden, filled with what appeared to be bales of fresh hay.

Betty stopped the landrover at the crazily awry front gate and eyed the rain washed scene with trepidation. Was she making a complete fool of herself? The geese honked loudly and stretched their necks at her. A swarm of cats swept towards her, all meowing loudly, tails in the air. The old donkey began hee-hawing, the noise seeming to echo over the desolate landscape.

Betty descended from the Landrover, pulled her oilskin cap over her head and approached the gate. The geese came at her, necks taut, complaining. To the unitiated, their performance would be threatening. Betty ignored their pecking, stepped around the cats and walked to the front door. It opened when she was ten feet away.

Everybody considered Funny Fanny to be old. At least, that was the myth. Close-up, Betty saw a youngish face, high cheek-boned, narrow chin, wide-spaced eyes, obsidian, penetrating. A mane of black hair without a trace of greying parted in the centre, fell each side of her face. She was clad in a long tweed skirt, a black blouse, cardigan and a loose-knit woollen shawl around her shoulders.

"I've been expecting you." Fanny spoke with a faint accent, a kind of sing-song, musical.

"You have?" Betty stopped, taken aback, "But.. how did you know?"

Fanny smiled, showing a set of almost perfect teeth. "The airwaves. Come on in," She beckoned.

Betty didn't know what to expect inside the cottage. The cats followed her in, the geese seeing their warning ignored wandered off. The donkey ceased it's complaining as if aware that its owner was in charge.

The interior was warm, a log burner blazed at the far end of the large room. Rush carpets covered the floor, rough pine furniture filled every available space not occupied by sofas, settees and armchairs. Cats sat, slept, lay on every single article of furniture, giving her the evil eye. She estimated there must have been upwards of fifty cats in the room.

"Take your coat off, Mrs Lewin," invited Fanny. "Sit down! The cats will move."

Betty sniffed suspiciously, surely with all these cats, she thought.

"Cats are very conscious of dirt, Mrs Lewin. They like to be clean." It was as if Fanny had read her thoughts. The rumour went that Fanny was a mind reader. "Would you like tea? My crockery's clean, I assure you, no cockroaches, spiders or flies."

There was mockery in her black eyes, "The water's pure from my spring."

"Oh yes, thank you that would be very nice." Betty felt uneasy as she looked round the room as if expecting something unseen to jump out at her. The walls were covered with framed animal pictures, cats dogs, horses, donkeys, birds.

"Hello!" croaked a voice in her ear.

Betty jumped a foot in the air.

A huge parrot stood on the back of the armchair she had made for it. "Sit down! I don't bite!" invited the bird, nodding its head and lifting one claw to indicate the seat.

"You frightened Mrs Lewin, Oscar, that was naughty! Go and sit somewhere else!" The mockery was still in Fanny's voice, titillated by amusement.

The parrot ambled off the chair to sit on the windowsill. It was at that point Betty saw the Irish Wolfhound lying in front of the wood burner. The animal was huge covering the surface of the mat. It raised its massive head to examine her, stared at her for a full ten seconds, eyes yellow, unwinking.

"It's alright, Damien, Mrs Lewin is a friend" cooed Fanny, working a pump over the sink.

The dog lay down again, making satisfied gruntings.

Fanny placed a kettle on the woodburner. "Dark in here, isn't it?" The words echoed Betty's thoughts.

Fanny lit a paraffin burning lamp, pumped it vigorously. The lamp hissed and cast long shadows around the room, a warm glow permeating the space.

"God! What's that?" Betty nearly screamed with fright.

A massive spider crawled from under the dresser and ran across the floor to stand before Betty, palps waving, its bank of eyes glittering in the lamplight.

"That's Tweety, she's a Brazilian tarantula, quite old now, come to say hello, haven't you Tweety? Quite harmless unless you threatened her, aren't you darling?"

Fanny stretched her hand down. The spider ran onto her hand then ran up her arm and sat on her head like an obscene hat. Betty shuddered in horror as the creature seemed to be observing her with an objective stare.

"I have a horror of spiders" she stuttered, her legs like jelly.

"Many people feel like you. Arachnids have been around a long time, as long as people. They're very sensitive creatures, highly developed nervous systems. Tweety likes Beethoven, don't you darling?"

Fanny lifted her hand to her head. The Spider ran onto her hand, "You'd better go back to your bed, you're frightening our guest, there's a good girl!"

The spider ran over the sofa and vanished under the dresser.

"She won't come out again, she was just curious about you!"

Betty felt nauseous, quivering with fright .The thought of that thing crawling all over her made her feel ill.

"Sit down! Sit down woman!" intoned Oscar from the sill, "Don't get your bowels in an uproar!"

"That's very rude, Oscar!" admonished Fanny, "Say you're sorry!"

"Sorry lady" squawked the bird, dancing from one foot to the other.

The kettle was hissing, Fanny filled a teapot, covered it with a cat cosy, laid sparkling cups and saucers out on a glass covered tray, "You don't mind untreated milk Mrs Lewin? I have pasteurised if you wish?"

"I'm used to it from our cows" said Betty, still apprehensive about Tweety under that dresser. The size of it alone horrified her. She watched Fanny prepare the teacups with milk, noting the almost masculine hands, yet without any semblance of muscularity. The woman handed her a cup the milk added in just the precise quantity that Betty approved. There was something odd about Fanny Legge, Betty decided, super-human. She was reluctant to admit it to herself, but acknowledged that this woman had more than normal power. She felt Fanny's eyes on her as she accepted the cup and saucer. It seemed as if they were penetrating her brain, probing like a laser into her innermost thoughts. It wasn't an uncomfortable experience, but disturbing nonetheless.

"You want me to have a look at Mr Lewin's back."

It was a statement. The very baldness of the prediction was breathtaking.

"How did you know?"

Fanny smiled showing those near perfect teeth, "Nothing very mysterious about that Mrs Lewin. You've come all this way on a very miserable day just to say hello? Of course you haven't. You want something from me. Don't worry about it," she added hastily as Betty was about to protest. "I don't mind, I am used to people being wary of what they see as my eccentricity"

Betty decided she wasn't dealing with an uneducated woman possessing extraordinary gifts. Fanny was far too eloquent and, well, prescient. No other word described her ability to divine thoughts as she had.

"I can help your husband, if he would like my help and he also believes I can help him. I can't help people who are sceptical and doubtful. I'm not a witch."

"He would like you to come and see him, Miss Legge. Orthodox treatment hasn't worked."

"Miss Legge, I'm a spinster. Your husband has talked to Mr Watson, he knows how I helped him with his problem."

Again it was statement, not a question.

Betty nodded. The tea tasted special, as if itsparkled, refreshing. Not the normal dead liquid that she accepted as the norm.

"We'll pay you of course," she said quickly.

Fanny smiled again, "It's odd how people believe that money is the answer to all effort. If your husband wants my help, I will try my best. I don't need money."

"You have to live, pay rates, electricity, water." Betty remembered the hissing paraffin lamp. There was no electricity in the house. The pump provided water.

"I manage with what the earth provides, freely, if you make the effort Mrs Lewin," Fanny stood up, "When you've finished your tea I'll come with you. See what I can do for your husband's back."

"That tea is something very special, Miss Legge," Betty handed back the empty cup.

"Fanny, please, Miss sounds so banal and sterile, doesn't it?"

"If you return to your vehicle, I'll be out in a moment. Have to make sure all my animals know what I'm doing. They'd get worried otherwise."

Betty pulled on her coat and walked out into the slanting rain, cold wind, got into the Landrover and started it up. The cottage had been so warm the contrast was noticeable. The marsh stretched away into infinity, the grey mist cloaking the dykes and leaning hawthorn hedges. The marsh had always made her apprehensive. There was something untamed about it that disturbed her, despite twenty years of living in Babingley. It was as if the marsh tolerated humanity because it wished to. It could easily rescind its charity at any time. The chill wind was a constant factor in the Fens. At its best it was clean, at its worst it was diabolical, roaring like some obscene beast, bending everything to its will.

Fanny appeared in the doorway, a kind of shawl around her shoulders. Betty saw her lips move as if speaking to the cats that wandered around the garden, then moved to the gate. She got into the passenger seat without effort. There was something odd about her appearance, Betty thought. It wasn't until they were driving down the lanes to the main road that the answer came to her. Fanny's hair was dry! No sign of dampness from the rain!

****

4.

Monday, March 1st, 1983.
Lewin's Farm, Babingley,
King's Lynn, Norfolk.

Betty drove up to the front door of the house, still in awe of the mysterious Fanny Legge and her ability to keep her hair dry in a slanting downpour!

Fanny exited from the Landrover without a word and was in the house before Betty had even switched off the engine. Jim Lewin wasn't even aware of anyone in the kitchen when Fanny seemed to materialise before his eyes.

"Hello" she said, "You want help with your back problem?"

Jim was so startled at Fanny's sudden appearance he stuttered and gabbled for a second or so. Betty entered, removed her waterproof cape and hung it up. "This is Miss Legg, Jim" she said unnecessarily, "She says she can help you with your back problem!"

"You want help, Mr Lewin?" Fanny stood immobile before him, looking down at him, her eyes seemed to penetrate his brain, "You believe I can help you?"

"Well, you helped Bill Watson with his disc, said he'd never felt better, been to chiropractors, osteopaths, drugs, traction, nothing helped much. If you did that for him and he says you did, yes, I'd like you to try!" said Jim.

Fanny nodded as Ellen entered the kitchen, still in her dressing gown, hair a titian cloud, feet bare.

"Hello Ellen" greeted Fanny.

Ellen was as startled as Jim and Betty. "How did you know my name?" she gasped.

Fanny shrugged, "You look like an Ellen" she smiled. "I could have been wrong."

She touched Jim on the shoulder with her right hand, "Bend forward Mr Lewin"

"I don't think I can, Miss..er..?" said Jim, his face twisted with pain.

"Try," urged Fanny gently. Her left hand pressed him softly.

Jim bent forward. "Jesus!" he gasped, astonished, "I didn't think..."

"I want you to lift your gown up, bare your back for me, "said Fanny softly.

Betty and Ellen were as surprised as Jim. There was no way he could have bent forward like that a few minutes before. Betty came forward to assist.

Fanny checked her, "Let him do it" she said softly.

Jim eased the dressing gown up over his buttocks. Fanny pulled it up so that it covered his head, his back still bare.

"When I press, I want you to straighten up, you understand?" she said. She didn't raise her voice, but the authority was plain.

Jim nodded, his head concealed by the dressing gown, "If I can," he mumbled.

"You will."

Ellen and Betty watched as Fanny's fingers explored the lum-ber area of Jim's back,touching,caressing,her head on one side as if listening to some silent music.She then placed both hands over Jim's spine,pressed"Now!"she said sharply.

Betty and Ellen saw Jim straighten up. The pained expression on his sallow features dispersed. Betty later swore she saw a kind of shadow travel over her husband's back, upwards then vanish into the ceiling. Ellen declared that she felt a kind of shock wave pass her en route to the ceiling. Jim sat still for a full ten seconds, then arose from his chair, a beatific smile on his face, "It's gone!" he said, wonderingly, doubtfully, then suddenly gave a whoop, danced round in sheer joy. "It's gone! I'm cured! Christ! It's a miracle!"

He stretched, then touched his toes several times, then straightened again," It is a bloody miracle! How did you do it Miss Legge?"

"You wanted to be well, I just exploited the natural energies all around us" said Fanny, softly.

"I don't know how to thank you," crowed Jim, "Billy was right, you're a magician, a healer, you're divine!" He did a dance round the floor, grabbed Betty and did a kind of dance with her.

"Shouldn't he be careful for a few days Fanny?" Betty was dubious, expecting her husband to double-up again any second. The actuality of Jim's recovery was almost too much for her to grasp.

"No need, he will be fine now," Fanny was motionless, staring into the distance.

"How much do I owe you Miss Legge?"

Jim went over to the bureau, extracted a cheque book, "You name it, it's yours! I do not recall ever feeling so good."

"I don't want money Mr Lewin" Fanny was still standing still a faraway look on her features.

"You must accept something," insisted Jim.

"You can give me some hay for Willow, a bale or two."

"Willow?" Jim echoed.

"My donkey."

"You can have as much as you want Miss Legge. Any time you want hay just let us know, we'll deliver a load for you. Are you sure that's all you want?"

"A few carrots when you can spare them. Willow enjoys carrots."

Consider it done," Jim pressed his back, still unable to grasp the fact that he was cured.

"Well, I'd better be getting back, my animals need feeding."

Fanny moved to the door.

"I'll run you back," offered Jim.

"Sure you're OK?" Betty was still dubious.

"Right as rain, I'll put a few bales in the back of the landrover to be going on with, and a bag of carrots."

"You're not going to lift haybales again, Jim!" cried Betty," You'll do your back in again you fool!. Let Bobby do it when he gets back from the Hump!"

Fanny looked at Betty suddenly, her eyes sharp, "Hump, what Hump?"

Betty shrugged, "It's a kind of hill over near the church. Every time we take Freda over it she breaks down. We've been meaning to flatten it out for years, never got around to it, always other things to do, more important."

"Freda?" Fanny's eyes were intent. "Our tractor, whenever we take it over the Hump, it's a short cut to Slade, she breaks down!"

She'd barely finished speaking when they heard the sound of a tractor approaching. The massive machine pulled up at the door. Behind was Wally's ancient Renault van.

Bobby jumped down from the enclosed cab and entered the kitchen.

"Take those boots off!" screamed Betty, "and those oilskins!"

Wally Thompson paused at the door, saw Fanny and waved, "How're yer Miss Legge? Find what you were looking for on the marsh yesterday?"

"Yes, thank you Mr Thompson," Fanny seemed to be in a daydream.

"Won't come in, gotta cylinder head on a Jap job to fix. Freda's OK now, went like a dream as soon as we got her off the Hump. Needs a service like yesterday, up to you Jim."

He looked again, "I thought you had a bad back?"

"Miss Legge gave me some treatment, better now," said Jim, looking sheepish.

"You fixed Billy Watson's for him, didn't yer Missus?" Wally rolled a tailor-made as he stood in the doorway.

Fanny didn't seem to hear Wally. The mechanic shrugged, scratched a match on his overalls and applied it to the end of his cigarette. It didn't light.

"Bloody matches!" said Wally, trying another. It still wouldn't light, "Stone the bleedin' crows! Wassa marrer with the bloody thing?"

"You shouldn't smoke that evil weed Mr Thompson," said Fanny. "You will become ill."

"Getaway, me old man smoked all his natural, lived til he were ninety, never did him harm." Wally put the cylinder behind his ear, "I'll smoke it later, gotta go. Bring Freda in soon or you're goin' ter have problems." He drove off.

"Thank God for that!" breathed Betty, "That awful smell, just like ..."

"Horseshit" said Bobby, grinning.

"Hadn't you better get on with it?" demanded Betty, as Bobby was in the process of divesting himself of the oilskins.

"I'll do it," said Jim, "You go and meet Tracy, I'm fine now!"

"Jesus, how did that happen? Your back? You were stuck in that chair earlier?" Bobby looked at his Father, suspiciously.

"Miss Legge fixed it for him," said Ellen.

"Must be a miracle, the last time you did it in you were laid up for a week!"

"Get on with Slade, never mind that Tracy Middleton!" said Betty.

"Let the lad go, I'm fine now love," said Jim, "You take Miss Legge home.

"He's done nothing this week exept laze around," stated Betty.

"He's shagged Tracy at least half a dozen times," said Ellen.

"That's a useful contribution to the nation's feel good factor, I'll bet she's well into the club by now!"

"Ellen, that's enough of that. Whatever will Miss Legge think of you?"

"I expect Miss Legge could confirm that Tracy's got a bun in the oven for us, couldn't you Miss Legge?" Ellen was defiant.

"Excuse her Miss Legge, it's all this spurious education she gets at Nottingham. Pity they don't teach them decorum and good manners."

Betty picked up the mug Wally Thompson had drunk from, looked at the black fingermarks disgustedly, "I'll take you home now if that's what you want?"

"I'd like to see this Hump, if that would be in order?"

Fanny seemed to have emerged from her reverie. "Take Miss Legge down there Bobby," Betty stood by the Aga, toasting herself.

"You really want to go down there Miss Legge? Bobby looked at the slanting rain, "You could come back another day when it's not raining and cold."

"Today, if that's convenient?" Fanny gave Bobby an appraising look.

"Of course it is, get going Bobby."

Bobby sighed, began pulling on oilskins again, "You'd better put this on, you'll get soaked down there," He held out a waxed jacket with a hood.

"I'll be alright, really," Fanny shook her head.

Betty recalled Fanny's head not even damp in the pouring rain outside her cottage earlier. Strange woman, and those eyes, as if seeing beyond time and distance. She shuddered a little, smacked of witchcraft and the occult. Still, a woman unmarried, living alone with cats, an Irish Wolfhound, a parrot and a spider, Ugh. She shivered again on recalling that hideous creature crawling around the room and on top of Fanny's head! It was obscene.

"Kevin Wilson says it's a tumulus," Ellen said.

Fanny turned to look at Ellen, "Now that is interesting Miss Lewin. I know Kevin, very knowledgeable about these things."

"He says that there are ley-lines crossing at St Mary's and at the Hump" said Ellen.

"Come on Elly, don't go giving Miss Legge all that occult crap," said Bobby, "The Hump is just an old slurry heap from way back."

"It sounds like something out of black magic, Mr Lewin. I can assure you they are very real," Fanny was quiet.

"Kevin says every church is built on one of these ancient sites where ley-lines cross because the early Church wanted to bury all the ancient wisdom since it threatened their religion."

"Like I said, Kevin is very knowledgeable about these things. The early Church did a great deal of damage to our understanding of the old world and they thought that by building on these ancient sites they'd cover up any vestige of the old knowledge remaining, consolidate their power."

"You really believe all this stuff about old civilisations and knowledge Miss Legge?"

Betty felt faintly uneasy. There was more to Fanny than she had suspected. The rumours that were standard about her were that she was slightly crazy and a little stupid. Betty had altered her views on that judgement in the past hour. Jim's back was nothing short of a miracle and she evidently knew more about the old ways than people gave her credit for.

"As Shakespeare stated, there are more things in heaven and earth than we are presently aware of, Mrs Lewin. I know my reputation amongst the people in Lynn, I'm an eccentric, slightly cranky, living alone with my cats and things, perhaps crazy, mad, some say. If you'd like to know more about these things, I would be delighted to explain."

"That's very kind of you Miss Legge. We might take you up on that offer someday," said Betty hastily, superstitiously crossing her fingers. The last thing she would want was to be confused by a load of guff about the occult. She wasn't too happy about Ellen and that Kevin Wilson feeding her all this witchcraft rubbish. She didn't want a daughter believing all the tripe Kevin came out with, ley-lines, God! Whatever next.

"I'd like an opportunity to talk to you Mrs Legge," said Ellen. "I find the subject fascinating."

"Everybody knows where I live Miss Lewin. You're welcome any time."

Fanny turned to Bobby, "Can we go now?"

"I don't know how to thank you for my back Mrs Legge," said Jim, "Feels great, no pain, no stiffness, nothing. Sure you won't take some money for your trouble?"

"Just the hay for Willow Mr Lewin," Fanny smiled. Her teeth were very white in the gloom of the vast kitchen.

"Put half a dozen bales in the Landrover, Bobby. That enough to be going on with? I'll deliver some more tomorrow for you."

"Miss Legge, Mr Lewin. I'm not married." She moved to the door.

Bobby went out to the Landrover, Betty and Jim watched Fanny get in.

She seemed to glide without effort.

"That's one weird woman love," Jim echoed Betty's own opinion.

"You should see that cottage she lives in, a dog, parrot and believe it or not a spider the size of one of those dinner plates, called Tweety. I nearly fainted when I saw it, she let it crawl up her arm, sit on her head! God, It makes me feel queasy just remembering it, and all this ancient wisdom rubbish, ley-lines, tumulus..."

"You might think it rubbish Mumsy but she cured Dad's back didn't she? Didn't get that out of medical school, or a book. So where do you think she got it from?" Ellen was excited.

"Some people have a gift for laying on of hands," Betty knew it sounded weak.

"Come off it Mumsy. She didn't incant, mutter anything cabbalistic, did she? Just put her hands on Dad's back and pressed."

"It felt funny love," said Jim, "Hot at first, then as if something was sucking the pain away. It feels better than it's felt in years. She could ruin Barry Lassiter's practice if she set up. She could be rich in no time curing people's back problems, look at Billy Watson. He thinks she's one step down from JC."

"Well, this isn't getting Slade ploughed over is it?" Betty felt some pragmatism was required to restore a sense of reality to a very odd morning.

****

5.

Monday, March 1st, 1993.
Lewin's Farm, Babingley
King's Lynn, Norfolk.

"How's it going John?" Jim Lewin walked up to the edge of the building site, surveying the excavations.

John Foster growled, "The answer to that one is that it isn't going at all. That bloody 'dozer has broken down half a dozen times in the past week and every time Wally Thompson comes up here to fix it, he tows it off the site and it works. It's bloody weird. The lifter doesn't work, the hydraulics don't work and as you can see we ain't any further forward than we were two weeks ago. Costing me a sodding fortune. The mixer won't work, it keeps stopping as soon as I start it up. I've had four blokes off sick, complaining about headaches every time they start work. The place is jinxed mate. Charlie says that the markers were all taken out on Friday, had to call Johnstone out to re-do them. He rings me up gives me some horrible shit about couldn't drive the stakes in because there's a load of concrete under the topsoil. So I get Paddy to dig it out, and he tells me there's nothing there, and he wasn't pissed either. I get back to Harvey and tell him he should take more water with it. He comes down here with his blokes, all red in the face. I'm standing where you are now watching his blokes trying to drive those markers in. They try all ways, can't do it. I tell you if it goes on much longer I'm going to have to call it off mate. I'm going to make a loss on this job as it is."

Foster took out a large cigar, bit the end off, stuck it in his mouth and flicked a gold plated lighter. He tried several times, it wouldn't operate.

"Jesus fucking Christ! There just has to be something odd about this place. It worked in the car coming over."

Jim Lewin gazed at the half levelled site and the workmen sitting in their tin hut drinking tea, "For Christ sake John. Ellen and my son-in-law are due to move in any time now. Betty's getting real pissed off with them livin' in with us this last six months. Now you tell me you wanna jack it in, for Fuck's Sake. I gave you the job because your quote was not the best, but I know you from the Chamber and you don't cut corners, no names, no packdrill. "

"I know all about that Jimbo." Foster put the cigar back in his pocket, "You think I enjoy standing here telling you this? I've spent a fucking fortune on these footings. You can see for yourself, we've made no progress at all in the past two weeks, even my cigar lighter won't work round here. This place is jinxed, I'm sure of it!"

"So what're you telling me? You wanna cry off?" Jim was angry.

Foster hitched his trousers up over his massive gut, "I'll tell you what Jimbo, I'll cut my losses if we can move the site down there on Slade, start again. There just has to be something wrong with this place."

"But we'll have to go all through planning again and those twats in the Town Hall are about as turned on as a load of junkies, it'll be bloody months before we even git started."

"I'm being fair Jimbo, I'll stand this loss to date, but I can't go on paying out blokes sitting on their arses waiting for fucking Goddo because the bloody machinery doesn't work and every time that bastard Thompson comes out to fix it he grins, tows it fifty yards down the road, turns the key and it starts! I tell you it's like fucking witchcraft, and I ain't superstitious, at least I wasn't until I started in on this. I ain't too sure now."

A large man emerged from the site hut, walked over to where Foster and Lewin were standing. He crossed himself as he passed the site.

"What's up Paddy?" Foster hitched his trousers up again.

"Mick isn't feeling too good Mr Foster, I'm going to have to send him home."

"Hells fucking bells Paddy, he's the third bastard this week. What's the matter with your blokes? Mick's never sick."

Foster tugged at his black beard in fury.

"Been complaining all week about his stomach, cramps, or something. I don't feel so good meself, must be the marsh air or something Mr Foster."

Paddy was over six feet, burly, raw-boned and looked tough as old leather.

"Don't you start in on all that Jesus freak crap Paddy, this means we call it off today until Mick feels better."

Paddy looked apologetic, "Sorry Mr Foster, but nothing's gone right about this job. Those markers keep coming out even when we prop 'em up, the mixer isn't workin' and the dozer breaks down every time we moves it onto the site, and the blokes get sick. Ain't happened before on any other job."

Foster turned to Jim, "See what I mean? Even this fucking bograt's got the jinx," he snarled.

"All the cement's gone solid as well. "Paddy looked sheepish.

"What cement? We haven't mixed any yet, for Chrissake," Foster snorted.

"In the bags," Paddy pointed to the site hut, "Come and see for yourself."

"You been on the juice, Paddy?"

"Haven't touched a drop Mr Foster."

"I have to see this," moaned Foster. "Show me!"

Jim, Foster and Paddy entered the site hut where around fifty bags of Blue Circle cement were stacked in the corner. The workmen sitting drinking tea looked up at them as they passed.

"You OK Mick?" asked Foster of a small man with a cast in one eye.

"Don't feel so good Mr Foster, tummy's playin' up, never had any trouble before, just since we started here. It's OK in Lynn, right as rain, starts givin' me gyp as soon as I walk onto the job."

Foster made no comment, walked over to the pile of cement bags and felt the top one.

"Christ, it's solid!" he exclaimed, "Has it been damp?"

"Well the heater don't work, hasn't since we started here, but the place ain't that damp," said Paddy

"Let's have a look at the others lower down," ordered Foster.

Two of the men came over and lifted the top layers of bags to the ground.

"I don't bloody well believe this," bawled Foster, "It must've been like this when Blue Circle delivered it."

Paddy shook his head, "Perfectly OK Mr Foster. I wouldn't have accepted it if it had been queer."

Foster nodded then felt over the bags. Jim felt some, they were like rock.

"Must be the little people Mr Foster," said Paddy.

"That's all I need, fucking leprechauns, just about makes my day," yelled Foster. "Two hundred quids worth of cement like fucking rock. I'll have to have my fucking head read, it just doesn't make sense."

"Have you seen the water Mr Foster?" Paddy looked uneasy.

Foster held up a hand, "Don't tell me it's black and oily and it groans when it comes out of the tap!"

"Come have a look" invited Paddy.

The tap was set against the site hut, lagged with sacking. Paddy turned it on. An ooze of mud came out, spluttered, coughed, then turned red.

"Feel it" said Paddy.

Foster put a finger under it and rubbed his thumb across it. "Have you contacted the Water people?"

"They can't understand it. Tried some tests, wouldn't come any different." Paddy dipped his finger under the tap and rubbed it, "It's like...."he stopped, looked at Foster.

"Blood" Foster finished for him.

"Come on John," Jim stuck his finger under the tap, put it to his lips and spat it out, "It's salt!" he cried.

"And warm!" Foster looked pale.

"We've had to buy bottled stuff for the blokes," said Paddy inconsequentially.

"That's it Jimbo, I can't take any more of this, I'm calling this off, fucking ridiculous. You won't get charged and I'll refund your deposit. You'll have to get somebody else to build your house."

"Who will take it on once the word gets about?" wailed Jim.

"One of the big boys'll do it for you Jimbo. They can stand the losses, I can't. Twelve weeks this was going to take, on this record it will take forever. The place is jinxed I tell you. Christ, who's this coming?"

An ancient Renault van lurched and bumped its way down the dirt road.

"That's Wally, come to fix the mixer again" said Paddy.

"God, that's another cost I didn't allow for," said Foster.

Wally Thompson came out of the driver's seat. His complexion was waxen, he had to steady himself before walking over to where Foster and Jim stood. "Came as soon as I could mate," he croaked. "Not been feeling too kosher. Chest playing me up this last few months." There was the stump of a tailor-made in his ear.

"Well you don't have to worry about this lot again Wally," Foster said grimly.

"Why? What's up? Buying new stuff?" Thompson coughed painfully.

"I'm closing the site."

"Ain't like you to make a loss Johnny. What's up?"

"For a start I can't keep paying your bills, coming out here three or four times a week. We've had nothing but problems ever since we started, bunging the costs up."

Thompson looked round at the raw ground, "This is the old Hump, ain't it Jimbo? Just realised it."

Lewin nodded, "That's what we used to call it."

"Hump, What's this Hump?" Foster was irritated.

"Just an odd piece of land we used to give a name to," Jim was dismissive.

"Freda always used to break down on this stretch if I recall rightly back, let me see, must be ten year ago, when Ellen was still at Nottingham."

"Freda, break down? What's all this crap? What're you rabbittin about Wally?"

"Jim had an old Massey Fergusson tractor in them days, before he got rich, kept on breaking down. I used to tell him he never had it serviced."

"What's that gotta do with this Hump?"

"Everytime it broke down it was over this piece of land, I've just remembered. Soon found out that all I had to do was tow it off the Hump and she started, no trouble at all." Wally coughed again, held his chest and massaged it gently.

Foster glared at Wally, "So all we have to do is move that bloody mixer off this site and it works?"

"Let's try it," offered Wally, "Get your blokes to move it fifty yards up there." He pointed to where the site sloped gently.

"That's where I used to tow Freda, looks so different now that this is all roughed up."

"Paddy!" Foster called, "I want you to try something."

"What's that?"

"Get your blokes to shift that mixer over there!"

Paddy looked as if he might refuse, he shrugged, then signalled his men. They heaved the mixer along the broken ground.

"OK, that's far enough," announced Wally.

"See if it starts Paddy," ordered Foster.

Paddy gave the starter cord a pull. The engine caught first time and began firing away.

"Well, fuck me stupid!" Foster automatically pulled the cigar from his inner pocket and flicked his lighter.

"I don't fucking well believe this," snorted Foster.

"You want some advice?" Wally had another choking fit, whilst Foster puffed away, a satisfied look on his florid features.

"Well?"

"Get Funny Fanny out here. Let her give you her opinion," said Wally, holding his chest, breathing torturously.

"Is that a joke, mush?"

"I ain't kidding mate. She'll tell you all about it."

"All about what?" Foster looked peeved.

"Remember when she fixed your back Jimbo? What, must be ten years ago? She came here with Bobby to take a look at the Hump."

"Go on, I like fairy tales, especially when they cost me money."

Wally shrugged, "Suit yourself tosh, no skin off my nose."

"OK, keep your shirt on. What's that old crone gonna do for me?"

"Save you a bob or two for starters, since you've fucked-up here"

"Very funny" Foster dragged on his cigar thoughtfully, "OK, so what will she do?"

"I didn't hear everything she was telling Jim's son Bobby, It was pissing down like plate glass. She reckoned this place is where ley-lines cross and under there is a tumulus. An invisible current passes over it all the time."

"I had you fixed for a bloke with his head screwed on Wally. You believe all that shit?"

Wally shrugged again, "Pull that mixer back onto the Hump, see if it starts."

"Paddy, move it back where it was."

Paddy and his men were looking bewilderedly at the mixer chugging away merrily. Paddy switched it off, helped his men manhandle it back to its original position.

"Start it," ordered Foster.

The machine started first time. Foster broke into a guffaw of laughter, nearly choked on his cigar, "Fucking witchcraft and you swallowed all that crap. Fucking marvellous"

Wally looked askance at the mixer, the pan whirling away.

Foster poked him in his stomach, "There's one born every minute they tell me. Wally, I reckon you've been ripping me off sunshine. How does that grab you?"

"You can always go to Lyons pal. See what they charge you for a callout. That should make your day, I'm off, see you around."

"Not if I see you first."

Wally broke into a fit of coughing. His face was sheet white, he barely made it to his old banger, hanging onto the door handle, gasping for breath.

"You alright Wally?" Jim ran to his side and aided him into the seat, "I'll run you home if you hang on a minute."

There was a sheen of perspiration over Wally's features, "I'll be OK Jimbo, I'd get that site moved if I were you. Fanny said these places shouldn't be disturbed."

Jim watched him drive off, then walked back to Foster and his men.

"Funny Fanny, Christ, whatever next," scoffed Foster.

"Fanny fixed my back for me John, that was ten years ago. Just ran her hands up my back, never had any problems since."

"You and Billy Watson are a pair," jeered Foster, "Into the witchcraft, are we?"

"Witchcraft or not, she fixed it and good. Bob Lassiter never did me any good, all that traction, pills, manipulation, osteopaths. Have a laugh. Hope you never have a back like mine."

"Never have back problems, too fit, mush, an hour a day in the gym, keeps you young. Fuck it! This thing has gone out again."

He examined the end of the cigar, shrugged his shoulders and brought out his lighter, then flicked it. It wouldn't work.

Foster flicked it furiously, not a spark.

"Bloody Taiwanese crap, should've bought a good one."

The mixer stopped running.

****

6.

**Monday May 1st, 1993.
Lewin's Farm, Babingley
King's Lynn, Norfolk.**

"What're you doing Paddy?" roared Foster, "Let the bloody thing run."

"Didn't touch it," said Paddy, dourly

"You must have, it can't stop on its own." Foster was still trying to get his lighter to work.

"I told you, I didn't touch it," Paddy's face was red with suppressed anger.

"Well, start it up again"

"Tell you what boss, you do it. Me and the blokes have had enough of this site, you and your bloody company. You pay peanuts, expect miracles and have as much idea of management as Adolf Hitler. So fuck you and your job, we're off. Lyons pay better than you and Harry Farraday knows how to treat his workforce. Up yours!" Paddy gave a double sign of the two digits, then stomped off and signalled to his crew. Foster watched speechlessly as his workforce got into the minibus and drove off.

"I'll fire that Irish bograt," cursed Foster.

"Looks like he fired himself John" said Jim.

"Don't you start Jimbo," snarled Foster, watching the minibus lurch over the uneven ground towards the lane.

"Well, since we're in the business of soul searching, you can get off my land as soon as you like. Your man management skills, as Paddy said, are minimal. Why those blokes have stuck it this long beats the shit outa me. You're pigheaded, brash, rude and enjoy a brain the size of a pea. You can remove your gear at your earliest and consider our contract defunct. If this stuff isn't off my land by the end of the week I'll flog it. How's that grab you?"

Foster looked unhealthily angry, "You can't do this," he choked

"You obviously haven't read the small print in our contract sunshine. I wanted Ellen and Kevin to move in in six weeks. You said you could do it.

Says so in the contract. It's now two months, two weeks over, and you haven't even got the footings in. If you wanna sue me be my guest. Look good in the Advertiser and the freebies. Do your business a world of good."

Jim walked over to his Landrover and drove off. He could see Foster via his rear view mirror, almost doing a war dance in frustration.

"What's up love?" Betty was in the conservatory, reading the latest Barbara Cartland. She looked up over her spectacles.

"I've just fired Foster."

"I approve, he's a rude man, treats me like something out of a workhouse. Thinks women should not have been let out of the kitchen. It's been eight weeks and no sign of any foundations let alone a house. Whilst I love my daughter dearly, having her and that Kevin around in our house is just about driving me hairless. That was supposed to be their wedding present."

"You don't have to remind me love," Jim removed his boots and sat down in a padded garden chair, sighing wearily.

"Want some tea?" Betty stood up.

"I'll make it in a moment."

"Sit down, I'll make it." She disappeared into the kitchen.

Jim picked up the phone and dabbed at a number. "Harry Farraday please love. Harry, Jim Lewin here, how'd you like to build me a house? I fired him. I won't tell anybody what you said, he'd probably sue you for defamation of character, yeah, would be difficult. I know, I needed my head read. He gave me a better quote than you, I know that now, so don't rub it in. When do you want to start? I've got my in-laws living with me and they are driving Betty and me up the wall. I know it's a big house, Christ knows what we'd do if it was a council job, both be in the funny farm. What rumour have you heard? The only thing that's jinxed is Johnny Foster and his man management skills, well do you want the job or don't you? Now? OK, can't grumble about the response, can I? See you in an hour."

"Who was that?" Betty handed him a mug of tea.

"Harry Farraday."

Betty sat down, placed her own mug on the coffe table, "You reckon they're going to be able to finish it?" She was quiet.

"What's that supposed to mean love?"

"As much as I dislike John Foster, I can't help feeling that it hasn't entirely been his fault.

"Oh no not you as well?" groaned Jim, pulling a face as he sipped his tea.

"What's the matter with it?" Betty's eyebrows came down in a frown.

"I don't know, I spent a bloody fortune on that new kitchen, yet the tea never tastes as good as it did when we had the Aga. Nothing to do with you love, you make good tea."

"You're just upset about John Foster."

"I guess we were rash about choosing the Hump as a site for the house," said Jim.

"So you admit it, at long last?" Betty grinned.

"I was down there just now. Wally comes to fix the mixer, moves it off the Hump and it starts. Take it back on and it stops. Johnny can't light his cigar. As soon as he moves off it lights, good as gold. Those markers won't stay upright, and the whole load of Blue Circle Johnny had delivered was rock solid, hadn't even been out of the site hut. I'm beginning to believe the place is haunted or something."

"Ellen and Kevin told us it wasn't a bright idea building a house on the Hump last year when we put planning application in."

"We should have listened, as much as that bloke gets my goat. Sorry love, but why our daughter wanted to marry that freak is beyond me. He looks like a refugee from the funny farm and all that weird gear in their room .makes me wonder whether he's got all his marbles."

"I have to point out that he earns more than we do, despite all the hard work you put in. I feel the same way about computers, but that's the way things are going, and he's good at it. Lilly Simpson told me that they think he's a wizard at Wards, key man."

"I wonder how Lilly Simpson knows that?" grinned Jim.

"You've a dirty mind Jim Lewin. She and Lance Ward are just good friends."

"If you say so, anyway, Harry Farraday is coming up to have a look at the site."

"You'll have to tell him."

"Tell him? Tell him what?"

Betty picked up the novel, replaced her spectacles on the end of her nose and looked at him, "All about the funny goings on, machinery breaking down, men getting sick. If you don't we'll be back to square one in another eight weeks, and I don't have any confidence regarding my sanity if

I have to endure much more of them in the house. I thought it would work out, I was wrong. So tell him about it."

"He's heard the rumours already."

"Confirm them for him."

"He'll cop out," Jim put his mug down, pulled a face, "Must be that fancy purifier we had put in, tasted better with a little slurry in with it."

"Better he cops out now than eight weeks down the line," She sat back.

"Wally said we ought to get Fanny in, let her smell round."

"Good advice love. If we have to move that site, better we know now than wait another two months and then start the process all over again. Planning permission, surveying, we have already spent a fortune on this project."

"It's a bit like, well you know, acknowledging there is something at work on that site. I feel embarrassed."

"Better a little red face than an overdraft," Betty was tart.

"Remember Freda? Broke down every time on that Hump. As soon as Wally towed it off, she started. There just has to be something odd about that Hump, even our son-in-law bless him, warned us about it, ley-lines crossing, tumulus site, mystic energy."

"I know love, but if he was normal, I could accept it, but let's face it he's a weirdie, and what excuse do we give to the Planning Department wanting to move the site? Fanny Legge says that ley-lines cross and it's the site of a tumulus, whatever a tumulus is? Can you imagine the smirks in the Town Hall? Jim Lewin's losing his marbles, you know, on the say so of the local witch doctor, poor chap, can't help it, look at his son-in-law, member of the local Wizard Society, dressing up like Klu Klux Klan men, holding rites out at Bawsey Ruin on midsummer day, sex orgies, drugs, booze, I'd never live it down."

"Like I said earlier, better to let those jokers in the Town Hall have a smirk or two than have an overdraft like a toilet roll. Let's get her in, she did your back for you, did she not? Call that witchcraft? You haven't had any trouble for ten years. Billy Watson the same, and a few more since. Call her a witch if you want, she could earn a million in Harley Street, let's hear what she has to say. We can always ignore it?"

"Have it your way love. I suppose it can't do any harm, as long as you don't tell Lilly Simpson. It'd be like the bloody oil slick from the Exxon Valdez, all over Lynn in less time than I spend in the toilet."

"The least said about that the better love"

"I like a comfortable crap, I get my best ideas in the loo."

"Pity you didn't have a revelation about the Hump last year."

"Very funny, Christ, Harry Farraday's here already, he must have shit the bed."

"That's where our daughter gets all that bad language from."

"Relieves tension."

They both watched a nearly new Jaguar pull up at the door. Harry Farraday was tall, athletic, broad shoulders, no paunch, with greying hair cut short. His square face was clean cut, no jowls, and Ice blue eyes in a high cheek boned setting. He was tanned.

"Nice" he commented in unaccented English, looking round at the conservatory, "Who did this for you?"

"Norries" said Jim, "Two years ago."

"Must be money in this farming business," grinned Farraday. "How are you Betty? Looking beautiful as ever. If Jim hadn't beaten me to the punch I'd have carted you off to the altar." He took her hand and kissed it.

Betty blushed, obviously impressed by Farraddy's galantry. "You always were a bullshitting bastard Harry. How the women swallow all that crap, I can't imagine."

"You've lost your sense of romance Jimbo lad. The ladies appreciate it, don't they Betty?"

"Well you won't look very romantic after you've been down at the site, with those shoes and that suit," said Jim, piqued.

Farraday's suit was tailor-made, hand-made blue shirt, tooled leather grey shoes.

"I've come prepared Jimbo," he said.

"You want some re-cycled urine before we go down there?" Jim held up his mug.

"Not my scene at all" Farraday shook his head.

"How are you Betty? Lilly Simpson told me you were as beautiful as you were when we were together as a gang. She was right. Jim's a lucky man."

"Jesus, do you keep this up all the time Harry?" Jim sighed.

"A little praise makes the world go better Jim, you should bear that in mind."

"Well, let's see if you can find anything to praise about the Hump sunshine." Jim made for the door, pulling on his old anorak.

"What happened to Freda?" Farrady looked at the near new Massey Fergusson in the barn.

"That's a good memory," Jim was impressed, "Still got her, pensioned off now."

"Bullshit plus a good memory created business Jimbo," said Farraday," And a late registered BMW, very nice. When did you acquire that? Let me get my wellies out of my heap."

Farrady brought out what looked like a brand new pair of Wellingtons from the boot of his Jaguar.

"Don't be so bloody nosey. That's the reward for twenty years graft, creating something out of a run down heap that old Garrard left behind when he died."

"You've done wonders Jim, I reluctantly have to admit. The old church still standing?"

"In the middle of Slade where it always was, ploughed up now of course."

"Had some great times in there didn't we?"

"You mean you did, shagging Lilly and all the others, you randy fucker. It was always a wonder to me that you didn't drop a bun in."

Harry grinned as he climbed into the Landrover, "You were a bit naive with the ladies Jim, thought a condom was a fancy balloon."

"Or clap," added Jim, starting the vehicle.

"Jimbo, how can you denigrate the ladies of Lynn in that disgusting fashion. They didn't have that going for them."

"Fuck your luck, mate. I'm only envious. Had to work hard to get my end away."

"I had the ability to sweet talk them sunshine. You were always a bit gauche, shy"

"Well,that's enough of Memory Lane, that's the Hump over there." Jim pointed to where Foster's site hut stood.

"No access road? What're you intending about that?" Farraday became professional

"I thought it would be best left until the bungalow was finished."

"More costly, I'd have thought Johnny would have told you that."

"What with all the other factors, that's why I've called you in," Jim manoeuvred the Landrover close to the Hump.

"Why are you stopping here? Why can't you drive onto the site?"

He saw Jim's hesitation, "Come on, I've heard all the rumours. What's the problem with this? Better tell me now than get way down the road and we have to backtrack" Farraday was business-like.

"We've had problems, or rather Foster had. Machinery wouldn't operate on the site, his blokes falling ill all the time, and I'll show you something you'll find hard to believe."

"I'm glad you told me, Jimbo. I'd heard Johnny had trouble. I thought it was of his own making, cutting corners, as usual. He never learns. Those houses he finished along Saddlebow. All got subsidence because he cut corners on the footings. In fact Friend Johnny is bad news for us contractors. Gives us a lousy name. He should be struck off, that's between you and me. When I heard you'd given him the contract I had grave doubts. He's a cowboy, of the worst kind."

Farraday pulled on his wellingtons, carefully folding the turn-ups of his trousers. Jim watched this performance with amusement.

"I should have brought my overalls. When was the last time you cleaned this crate?" Farraday brushed dust from the seat of his pants.

Jim followed him onto the site. "What's the matter with the markers?"

"That's another problem Johnny had. They wouldn't stay put."

Farraday looked at Jim, "Is that a joke?"

"You think I enjoy looking at this fucking mess eight weeks into his contract, and not a bloody brick to show for it?"

"OK, so what was his problem?"

"Every time he tried hammering them in they'd be out the next morning."

"Vandals" said Farraday.

"I wish it was that simple," Jim walked over to the site hut. "Take a look at this"

Inside the hut Jim indicated the pile of Blue Circle Cement bags, "Feel them," he invited.

" They must have been damp on delivery," said Farraday, feeling the hard mass.

"Johnny said they were OK, and Paddy said he'd never have accepted the load if they'd been like it."

"Murphy is a reliable bloke, I believe him, this is really something." Farraday stared at the pile, wonderingly, "Did he say what caused it?"

"They don't know, .it just went hard."

"I'm beginning to believe the rumours that this site is jinxed," Farraday ran his hand over his forehead, "Must have a migraine coming on. I don't feel so good, have to sit down a minute. Jesus!I feel sick, I'm going to throw up." He exited from the hut. Jim heard him retching violently.

****

7.

Monday, May 1st, 1993.
The Hump, Lewin's Farm
Babingley, Near King's Lynn, Norfolk.

When Farraday re-entered, he was pale and shaking.

"I still don't feel so good. Don't know what's the matter with me, I was as right as rain a few minutes ago."

"That's what Murphy claimed was happening to his crewmen, every time they came on the site they'd feel bad."

"I wouldn't have believed it, now I do. Must be something about this site, as reluctantly as I am to admit it."

"Well? What do you think?" Jim felt sorry for Farraday, he looked so ill.

"Let's get out of here before I throw up again, all those oysters at lunch, waste of money," gasped the contractor, mopping his face with a handkerchief.

They walked back to the Landrover.

"That's odd," said Farraday.

"What is?"

"I feel fine now. This is bloody weird, almost as if..." he hesitated.

"As if what?"

"I'll sound like Funny Fanny," Farraday was embarrassed.

"There's only me and thee mate. I won't say anything, not in my best interests to do is it?"

"Almost as if some force is at work here."

"Well, you can commiserate with Johnny Foster then can't you?

"I've seen enough, I'll get Harvey down here to give me a run down, then let you know what the score is."

"Harvey won't be too pleased about that, he did the original survey. Got his blokes to mark out the footings, couldn't get the stakes in, he claimed there was concrete under the top soil."

"What happened?"

"Murphy dug it up, found nothing. Harvey propped the stakes. Every morning they were flat."

"Well, I'll get it from him. I don't believe in witchcraft and there must be another simpler explanation for all this business."

"I'd be delighted if you come up with the solution. I want those two out of my pad and into their own place, tout suite. Betty and I have had enough of them. I know Ellen's my daugher, but Jesus, a joke's a joke. I don't want a bloody pantomime."

"OK, let's go before I begin to believe all that shit."

They arrived back at the house. The BMW was missing from its parking place.

"Betty must have gone out, you want a drink?"

"Some water, my mouth feels like a country shithouse in the summer."

"Pure H-two-Oh." Jim handed him a glass. "Had that purifier put in when we had the kitchen done, tastes marginally better than the run-of-the-mill stuff."

Farraday drank it down, "Feels better, I find it hard to believe, seems basically as you've experienced it. I've never been sick before, I'll see what Harvey has to say tomorrow, then we'll have a chat about the site."

As he was leaving Farraday said, "You say Funny Fanny cured your back?"

Jim nodded, "Must be ten years ago now, suffered for years with it, not had any problems since. Bill Watson had a similar condition, she cured him too."

"I've had disc problems for years, I'm wondering."

"What have you to lose?" Jim saw the BMW approaching. There were two people in it, "Speak of the Devil, that looks like Fanny with Betty, stop and ask her."

Farraday got out again as Betty pulled up at the door.

"Hello Mr Lewin, how's your back?" Fanny was clad in her customary long skirt, her hair was long and hanging in two wings either side of her face.

"Fine since you treated it all that time ago. I don't know how to thank you."

"You've been generous with the hay ever since, I'm also grateful. I'm afraid I had to have Willow put down, old age finally got her. I have another rescue animal, a mule, badly treated. I'll have to start paying you now for your material."

"Nonsense my dear lady, It's no trouble, I'll continue the treatment as usual."

"You're very kind, "Fanny looked at Farraday, "You're a building contractor aren't you? Suffer with your back don't you?"

Farraday looked startled, "How did you know that?"

"It's written on your face Mr Farraday. Mr Lewin would like me to look at it for you?"

Jim's turn to be surprised, "I'm sure Mr Farrady would appreciate your time, Mrs Legge."

"Can we go inside?"

Betty led the way.

"Strip your shirt off," ordered Fanny.

"Eh?" Farraday was disturbed.

"If you want me to look at that disc, I have to be able to examine you systematically." Fanny patted Jim's chair, the same chair in which Jim had been seated when Fanny had treated his back ten years before.

"We'll go into the conservatory Harry. See you in a few minutes," said Betty, as Farraday began stripping off his shirt.

"What's she here for love?" asked Jim, "I'm not complaining, just want to know."

"She's going to tell us about the Hump," Betty looked determined.

"That'll go down well with Harry, just about to take over from Johnny Foster, a dose of witchcraft."

"Better we know now than let him get started. Paddy Murphy and his mates will spread the word, nobody will want to work on the site."

Jim had to admit the logic, still concerned about Farraday's reaction to Fanny Legge's predictions.

"Have you noticed anything about her?" asked Betty as they sat down.

"For example?"

"Anything."

"Still looks like a witch, is that what you mean?"

Betty shook her head, "Her appearance."

"Same clothes, same style, I mean long skirts, shawl, brogue shoes, hair done the same way that I recall."

"Her face," insisted Betty.

"What about it? Looks the same to me."

"Exactly. She looks the same as she did when she came here ten years ago. No grey hairs, no lines or wrinkles, in fact she hasn't aged at all," Betty was triumphant.

Jim thought about it for as minute and then nodded, "You're right love. I knew there was something about her, odd, couldn't put my finger on it, like that bloke in the play, what was his name? Can't think, Oscar Wilde."

"Dorian Gray," finished Betty.

Jim gulped, "It's weird, I always feel funny when she's around."

"At least she hasn't got that spider, Tweety any more and there's a new dog, another wolfhound, Darren or something like that. Everybody round her dies, but she remains the same just like the play."

"Stop it love, you're making her sound like some alien being, she's human like all of us."

"She has powers that nobody else has that I'm aware of, your back, Bill Watson's and now Harry in there, orthodox medicine didn't cure your complaint, she did. What do you make of that?"

"Lot's of people have these powers, hands on faith-healing and all that kind of thing. I didn't believe any of it before she treated me, can't get away from the proof. She has some extraordinary abilities none of the medical people have, but alien, that's going a bit far."

"Kevin reckons she's from another world," said Ellen from the doorway.

Jim snorted, "Your husband is as weird as Fanny, a wizard and all that funny get-up, rites in Bawsey Ruin at midnight on midsummer's day and all that."

Ellen came in and sat down, "You can laugh, she told Bobby about the Hump all that time ago. Nobody believed her, yet look what's happened on the site, all those weird happenings. How do you account for that?"

Ellen had matured into a very attractive young woman, Jim had to concede looking at her, credit to both he and Betty. The only fly in the ointment was the man she had chosen for a husband, definitely odd, as odd as Funny Fanny.

"I can't love," admitted Jim.

"Kevin reckons that the same ley-line runs from the old church through the Hump to Bawsey. Another crosses at the old ruin and another through the church. He says that we'd have the same problems if we interfered with the church or Bawsey."

"As much as I appreciate Kevvy darling, and I know he's your husband, but that young man is definitely odd. I know we've had some problems over your bungalow but Kevvy takes all this sort of thing too seriously."

"How do you account for all the things that have happened down there? Eight weeks Foster's men have been there and it hasn't improved one bit from when they started. How do you account for that?"

"Well, that's what Fanny's here for today," Betty looked embarrassed.

"To tell you not to build on the Hump? "Ellen looked triumphant, "You can't get away from the fact that something's very strange about that Hump, something is telling us that we shouldn't disturb it."

"You're going to tell us all about these tumulus's or what-ever they're called," said Jim, "Another of that husband of yours weird theories."

"I know you don't approve of Kev Dad, because he's a wizard and he digs into the occult, but he told you about the Hump long before you got planning permission to build on it. Give him credit for that."

"She's right Jimbo," said Betty, "Kevvy did say it wasn't a good idea."

"And I pooh-poohed it, alright so Johnny's had some problem over there, doesn't make it an alien powerhouse or whatever he calls it, a beacon for space ships, flying saucers from other star systems, and all that sci-fi crap."

"I think you should stop trying to build on the Hump, get permission to build on Slade," Ellen was serious, "It's nearer the lane than the Hump, cost less to put a road in and you might get permission to put a whole estate on it, that would make a difference to your situation wouldn't it?"

"She's right you know Jimbo," Betty sat up straight, "We could get quite a cash sum for that land if we got planning permission. It's not that much use for rape or wheat, barley or corn. Harry would give us a lump sum, solve our cash crisis."

"I'm being ganged up on," groused Jim, irritably.

Farraday appeared in the doorway. He looked baffled, pleased mystified and puzzled all in one expression.

"How'd you get on Harry?"

"It's a miracle," Farraday felt his lumbar region, "I've had nothing but pain here for years, always had that brace on otherwise I couldn't operate, it's gone completely. Mrs Legge says I can throw away that brace it won't recur, I can hardly believe it, all this time I've suffered and five minutes with her and I'm cured. I'll have to wait a few days, see if it does come back. I can't believe it's that simple. All she did was feel my back."

"And you felt as if some power was operating," finished Jim.

Farraday nodded, "I'm sure..."he stopped and shrugged his shoulders.

"Well, tell us Mr Farraday," prompted Ellen, "You felt something go out of you, travel past you towards the ceiling?

"I don't know," Farraday was plainly embarrassed, "It was a funny feeling, sounds like...."

"Witchcraft, Mr Farraday?"

Fanny stood in the doorway, that enigmatic smile on her face.

"I'm sorry Mrs Legge, but I've suffered with that disc for years, had all sorts of treatment for it, cost me a fortune, then you come along and in less than two minutes, cure it. It is a miracle, I don't know how to repay you."

"Nothing miraculous about it Mr Farraday, I've just repaired the circuitry in your body, your own body completed my work."

"Call it what you like Mrs Legge, I consider it a miracle. Let me pay you something for your expertise?"

"Miss Legge, please, I'm not married Mr Farraday and I don't want money."

"Surely there's something you could use?" protested Farraday.

Fanny nodded, "There is one thing."

"Name it, if I can do it I will." Farraday unconsciously felt his back again.

"The pain won't recur, I promise you."

"What can I do for you?"

"Persuade Mr Lewin not to build his house on the Hump."

****

8.

Saturday, 1st June, 1995.
Lewins Farm, Babingley,
King's Lynn, Norfolk.

Trestle tables were overlaid with crisp white cloths. Plates of food covered every inch and bunting stretched between temporary poles. A band from the Royal Norfolk Regiment played on the patio, while crowds of people milled around the stalls and tents of the various exhibits. A fairground had been laid out for the children with rides, slides and more stalls. The music from this area competed with the noise of the PA system and the MC's voice.

"It's awfully good of you to organise this fete Mrs Lewin."

The Reverend Charles Gates looked like a cadaver, and smelled somewhat of decay, Betty decided. His scrawny neck protruded from his collar like a turkey's crop, his bald head shone with unhealthy paleness, goggly eyes in shallow sockets thin blade of a nose with flared nostrils and teeth already in an advanced state of pyrorrhea that stuck from inflamed gums like horses. His hands reminded Betty of Fanny Legge's pet spider, Tweety, gave her the creeps. In fact everything about the Reverend disturbed her, especially his BO and halitosis.

"Well hopefully we can get enough money to help you restore St Mary's after what, nearly eighty years?"

"It's a miracle Mrs Lewin, God's work and one of his more mysterious ways. Who'd have thought there'd be a whole community in Babingley again, potential parishioners for the restored church...all down to you and your husband's foresight. Slade Estate is a very model of what a modern estate should be. Everybody is very grateful to you both for your prescience and planning," The Reverend breathed dead crab odours all over Betty. "The Bishop will be here shortly and I'm positive he will want to thank both of you personally for your handsome contribution towards the restoration fund. I'm positive the shortfall will be made up today. Most of the business community is present today. Ah, here's the Bishop now."

A portly man clad in all the regalia of his rank approached the patio accompanied by a bevy of reporters and hangers-on. A faint rime of perspiration covered his forehead, which was delicately dabbed at with a crisp white handkerchief. The Bishop deMaunary was breathing strenuously as he mounded the steps to the patio, assisted by his aide.

Betty decided that if the Reverend Gates looked like a four-day old corpse, the Bishop resembled a dead Vietnamese pig. Pouchy eyes stared myopically from puffy cheeks that appeared to squash his mouth into a thick trumpet from which two front teeth could be seen. Jowls unfolded like curtains over his cravat. There were several rings of gold and diamond on his fat little fingers. Dead blue eyes decorated with a road map of capillaries stared at her and Jim.

"I would like you to meet Mr and Mrs Lewin Bishop, the owners and organisers of this fete. We owe them quite a debt of gratitude for their work and contribution towards restoring St Mary's. Our fund had already passed the half million mark thanks to their own handsome contribution and that of the business community of Lynn and surrounding disctrict."

The Bishops' hand was cold and clammy despite the heat of the day. He held Betty's hand longer than she deemed propriety required and stared at her with those dead eyes as if seeking to hypnotise.

"The church is very grateful to you both Mr and Mrs Lewin. If it hadn't been for your initiative our church would eventually collapsed into ruin. The new Slade community will breathe new life into the area. I hope I shall be given the privilege of re-consecrating the restored edifice in due course," The Bishop's voice was wheezy, breathless and not from the climb up to the patio.

"We sincerely hope you will be able to attend the opening ceremony Bishop. Perhaps you'd like to meet the gentleman who will be responsible for the restoration work?"

"I most certainly would."

"Harry!"called Jim loudly.

The Bishop shuddered slightly as if the additional noise over the fairground and PA background was an affront. Harry Farraday approached, accompanied by his wife Fiona. Betty saw the Bishop's piggy eyes light up on seeing Farraday's second wife. He licked his lips unconsciously as he gazed lasciviously at the lithe body clad in a short dress. Her carefully coiffed blond hair coiled thickly around her head.

"Pleased too meet you Mr Farraday," said His Excellency, Bishop deMaunary, not looking at Farrady but at Fiona's spectacular milking machinery that bulged dangerously from her up-lift bra. He shook hands with her, holding her slim hand for an uncomfortable period.

Betty didn't entirely approve of Fiona Farraday. It wasn't entirely due to her remarkable good looks and perfect chassis with its ripe sexuality. Lilly Simpson, at one of that lady's famous coffee mornings held in the drawing room of the Simpson's half million pound mansion along the Wootton Road, Gaywood had inferred that Fiona's bedtime activity was not reserved entirely for her husband's amorous advances. She, so Lilly implied, was having it off with John Foster and had on one occasion been seen in compromising circumstances in a Norwich Hotel with that gentleman. How Lilly had acquired this unethical intelligence had not been revealed. Betty had no moral judgements on Fiona's extra-marital romps, she merely disapproved of her choice of partners. John Foster, ever since his failed attempt to build the bungalow on the Hump, had not filled Betty with unqualified respect.

"Nice to meet you Bishop," said Fiona, making no attempt to remove her hand from the Bishop's grip. She smiled, showing her perfect dentifrice, giving His Excellency the full treatment.

It was Harry whose opinion of the Bishop had collapsed into dubious doubts about the Bishop's intentions regarding his wife who broke the grip.

"Delighted you could be present today Bishop deMaunary. We shall be commencing work on St Mary's within a week or so. The work is scheduled to be completed by the end of next year. I have worked closely with Reverend Gates over the plans. I trust they meet with your approval?" Harry was shaking the Bishop's left hand vigorously in the hope of dislodging the prelate's grip on Fiona's hand.

The Bishop, whose sexual preferences were more for teenage choirboys than for sexually ripe females of whatever age, released Fiona's hand under Harry's enthusiastic assault, and gave him the benefit of an icy glare. The Bishop was bi-sexual biased in favour of young males, but didn't spurn the opportunity of delivering equally appropriate young females from the clutches of the ungodly by introducing them to his special form of deliverance from the paths of sin.

"I have seen the proposals Mr Farraday," he wheezed, his eyes still on Fiona's breasts. "I thoroughly approve. It will be a tremendous fillip for

God's work in the restored Parish of St Mary's. I understand the last service held in St Mary's was in 1918."

Betty and Jim moved towards Ellen and a group of the younger set who had all purchased houses on the Slade Estate. Lilly Simpson intercepted them. Five feet ten and weighing nearly two hundred pounds, Lilly Simpson could not be ignored. She was clad in a richly flowered dress that resembled an Army bell-tent, wholly unsuitable for concealing her full figure. From beneath the ankle-length dress protruded silver high-heel shoes. She believed in the confirmation of matriarchal authority by sporting her white hair decorated by a blue rinse, spurning all attempts by her hairdresser to head her off from such dating processes. Like the Bishop, gold rings were glued to every plump digit. A double pearl necklace hung from the plunging neckline, dangling into the valley of her enormous breasts.

"Ah Betty, caught you at last!" There was no doubt about Lilly's pedigree, Roedean and one of the best female Oxford Colleges. She projected her voice like a Dogger Bank fog horn.

"Just wanted to thank you and James for your sterling work helping restore St Mary's, and to give you Demetrius's contribution to the restoration fund."

She handed Betty a folded cheque removed from a crocodileskin handbag, "He would have been present but had an important board meeting in London. He asked me to give you this without too much ostentation."

Everyone within a hundred yards radius had heard her, including the local press reporter, Rory Calhoun.

"It's only a modest contribution of a hundred thousand, but it was the thought that counted wasn't it?"

Lilly's dentures had been fashioned by an expert and looked like natural teeth. She flashed a warm smile at Jim, "How's your charming daughter these days? I understand that Tracy and Bobby are around somewhere with Troy and Pamela Middleton? Haven't seen Pam at our coffee mornings for some time, I believe she is a surrogate Mother for Tracy and Bobby's daughter, Laura? Tracy does modelling full time doesn't she? Hasn't lost her figure after that remarkable pregnancy so soon after their marriage."

"Could we have a photo Mrs Simpson please, you and Mr and Mrs Lewin together?" A young man with long hair asked. His thin torso was festooned with camera equipment, "Perhaps you could hold out Mr Simpson's cheque Mrs Lewin? Our readers will want to know that Mr Simpson's contribution was generous."

The group posed self-consciously, save for Lilly who adored media attention. She dominated the group by sheer size and presence.

"Let me have a copy young man," ordered Lilly as he went his rounds to the next group.

"Hi Mum, Dad, how's it going?"

"Looks successful doesn't it love?"

Bobby and Tracy with their ten year old daughter came up. "You've performed miracles Mother," said Tracy, giving Betty a kiss, "You are a remarkable organiser."

Tracy Lewin looked like everybody's idea of a model. Tall, slender, dark hair carefully coiffed. The sheath dress encased her curves with casual grace. Her perfume was subtle yet pervasive and her gentian blue eyes were large, her nose a perfect line and mouth ripe, yet controlled.

"Thank you Tracy, where's Troy and Pamela?"

Betty hadn't approved of Tracy during the shotgun wedding of her son to the local millionaire's daughter ten years before. She had since modified that opinion and she and her daughter-in-law had become firm friends. "Hello Laura, are you enjoying our fete?"

"Quite frankly no Grandma. I'd sooner be with my horses. I find humanity in this amount quite off-putting." Laura looked more like her Father than Tracy, she had Bobby's build, fuller and more robust-looking.

"Why don't you sneak off love? Nobody's going to miss you," said Jim, "I can get Miller to drive you over to the stable?"

Jim was fond of his granddaughter. A feeling reciprocated.

"That would be nice Jimbo," Laura gave Jim a grateful smile, "I'm sorry I find these functions boring Grandma, but one can't help one's nature can one?"

"Don't overdo it Laura," warned Bobby, clad in sports jacket and slacks, "Grandma and Jimbo have worked hard for this, when they're not on their eighteen hole golf course, naturally."

"Don't knock it son, the EU provided the money to take the farm out of production," Jim grinned.

"Soon rival Sunningdale Dad," said Bobby, grinning in turn.

"About time that place had serious competition."

"Have you seen Ellen lately?" Betty looked round the crowded field.

"You mean lately, as in weeks, or as in today?"

Bobby opened his collar, jerked his tie down, "Christ it's hot, who'd have thought June would be as hot as this?"

"I mean today."

"I saw Aunty Ellen and Uncle Kevin with that bunch of weirdies over by the Fortune Tellers tent," said Laura.

"Shh, you mustn't talk about your aunt and uncle like that, you saucy girl," admonished Bobby, "Just because they happen to believe in wizards and witches doesn't make them weird."

"Granddad says they are," Laura was defiant.

"Your Granddad is apt to open his big mouth at the wrong time," said Betty, still looking round, "Oh God, look who's headed our way," She nodded in the direction of John Foster and his wife approaching their group.

"I wonder that bloke is still in business," said Bobby, "Selling cars is about his style since he went out of building."

Foster arrived, his mousy wife in tow, "Hi Jimbo, how's it going? Got your fund target yet? I see the thermometer is rising satisfactorily," he pointed to where a model of a thermometer stood at the entrance to the fete grounds.

The young reporter who had taken Lilly's photo a few moments before was hanging around in the vicinity, taking photos of various local prominent business people.

"Hi Lilly, how's Demtetrius? Made his fourth million yet?"

Foster looked as if he might administer a slap to Lilly's ample shoulder, then thought better of it at the last moment, "How's that vehicle your son bought off me going?"

Lilly gave Foster a sour look, "As a matter of fact he's had problems with it," she said.

"Tell him to bring it in, I'll have my chaps look it over for him. It's under the Foster warranty, same as all the cars I sell, got my reputation to maintain you know. That's a nice dress you're wearing Mrs Lewin," Foster was staring at Tracy's breasts, eyes peeling off her clothes. "We saw your photo on the front page of Vogue last month didn't we Jeannie?"

"Very impressive Mrs Lewin," gabbled Jeannie, "You must have a very glamorous lifestyle being photographed all the time, posing for films, adverts and clothes."

Tracy shrugged, "Hard work Mrs Foster, long hours like any other profession."

"You got that right love," said Foster, reaching into his inner pocket, bringing out a folded cheque, "Just thought I'd give you my little contribution to the old church fund Jimbo. How about that? Ten thousand nicker should help the old therm up a bit shouldn't it?"

Foster held up the cheque theatrically. The young press photographer took a series of flashes of Foster handing it to Jim.

Foster made sure that Tracy was in the group included in the photo, "Result of hard work in another commercial field eh?" He put his arm round Tracy's shoulder, "We're all in business aren't we? Jimbo there making money out of land and his fancy golf course, and me grafting away at my car business. I see you've awarded Harry with the restoration contract? Good bloke Harry. He does all the body work for me in his works, when it's necessary, of course, little dents and knocks all used cars acquire in the course of life. Very reliable, Harry's repair crew."

Tracy moved out from under Foster's arm, a look of distaste on her classic feature.

Foster wasn't abashed, he grinned at her, "Let's go talk to the Bishop, love shall we? See if we can get absolution on special offer this week, guaranteed for life?"

Foster waved his arm to include the field, the roofs of the houses on the Slade Estate, "Bit different to ten years ago mate, ain't it Jimbo? Had a hard time scraping the money together for that bungalow that never was, huh? Good old EU wants more golf courses than farms, made it into the big time haven't you? See you around folks."

He walked off, Jeannie hurrying after him after giving a nervous smile.

"What an obnoxious creature that man is," said Tracy.

"At least he's not in the jerry-building business any more," said Jimbo.

"Doing more damage killing people with his second-hand cars," said Bobby, "I shouldn't tell you this but we've got two sets of litigation going as a result of faulty workmanship on cars he's sold to locals."

"That's confidential info Bobby," said Betty, "As much as I disapprove you shouldn't spread rumours like that around and you a lawyer into the bargain."

"We're all family here," Bobby looked embarrassed.

****

9.

Saturday, June 1st, 1995.
Lewin's Farm Fete, Babingley
King's Lynn, Norfolk.

"Hi Jimbo, how's it going?"

"Wotcha Bill, long time no see, how's the old back?"

He greeted everybody with affability in turn. Bill Watson was a big man, over six feet tall, broad shouldered, craggy featured with beetling eyebrows, a large mobile mouth and yellowing teeth.

"Never had a problem since Funny Fanny gave me her treatment, what, must be over ten years ago now. I told her then and many times since, she could earn a fortune in Harley Street. Did the same for you didn't she?"

Jim nodded, "Never had problems since, touch wood. Bloody miracle, one minute I was agonised, next all gone, never comes back."

Watson nodded, "Same here mate, it is a miracle. I tell everybody about her when they start in on all this witch business living with spiders, dogs and all those cats. Not everybody's idea of a lifestyle but there we are. You had her in over that Hump business didn't you? I seem to have heard something about it in the local rag, ancient burial site isn't it and that's why Johnny Foster, that snide bastard had all those problems with the footings."

"Tumulus Mr Watson," said Bobby, "and ley-lines cross at that point. Nobody's ever got to the bottom of that problem, just why that cement went hard and the markers wouldn't stay put. It's still as it was then, we don't go near it. Fanny said there are ancient energies at work around it"

"Read the article in the 'Advertiser' some years back about these ley-lines, couldn't swallow it me-self, but there we are. If Fanny cured my back and yours and she believes all that crap, don't do no harm. You say you haven't touched that Hump since?"

"I fenced it off, just as Johnny Foster, Paddy Murphy and his blokes left it," said Jim.

"Memorial to Johnny's lousy workmanship eh?" Watson grinned.

"My son bought a car for his missus off him, had nothing but trouble with it, clutch, gearbox, steering, brakes, been back to Harry Farraday's place more often than she's driven it. You hear about poor old Wally?"

"Wally Thompson?"

"Yeah, poor sod's in dock, lung trouble, reckon he's got lung cancer through smoking, in a bad way he is."

"Didn't Mrs Legge say something to him about smoking that time she came to our house Jim? That was in '83, said Wally would become ill if he didn't give up smoking, I remember it well. He didn't look good then, poor Wally. He always came to see to Freda when she broke down, I'll go and see him."

Jim nodded, "Yeah the time she did my back for me, said you will become ill Wally if you smoke that evil weed. There's something strange about that woman."

"You ain't-a-kidding Jimbo. She warned my son's wife about that car when she was thinking of buying it, said the spirits were not good about it. Like we all do, we dismissed it as hokum, she was dead right though."

Watson looked round the crowded field at the milling crowds, the roundabouts, swings and stalls. "I can see someone coming our way you'll be pleased to meet coming to give you his company's contribution to the Fund."

"Who's that?"

"Lane Ward, Lilly's unofficial amour," grinned Bill. "I'll be off, try and find that wife of mine before she spreads any more scandal, see you around." He waved a hand and moved off.

Lane Ward, MD of Ward Electronics, Lynn's electrical discount store occupying an out of town site on the Saddlebow Industrial Estate, was late fifties, heavily built, with incipient jowls, thinning hair carefully combed over his scalp, fleshy mouth and eyes displaying the ravages of thyroid problems. His wife had died several years before and his liaison with Lilly Simpson was a village joke.

"Hello folk, nice shindig you've organised Betty," he grinned. "If you ever want a job come and see me, I can use managerial talent like this, rare commodity. How're you Jimbo? How's the old back these days? I saw Billy walk off when he saw me coming, one of his attractive traits. Both of you go in for witchcraft from Funny Fanny, treating back pain. I reckon it's all in the head, psychological auto-suggestion."

"Well I hope you don't have the pleasure of a back injury mush," said

Jim," And if Fanny's treatment of my back and Billy's was witchcraft, I'm glad I tried it."

"Ouch! hit a nerve have I? I was only joking, I've heard all the tales about Funny Fanny and her activities, thought it was just that, rumours. She actually cured it for you did she?"

"Completely and it wasn't just my skull playing up either."

"OK, sorry, seems Fanny has some admirers. I saw her down by the dipper just now, had that bloody dog with her, he looks like a small donkey, a wolfhound or something, frightened six colours out of me. You invite her? She won't make much of a contribution to the fund, might drop a tarantula in the collection box for fun, no bread."

"How about your contribution Lane?" Betty was sour, "We're publishing a list of all the firms who gave to the fund, that should give you food for thought. Lane Electronics not on it wouldn't do your image much goodm would it?"

"Speaking of that matter Betty, I just happen to have my chequebook with me, how much do you want?"

"Well, I can see the thermometer from here, looks like we're short of a hundred thousand to make our target,"said Betty.

"Look good next to Demetrius' contribution in the 'Advertiser next week," Betty ignored Jim's nudge.

"You're joking of course lady?" Ward's goggly eyes almost popped from their sockets.

"Up to you of course Mr Ward, even Bill Watson had given a substantial amount."

"I don't get subsidies from the EU," Ward scowled.

"Opening another store in Downham next month aren't you?"

Jim grinned, "Salve your conscience, get blessed by the Bishop as well, Lilly can always give you a hand-out if you're ever short of cash flow."

"Lilly and I are just good friends," Ward looked shifty.

"We believe you Lane, it's the others," said Jim, warming to the idea of Ward Electronics making up the shortfall in the fund after the initial shock of Betty's suggestion had worn off. "We buy all our goods from your discount house, good prices, better than Dixons or Comet, don't know how you do it. Demetrius isn't subsidising you is he? Not being funny but if the big boys have problems with margins you must be working on a low profit."

"Good financial management Jimbo. If you ever want advice on how to make money out of your EU hand-out for that fancy golf course of yours, let me know."

"Well how much?" Betty twisted her fingers," A hundred thousand chicken feed for you. Lilly would approve of such generosity."

No wonder you've come into the money, sunshine," snapped Ward, "With a pushy wife like Betty it's a foregone conclusion."

"When Demetrius finally pops off you'll be in clover Lane, marry Lilly who'll inherit the lolly from the beer and lager," said Betty in a hard voice.

"Christ, you're a real bloodsucker," Ward pulled his chequebook from his inner pocket, scribbled rapidly and handed the cheque to Betty, "Satisfied?"

Betty scanned it, smiled "This is true heart-warming generosity Lane, I'll see you and Lane Electronics gets special mention on our list of contributors, free advertising for you. If you'd like to submit a three column ad I'll see it goes in, pride of place."

"Thanks" snapped Ward, 'I'll see you around." He stomped off.

"How much?" Jim strained to look.

"We've done it!" exulted Betty, waving the cheque, "The Fund has met it's target"

"How much?" insisted Jim.

"There it is, a hundred grand. I was only joking as well. His conscience must be worrying him."

"Shit, he must have got out the wrong side of bed this morning," Jim looked at the scribble, "Hope he doesn't have it stopped when he recovers."

"He wouldn't dare."

"You putting the mockers on poor Ward Lane Mumsy?"

Ellen stood behind them. She was clad in a short skirt and halter, bare feet in sandals, her titian hair thickly coiled.

"Nothing poor about that man love, he's a multi-millionaire, " said Betty, "Where's Kev? Isn't he with you?"

"He's with the other wizards of the Coven, planning the summer solstice at Bawsey in the house."

"I wonder why you put up with all that crap sis," said Bobby. "They're all weird like those freaks at Stonehenge on Midsummer morning."

"Leave her be Bobby," admonished Tracy, "Everybody's got at least one hang-up. Dressing up in funny gear is not that bad."

"Thanks Tracy, your husband was always anti-unusual. He's a fully paid up member of the Establishment," Ellen grinned at her brother to remove the sting.

"There must be some connection between working with computer programmes and the occult," Bobby was not to be gainsaid, "Something to do with VR, how's the mint tea and vegies?"

"You really are an eighteen carat asshole brother. Kev holds down a responsible job at Marshall's. He'll be Chief Programmer soon when Merv Hudson retires," Ellen patted her thick hair in place.

"If I recall Merv Hudson he must be around forty plus now. How can he retire? He's got another twenty years to go."

"Forty is old now in the computer business."

"What's he going to live on in his enforced retirement? Bobby was contemptuous.

"Just because lawyers go on until they die from hardening of the arteries sunshine, or die from inhaling dust from the archives, you mustn't think the world revolves around law. If I were you Tracy I'd be looking round for some sugar daddy to replace your husband when his sex drive dries up. Should be any time now."

"You always were a saucy cow," said Bobby good naturedly. "There is nothing wrong with my libido system."

"I'll have to have a private discussion with Tracy on that subject. Kevin has some potions that can stimulate tumescence in males."

"Made from frogshit and weasel blood?" scoffed Bobby.

"Oh stop it you two," commanded Betty. "Ellen, go and tell the steward we've met our target and get him to alter the thermometer."

"Not a good idea Mumsy, it'll stop other people giving if they see you've topped the million mark," said Ellen, "Defer it until the fete's over."

"She's right love," said Jim, "There could be more money around, Harvey's over there and there's Barry Lassiter and Troy has not donated yet, wait a little while longer."

"I thought it would stop these two going at one another," said Betty, "I thought they'd grow out of it."

"She gets her quarrelsome nature from you Mumsy," said Bobby, "The way you browbeat poor Ward is typical of the irascible nature of the Lewin women."

"You can ask Daddy now about his contribution," said Tracy, "He's headed in this direction."

"Hello James," Troy Middleton was tall, a human lamppost, sagging slightly around his middle. His bald head gleamed in the sunlight, rimless spectacles. Incongruously, his features were delicate, almost feminine. He wore a tailored bush jacket and serge khaki trousers. "Thought you'd want this from me," He held out a cheque to Betty, "I hope that's adequate?"

"Goodness me, it's very generous Troy," said Betty, glancing at the amount.

"He's building up treasure in heaven Elizabeth."

Pamela Middleton was ex-St Pauls and it showed. Her two-piece in soft lemon was not off the peg at M & S, it highlighted her dark good looks. Made Betty's silk frock look like Salvation Army handout.

"Thinks if he gives to good causes God will give him pride of place in the hereafter."

"She always suspects my motives Elizabeth." Troy Middleton was soft spoken, his rivals in the transport business had often taken this for lack of drive or old fasioned guts. The fact that Middleton Freight PLC carried most of the distribution network of the main supermarket chains belied suggestions of being a soft touch. His casual manner concealed a hard-nosed acumen that made rival firms envious.

"Perhaps we can persuade Bishop deManaury to put in a good word Pam," said Betty, "When he sees this he'll be overjoyed, with due ecclesiastical decorum naturally."

"Have you reached your target yet?" Pamela was as shrewd as her husband, the power behind his throne.

"Haven't checked recently, but we must be almost there," lied Betty, "This should help enormously," She replied, waving the cheque.

"Don't be so devious Mumsy," reproached Ellen. "She reached her target with Lane Ward's contribution Mrs Middleton, that will put it way over."

"Well, better late than never my dear?" Pamela Middleton's smile was forced.

"How's the old lumbar these days Jimbo?" Barry Lassiter looked like a refugee from a fancy dress ball. Clad in a shepherd smock-type garment, wearing a trilby and heavy boots, it was difficult to associate him with medicine.

"Fanny Legge did for me what you quacks never did," said Jim. "You should send all your back sufferers to her, she cures people, you just give them palliatives so they keep coming back for more treatment. How's Wally Thompson doing? Is he as bad as Billy Watson says he is?"

Lassiter sobered, "He's very ill Jimbo."

"Perhaps you should invite Funny Fanny to look him over? Perhaps she could do something for him that you and your mates can't do?"

"That's slanderous, you heard that Harvey? Casting aspersions on my competence on the medical profession."

Harvey Johnson was a small man, barely five-five, even smaller build with rounded shoulders and pidgeon-toed. He wore a pin-stripe suit, black shoes and sported a collar and tie. Ellen had more than once described him as resembling a tortoise.

"She cured Bill Watson's back as well Barry," Johnson's voice was powerful coming from so small a man. "You could do worse than co-opting her on your team."

"Another traitorous bastard in my circle of friends," said Lassiter, "You're supposed to be on my side you snide sod."

"A little witchcraft would help your practice mister," declared Johnson, "Enliven your image create interest in local medicine."

"Get me struck off as well," said Lassiter, "The BMA doesn't approve of mavericks."

"Like Pasteur Lister and Roentgen," said Johnson, brushing his thick hair back.

"They didn't live with two dozen cats, a dog as big as a bloody pony, and a pet spider as big as a dinnerplate, and a lame donkey," said Lassiter.

****

10.

Saturday, June 1st, 1995.
Fete, Lewin's Farm, Babingley
King's Lynn, Norfolk.

"That might go down well with your customers," said Johnson.

"Like I said I thought you were on my side?" Lassiter was staring over the diminutive Johnson's head, "The witch in question is heading this way, I'm off. Dogs that big frighten six colours out of me, here's my cheque Betty as much as I can afford with all my commitments." He handed her a cheque and made off into the crowd.

"Mine also Mrs Lewin," Johnson handed over his cheque, "I'll see you around. I don't know how to handle the occult."

He walked off just as Funny Fanny arrived with her dog, Darren. The animal was huge, Jim had to concede, it reached Fanny's waist.

"Sit Darren," ordered Fanny.

The dog obediently sat.

"Looks as if you have had a successful day Mrs Lewin?" Fanny's voice was soft, even melodious.

"I think we've reached our target Miss Legge," said Betty, eyeing the wolfhound with caution. It looked ferocious.

"You passed that point a short time ago," said Fanny.

Jim and Betty exchanged looks, the woman was truly a witch. How on earth could she have known that? It all tied in with the woman's uncanny ability to read minds.

"This isn't your scene at all is it Miss Legge?" said Betty.

Fanny shook her head, "I'm interested in what you propose doing to the old church with all the money you've collected."

The Middleton's were gazing at Fanny with something akin to awe. Betty had to admit there was something about Fanny Legge that commanded attention, but was hard put to identify just what that something was. She recalled her son-in-law Kevin saying something about an aura. Just what an aura was he'd been vague. She had to admit that whatever it was,

Fanny Legge had it.

"You'd have to talk to Harry Farraday about that kind of detail Miss Legge," said Jim.

Betty sensed that her husband had also become aware of this mysterious 'aura'. Indeed so had everybody present.

"I don't mean the detail, I meant the structure." Fanny Legge had this awesome ability to remain totally immobile, yet the impression she gave was one of immense vitality.

"I believe the intention is merely to restore the fabric of the building, replace the stonework where it's needed, but mainly bring it back to something usable as a place of worship again," Jim was uneasy. He couldn't meet Fanny's black eye gaze, it was as if something was probing inside his skull.

"Ley-lines cross at St Mary's Mr Lewin, as well as the place you call the Hump."

The announcement was quiet, yet everybody heard it.

"Are you telling us that we're going to have the same problems that we had trying to build our bungalow Miss Legge?" asked Ellen, an eagerness in her voice.

"Do you know why that church was abandoned Mrs Wilson?" Fanny turned her gaze on Ellen.

"Lack of parishioners. There weren't many people round here in the first place, I suppose the First World War finished the process," said Ellen. Everybody was looking at her.

Fanny shook her head, "It would be worthwhile looking up the old records for that period before you commence any work on restoration Mr Lewin."

"Can you be a little more specific?" asked Jim. Alarm was flickering inside his head. Fanny's question sounded like a warning. He knew Betty had picked up the vibes as well as Ellen.

Fanny shook her head, "I just feel you should," she said, "I'm glad your back is not troubling you anymore."

"Never had a spot of bother since Miss Legge," Jim assured her hastily.

Fanny turned her gaze on Troy Middleton, "You have the same name as an American General in World War Two Mr Middleton. Were you aware of that?"

Troy looked very uneasy at being subjected to an inquisition by the local witch. His calm, assured manner seemed to have deserted him.

"His Father was an admirer of that soldier Mrs Legge," said Pamela, "Always told Troy's Mother that if they ever had a son they would call him Troy."

"You've been feeling unwell recently Mr Middleton," Fanny ignored Pamela, it wasn't a question.

"Nonsense, Troy's as fit as a fiddle Mrs Legge," stated Pamela, "Never had a days' illness in his life."

Betty saw Pamela visibly wilt under Fanny's gaze as if she'd been struck by some force.

"Seems I'm mistaken," Fanny's hand waved. The wolfhound rose and he two of them walked off without saying another word.

"Peculiar woman," said Pamela in a strident voice. There was an element of uneasiness in her tones, "Trying to alarm us, I've heard all about her abilities, this mysterious healing power. Utter nonsense of course, just rumours invented by ignorant peasant types."

"They aren't rumours Pamela, she cured my back, as well as Bill Watson's, that was ten years ago, I've never had problems with it since she treated me."

"Are you sure it wouldn't have got better on its own without her James?" Pamela's voice was assertive, as if trying to restore her lost dignity in face of Fanny Legge's powers.

"Jim had suffered with that back ever since we were married Pamela," said Betty, "Barry Lassiter had given him treatment. The hospital had tried traction, we spent a fortune on chiropractors, osteopaths, but nothing worked. She just massaged Jim's back and he's never had trouble since, and that was back in '83. That can't be rumour."

Pamela sniffed dismissively, "I still think people believe in witchcraft and because she's eccentric they invest her with all sorts of weird things outside normal experience, all hyped into legend."

"I think we ought to do as she suggests Mumsy," said Ellen.

"What, look at the records?"

"Do we know why St Mary's was abandoned? The truth, not hearsay, and that business about lack of congregations? Was that the real reason?"

"That would take months love, Harry is anxious to get started, it hold up his schedule," said Jim.

Ellen shrugged, "I just have this feeling that that was a warning. We don't want another Hump do we?"

"You're subscribing to these peasant rumours Ellen," said Pamela, "It's all in the mind of unlettered ignorant types."

"The trouble we had with the Hump wasn't just rumour or the hysteria of peasant types Pamela," said Ellen, "We had to abandon building our house on that site because of the things that happened to people and machinery on the site."

She didn't care for Pamela Middleton, or her daughter for that matter. Pamela was aware of this fact, the animosity was mutual.

"I think she's right Jim. The Reverend can do a lot of the legwork, he'll have access to the Parish records," said Betty.

"I don't think that's a bright idea Mumsy," Ellen had her back to Pamela.

"Why not?"

"Let's assume there is something odd about why St Mary's was abandoned. Is he likely to tell us the truth? He wants the church restored. If there was anything in the records likely to inhibit the restoration he'll either play it down or not tell us. Harry Farrady'll get started and then we have all the hassle of the Hump all over again. You know how reluctant Harry's men were to even come near Slade because of the things that had happened at the Hump. He had to give them bonuses before they'd start."

"I don't think the Reverend would deliberately varnish over something bad Ellen," Pamela was determined to have her say, "He isn't the type."

Ellen gave Pamela a caustic look, "I'm afraid I haven't your confidence in our local vicar where financial benefits are concerned Pamela. The Church is short of cash and the pension of all priests are at risk."

"That's not a very nice thing to say about Gates Elly," said Bobby, "All that ley-lines business is strictly for the birds. Fanny loves all that occult crap, spreading despair and despondency."

"She saved Dad from spending useless money on the Hump site brother dear. Kev and I would still be living with Mumsy and Dad."

"Perish the thought dear girl," Betty crossed herself, "You alright Troy?"

Middleton had turned very pale, he looked shaky.

"Feel slightly peculiar Mrs Lewin," he said, massaging his abdomen.

"Barry's over there by the thermometer, I'll call him over. If we have a professional on tap even if he is off-duty, he can take a look at you," said

Betty.

"I'll go get him fix the thermometer at the same time," said Ellen. She walked off.

"I'll have to sit down love," said Troy, "I feel most peculiar."

"I'll get you a chair from the bandstand, hang about," said Jim, hurrying off.

Betty decided that Troy Middleton did look bad. He was ashen and in obvious pain.

"It's all that curry you had at lunch dear," Pamela wasn't very sympathetic, "You know you can't take that spicy food. Those Indian places always make me suspicious."

Jim returned with a chair. Middleton sat down and Jim and Betty exchanged glances.

"Fanny said he looked ill," muttered Betty.

"Looks as if she got that right, as well. Here's Barry now."

Lassiter bustled up, his shepherd-type smock looking absurd. "What's the problem Troy?" He put his hand on Middleton's forehead, "Hmm, slight temperature. Where do you feel bad?"

"Around here," Middleton indicated his midriff, "Feels tender."

"Lift your shirt," commanded Lassiter.

Middleton was self conscious, but complied with the request. Lassiter felt his abdomen, pressing here and there gently, Middleton winced.

"Painful?" Lassiter looked round, "Could someone fetch my bag from my car for me? It's in the main car parking area, Grey BMW."

"I'll go," offered Bobby, taking Lassiter's car keys.

"I'll go with you Daddy," said Laura.

Lassiter lifted Middleton's eyelids, and peered inside his mouth.

"Feel nauseous?"

"Slightly," Troy nodded, "I feel like lying down."

"You can't do that here Troy, not on the grass," Pamela looked shocked.

"If he wants to lie down Pam, let him," said Lassiter.

"Every body will see him," wailed Pamela, looking round apprehensively.

"Lie down Troy," said Lassiter, ignoring Pamela.

Middleton lay down and groaned faintly.

"What's wrong with him?" Pamela looked apprehensive.

"Looks like liver, it's distended marginally."

"Is that bad?"

"It's unusual, put it that way Pamela."

"God! People are already looking this way, it'll be awful having those peasant types gawping all round us."

"Get a grip on yourself woman. Your husband needs your sympathy, not your social hang-ups," snapped Lassiter, looking over to the car park.

Bobby was rooting around in the boot, trying to find the plastic bag. Lassiter tutted impatiently. Middleton meanwhile had turned a ghastly yellow and was groaning, holding his abdomen.

"Should we phone for an ambulance Barry?" asked Jim.

"I'll examine him first," Lassiter stood looking at Bobby, who was still busy at the boot of the doctor's car, "What in hell is keeping him?"

"Well do something man. You're a doctor aren't you?" snapped Pamela.

"Pamela, when I am sure what it is I will then do something." He was restrained.

A small crowd attracted by the almost bush telegraph effect of bad news had now gathered.

"God! This is awful," moaned Pamela, "We'll be the laughing stock.

"Why don't you go and help find Barry's bag Pamela? Looks as if Bobby is having difficulty," said Betty.

"That's what you'd do isn't it?" Pamela turned on Betty.

"I'm trying to be helpful Pam, and if you keep this up you'll attract more attention, s o why don't you go help Bobby?" Betty suppressed her anger.

Bobby returned without a bag, "There's nothing in there Barry, I've looked all over the vehicle."

"Oh God help me!" growled Lassiter, "Keep him warm, I'll go and find it."

Betty felt Troy's forehead, it was cold, clammy, "He's getting cold," she announced, looking helplessly around for something with which to cover the sick man, "Has anybody got a blanket?" She appealed to the crowd.

One of the onlookers volunteered to fetch one.

"Can I help?"asked a voice.

Fanny Legge stood inside the circle of people, the wolfhound at her side.

People moved away from her uneasily, as if frightened of being contaminated by some spell.

"I don't know Mrs Legge. Doctor Lassiter says it's his liver," said Betty.

Fanny nodded, "It is, an I have a look?"

"Oh God this is all we need, a witch," moaned Pamela.

"Don't be rude Pam," snapped Jim, "Let her have a look."

Fanny knelt down beside Troy, her slender strong hands probing under Troy's shirt.

"We'll be the laughing stock of Wootton," cried Pamela, angrily.

She made to pull Fanny away. The wolfhound growled menacingly. Pam jerked away, her eyes dilating in fear.

"I'm going for the police," she announced hysterically, "That woman is evil. No business having an animal like that, it's dangerous!" She departed, pushing her way through the crowd.

Fanny had both hands over Troy's abdomen and began pressing gently, a faraway look on her face.

To Jim and Betty's astonishment the colour returned rapidly to Troy's face, the yellow disappeared and his groaning ceased. He looked relaxed, at ease. It was at this point that Barry Lassiter returned, holding a black leather bag. He stopped in his tracks on seeing Fanny kneeling beside Troy Middleton,

"What the devil...?" he began.

"Hold still Barry," said Jim, firmly, "Don't interfere"

Lassiter could see the change that had occurred in Middleton's skin colour, the fact that he looked easier and had stopped moaning. He looked down disbelievingly at the kneeling woman, eying the huge dog speculatively. It sat beside Fanny, it's yellowish eyes baleful.

Troy opened his eyes and saw Fanny, he started to move nervously.

"Stay still for a minute Mr Middleton," said Fanny, gently pushing him back, one hand still on his abdomen.

He lay still, embarrassed at the crowd around him.

Fanny removed her hand, "I think you'll be alright now Mr Middleton, you can get up if you wish."

Jim aided Middleton to his feet, "How'd you feel Troy?" he asked.

"I'm fine, that was most peculiar." He looked perfectly fit and smiling.

"You have Mrs Legge to thank Troy," said Jim as Middleton looked at Lassiter.

The doctor was standing there, bag in hand, a dazed look on his face, shaking his head faintly. "I don't believe this," he muttered.

"Bloody miracle," said someone in the crowd.

"Raising Lazarus," said another.

There were murmurs of astonishment and disbelief.

"You sure you feel OK Troy?" asked Betty.

"Fine, I assure you. Must have been a funny turn."

"You looked awfully ill before Miss Legge attended you Troy," said Jim, "You owe her your thanks. Where is she?"

"Went that way," said one of the crowd, pointing.

"She must be a bloody witch," said another, "I ain't ever seen anything like that before."

Jim pushed through the crowd, there was no sign of Fanny Legge or her dog. Pamela was hurrying up, accompanied by two duty police officers.

"Where is she?" Pamela demanded, face distorted with anger.

She stopped, seeing her husband standing, looking fit and well again, "How did you...?"she began.

"Where's this dangerous animal Madame?" demanded one of the young policemen.

"She's a little distraught officer," said Betty, "There's no dangerous dog here as you can see."

"You cured him?" Pamela was bewildered and distressed. She addressed Lassiter who was still standing there, a bemused expression on his face.

"Eh? No, I did nothing at all Pamela," he muttered.

"You must have done, look he's well again," Pamela pointed to Troy who was brushing the dust from his clothing.

"I had no hand in it whatsoever, that woman Mrs Legge cured him. He looks fine to me now, I never believed in miracles before but this is an astonishing feat. Faith healing, you'll have to thank her Pamela. Troy looked very ill to me a short time ago, I had grave doubts about him."

"You're making all this up," Pamela accused him.

"He ain't missus, the witch cured him," said one of the crowd. "Saw it with my own two eyes, I saw it, bloody miracle, like he said."

Pamela huffed at the woman and turned away in disbelief.

"Cheeky bitch," muttered the woman, "Typical stuck-up cow, think money gives 'em airs."

"So there's no mad dog?" The two policemen were looking at one another. One raised his eyes heavenwards.

"No mad dog Officer," said Betty.

"Let's go Buck," urged the policeman to his colleague, "Bloody waste of time."

****

11.

Saturday, 8th June, 1995.
Lewin's Farm, Babingley Marsh,
King's Lynn, Norfolk.

Jim sat reading the Lynn Advertiser's account of the Fete the previous week. There were photos of all the local personalities, business, social and religious. The Bishop deManaury was prominent as was the Reverend Gates. Lilly Simpson was seen posing ostentatiously along with Lane Ward. There were half page photos of scenes from the fete with stylised photos of himself and Betty as hosts of the Fete. The news that the target money for the restoration of St Mary's Church had been reached via the generosity of local business people like Lane Ward, Demetrius Simpson, John Foster, Harry Farraday, Troy Middleton and others was prominently featured. It had evidently been a big event in the local calendar.

Jim turned the page, the headline jumped out at him. 'Local Man cured by witchcraft!' There was a lurid and not at all accurate account of Troy Middleton being cured by the community witch, Fanny Legge. Somehow the writer had secured a photo of Fanny and her wolfhound. This was given full coverage with an obviously faked Troy Middleton being observed lying down by a puzzled Barry Lassiter. There was a blank space on part of Troy's body, as if something had covered that part of his anatomy. No sign of Fanny Legge. The writer had permitted his ripe imagination to run riot with exotic stories of bringing Troy back from the dead and Fanny Legge practising Black Arts in the garden of her North Wootton cottage. There was even a cauldron suspended on a tripod over a stick fire. An artist had sketched a picture of Fanny Legge stirring the brew, a satanic expression on her face.

"Have you seen this love?" Jim called to Betty from the conservatory.

Betty gazed at the lurid pictures and story horrified, "That poor woman, she'll be hounded by the media now when that story is syndicated."

"I bet she's already sussed that out, won't be around when they turn up," said Jim. "It was a miracle, I've no doubt about that. Troy is as right as rain now, if I hadn't seen it I'd have not believed it."

"I agree, whilst I am pleased about Troy, I can't help feeling a little uneasy about the power Fanny possesses, it's awesome. The way that Barry reacted, as if all his skills learned the hard way, medical school, hospital, then locum and finally his practice, years of experience are all worthless in the face of Fanny's magic. No wonder he got drunk last Saturday."

"Oh come on love, it was only a one off. She doesn't go around performing miracles everyday, she just happened to be there."

"I can still appreciate how Barry felt, helpless," Betty picked up the Advertiser, scanning the article on Fanny Legge, "This lot don't help."

"You can't blame them love, I mean it wasn't as if she did the thing in private. There was a crowd and they all witnessed it, like the raising of Lazarus. One minute Troy's half dead, the next he's walking around cured. Bound to start people fantasising about it like Chinese whispers."

"That poor woman's going to be hounded by the media, TV, national newspapers, magazines, the witch of Lynn, or something like that and as soon as they get wind of spiders and cats, lame donkeys and see her cottage..."Betty left it hanging.

"I have the feeling that she can handle it love."

"Handle what?" Ellen stood in the doorway of the conservatory.

"Hello love, what brings you here at this time of the day? Why aren't you at work?"

"I've taken a few days off, felt like it."

"Just like that?"

"I'm not indispensable Mumsy and Paul said he can manage for a week without my expertise."

"As long as the members don't suffer as a result of your absence."

"You think they care about what goes on behind the scenes? All they care about is the eighteen holes in good order and I don't think you can complain about that. The membership has increased every year since you set it up and Paul is a good manager. Runs the place like a military operation."

"Glad to hear it love, help yourself to some coffee."

"I've just dropped Laura off down at the stables. That young woman is horse mad."

"There are worse things to get excited about love," said Jim.

"If I was Tracy it would worry me," Ellen helped herself to coffee from the percolator.

"Why, for goodness sake? The child has been riding ever since she could walk," said Jim, "Got more medals and credits than anybody else in Lynn."

"Have you see that horse she's riding?" Ellen sat down next to Betty.

"What's wrong with it?"

"You haven't been down at the stables for yonks have you?"

Jim grinned, "Merry runs it efficiently, doesn't like me poking my nose in, not that I want to. All those plummy women kissing horses noses, obscene!"

"What's wrong with the horse?" Betty frowned at Jim.

"It's seventeen hands, a stallion, and very lively," said Ellen.

"I hope Bobby has vetted it, and approves," said Betty.

"I don't think my dear brother knows anything at all about it, none of us are horsey, he just indulges Laura. I'm probably making mountains, but there you are, that's me with horse riding. I'm like you, think there's something slightly weird about those women lavishing all that affection on half a ton of unstable dynamite," Ellen picked up Jim's discarded Advertiser, "God, poor Fanny, have you read this?"

Betty and Jim nodded.

"This is obscene if ever anything was. The poor woman will be hounded now by all those media freaks from TV, witchcraft and raising Lazarus, Christ, they've really gone to town on this. Why don't you have a word with Jeff Patten? He's at the Club House now playing his daily eighteen holes."

"Even if I did he'd tell me to mind my own business and it's slamming the door after the horse has bolted. He's in the business of selling papers and a local St Bernadette is newsworthy stuff. I'll bet the circulation has jumped this week."

"I'm thinking of the effect on Fanny, the National media are bound to jump on it, anything weird and they're like ghouls." Ellen sipped her coffee, still scanning the article on Fanny Legge.

"It's a nine days wonder love," said Betty, "There'll be something else to attract their attention tomorrow. That's one consolation about TV, doesn't last long."

"Every sick person in the UK will want to know about Fanny if she can cure them," Ellen was angry, "She'll be hounded."

"Why're you so concerned about Miss Legge?" Betty refilled her cup.

"I like her, for all her odd habits and lifestyle, I'd hate to see her hassled by media freaks and crowds of hypochondriacs with bumps and swellings."

"The damage has been done love, there's nothing we can do," Jim held out his cup for Betty to fill it.

"Help yourself mister, I'm not your skivvy," said Betty, tartly.

"Should never have let 'em out of the kitchen," groused Jim, walking over to the percolator. He turned after filling his cup, "What brings you here at this time of the day, apart from filial devotion, I mean?"

"I've been looking at Parish records," said Ellen.

"What on earth for?"

"Remember what Fanny said last Saturday, about the church restoration?"

"You mean about looking up the records before Harry Farraday starts on the restoration work, I'd forgotten all about it."

"There's been a load of gear delivered all outside the old burial grounds, Farraday hasn't lost any time getting started."

"Sounds like efficiency to me love," said Jim, "Doesn't mess around like Johnny Foster used to."

"Remember what Fanny said about ley-lines crossing at the church as well as the Hump?" Ellen sipped her coffee.

"Oh God, not that again?" Jim moaned.

"Kev reckons there's a definite alignment between St Mary's, the Hump, Bawsey Ruin and Reffley Spring, with lines crossing at each of those points."

"And what conclusions does your hubby draw from that intelligence?" Betty sounded sceptical.

"Apart from Parish Records, I persuaded Ray Hammond to let me into the archives section of the Library. He and Kev went to Grammar together."

"And?"

"Fascinating, all those old tomes, leather bound, paper flaking, tons of local history all recorded by all sorts of people, some of it never published."

"Well?"

"Hang about, I also went to see Jeff Patten, to let me have a butcher's at his records."

"You doing this deliberately to build the suspense?" Jim was irritated.

"St Mary's wasn't closed for lack of congregation," said Ellen

"God, you're just like your Mother woman, bloody irritating," snapped Jim, "What was the reason?"

"There was an influenza epidemic in 1918, worldwide, killed a lot of people."

"Get to the point."

"Fifty people died in Babingley village, as it was then, accounted for fifty percent of the population, half of them. No other village suffered that kind of devastation."

"So there weren't enough parishioners to keep the church going, simple," said Jim.

Ellen pulled a folded paper from her handbag, "I copied this from the Advertiser, June 21st, 1918. You can see the date at the top," she handed it to Jim. "Local Church Infected by Plague," was the headline.

"You were talking about influenza, what's this got to do with anything?"

"Read it," said Ellen, "Fifty people attended evening service on the previous Sunday, three days later they were dead, not from influenza, but plague, bubonic variety, at least that's what the coroner said after the inquest."

"Well?" Jim handed the copy to Betty.

"There were some private papers in the Library, written by the last parson of St Mary's around the same date. He officiated at the service on that Sunday."

"You're loving this aren't you?" said Jim.

"It's fascinating," agreed Ellen.

"What did he say?" Betty finished reading the photocopy, handing it back.

"He claims there was a flash of lightning, at least that's how he described it during the service, it lit up the whole church for around twenty seconds, the lanterns went out and there was a smell of burning cloth. By the time they'd re-lit the lanterns, no electricity then, people were complaining about feeling ill. He called the service off, three days later all fifty of his congregation were dead, from this mysterious plague, all at the same time, noon on June 21st, 1918. A week later, he and his family were all dead, again the coroner claimed it was bubonic plague."

"I suppose he knew what he was about?"

"The local doctor was called in to several of these people on the Monday, June 18th. He couldn't identify any of the symptoms, or why these people were so ill. None displayed any symptoms of bubonic plague, no swellings, nothing.

They were just ill, sweating, with high temperatures and sore throats. The whole family was affected, not just the ones who'd attended the service on that Sunday. The doctor who had been called in also died, and his family."

"Sounds like a Mafia vendetta," said Betty.

"How long is it since you visited the old churchyard?"

"Yonks," said Jim, "not since we fenced it off to keep vandals out, why?"

"They're all buried there, I looked. There are some old graves but most of them date from that June 1918. It might sound like spooks but I had this funny feeling whilst I was in there."

"You always were a little odd love, even as a child," said Betty.

"What kind of feeling?" Jim was sceptical.

"That I was being watched," She shrugged, "I know it sounds daft and it might be all inside my head, but I don't think so."

"You'd been influenced by what you'd read."

"That's what I kept on telling myself. The feeling grew stronger, I simply ran out of the place," Ellen looked shamefaced. "As soon as I was clear of the fence we had put round it, the feeling went. I told myself not to be so stupid, so I went back. It was even worse, just as if someone was standing behind me. It was even more spooky by virtue of the fact that it was brilliant sunshine, birds were singing, it was hot and yet the place was gloomy. I know the trees have grown up around it, but it didn't account for the shadows inside and it was cold, damned cold."

"Your imagination playing up love," said Jim.

Ellen shrugged again, "It was very real whilst I was in there. There was something else, and I know you're going to think I'm going round the twist, but..." She stopped, raising her arms helplessly.

"You were just hyped up love. Imagination plays tricks," said Betty.

"Well what was it?" Jim was amused at his daughter's over sensitivity.

"I heard this sound," Ellen was embarrassed, "I know it sounds like something out of a Roald Dahl story and you're forgiven for thinking it was my imagination working overtime."

"Come on then, what did you hear?"

"It sounds daft now."

"Come on don't keep us in the air," Jim was exasperated.

"When I got near the bricked up entrance to the crypt, I heard this moaning, it rose and fell like the wind in some attic. I freely admit it, I was frightened shitless. Nobody around for miles, sun blazing down, birds singing and then this noise. I didn't stop running until I got back to our house."

"No need to feel embarrassed love, if I'd heard groans coming from the crypt I'd have done a bunk as well," Jim could hardly prevent the grin.

"You may laugh Dad, it does sound funny, illogical, the response of a nervous female alone in a spooky environment, it was very real."

"Never mind your Father love, he's totally insensitive," said Betty scowling at Jim.

"Is that it?" asked Jim.

"One item I found in the back-issues of the Advertiser and in the Parish records. You aren't going to believe this," Ellen looked even more embarrassed.

"Well, what was it?" Jim was impatient.

"Guess who's buried in that crypt?"

"From what I recall when we used to play down there as a kid, there are several people down there, old families who lived in Babingley during the seventeenth century," said Jim, "Did a bit of courting down there as a lad."

"Who's down there love?" Betty was sympathetic.

"Myfanwy Legge!"

****

12.

Monday, 15th June, 1995.
St Mary's Church, Babingley Marsh,
King's Lynn, Norfolk.

Harry Farraday knew there was something wrong the instant he turned the bend in the track leading to St Mary's past the Lewin Farmhouse. The scaffolding was almost in place round the old church and the plastic sheeting had been secured over the roof of the nave. The old tower stood proud over the surrounding marsh. What in hell was wrong?

Harry slowed, was tempted to call in to see Jim Lewin before travelling on to the church. He dismissed the idea, if there was something wrong the sooner he was aware of it the sooner it could be handled. He stopped his BMW when he was still half a mile from the church, stared out over the golf course that now occupied what had once been fields of rape, corn, barley and wheat. The Club House was half concealed behind a screen of mature cypress that Lewin had imported at great expense to soften the image of the raw building surrounded by the vast expanse of sky and marshland.

St Mary's stood out like the proverbial sore thumb on the landscape. It always bothered him why anyone would want to build a church in such an isolated position. Apart from the Club House and Jim Lewin's farmhouse there wasn't another dwelling until one reached the old Hunstanton Road that meandered along the pine clad escarpment two miles behind him. He knew there had been in the remote past, a village of Babingley, with several families living in close proximity to the edifice. But that didn't appear to justify the church builders of the fourteenth century building such a monument to religion in such a remote location.

The new Slade Estate, all modern four bedroom, mini-mansions, way out to his right had always seemed to him to be an obscenity, an affront to his sense of what was justified in terms of planning. It was new, relatively speaking and the trees planted around it would soon soften the outline. Even so how Lewin had ever got permission to build from the Council Planning Department was a baffling mystery. He'd suspected bribery when

Lewin had informed him that he'd gained planning permission to build on Slade, especially after John Foster's disastrous attempts at building on what was known as the Hump. Being basically pragmatic, he didn't wholly swallow the lurid tales, embellished through repetition in the local pubs, of mysterious events, machinery not working, men falling ill, cement bags going hard and tools going missing. Paddy Murphy, who had become one of his most respected site managers, swore on oath that it had all happened and that he wasn't exaggerating, that it was fact.

Murphy was now in charge of the restoration work at St Mary's. He was a hard worker, made his men toe the line, he did not tolerate slacking or shoddy workmanship. Malingerers or ne'er-do-wells that had been integral to construction industry in former times, he would not countenance. In fact it had been a boon to his company that Paddy Murphy had transferred his allegiance from Foster Development to the Farraday Construction Company way back in '83. Despite the rumours that accompanied Irish workers of drinking, slackness, shoddy work, Murphy was the exception. If a job was assigned to him Harry knew he could safely leave him to execute it with despatch and efficiency.

What was wrong?

It took him a good five minutes staring at the scaffolding surrounding the church before it hit him. There was nobody working!

"What the hell is Murphy thinking about?" he said it aloud. He re-started the car and drove slowly towards the church, expecting to find his worst fears unjustified, he'd imagined it.

As he entered the fenced off area he saw the site hut with the men all sitting round, apparently doing nothing, that he knew his fears were confirmed.

Murphy came out of the site office, the instant Harry turned his car into the compound. He looked worried and he hardly dare admit it to himself, the man looked positively frightened.

"What's up Paddy?" He dragged his rubber over boots from behind the passenger seat, removed his office wear and pulled on the boots.

Murphy didn't answer. Close up, Harry's fears were confirmed. The man looked frightened. A nasty feeling knotted inside Harry's stomach. Murphy had come a long way in the ten years he'd been with Farraday Construction. He was no longer the slovenly bograt from impoverished Ireland. He was smartly turned out even on site, didn't drink or smoke, he swore like a trooper it was true, but what construction man didn't? His paperwork was immaculate, his man management techniques a model for any smart-ass consultant to copy. What had got him into this state?"

"Better have a chat Harry, in the office," Murphy said at last

The twenty or so workers all stared at Harry as he and Paddy entered the site office. Harry thought they didn't look too happy. No leg pulling, no smiles and they weren't working.

"What's wrong Paddy? Why aren't they working?" Farraday swallowed his irritation. Murphy was not the man to permit this lack of activity without good cause.

"You ain't going to believe this Harry," Paddy held up the coffee pot enquiringly.

Harry took a look at the stained mugs, shook his head. Paddy helped himself, sat down in his swivel armchair and wiped his forehead with a clean handkerchief. It was warm in the office despite the fan.

"Convince me I'm not dreaming Paddy."

"It sound like something out of a fuckin' Irish fairy tale, you know,l leprechauns, the little people?"

"Tell me, see if I believe it," Harry brushed dust off the chair.

"The fellers say they heard sounds coming from that bricked up crypt," Murphy looked embarrassed, expecting Harry to give a belly laugh.

Harry repressed his urge to yell, this wasn't the way to handle Paddy Murphy, "Sounds from the crypt?" he echoed, "What kind of sounds do they think they heard?"

Murphy was plainly deeply self-conscious, unwilling to say more.

"Come on Paddy, this job is not one we can fall down on. It's prestige for us, we got the job in front of a lot of high-powered competition. If we louse-up we're in deep shit."

"Have I ever muffed a job Harry?" Paddy's blue eyes were hard.

"You haven't, so what's with this fairy tale crap?"

"When Boxall came in to tell me I was all for kickin' ass, firing the bastard, I'm not too sure about him anyway."

"What convinced you?"

"He was scared shitless and so were his crew," Paddy took a quaff of his coffee, "..and he wasn't putting it on, I assure you."

"So Fred Boxall heard sounds coming from the crypt?" Harry had to control his desire to bawl Murphy out.

"I told you you'd have a hard job believin' it. My first reaction like I said was to kick ass, tell him to get his act together or else."

"Why didn't you?"

"Fred might be an eighteen carat wanker but he doesn't scare easily."

"So you had a butcher's yourself?"

Paddy nodded, said nothing.

"And?"

"It was like a moaning groaning noise that rose and fell," Paddy looked embarrassed, "Frightened six colours outa me Harry," he said, quietly, "I don't know how long that place has been bricked up. By the look of the mortar I'd say twenty years at least and you hear noises?"

"Blow hole somewhere," said Farraday.

"I thought about that, I had a good look round the outside wall First there isn't any wind and second I couldn't find anything that looked like a hole."

"So what do we do? We can't just stop work because of a few bloody noises. Like I said we got this one in front of some high-powered opposition. We can't afford to fuck-up, we'd never live it down and if Jeff Patten gets too hear about this we'd get media attention that would give us all red faces."

"None of them will go near the place Harry."

Farraday stood up, "That leaves you and me Paddy," he said, "I'll get my gear on, you get a drill set up, I've got around an hour before I have to go."

Paddy looked as if he might refuse, he thought about it, then nodded. "OK"

Farraday went out to his BMW, passing the lounging men en route. He heard Paddy ordering the men to set up a pneumatic drill inside the church.

Harry stripped off to his underpants, pulled on an engineer's overall, picked up a hard hat and went back. "All set?"

Paddy nodded, he looked uneasy as he followed Harry into the gloomy interior of the decaying church. The entrance to the crypt was via a bricked up door beside the altar.

"OK, let's get started," said Harry, picking up the heavy drill.

Paddy signalled, the compressor started up. It took Harry less than five minutes to pierce the crumbling brickwork, Paddy removed the debris. In ten minutes they had made an aperture wide enough to allow entry. A musty smell emerged from the hole. The men had gathered round to watch, wheeling the debris from the body of the church in wheelbarrows. At a signal from Paddy the compressor was switched off.

"Arc lamp fellers," ordered Harry.

The men had been impressed on seeing Farraday's firm example of leading from the front. They'd also been influenced by his expertise at handling the drill.

"You coming down with me Fred?" asked Harry of Fred Boxall, the foreman who'd been responsible for the stoppage.

Boxall was a small man, lean and dark with Celtish blood.

"No way sir," He shook his head.

Harry looked round at the men gathered behind him. They all shook their heads, moving back slightly.

"That leaves me and thee Paddy," said Harry as two men came in with a cable reel and a powerful arc lamp.

"Murphy knew that to be seen to refuse would ruin his authority with his men forever. They'd never accept him as boss again.

He was uneasy, but nodded. Harry stepped into the aperture, treading warily down the stone stairs. The powerful light showed all the ancient stone walls, cracks and crumbling mortar. The stairway wound round a bend.

The two men arrived at the foot and stepped fully into the crypt. Harry shone the lamp round, there were several catafalques in niches in the walls. The place was musty but dry. A single massive catafalque occupied pride of place on a plinth in the centre of the floor. It was constructed of stone, carved with ornate symbols. Harry shone the torch on the side of the massive stone coffin. A brass plate had been fixed to the side. A name was engraved in Gothic script.

Harry cleaned the dust from it with his hand, "Myfanwy Legge, June 21st, 1796."

"Well, there's nothing down here, save a few old stone coffins Paddy," said Harry, his voice echoed. The name didn't ring any bells, some local dignitary from ages past, he thought, "Satisfied?"

"I definitely heard the moaning, Harry," said Paddy. His expression was tense in the reflected light from the arc lamp.

"Well there's none now." He walked to the foot of the stairs

"Come on down you blokes, take a butcher's, see if there's anything to be scared about."

They took some persuading until Fred Boxall finally descended, followed by a small group of his fellow workers. They looked around the musty crypt with awe, inspected Myfanwy Legge's massive catafalque.

"Isn't that the name of that witch who lives in North Wootton," said one of the men, inspecting the brass plate.

It struck Harry then, Funny Fanny! The woman who had cured his back and that of Bill Watson and Jim Lewin, she was known as Fanny, which was easily a corruption of Myfanwy. One of her relatives buried in the crypt of St Mary's. So Funny Fanny had relatives in Babingley as long ago as 1796. Odd, but not impossible. He'd never heard of any other Legge in Lynn and Funny Fanny always insisted on being called 'Miss'. He dismissed the thought. Without going through Parish records, finding an entry that confirmed that Legge's had indeed lived in Babingley when there had been a village. But what was the point? So her ancestor shared the same name, nothing odd about that. Lots of people were lumbered with family names they did not particularly approve of.

"Satisfied gents?" demanded Harry, "There's nothing down here save a few mouldering corpses, "You Fred?"

"Looks like we've been a load of old women Boss," said Boxall.

"I'm sorry."

"OK, now perhaps we can get on with it, can we?" Harry avoided criticism, that would merely inflame the situation, cure nothing.

There were grunts of approval. Just then the light went out.

"Shit, that fucking generator's been playing up," said Paddy.

"Don't panic," said Harry from the dark, "I came prepared." He fished a hand torch from his overall pocket.

Just then they heard it, a grisly moaning that started as a groan, then rose to a wild, unnerving shrieking that went on and on!

****

13.

Saturday, June 15th, 1995.
Lewin's Farm, Babingley Marsh,
King's Lynn, Norfolk

"What in hell is that?" Jim stared out of the window towards the dirt road leading to the Hump and St Mary's.

The hee-haw of a siren echoed mournfully fading as it past the house. Jim caught sight of an ambulance as it hurtled past the Hump, en route to the Church.

"Somebody must have been injured, masonry falling from the roof," said Betty.

"Can't be that, unless Harvey got it wrong. He said it was safe enough until the scaffolding was in place," Jim strained to see in which direction the ambulance had gone.

"Could be someone in the Slade and the driver's gone the wrong way. They all think they can get this way instead of along the new road," Betty joined him.

The siren was cut off suddenly.

"It's got to be the church," said Jim, "I thought I saw Harry go down there a short time ago, I think I'll go take a butcher's."

"I'll come with you," Betty pulled her cardigan around her shoulders.

A Jaguar pulled up at the front door just as they exited. It was Bobby. "Going someplace folks?" he grinned.

"Down to the church, an ambulance has just gone down there." Betty was impatient.

"Hop in, I'll take you," He reached over flung open the passenger door. "You sure about the ambulance?" he asked starting off.

"I saw it" said Jim, leaning over to observe the church tower with its scaffolding and plastic covering.

"Who's down there on a Saturday morning?"

"They started work on the restoration yesterday," said Betty.

"I hope nobody has been injured."

"Somebody stuck his hand in the mixer," joked Bobby, "Construc-tion is only marginally more dangerous than horse riding."

They saw the ambulance then, backed up to the main door of the church. The medics were carrying someone out on a stretcher.

"Must be serious," said Jim.

Bobby pulled up as close as he could get to the surrounding perimeter security fence. The medics were closing the door of the ambulance as the three of them went forward. Harry Farraday was standing talking to his workmen. There were scared expressions on the faces of the workmen. Harry saw them coming, he left his men as the ambulance drove out through the gate and approached them.

"Trouble?" Jim squinted against the morning sunlight.

"Paddy Murphy, think it's a coronary."

Farraday looked dazed half aware of what was going on. His men were packing up their belongings, heading out to their cars and other transport.

"How did he get that? He looked fit as a fiddle," said Bobby.

The men called out farewells as they passed. Jim noticed Farrady's hand trembling. He was pale, looked totally drawn.

"You OK Harry? Come up to the house have a drink."

Farraday didn't seem able to grasp the import of Jim's offer, as he looked blankly at him.

"I'll lock up Fred," called Harry as the works foreman closed the gates. Boxall waved. he also looked scared and shaken.

"You're closing early aren't you Harry?" said Bobby, "What're you togged up in that gear for?" He indicated Farraday's overall and hard hat.

"Let them get off the site, I'll tell you," said Farraday, leading the way into the site hut.

He waited until the last car in the cavalcade had passed en route to the main road. He was shivering and looked ill.

"Sure you're OK Harry?" Betty pushed him into Murphy's chair, "I'll make some tea."

Farraday sat silently watching Betty operate the Calor gas stove, making the tea in four mugs.

"Well?" said Jim as they all sat down.

"I came in early and saw all the work had stopped, unlike Paddy to allow it," said Farraday, "Murphy met me said his blokes including Fred Boxall were scared, they were downing tools."

"You're joking of course?" said Bobby.

Farraday shook his head," I was miffed. I want this job completed on time and properly, in view of the Opposition's interest. I swallowed my anger, asked the reason," Farraday shook his head slowly, "I still find it hard to believe."

The Lewins waited, Farraday seemed trying to regain some composure.

"Take your time Harry," said Jim.

"Fred said he and his men had heard noises coming from the direction of that bricked-up crypt in there." He nodded towards the body of the church. He looked at them, as if challenging them to laugh or sneer.

"Noises from the crypt?" echoed Bobby, "That was bricked-up when I was a kid. Dad thought it was dangerous for us to go playing down there. The stairs were crumbling and the floor of the church could easily collapse, that correct Dad?"

Jim nodded, "Let Harry finish," he said.

"I nearly laughed as well, sounded like excuses for not wanting to work. Boxall is a barrack-room lawyer, always working the blokes up. Anyway, I went in there, I couldn't hear anything. Fred and the blokes were obviously upset so I got togged-up. Paddy and I took the bricked-up door down with a pneumatic drill. I didn't want work stopped for stupid reasons like noises from a crypt, sounded like Roald Dahl to me. I went down with an arc lamp, Paddy came with me. I expected it to be damp, being below the water table of the marsh, but it was dry. I guess you know what's down there?" He appealed to Bobby.

"Some tatty old catafalques in niches and one in the middle of the floor if recall correctly," said Bobby, "On a plinth."

Farraday nodded, "I called the blokes down to see for themselves there was nothing, no noises, nothing that could make a noise, except a few mouldering corpses mummified by time," He paused and shivered.

"Don't tell me you heard noises Harry?" Bobby was scornful.

"You saw them carry Paddy out didn't you?" Farraday's hands were still shaking, "It was like nothing I ever heard before. A strangled kind of groaning that rose to a scream." Harry passed a hand over his forehead, "I'm not an imaginative bloke, but that noise in that atmosphere frightened six colours of shit out of me. It's the kind of thing you hear in a horror movie not in real life, at ten o'clock in the morning on a bright summer day." He paused again, saw the incredulous expressions on his listeners' faces, "I know, sounds like the most idiotic scenario you ever heard. Paddy went down like a pole-axed cow. The other blokes did a bunk like frightened kids up the stairs. To cap it all the generator packed up and I was left down there in complete bloody darkness with an unconscious man. Not something you can easily cope with. I couldn't see a thing without a light. I left Paddy and found my way out. Tried to get the blokes to come back with me with hand torches to get Paddy out. They were like frightened rabbits. None of them would go into the place, let alone down into the crypt. I used my mobile to get an ambulance. The medics went down brought Paddy out, said it looked as if he'd had a major heart attack and no, I didn't tell them what had caused it. Can you imagine Jeff Patten hearing that? The media would have been here in droves, making life more of a hell than it is right now."

"Didn't the medics hear anything?" asked Bobby.

"If they did they didn't say anything."

"Didn't they want to know what Paddy was doing down in the crypt?" asked Jim.

Farraday nodded, "I told them he was making structural evaluations for the restoration work. I know what you're thinking believe me, I swear it was true, that noise was awful," He dabbed at his forehead with a handkerchief, "Came from the direction of Fanny Legge's catafalque."

"That is a joke isn't it?" Bobby tried to stifle a grin, "I saw Fanny Legge only yesterday in Lynn, she'd hardly have risen from the dead."

"There was an old brass plate on the side of the coffin. I forget the date but it said Myfanwy Legge alright."

"Forgive me Harry but there's nothing on the side of that coffin, certainly no brass plate. I've played down there as a kid, I'd have remembered that. Dad will corroborate that won't you Dad?"

"I don't recall seeing a brass plate I have to admit Harry. You sure about this? I mean you must have been in a state, so to speak, you could have imagined it."

"I seem to recall the date was some time in the late seventeen hundreds. I know the month was June and yes, the twenty-first of June, seventeen...let me think.. ninety-something, that's it 1796."

"You got a torch? I have to see this for myself. Be quite an experience going down after twenty years, nostalgia and all that," Bobby looked sceptical.

"You think you should Bobby?" asked Betty, uncertainly.

Bobby laughed, "What do you think I'm going to see, a reincarnation of Dracula or Fanny Legge looking like Tutenkhamun? I want to see this brass plate, there was nothing on that catafalque when we used to play down there. I wonder if that is Funny Fanny's real name? Sounds Welsh..Myfanwy."

"I could hardly have made that up could I?" Farraday was peeved at Bobby's scepticism.

"I'll come with you son. I don't remember any brass plate and we never knew whose catafalque it was," said Jim, "There's nothing in it anyway. I seem to recall we removed the lid just before we bricked it up, not even bones or bits of clothing."

"Go and see for yourselves, there's my torch," Farraday pointed.

"Won't be long love," Jim picked up the torch.

He and Bobby entered the church careful to avoid bumping into the scaffolding and made their way to the entrance to the crypt.

"I reckon Harry's having hallucinations in his old age," said Bobby, "I've heard some fairy tales in my short and happy little life but moans from a coffin..."

"He's not usually prey to things like that," temporised Jim, "Watch these stairs, they're crumbling."

They entered the crypt and Jim shone the torch round. The arc lamp was lying on the floor near the central catafalque where Harry had dropped it. Jim shone the torch on the stone coffin.

"Told you so, Harry's having hallucinations," said Bobby, "There is no brass plaque."

"Where did he get the name from though? Myfanwy Legge and the date, seventeen ninety six was it, or seven?"

"Probably an association of ideas, Funny Fanny fixing his back at the fete a couple of weeks back, miracles, ergo something occult, whatever. You can see there's no brass plate is there now?" Bobby's voice echoed in the crypt.

"Funny he should pick that name and date. You're right though, no brass plaque and I don't remember seeing one when I had Johnny Foster brick it up."

"He's in a state of nerves Dad. We don't want to make things worse, let him get over his fright then we can tell him, or he can come and see for himself."

"What do we say now then?"

"Say it's difficult to see properly, could be a plaque but we couldn't find it. Come on let's get out of here before we start hearing groans and screams," Bobby chuckled, "I can't get over it, a mature bloke like Harry and that Paddy fellow, hard to imagine him having a heart attack, big, strong, plenty of exercise."

Jim picked up the fallen arc lamp, the cable still attached and carried it up the stairs. He stopped Bobby as they exited from the crypt, "If Murphy starts blabbing about it when he comes round we'll have some unwelcome media attention, Anglia TV, newsmen, Christ it would be awful, paranormal freaks, ghost hunters..."

"How do we stop him? He's bound to tell what he believes he saw and heard?"

"I'll have words with Barry Lassiter, imply that Paddy's been under a bit of strain, tell the hospital staff not to take much notice of his explanations."

"I can't imagine any self-respecting consultant swallowing that tale," said Bobby as they exited from the church, "Sounds like the worst bloody fairy tale you ever heard. Oh,Christ!"

"What's up?" Jim looked at his son.

"Your daughter has arrived, I suppose we'll get a visit from the Advertiser bloke, what's his name? The one taking photos at the fete, Gary, Rory, Morrie...fucking weirdo, long hair tight jeans, medallion hanging round his neck."

"Calhoun?"

"That's him, he'd be all we need."

They entered the hut, Ellen was making more tea, Betty and Harry Farraday were talking.

"The grave robbers come to steal the gold from the tomb," greeted Bobby, "How's the freaky husband, ready for the solstice at Bawsey is he?"

"Very funny sonny," Ellen wasn't amused.

"Well, did you find the plaque?" Farraday looked up eagerly.

"Difficult to see with this little object," said Jim replacing the torch, "Could well be, have to wait until we get some proper lighting down there, we found your arc lamp though."

"You're prevaricating Jimbo, trying to make me feel better," accused

Farraday.

"I heard those sounds," said Ellen, "Harry's imagination wasn't working overtime. Remember me telling you about it last week? and there is a Myfanwy Legge buried in that crypt, according to the Parish records and the old issues of the'Advertiser, remember me telling you?"

"What was the date?" asked Bobby.

"Late seventeen hundreds," said Ellen.

"Seventeen ninety-six?" said Farraday.

"I believe it was around then, can't recall precisely."

"So I wasn't dreaming it?"

"Not if the Parish Records are correct," Ellen was glaring at Bobby and her Father. "You say you couldn't see a plaque on the coffin?

"It was difficult with that torch Harry," Jim looked uncomfortable.

"If Paddy starts talking in hospital Harry we'll have bigger problems," said Bobby, to head Farraday off from probing. "The media ghouls will be down here in large numbers. They love stories about witchcraft, the occult and funny goings on in a derelict crypt would be manna from heaven. You'd better warn him as soon as you can not to talk too the media, least of all someone like Calhoun. That gentleman has ambitions to become another Robin Day.

"And warn Fred Boxall not to open his mouth in the pub," added Jim.

"I'm going to have problems with the blokes over this." Farraday seemed to have forgotten the issue of the brass plaque.

"They aren't going to be happy about working in there in future."

"You want to cop out of the contract?" Jim seized the opportunity to further divert Farraday, "Mason's could take it over, glad of the work I suppose, bearing in mind the state of the industry right now."

Farrady shook his head, "No way, I'll handle Freddie and the blokes." He seemed to be recovering from his shock, "I don't need Calhoun and his ilk around making hay out of this situation, that would be awful. I'd better get cracking now before those fellows start talking."

"We'll lock up for you," offered Jim, "You carry on, you know where they'll be?"

"Rising Sun, you know it?"

"Along the Wootton Road?"

"I'll try there first, make sure the gates are locked, we don't need Calhoun snooping round on his own," He hurried out.

"What was all that about?" demanded Ellen, "You were trying to bluff him about that plaque weren't you?"

"There was no plaque love," said Jim.

****

14.

Sunday, June 16th, 1995.
Lewin's Farm, Babingley Marsh,
King's Lynn, Norfolk.

"More toast love?" Betty poured her husband another mug of tea.

The sun was warm through the conservatory glass at just eight am.

"Eh?" Jim was reading the Sunday papers.

"Tea" Betty said sharply, "More tea?"

Jim put down the paper, "Thanks love," He pulled the mug towards him. "I think you ought to ring Harry Jimbo. Make sure he caught that Boxall fellow before he starts talking in 'The Rising Sun."

Jim picked up the mobile, "I was about to do that anyway, thank for the reminder."

"Oh no," Betty was staring out of the window.

"What's up?"

"Isn't that that chap from the 'Advertiser'?" She pointed.

A vintage Volkswagen Beetle, painted a bright yellow with oversize tyres had pulled up in the driveway. A young man in his thirties had stepped out carrying camera equipment in an aluminium case.

"That's him" Jim swore, "No need to phone Harry," He compressed the phone aerial. "Harry didn't catch them in time, we need him like a dose of Legionnaire's Disease."

The young man, clad in washed denim with long hair and dark glasses stood looking round for a minute before walking up the drive. Jim met him at the door to the conservatory.

"Can I help you?"

"I believe so Mr Lewin, we met at your fete a fortnight ago?"

"Calhoun isn't it?" Jim was short.

"That's me Mr Lewin, can you give me a few minutes? I know it's early."

"Come in Mr Calhoun," called Betty, "Want some breakfast?"

Calhoun smiled showing good teeth, "That's very civilised of you Mrs

Lewin, it would be nice."

"Come in and sit down," invited Betty, clearing the breakfast debris from the table, "You'll have to talk to me I'm afraid. My husband has some urgent work in the barn."

Jim was about to argue but thought better of it and exited from the conservatory.

Betty pushed the Sunday papers over to Calhoun, "I'll be back in a minute or so, bacon and egg alright? How'd you like it?"

"Sunnyside up Mrs Lewin, thank you."

"Coffee, tea?"

"Coffee if that's not too much bother."

"What're you up to?" hissed Jim in the kitchen, "That creature is a man-eating reptile."

"We start looking guilty and he'll draw his own conclusions mister," whispered Betty sharply, "Now leave him to me, go and see Ellen or Bobby for an hour."

"I hope you know what you're doing," Jim groused.

"I know precisely what I'm doing, go on get lost," She busied herself at the Aga with the frying pan.

"Here we are Mr Calhoun," she announced ten minutes later, coming in with a tray.

"That smells good Mrs Lewin, I didn't anticipate this."

"We have to keep on the right side of the Press," Betty smiled.

"That's not the view everybody would endorse Mrs Lewin," said Calhoun, starting on the breakfast.

"You married Mr Calhoun?" Betty sat opposite.

"Fraid not Mrs Lewin, is that bad?"

"I'd have thought a good looking young man, good job in the media would have attracted some young lady. How old are you? Thirty, thirty-five?"

"I'm supposed to be interviewing you Mrs Lewin," Calhoun grinned, stuffing his mouth with egg and bacon.

"Female curiosity," said Betty, "Like vintage cars, do you?"

"You mean my Beetle? I do like old cars, although vintage would be a trifle exotic."

"Where do you live?"

"I have a flat in the North End, bachelor stuff, very untidy, full of hi-fi and photographic equipment."

"Where do your parents live?"

"Norwich."

Betty didn't let up for the duration of Calhoun's meal.

"That was great Mrs Lewin," Calhoun put the plate back on the tray, "I've never been interviewed before, you did a grand job."

I'll have to tell Jeff that if we need another reporter, I can recommend a good prospective candidate."

"I haven't the figure or the looks," said Betty, modestly.

"People like talking to more mature reporters, dollies put them off."

"What can we do for you Mr Calhoun?" asked Betty abruptly.

"Rory please Mrs Lewin, the mister bit makes me feel old."

"Rory," said Betty.

"I was in the Rising Sun yesterday lunchtime Mrs Lewin, there were some workers in there, they work for Harry Farraday. I know Fred Boxall, he and my father went to St James's."

"What has Fred Boxall got to do with us?"

"Farrady's got the contract to renovate St Mary's, Fred said they'd just come from the site. The site manager had been taken to Lynn General suffering from a coronary as a result of something they'd seen in the crypt of St Mary's, you know anything about it?" Calhoun's easy manner had gone.

"Paddy Murphy you mean?"

"That's him, been with Farradys ten years, used to work for Foster's before John Foster copped out of building, went into used cars."

"What's the connection Mr Calhoun?"

"Can you tell me what happened in that crypt to give Paddy Murphy a coronary?"

Betty smiled, "Oh that? Very simple and very mundane I'm afraid."

"Not what Fred Boxall told me, Mrs Lewin."

"What did he tell you?"

"They saw a ghost down there."

Betty giggled, "You believe that?"

"No, but something must have frightened Paddy, what do you think it was?"

"The TV has a lot to answer for, all those horror movies, Alien,, The Living Dead and all that and in a crypt, just the atmosphere to create fears.

Murphy must have had a condition to start with."

"Granted, Boxall said they heard noises coming from the crypt, Betty laughed, "I'm surprised at a hard-headed young man like you believing that."

"I think Freddie was serious Mrs Lewin, he said when they investigated there were screams and groan from a coffin and Paddy saw a ghost."

"Tell you what Mr Calhoun, I'll take you down there, you can see for yourself what a peculiar tale Paddy has been spinning. How do you feel about that?"

Calhoun nodded, "That would be a good start Mrs Lewin."

"Let me get my coat," Betty went into the lounge. Jim was sitting reading the papers, "Come on, I'm taking Calhoun down into the crypt, let him see there's nothing unusual about it."

"Are you crazy, woman?" gasped Jim, "What happens if Paddy was right and there is something down there?"

"Well, we'll have it confirmed won't we? If you're frightened I'll go myself."

"No, I'll come."

"One thing though, let me do the talking."

Calhoun got up when he saw Jim, "Ah Mr Lewin, I'm Rory Calhoun from the 'Advertiser', your wife has kindly offered to let me see this crypt that Paddy Murphy was talking about."

"I know who you are Mr Calhoun"

"Do you mind if take pictures?"

"Be our guest."

On their way down to the crypt, they drove past the Hump.

"Isn't that the site of all those odd goings on, way back in 1985 wasn't it? John Foster packed it in because of all the weird events, machinery wouldn't operate, the men became sick and the foundations crumbling?

"That was his story Mr Calhoun," Betty didn't stop. Calhoun took photos of it as they passed.

Jim was becoming uneasy, he began to see the end product of Calhoun's visit, a garbled version of the Lewin Farm Story with all things taken out of context, exaggerated and media freaks running amok over the two sites. They arrived at the perimeter fence, Betty stopped the Landrover so that Jim could unlock the gates. She drove in and parked, the car. Betty took a large torch from the glove compartment, while Calhoun prepared his camera with flashes and various lenses.

"Watch your head on the scaffolding," warned Jim, as they made their way inside.

"Why is the other site fenced off?" asked Calhoun, stopping taking film of the interior of the church, "Is it dangerous?"

"According to our son-in-law it is an ancient burial site, tumulus, or something. We didn't want people treading carelessly over it," said Betty.

"Your son-in-law?" Calhoun squatted to take copious film of the nave and altar.

"Kevin Wilson."

"Oh yes, Kev and I used to go to school together. He was into the occult in those days, witchcraft, ley-lines, tumuli, ancient civilisations, the Pyramids, funny bloke."

He's got that right thought Jim, bloody wizards society, Bawsey, Summer Solstice and he's subverted my daughter, she is getting like him.

"You want to go down here?" Betty stopped at the entrance to the crypt.

"Most certainly, I find these places fascinating, why is it so gloomy in here?"

"Scaffolding, I suppose."

"Not that much of it, strange."

Jim took the torch from Betty and led the way, "Watch your step, the stone is crumbling."

They entered the crypt proper. "Christ, it's chilly down here," muttered Calhoun," Must be several degrees colder than outside." He took flash photos of the crypt from every angle, including the central catafalque on its plinth.

"What's the brass plate for?" Calhoun's voice echoed.

"What brass plate?" Jim and Betty stood back, allowing Calhoun to take film, standing near the foot of the steps.

"On this catafalque? Can you bring your torch over?"

"You're mistaken, there's no brass plaque," said Jim.

"What do you call this then?" Calhoun was pointing at the dull object on the side of the stone coffin.

Jim shone his torch in the direction of Calhoun's pointing finger. It was brass, dusty but plainly fixed to the coffin wall.

"Too much dust, can't read the inscription," said Calhoun.

He reached out to brush off the dust. There was a brilliant flash, Jim saw an electric spark jump from the plaque to Calhoun's hand.

The newsman was flung backward to the floor, his camera went flying and Jim's torch went out!

"Shit, the fucking torch has gone phut," snarled Jim, "You OK Calhoun?"

"What in hell was that?" came Calhoun's voice from the floor, "You got that coffin wired?"

"Is that a joke?" Jim wasn't sure what he'd seen.

"You saw the flash didn't you?" snapped Calhoun, "My hand is burnt, where the hell is my camera?"

Betty and Jim heard him scrabbling around, "Got it, I hope to Christ it isn't buggered, it cost me a fortune. What was that flash?" His voice echoed.

"Haven't the vaguest idea," said Betty, "Let's get out of here."

"Hang about, let me see if this camera works."

Jim and Betty heard him fiddling around.

"Here we go," The flash illuminated the crypt, "Still works."

"Come on, let's go," urged Betty, "I'm getting cold."

They had to feel their way back to the stairs. In the gloom of the main hall, Calhoun examined his hand. There was an extensive area of burnt skin around his fingers.

"Better come up to the house, I'll dress that for you," Betty was anxious to exit.

"Why do I get this feeling that people are watching us?" asked Calhoun, "At least it proves there's something odd about this place. Murphy wasn't totally imagining those things. An electric shock, must have been at least a thousand volts, from a coffin, made of stone at that. What a story and my burnt hand to prove it, Jeffrey's going to love this. All this film as well, great stuff, we can get the national media interested in this story. Christ, my hand hurts."

Betty started the Landrover and Jim tried the torch as they embarked, it still worked. The sun was hot, high in the sky as Betty drove back to the farm. Jim and Betty looked at one another as Calhoun examined his camera for damage. There was a Toyota parked next to Calhoun's Beetle.

"Oh no," muttered Jim.

"Something wrong?" Calhoun looked up from the rear seat.

"Nothing wrong, just an observation."

Ellen and Kevin were seated in the kitchen drinking coffee. Kevin Wilson was tall, painfully thin, with black hair combed forward to conceal incipient baldness in a Caesar quiff. He had a beaky nose, thin lips, acne scars all over his cheeks and beady black eyes half covered by thick black eyebrows.

"Hi Kev, how's it going? Long time no see, must be ten years, tempus fugit and all that."

Kevin nodded, "You got famous then, Calhoun, ace reporter for the local rag, congrats."

"What's wrong with your hand Mr Calhoun?" Ellen arose, picked Calhoun's hand up and examined it, "You need that dressing, sit down and I'll take a look at it for you."

"You must be Ellen, Kev's wife, Mr Lewin's daughter?" said Calhoun.

Ellen nodded and fetched the first aid kit from the cupboard. She dressed Calhoun's hand.

"Well you Wizards should have a field day in that church Kev, there's something definitely not kosher about the place, and that brass plaque on that catafalque needs earthing."

"What happened?" Ellen applied burn lotion and bandage.

"I went to see Paddy Murphy in dock yesterday, he had a heart attack whilst he was in that crypt, swears he heard noises and saw a ghost. Naturally, being innately curious about all paranormal activity, I came along here to have a chat with your Mum and Dad, ghosties and vampires, werewolves, they all make good news, get the circulation up. I didn't really believe Paddy, smacked of leprechauns and the Little People. After what I saw in that crypt a little while ago, I'm not so sure."

"Well, what did happen?" Ellen cut the loose ends of the bandage with scissors. She looked at Jim and Betty over Calhoun's head.

"I touched that brass plaque on the side of that stone coffin, the one in the middle of the crypt, there was a flash and a spark, must have been all of a thousand volts. It threw me on my back and I dropped my Nikon. Lucky for me these Nips make good cameras, no damage and I have some good film."

"But there's no brass plaque on that coffin," began Ellen. She saw her father shake his head.

"I saw one lady. How else do you think I got this burn?" said Calhoun, sensing a cover-up. "Is there something you folks should be telling me?" He rose from the chair and looked at each of them in turn, "You can tell me now before I write it up. If there's anything you don't want exposed I can withold it, in view of your co-operation and the fact that Jeff Patten is a friend of yours. This is going down big I promise you and when you see the photos on Tuesday in the rag, oh boy, is that going to create a sensation."

Jim looked at Betty, dismay on his face.

"What makes you so sure about the plaque Mr Calhoun?" asked Kevin, softly.

"I saw it, your Dad and Mum saw it, so what's all this about a plaque, you got it wired or something?" He looked at each of them in turn again, "Don't try and pull the wool by removing it when I've gone, that'll be most suspicious. Who's in that coffin anyway? I couldn't read the inscription. You know who it is?" His tone was hectoring.

"Mr Calhoun," Betty's voice was hard, "We treated you civilly when you arrived here a short time ago, fed you breakfast and gave you the benefit of seeing that crypt so that you could determine for yourself there's nothing unusual about it. We can't explain what happened down there, but don't start threatening us please. You're at liberty to print what you like, but don't anticipate co-operation from us in future. As far as we are aware there is no brass plaque on that coffin and we don't know for certain who that catafalque was made for, so if you don't mind, you are free to leave when you please."

"Ditto that, Calhoun. I don't care for your breed anyway and using that kind of language doesn't endear you to us," Jim was hard-faced.

"I smell a cover-up," Calhoun looked pale, "I know Jeff gave her permission to search the records," He pointed at Ellen, "If I find something odd I'll publish, I promise you."

"On your way mister, you've out-stayed your welcome," said Jim, coldly.

"You're covering something up Lewin, I can smell it in the air." He retreated hastily when Jim made for him, "You'll regret this."

He exited to his Beetle and drove off at speed, dust trailing it.

****

15.

Sunday, June 16th 1995.
Lewin's Farm, Babingley Marsh,
King's Lynn, Norfolk.

"Was there a plaque on that coffin?" Ellen faced her parents. "Or was he imagining it?"

Betty nodded, "There was something on the side of the coffin. I couldn't see properly before that kind of electric shock erupted."

"But Bobby and Dad checked it yesterday, they said there was no plaque and now, Calhoun says there was? Harry Farraday said there was one, with the date on it and now you say there might have been one when you took that creep down there?" Ellen put the first aid kit back in the cupboard.

"I'm confused and scared," confessed Betty, "The place was like an ice box, I was cold not just a chill, but icy cold and the torch wouldn't operate immediately after that fellow received that shock. I thought I saw something but couldn't be sure, it all happened so quickly. What do you think Jim?"

Jim shrugged his shoulders, "There was definitely something on the side of that coffin. Like your Mum said it happened so fast, I can't be sure what I saw."

"You know what that creep is going to do now don't you?" said Kevin.

"Start checking the records, since he knows Jeff Patten gave me permission to search," said Ellen.

"And the next thing that's going to happen is he's going to ring Anglia TV, get his article syndicated. There'll be an invasion of bloody freaks from the media and a lot of others interested in paranormal activity," said Kevin.

"What if there is a brass plaque on that coffin and Harry was right yesterday?"

"Let's go take a butcher's," said Kevin, "At least we can be sure of your facts."

"I'm not going down there again," Betty shuddered, "Gave me the willies, you can go if you wish."

"You coming Dad?"

Jim nodded, "If only to prove that there's nothing on the side of that coffin."

"Calhoun is going to find out about Myfanwy Legge buried in that thing," said Ellen.

"Then he'll check with Funny Fanny about her ancestors and all that jazz," said Kevin.

"I haven't told you," began Ellen.

They all looked at her, expectantly.

"Well? What haven't you told us?" Betty glared at her daughter.

"As far as I could see there are no records of Legge's living in Lynn apart from that one entry. None before, none since.

"You're kidding," said Kevin, startled.

Ellen shook her head, "I went back as far as the records go to find births, marriages, deaths of Legge's, there aren't any. I then went from the date Harry gave, June 21st, 1796 to the day the church was closed, nothing. I went through the old electoral Rolls, nothing again. There's only Myfanwy Legge, the one that Harry said he saw on this disappearing plaque."

"They must have come from outside the town," said Kevin, "Or you missed it."

"If they came from another town they'd be on the rolls, if nothing else," said Ellen.

"You missed it then," said Kevin.

"The only conclusion," Ellen looked at her husband, "She can't just appear, can she?"

"Fanny did say we should check the records before we started work on the church at the fete," said Betty.

"I wonder why she said that?"

"Well let's go, see if Calhoun did see a brass plaque that should confirm it one way or another," said Kevin, "Could be that entry about this Myfanwy Legge is up the creek. Does happen, and whoever was in that coffin wasn't a Legge."

"I'll get lunch ready, are you staying?" she appealed to Ellen.

"If you're inviting us Mumsy, thank you."

"I'll bring my torch as well," said Kevin, "At least we'll have a back-up."

They arrived at the church, the gates were open as they'd left them.

"It is cold in here," said Ellen, "Mum was right," She shivered.

They entered the stairway, Jim couldn't help feeling apprehensive. The feeling that something was observing them was strong. Kevin stumbled on the crumbling steps, Jim caught him. In the crypt proper they shone their torches on the catafalque.

"Well that proves it doesn't it?" said Ellen, "Nothing, he must have dreamed it."

"I saw it," said Jim, "At least that's what it looked like before Calhoun touched it and that flash occurred."

Kevin bent close to the stone coffin and shone his torch along the side, "No sign of fixings or drilled holes and the surface is too rough to glue anything. You got it wrong Pop."

Jim shrugged, Betty had been right, it was damned cold in the place, unusually so, bearing in mind the ambient temperature outside the church, in the lower eighties.

"Have you ever had a look inside?" Kevin was still examining the coffin.

"We took the lid off a long time ago, can't recall exactly when, there was nothing inside," said Jim.

"Give us a hand, let's have a butcher's" said Kevin, climbing onto the plinth.

"Should you do that?" quavered Ellen, uncertainly.

"My dear young woman when those media freaks descend on us as they certainly will, when that snide bastard Calhoun gets his story into the paper on Tuesday, they'll pull the place apart. Let's save them the trouble, come on Jimbo give us a hand I can't move it without help."

"I don't think we should disturb the dead, Kev," said Ellen.

There was a tinge of fear in her voice.

"Aw for Chrissake, I'm not going to stick my fingers into a load of corpse milk love. Anway, after two centuries there'll be nothing left but bones."

Jim reluctantly climbed onto the plinth.

"OK when I say heave, give it a whirl Jimbo," said Kevin, "Now!"

The two men strained, the lid wouldn't budge.

"Jesus, what in hell's holding it?" gasped Kevin, "Hand me that torch love, let's have a look."

Jim was breathing hard after his exertions. He watched Kevin examine the coffin from end to end by the light of the torch, "I can't see anything holding it, you say you had it off way back?"

"Came off easily if I recall, I was only a kid then], so if it had been hard we couldn't have done it," said Jim, uneasily. The feeling that they were being observed was strong and the chill was penetrating.

"Well it ain't coming off now, that's for sure."

"Leave it Kev, it doesn't matter," urged Ellen, her voice was shaky.

"Those media people will do it if we don't. Calhoun will say he's checked the records and Myfanwy Legge is incarcerated in here. Those ghouls will want film of bones, hair or something, to show the unwashed sitting front of their TV's."

"Don't you think you're exaggerating this event's going to create Kev?" Jim felt as if his chest was being constricted, he began having difficulty in breathing.

"I'm not joking Jimbo, I know Calhoun, he's an ambitious crud. If he has to bend the truth to get attention he will do it."

"You OK Dad?" Ellen focussed the torch on Jim's face.

"I'm having difficulty breathing, I have to get out into the open."

"So am I," Kevin sucked air into his lungs in a soughing motion.

"Let's get out of here Dad, Kev."

The constriction around his chest felt like a steel band was being slowly drawn tighter. Jim barely made it into the open, he fell to the ground sucking painfully. Kevin was similarly afflicted, he sat on a pile of stone dumped by Farraday's suppliers, his head between his knees, desperately drawing breath.

Ellen flapped round anxiously, "Shall I call Doctor Lassiter?" she asked, peering at her husband and her Father.

Jim shook his head and waved a negative arm, "I'll be OK in a minute, just getting my breath back now," he gasped.

Kevin, that much younger, was recovering more swiftly.

"It's because you attempted to remove the lid of that coffin," said Ellen a few moments later, "It's no good you sneering Kevin, I wasn't affected, only you and Dad."

"She's right you know, there's definitely something wrong with this place," said Jim massaging his chest. "First Harry Farraday and Paddy Murphy and then Calhoun gets nearly electrocuted touching that catafalque, and now we've been hit."

"And no brass plate on that coffin," added Ellen, "Either you, Mum and Calhoun were dreaming or there never was one."

"You say Harry Farraday saw a name and date on this mythical plaque and it ties up with your research love? This Myfanwy Legge who seems to have had no ancestors and no progeny." He rubbed his chest, "Christ my chest still feels sore, bloody painful in fact."

"Myfanwy Legge, June 21st, 1796, that's what was in the Parish records. I wrote it down and Harry Farraday could hardly be called psychic. How would he know that date unless he saw it as he described on that coffin plaque? Paddy Murphy and Harry both claimed there was a flash like lightning just before they heard the groaning and screaming"

"Listen, what's that?" Kevin held up his hand for silence.

"What was it?" Ellen didn't look at all happy, thought Jim.

Kevin shrugged, "I thought I heard cows moo-ing."

"Fat chance son, the nearest cattle are on Bill Watson's Tweedle Farm, a couple of miles away," said Jim, rubbing his chest once more, "I got shot of mine ages ago."

"There you are, there it is again," said Kevin.

They all heard it then, a soft lowing sound, rising and falling.

"That's not cattle," said Jim, listening intently, "Sounds like someone in pain."

"It's coming from inside there," said Ellen, looking scared. She pointed to the interior of the church.

"Rubbish love," scoffed Kevin, "You've been brainwashed by all this occult crap."

Ellen walked into the nave, they followed her. The noise was louder now, a gut-wrenching groaning.

"It's coming from the crypt," said Ellen, pointing.

The three of them moved over to the entrance to the crypt. The eerie wailing and moaning was rising up the crumbling staircase. It rose and fell like waves of sound on an aural ocean. Jim felt his bowels loosen, the sound was gruesome, awe inspiring.

"I'm going," Ellen ran for the entrance, her hands over her ears.

"Let's have a butcher's Jimbo," said Kevin.

"You kidding? No way am I going down there. Call it cowardice, fear, anything you like, but I'm not going back in there."

"But we can probably solve the mystery," Kevin had to yell over the noise of moaning.

Jim shook his head, "No thanks, fuck the mystery."

Without another word Kevin plunged into the dark chasm that led to the crypt, his torch wobbled as he attempted to keep his footing.

"Come back Kevin," yelled Jim, hoarsely, fear making it hard to breathe again.

He heard Kevin swear horribly, then the sound cut off abruptly.

"Kev, you OK?" Jim yelled, a premonition of something terrible gripping his throat. There was no response.

Ellen re-appeared, "Where's Kevvy?" she cried.

"He went down there," Jim pointed towards the crypt.

"The fool, the stupid crazy fool."

"If I'm not back in five minutes go for help love," said Jim, pressing the switch on his torch as he entered the stairwell.

He nearly went headfirst slipping on a crumbling stone step. Reaching the bottom he shone the torch round the crypt. Kevin was lying on the floor, rolling around, holding his head and sobbing with pain. An ugly-looking stain trickled between his fingers. Jim pulled him upright and held on to him or Kevin would have fallen.

"Let's get out of here son." He virtually carried Kevin up the stairs.

"Is he alright Dad?" Ellen was frantic.

"Don't know," he gasped, heaving Kevin over his shoulder in a fireman's lift, "Let's get out of here."

The sun was hot on their shoulders as they emerged from the gloom of the ruined church.

"Lie him on that heap of sand," commanded Ellen.

Jim eased his burden down onto the sand heap.

"Jesus!Look at that."

Ellen pointed to a six-inch long gash in Kevin's skull. Blood welled out in a dark ooze, they could see bone between the hairs.

"Let's get him to hospital love, quickly, you drive, I'll try and stop the blood flow."

Together they eased Kevin into the back of the Landrover. Jim pulled an old rag from underneath a seat and padded Kevin's head gently.

"Get going love, this is serious," urged Jim.

Ellen drove as fast as she could, past the Hump and onto the main road to the Slade Estate, emerging onto the main A149, headed towards Lynn. Headlights on full beam and with her hand on horn, Ellen passed all traffic to the junction with the A148 Grimston Road. She ignored furious horn sounds round the roundabout as she headed down the A149 to Holding's Hill Hospital and into Casualty, her hand still on the horn. Medical staff rushed out hearing the commotion and saw Kevin's injury. They quickly put him on a trolley and rushed him into an examination room. A doctor was summoned came almost immediately. A nurse pushed Jim and

Ellen out .of the way, "We'll handle this if you don't mind." Curtains were drawn and Jim and Ellen walked back into the reception area, unable to do anything more.

"He wouldn't listen love," said Jim, "He just rushed down there."

People were staring at them curiously. It was only then that Jim saw his clothes blood soaked.

"I'll see if I can get cleaned-up," he said, heading for the men's toilet. Betty arrived an hour later. Jim and Ellen stared, disbelievingly, for accompanying Betty was Funny Fanny Legge.

****

16.

Sunday, June 16th, 1995.
Holding's Hill Hospital,
Gayton Road, King's Lynn.

"How is he?" Betty looked harassed.

"Still doing a repair job Mumsy."

"Hello Mrs Legge," said Jim, "What brings you here?"

"That's not very nice Jim, you're being rude," scolded Betty.

"Sorry," mumbled Jim.

"I went to Babingley to see you and Mrs Lewin," said Mrs Legge, in her soft voice, "I was there when Mrs Lewin received your phone call, she invited me along. If I'm in the way I'll leave.

"Sorry, didn't mean to sound rude Mrs Legge," said Jim, "You're welcome to stay."

Betty stopped a passing nurse," Any news of my son-in-law, Mr Wilson?"

"He's being operated on at the moment, nothing serious, but he did need several stitches," said the young woman. "The doctor will be out shortly, he'll explain to you what's happening."

"That sounds promising anyway," said Betty, "I'll go find us some tea, how about you Mrs Legge?"

]"Nothing thank you."

Jim noticed the woman was clad in a long black skirt, maroon blouse, with a woollen shawl around her shoulders. Her shoes were little more than slippers, or moccasins.

'She doesn't look a year older than when she treated my back twelve years ago' he thought. Her hair was still dark, no greying, no lines on her face. 'She's weathered time better than I have'.

Betty returned carrying a tray with polystyrene cups. She was accompanied by a middle-aged woman who'd plainly been crying.

"This is Ruth Thompson, Wally's wife," said Betty, "She was on her own, I thought she could stay with us. Wally's in a bad way, not expected to live."

"God no," Jim couldn't believe it.

"It's true Mr Lewin, he's been suffering for years, finally caught up with him, he wouldn't give up smoking, even though he was warned." Ruth Thompson seemed composed but on the brink of more tears.

"In the general ward, is he?" Jim felt terrible. Wally had been a source of help during the hard times for Lewin's farm.

"Side ward, don't want to upset the other patients," said Ruth.

"I'll pop along and see him if that's alright with you?" Jim took a sip of the tea and pulled a face," Call me when there's news of Kevvy."

"May I come along Mrs Thompson?" Funny Fanny was also standing, "I'd like to see him please?"

Ruth looked suspiciously at Mrs Legge's strange attire, she shrugged her shoulders, "If you wish."

She led the way along a corridor. The door to Wally's single ward was closed. He was on an oxygen mask and a drip and looked terribly white and waxen.

"Some friends come to see you Wally," Ruth pressed Wally's arm.

Thompson opened his eyes and stared at his visitors blankly, then recognition dawned. He removed the mask.

"Jimbo, good to see you, how are you?" His breathing was ragged.

Ruth replaced the mask gently. "He can't breathe without it, you'll have to do the talking, Mr Lewin."

Jim rabbitted on inconsequentially until he ran out of steam.

Wally removed the mask again, "You're Funny Fanny, aren't you?"

Mrs Legge didn't flinch under the insult, she just smiled down at Wally

"Would you like me to help you Mr Thompson?" she asked.

"Help? how can you help? Bloody doctors have given up on me. I'm done for..kaput!"

"I might be able to help, I don't know, would you like me to try?"

"I don't bloody well care any more, I'm not long for this world, please yourself woman." Wally replaced his mask, his fingers were just skeletons with parchment skin stretched over.

"Is it alright Mrs Thompson?" Fanny appealed to Ruth.

Ruth shrugged, "There's nothing you can do Mrs Legge. If you think it will help, try by all means."

Fanny stepped close, "Give me your hands Mr Thompson please."

Jim had a feeling of deja vue., took him back ten years to the kitchen in his farm, Fanny pressing his back, the pain receding, the stiffness evaporating.

"Think of what you'd like most to do in the world Mr Thompson," intoned Fanny.

"Get out of this place," growled Wally through the oxygen mask.

"Concentrate on what you'd like to be doing right now," urged Fanny.

Jim was positive he felt some force brush past him. He saw a movement along Thompson's skeletal fingers, as if a wind was ruffling the loose skin. A pulse throbbed at Thompson's temple. The shadow that hovered over his face eased, his eyes brightened. The creases in his forehead smoothed out. Fanny was standing as still as a stone statue, her eyes closed, her lips moving as if in prayer. Jim was positive he saw a pulse of some energy flow from her into Thompson. Ruth Thompson was staring in astonishment as Wally's cheeks filled out, the waxen appearance of his skin faded and became clear. Colour returned to his cheeks, looking normal and healthy. His breathing became smooth, even via the mask. How long the scenario lasted Jim was unaware, so engrossed was he in the miracle being enacted before his very eyes.

Fanny released Thompson's hands gently, they were fleshed out healthy. The first thing Thompson did was to tear off the mask.

"God, that was bloody marvellous Fanny, I feel great." He sat up pulled the drip from his arm, "What did you do?"

Ruth Thompson was staring disbelievingly as Wally swung his legs out of bed and stood up, he looked fit and healthy.

"Hi love, I'm back!"

"I'm seeing a ghost," cried Ruth, bursting into tears.

"Hey, hey, what's that for love? I'm cured," cried Wally, taking her in his arms, "Does that feel like a ghost?"

"We can leave them now Mr Lewin," said Fanny quietly, "They'll want time together to adjust."

Jim shook his head, convinced he was about to awaken from a dream, "I don't believe this," he muttered.

"Let's go," urged Fanny, pushing him gently towards the door.

Via the glass door Jim saw Thompson release his wife to look for his clothes in the locker.

"What's the matter with you Jimbo?" asked Betty when they reached the reception area, "You look as if you've seen a ghost."

"I've witnessed a miracle love," stuttered Jim, "I still can't grasp it."

Betty looked at Fanny, who shrugged. "I think you'd better sit down until you feel better Jimbo," she advised.

"I've just seen Wally Thompson restored to health love," said Jim.

"Yes alright Jimbo, we all sympathise, gone has he?"

"He's alive and well, in full health love."

He saw Ellen tap her forehead gently.

"Hi there folks," came a voice from the door.

Thompson stood there, his arm around Ruth, dressed for the street. He looked fit and well.

"Betty stared mouth agape, as did Ellen.

"It's me Betty old girl, back to the land of the living, thanks to Mrs Legge here, worked a miracle she did." He did a kind of dance.

"Mr Thompspon, what are you doing?" The sister's voice trailed away. She stared, gave a strangled scream and rushed out of the room.

"Upset her Jimbo," grinned Wally, "Can't take a joke."

The door burst open to admit a two doctors clad in white coats. They stopped, the Sister who had seen Wally gave another scrambled scream and fled again.

The two doctors advanced on Wally, staring disbelievingly at him.

"It is Thompson isn't it?" the younger man choked.

"Me alright bozo," gurgled Thompson, "Given up on me hadn't you? There's the lady who performed the deed, the Miracle Worker." He pointed to where Fanny had been standing.

They all looked around for Fanny Legge, who had vanished, nowhere to be seen.

"Mrs Legge, she did it, took Wally's hands, held them tight and inside five minutes he was well again. What do you think to that? It's a miracle, that's what it is," Ruth babbled on incoherently, until Wally stopped her.

"Give us a lift home Jimbo?" asked Wally.

"But this is impossible," gasped the older doctor, "You were on...on." he stopped.

"My deathbed, huh?" Wally jabbed a thick finger into his chest, "Just goes to show doesn't it tosh?"

"We'll have to conduct some tests Mr Thompson," said the young doctor, "Make sure, sort of, I mean."

"Do your own testing mush, I'm discharging myself as of now. How about that lift Jimbo?"

"Eh? Yes of course," Jim came out of a trance.

"Off you go Jimbo. Ellen and I will take care of Kevvy," said Betty, still unable to grasp what she was seeing.

Wally chattered on about reviving his car repair business, getting back on the golf course, taking Ruth for a holiday abroad, buying a new house as they walked out to the Landrover, everything he'd always wanted to do.

"Take it easy for a bit Wally," said Jim, fighting to grasp what he had seen in that small ward. Fanny holding Wally's hands, and the mysterious power he had seen flowing from the woman to Wally Thompson. It was more than a miracle.

"Take it easy?" echoed Wally as they reached the vehicle, "I've been in that bed for the best part of six months. I just wanna get busy again."

"You don't want a relapse do you?"

"Do I look as if I'm gonna have one of them Jimbo?" snorted Wally, seeing the bloodstained rag in the back of the four-wheel drive. "That woman is a....I dunno what she is, but she cured me. I know it, feel it, I won't have any relapses."

Wally chattered on without cessation until they arrived outside his house in Loke Road, opposite the recreation ground.

"Hey I'm sorry Jimbo, I've been prattling on, how's Kev Wilson, your son-in-law? He'll be OK won't he?"

Jim stared at Wally, dumbfounded, "How'd you know about Kevvy, Wally?" he stammered.

"Well, you mentioned it didn't you? And you were at the hospital?" Wally came to a stop shrugged his shoulders, "I don't know Jimbo, what was the matter with Kev?"

"I haven't said why I was at the hospital Wally. Kev had an accident, cut his head badly, that's why that rag is in the back there."

Wally shrugged, "Funny, I just knew it concerned Kev Wilson, I don't know how. Sorry Jimbo, you coming in for a cuppa?"

"I'd better get back Wally. I'm delighted you're fit again, I still can't believe what I saw."

"Remember when you had that bad back, when was that? Way back in '83 and Billy Watson had one as well and I saw Fanny on the marsh collecting those herbs, she said the spirits were strong and that she knew you had a bad back, could cure it for you. You were sceptical and so was

Bobby.

But she did it didn't she? And Billy as well. I know everybody calls her a witch, livin' with all them cats, and a donkey and that bloody wolfhound, not to mention that tarantula, but she's worked miracles for lots of people. They still don't accept her as a person, think she's weird. She might be but she's OK by me. Mrs Miracle I'd call her. I hope Kev is OK Jimbo, thanks for the lift. You ain't got Freda no more, but if you need your vehicles servicing give us a bell. Don't let Johnny Foster get at them, fuck'em up for good, him and his cowboys."

"Thanks Mr Lewin," said Ruth. She looked dazed, unable to come to terms with her husband's miraculous cure.

Jim arrived back at Longley Hill in time to see Kevin in a small ward, his head bandaged and looking very pale.

"Going to keep him in overnight," announced Betty, "Just to be sure."

"Thanks for acting so promptly Dad," said Kevin, weakly.

"What happened exactly?"

Kevin shrugged, "Don't know exactly, I was at the foot of the stairs, shining my torch round when I felt this blow on my head. The next thing I remember is lying in that casualty ward with the curtains round me. Not much help am I? I remember that groaning noise stopping, that's about it."

"Kev, don't say anything to reporters if they hear about this will you?" cautioned Jim, "We don't want that kind of harassment."

"I've already warned him Dad," said Ellen, "I'll be here to head them off."

"You're staying on?"

Ellen nodded, "You get away home, Kev's parents will be coming in soon and all the Wizard Society members, not to mention my Guv'nor, Mervyn Hudson and his wife," Kevin grinned. "Gotta get outa here for the 21st Dad, we have to be at Bawsey for the solstice."

****

17.

Sunday, June 16th, 1995.
Lewin's Farm, Babingley Marsh,
King's Lynn, Norfolk.

"What happened at the church? Did you find that plaque?"

Betty was resurrecting the lunch, which had gone cold as a result of the hospital visit.

Jim shook his head, "There was no brass plaque love, Kevin wanted to see what was in the coffin. We tried to remove the lid, I remember doing it when I was a kid, easy as pie. We couldn't budge it and then I began to feel bad, I couldn't breathe, Kev the same, Ellen wasn't affected. We had to get out into the air, as soon as we were out I felt right as rain. Then we heard that noise, the one that Harry Farraday said he heard. We went to investigate, or Kev did, I was shit scared to go down there. I heard Kev cry out, then the noise stopped. I went down and found him lying on the floor with that cut on his head. Ellen drove whilst I tried to stem the blood in the back of the Landrover."

"That all?"

"That's enough isn't it?"

"So no brass plaque and you heard groaning?" Betty put a dish in the microwave and programmed it.

"That's it, love."

"You didn't see anything when you went down for Kevvy?"

"Not a thing, anyway, how did Fanny turn up at the hospital with you?"

"She just arrived here, I never heard her approach. She must have walked from Wootton, there was no car, she had come to ask if we'd had chance to check the parish records since she understood Harry Farraday was starting work on the restoration. She said that you'd taken Kev to Longley Hill with a cut head, I just got into the car and came down here. She just happened to come with me. Don't ask me how she knew about Kevvy, I don't know, I'm beginning to question all my prior experience. That woman is odd to say the least, her psychic power, healing, prescient, and we don't know where she came from, who were her parents, anything about her, and now Wally Thompson. That man was terminally ill, you saw him and then he walks out of that hospital half an hour later cured! Can you account for it? There's something else about her as well," Betty pulled the dish from the microwave.

"What's that?" Jim felt hungry.

"She doesn't age," said Betty.

"Oh come on love, I know she's well preserved, but some people are like that."

Betty shook her head as she bent down to the Aga oven, she pulled a hot tray out, "Sit down, we better get this before we get interrupted again."

"You were saying," prompted Jim as they sat down to eat, "about Funny Fanny?"

"Can you remember how she looked when she did your back for you?"

"Vaguely, doesn't look any different now," he recalled thinking that in Longley Hill earlier that day.

"Exactly," Betty was triumphant, "Just like a female Dorian Gray, she doesn't change, has no grey hairs, no wrinkles like me. I've won a few in the past ten years, but she looks exactly as she did ten years ago."

"What are you trying to say?"

"What does she live on? Where does her money come from? How can she pay the rates at least, I suppose she pays rates. She doesn't have electricity or gas and she has her own water. Has she any heating for hot water?"

Jim shrugged, "I don't know, is this relevant to anything?"

"She's unlike anybody else we know," Betty started on her food.

"She's demonstrated that love, but she doesn't do anybody any harm. She cured my back, Bill Watson's, and now Wally Thompson's lung cancer. For my money if there were more people like her around it would be great. I don't mind dumping a load of hay in her back yard every month, it's worth it when I remember how my back used to play me up."

The phone bleeped.

"Yes?" Jim picked up the mobile.

It was Bobby. "You OK? We just heard about Kevvy, Ellen phoned. Have they arrived there yet?"

"Has who arrived where?"

"The Anglia TV van?"

"Why should they?"

"They've just left here, wanted to interview us about the ghosts and psychic phenomena at the Church. Apparently they went to your place, nobody there. How they got my name beats the shit outa me but they did. I told 'em I knew nothing about anything, some woman reporter, I've seen her on the Box several times, right cow, asking all sorts of questions. They're headed in your direction again now, I just thought I'd warn you."

"What did Bobby want?" asked Betty.

"The media are on their way here, Anglia TV with that hard-faced bitch in charge, what's her name, Holly Summerfield, that's her."

"Oh no, we don't need that," Betty finished her dinner at speed, "Let's vanish."

She began clearing the table.

"Leave that we have to hop it double quick," urged Jim.

They made it as far as the Landrover before the Anglia TV Outside Broadcast van arrived, blocking their exit.

A young woman, blond, thirty-five or so descended from the cab, trailing a microphone. A cameraman hopped out after her, camera held on his shoulder.

"I'm Holly Summerfield from Anglia TV," she flashed a leather bound ID card at Jim, "You must be Mr Lewin?"

"We're just visiting," said Jim quickly, "They're in the house."

"He's lying Holly," said the cameraman, "We got his photo from the 'Advertiser', he's Lewin alright."

"That will do Ransome, we don't have to be rude to our interviewees," snapped Summerfield.

Jim had the feeling this was a put-up job on their part. The cameraman didn't look at all put out by Summerfield's tone.

"Well Mr Lewin, perhaps you would care to tell our viewers all about the mysterious happenings in Babingley? They'd welcome a frank appreciation of what we understand is a phenomena that could be called paranormal?"

"Get lost darling, go peddle your sensationalism somewhere else," Jim jerked a thumb in the direction of the main road.

Summerfield scowled, "Got something to hide have you Mr Lewin? Frightened of exposure are you? Up to some skulduggery?"

"I can't imagine you being that naïve madame."

"Tell you what Mr Lewin, let me put a scenario to you that I feel you won't enjoy one bit," Summerfield came closer. The perfume was pungent, cloying in fact. Close-up she looked older.

"You're wasting your time missus, there's no paranormal circumstances on my farm."

"That's not what Rory Calhoun told us Mr Lewin, it seems he was the main actor in a drama."

"Mr Calhoun displays all the normal media talent for gross misinterpretation of the facts."

Summerfield looked at her watch in theatrical gesture, a wafer thin gold Seiko, "In half an hour from now Mr Lewin, this road is going to be jam-packed with media people from all over the UK, your life will be pure purgatory. Some of our colleagues in the profession are not as scrupulous as Anglia. They will use methods that would make Genghis Khan blanche. If you want full media exposure be my guest, but be prepared to have a full and eventful life over the next few weeks."

"What are you proposing Miss Summerfield?" Betty stopped Jim opening his mouth again, "I assume you have a proposal that would be mutually advantageous to us both?"

Summerfield switched attention, "An intelligent lady, you are Mrs Lewin, I take it?"

"What's on offer?" Betty interrupted.

"A mercenary bitch," muttered Ransome.

"That's enough Ransome," ordered Summerfield, "For an exclusive interview with film and narrative what I'm prepared to do is keep all other media people out of your hair for a foreseeable period Mrs Lewin. If you believe that that's not worthwhile we'll bid you good day, let you enjoy the experience."

"What makes you think you could effect that privacy?" Betty signalled Jim to keep quiet.

"Guarantee it Mrs Lewin, nobody will attempt to subvert an exclusive, it would not be in their long-term interests."

"What about compensation for disruption of business?"

"We are prepared to pay you a retainer providing you render full assistance with our requirements Mrs Lewin."

"How much?"

"That will depend on the quality of the information and whether we get genuine co-operation, etc."

"For five thousand pounds we will give you full exclusivity as compensation for disruption of normal business," Betty was at the door of the Landrover.

"Done!" Summerfield smiled, showing a full set of healthy teeth.

"What happens now?" asked Betty.

"We would like to film this crypt in which Mr Calhoun suffered extraordinary burns from a metal plaque on a coffin and experienced other paranormal activities."

"Be our guests," Betty waved her hand in the direction of the church, "Get Bobby and Tracy over Jimbo, ask them if they'd help with refreshments for the Anglia people."

Jim dragged Betty on one side out of earshot, "Are you crazy or something love, she can't guarantee anything like that, how could she?"

"Trust me Jimbo," urged Betty, "You lay on the eats, I'll handle this meadow lady and her crew." She raised her voice, "If you'll kindly accompany me Miss Summerfield, bring your van along and please keep to the path, we treasure our environment."

"Got rich on it as well," said Ransome, sotto voce.

"Is he always as obnoxious as this Miss Summerfield? Got a hang-up about farms, or something?"

Summerfield had words with the burly cameraman in a low but hard voice.

Summerfield accompanied Betty in the Landrover, the Outside Broadcast van followed lurching and swaying over the uneven ground.

"Why is that place fenced off? Looks like an abandoned building site?" asked Summerfield as they passed The Hump.

"That was the where we had our first paranormal experience. We had planning permission to build a bungalow for my son in law on that spot. We had to abandon the project due to inexplicable happenings, men fell ill machinery wouldn't work and foundations could not be excavated."

Summer field faced Betty, "You exaggerating for effect Mrs Lewin?"

"You can check it out with Johnny Foster in Lynn, he runs a used car lot now. Went out of construction as a direct result of his experiences on the Hump."

"Stop the car," directed Summerfield urgently. She flagged down the following van.

"Get some film of that site Carl," she directed Ransome, "Can you open it up?" she asked Betty.

"Sure thing," Betty removed a bunch of keys from a hook inside the Landrover and unlocked the mesh gate then waved Ransome inside.

"Best of luck sonny," She gave him a smile.

The cameraman scowled, he entered the enclosure, followed by the sound engineer. Summerfield and Betty watched them set up the camera and recording equipment from the track. Betty watched Ransome testing the camera equipment, he fiddled around with it, she heard him grousing to the recording engineer.

"Get on with it Carl, we haven't got all day," yelled Summerfield.

"The fucking camera's kaput," snarled Ransome, "And Brian's mikes aren't working."

"Oh for Christ sake man, fix it, this is costing us money," bawled Summerfield.

"It was working back at the house, don't know what the hell's the matter with it," cursed Ransome, "Must be the batteries, get Dave to hook up on the generator will you?"

"Excuse me Mrs Lewin," Summerfield went over to the van. A big man in engineer's overalls jumped down from the cab and pulled a massive lead on a reel from a compartment on the side of the van. He unravelled it as he walked to the fence and threw the plug over.

Ransome plugged it in, raising his arms in an elaborate shrug to Summerfield, "Still won't work, get the spare over."

Two more engineers trundled a full size camera through the gate into the compound and connected it up.

Ransome beat it with his fist after a few seconds, "This fucking thing isn't working either Holly," he yelled.

Summerfield marched into the compound, her back rigid with indignation. Betty heard them enjoy a ding-dong row, as she grinned to herself. Ransome and his crew packed the equipment they had brought and put it into the back of the van.

Summerfield approached Betty, her features grim, "The bloody camera wouldn't work," she spat.

"I could have told you that," said Betty, "Try it this side," she said, pointing to the other side of the fence a few yards away.

Summerfield rasped out the orders.

Ransome swore, "The fuckin' thing's working now, wouldja believe?"

"What did you say?" Summerfield demanded of Betty.

"I could have told you nothing works inside that area, that's why Foster jacked it in. We had problems ten years ago with our tractor, every time we crossed that patch, it broke down."

"What do you want me to do?" bawled Ransome.

"Get some footage, I'll do a set piece, where's Daphne?"

A young woman dropped out of the van and began making Summerfield's face up.

"You too Mrs Lewin," said Summerfield, "Get cracking Daphne, I'll ask you questions, you just answer them ad lib about the history of breakdowns and stuff as I prompt you."

This last instruction was directed at Betty.

****

18.

Sunday, June 16th, 1995.
St Mary's Church, Babingley Marsh,
Kings Lynn, Norfolk.

Betty and Summerfield faced the camera, mike in hand and gave an impromptu explanation why Anglia's cameras would not work inside the fenced-off area. Betty responded to Summerfield's questions after she'd been introduced. It was plain to Betty that Summerfield had done some homework on the subject of ley-lines and ancient tumuli. It wasn't in depth, but she had a working knowledge, bringing in nineteenth century names of men who had first postulated the presence of such force fields over the face of the planet.

She then quizzed Betty, as the camera focussed on her, vis the history of machinery breaking down and the failure of a building contractor to fulfil his obligations due to the mysterious force that operated where ley lines crossed.

"OK, that was good. You are a good subject Mrs Lewin," Betty decided Summerfield wasn't giving gratuitous praise. It made her feel better despite her cynicism regarding media personalities.

"Frankly I didn't believe a word of what Calhoun told me Mrs Lewin," confessed Summerfield as the crew retrieved their gear and she and Betty drove on towards the church.

"I know him well, he's an ambitious crud with an outsize ego. He's had us on one or two wild goose chases to try and make the big-time. I daren't neglect this incident, the bastard might just have struck pay dirt, in that event Anglia would have been in deep shit, losing ratings to Central or Thames. I wasn't convinced about that burn on his hand either. He isn't above sticking his hand in a microwave to prove a point."

"Then why did you come here? He could have been romancing again," Betty had to concentrate on keeping the Landrover out of the ruts in the road.

"This is not for publication Mrs Lewin, but I've always been fascinated by this theory of ley-lines and the assertion that these are the remains of a vast printed circuit that covered the planet in centuries past with the Great Pyramid at Giza as the mains switch. I didn't need much persuading despite my misgivings about Calhoun."

Some of Betty's own reservations regarding the sincerity of the presenter had dwindled over the past minutes, there was more to the woman's personality than mere aggressive ambition. This admission regarding her belief in ley-lines had invalidated Betty's initial response to the woman. A vestige of suspicion still lingered that this might be a subtle ploy to disarm her, get to disgorge more information than she had intended.

They arrived outside the perimeter fence around the church. The scaffolding looked somehow sinister, enhancing the sensation of a brooding menace that seemed to encompass the building.

She divined that the same unease afflicted Summerfield. "Looks foreboding doesn't it?" Betty was startled by this disclosure of sensitivity on Summerfield's part.

Ransome hopped out of the van and approached, "How do you wanna play this Holly? We don't want another fuck-up, do we?"

"Beautifully put Carl." There was a tinge of sarcasm in Summerfield's voice, "Get all the gear ready whilst Mrs Lewin and I have a butcher's at this crypt."

"Cheeseman's going to bust a valve when he sees the cost of this caper," groused Ransome.

"You've made your point Carl. I suggest you stick to the technical problems, leave the financial considerations to me, huh."

"All this is a load of crap missus," said Ransome, "These geezers fixed that Hump to screw that five grand out of you."

"If they can bugger-up your cameras in that fashion Carl, I'd like to learn the trick, now get cracking please and no more bitching."

"Fucking women," Betty heard him mutter, "Should never have to let 'em out of bed, only good for one thing and she ain't very smart at that."

"He has a hang-up about females," grinned Summerfield, "Especially when they are in positions of authority."

"Sad," said Betty.

"Let's see Calhoun's crypt Betty, OK if I call you that? I was impressed by your demeanour in front of that camera, you are a natural. I shall have to watch you, you'll be after my job."

They entered the nave via the main entrance, Betty felt those unseen eyes observing her as they made their way to the entrance to the crypt.

"Christ, it's chilly in here," Summerfield's silk dress was not suitable for this adventure decided Betty.

"It's unnatural," said Summerfield, shivering, "It's seventy plus outside."

The sense of being watched was strong, Betty shivered also, yet it was not from the cold, her woollen dress was adequate protection from normal temperature changes. The experiences with Calhoun in the crypt earlier that day was still powerful in her mind. Trepidation seized her, a nameless fear she tried hard to dismiss seemed to grip her.

"Shit, it's bloody dark down there, I should have brought my torch," said Summerfield. She raised her voice, "Bring the Anson Carl, and my jacket."

It was Daphne who brought the articles, "He says he's not an errand boy," grinned the girl. "God, it's cold in here," She shivered, "It's funny."

"What is?" Summerfield shrugged into the fleece jacket and took the Anson light from Daphne. "You'll think me a nutter."

"I promise I won't, dear girl."

"I got this feeling..."

"Do spit it out Daphne, I will make allowances for your extravagant sensibilities."

"I had the feeling that someone was watching me," Daphne delivered this hurriedly as if anticipating Summerfield's scorn.

"Join the club darling," said Summerfield, "This place is definitely spooky."

"You felt it too?" Daphne seemed surprised, he looked round the gloomy nave, "It's dark in here as well."

"Thanks Daphne you have a reassuring bedside manner."

"If you don't mind Holly I'll go outside, I'm getting vibes about this place," She continued her apprehensive looks round the building.

Summerfield waited until the girl's high heels clattered into silence and switched on the powerful light, "Let's go have a butcher's Betty."

The two women trod carefully down the stairs, the Anson light illuminated everything starkly.

In the crypt the chill penetrated even Betty's dress.

"This isn't natural, the cold I mean," Summerfield was almost whispering, her voice echoing, "It's freezing."

The Anson light cast weird shadows over the rows of catafalques in their niches.

"Who's in there?" Summerfield directed the light onto the central plinth.

"We don't know," Betty couldn't help the feeling of menace that pervaded the crypt. It was as if some potent force was all around them, awaiting the moment to demonstrate its power.

"There's a plaque on the side, that shit Calhoun was right about that."

Betty had a hard time convincing herself that she wasn't dreaming. The brass plaque gleamed in the light.

"Myfanwy Legge, June 21st 1796," Summerfield read it out loud. Bending down to peer at the plate she continued, "Isn't there a supposed witch in Lynn with that name.. Funny Fanny, or something?"

"There is a Mrs Legge," said Betty, still thinking she was dreaming, "Whether she's a witch or not is debatable."

"Peculiar" muttered Summerfield, swinging the Anson round the crypt, "Decidedly spooky. I can't bring myself to touch that plaque, despite the fact I think that crud Calhoun was lying."

"As you can see there's nothing sinister down here," said Betty, trying to stop shivering, "A few old catafalques and stone coffins," her voice echoed.

"Has anyone ever had a look inside that thing?" Summerfield indicated the central coffin.

"My husband took the lid off when he was a boy, there's nothing in it."

"No bones, clothing or artefacts?"

"Empty, he says," said Betty, wishing Summerfield would terminate the visit. She was shivering so violently that her teeth were chattering.

"This cold is unbelievable," Summerfield was also shivering despite the thick jacket, "I've seen enough, we'll get the cameras down here and just take some footage before I die of exposure."

"You down there Holly?" It was Ransome's voice from the top of the stairs.

"Bring the gear down Carl, you'll need some thick clothing, it's bloody cold down here."

"It's cold up here dear girl," Ransome didn't seem too keen on entering the crypt judging from his tone, Betty decided.

They heard him yelling to the heavies to bring in the equipment. A few minutes later the porters began bring down tripods, camera gear and lighting equipment and lengths of thick cable and began assembling it. Ransome, clad in sheepskin jacket supervised the placement of all the equipment.

"If you don't mind I'll leave you to it, wait up above, I'm just about freezing," said Betty, hardly able to articulate for her teeth chattering.

"Of course, I can manage now."

"Spooky isn't it?" said Ransome, "The cold doesn't help, must be twenty degrees less than the ambient temperature."

The lighting flooded the crypt suddenly as the generator in the van began operating. Shadows were sharp, corners and the shape of the coffins in the niches were starkly outlined.

Betty arrived out in the hot sunshine, rubbing her arms vigorously, the cold seemed to have penetrated her bones.

"What's it like down there?" Daphne, the make-up girl came up to her.

"Why don't you go take a look?"

Daphne gave a theatrical shudder, "I can't stand those places, I'd have nightmares."

"Just a load of old stone coffins, that's about it," Betty was anxious to get warm by the Landrover's heater.

"You look frozen Mrs Lewin," said Daphne, "I've a thick jacket in the van, would you like to borrow it?"

Betty nodded, still shivering violently.

Daphne brought a suede jacket, lined with lambs wool, it fitted slightly tightly, but the feel was reassuring.

"I just want to contact my husband, I'll use the mobile in the Landrover," said Betty.

Jim answered immeadiately, "What's happening down there?"

Betty gave a resume of the events at the Hump and described the activity down in the crypt. "You aren't going to believe this Jimbo," said Betty, only just beginning to feel warm.

"Try me," There was something monumentally comforting about her husband's calm voice, she felt a surge of affection for him. The trials they'd been through together had cemented their bond of marriage firmly, from the early days of their struggle to make ends meet to their present opulence.

"That plaque is back on the cataflaque,"

"You ain't kidding us are you?"

"Us?"

"Bobby and Tracy are here, helping get the snacks ready for that TV crew, Laura's here as well."

"I'm not joking Jimbo, I couldn't believe it myself at first, but the light they've got down there you could see a gnat's balls. That plaque is there alright."

"What's it say on it Mumsy?" came Bobby's voice.

"Myfanwy Legge, June 21st 1796."

"You know what Ellen said, about her researches, that there is no record of any Legge's before that date or after in King's Lynn?" Bobby sounded sceptical.

"I'm just telling you what's inscribed on the plaque."

"You sound as though you are shivering love?" Her husband enquired.

"It must be below zero in that crypt, I can't seem to get warm."

"Where's that Summerfield woman?"

"They're all down there taking film of the crypt and the coffins, I've come up get warm."

"Uncle Kevin says that all paranormal places are colder than normal Grandma," came Laura's light tones.

"Well Uncle Kevin got it right as far as that crypt is concerned love."

"Shall I bring you some hot tea in a flask Grandma? I have Bella outside, it would only take me a minute to gallop down there."

"If you can manage it love, it would be nice, I'm so cold I don't seem able to warm up."

"Be there in a min, Grandma."

Even if Tracy is a snooty daughter-in-law, at least her offspring is more like a Lewin, Betty told herself. She turned the heater up to maximum with the fan on full. 'Christ, this bloody cold is killing me'. She realised she was swearing to herself, learning bad habits from Ellen, that brought on a thought about Kevin and the gash on his head, there was no rational explanation for the injury. She hadn't noticed any fallen masonry inside the crypt, that injury could only have been caused by something truly heavy. She turned on the radio to the local station in time to hear a news item that gave her another shock.

The cheery voice of the DJ on Radio Lynn was saying, '...Anglia TV are presently engaged in investigating what has been reported as paranormal and psychic phenomena in the old crypt at the derelict St Mary's church in

Babingley. The building has recently been the subject of a campaign to raise money for its restoration. Mr and Mrs Lewin, the present owners of the land on which St Mary's stands were the organisers of the function. The precise figure has not been disclosed, but our reporter Rory Calhoun, who first reported the presence of paranormal activity at the old church, indicated that well over five hundred thousand pound sterling has been contributed by local people and business. Restoration work is being carried out by the Lyons Group. There have been several instances of unusual and paranormal activity around the Lewin property. Lyons site foreman, Mr Paddy Murphy, is presently in Longley Hill Hospital, suffering from a heart attack as a direct result of inexplicable experiences whilst inspecting the crypt at St Mary's. Our reporter, Rory Calhoun, is with Mr Murphy right now as I speak, getting his version of the incident, we'll have an update on his interview later on today and Rory will be here in person to tell you all what his experiences were in what he described as a prime example of paranormal activity'.

"Damn!" said Betty, aware that this kind of publicity would inevitably result in hordes of gawping visitors, anxious to see the crypt for themselves. It would also attract the attentions of all the freak community, anxious to prove their own pet theories of paranormal activity.

She switched off the cannibal noises that emanated from the Landrover's massive speakers, appalled at the likely result of such publicity. That Calhoun had not wasted an instant to broadcast his experiences inside the crypt. He had evidently seen this as his chance to become a celebrity in the world of journalism. She nearly had a heart attack herself as someone knocked on the driver's window. It was her granddaughter Laura, riding Bella, her palomino pony and holding a large vacuum flask out to her.

Betty got out of the car, "Hello love, his is very good of you."

The pony was restless, Laura having a hard time keeping it still, "I don't know what's the matter with her, she's not normally as twitchy as this," said Laura, shaking her long dark hair back from her face as she attempted to keep the pony calm. "It's only when I ride her near the church and the Hump, I'm sure she senses something."

"Thanks for the tea darling, you'd better take Bella away from the bad influences," said Betty, pouring tea into the plastic top.

"Are they bad Grandma?"

Laura had Bobby's features Betty thought, illogically, 'I'm glad about that', she thought, also illogically. "Bad for Bella I meant darling," Betty hastily assured her.

"Where are those TV people and Miss Summerfield?"

"Taking pictures down in the crypt, they've got their cameras down there."

"I'd like to do something in television," said Laura, reining the restive animal in with skill. The pony was plainly upset about something, his eyes were rolling, his ears back.

"Have a word with Miss Summerfield when she comes up to the house, she could give you some advice," said Betty. The hot tea was restoring life to her frozen limbs.

She was startled to see the cameraman, Ransome emerge from the church entrance. He was yelling incoherently, waving his arms around. Even from
two hundred yards away Betty could see his eyes wild with fear.

****

19.

Sunday, June 18th 1995.
St Mary's Church, Babingley Marsh,
King's Lynn, Norfolk.

Laura's pony, Bella, began plunging and rearing, almost unseating Laura as Ransome's frantic yelling echoed around the old church.

"You take off love before Bella gets more upset," said Betty, stepping aside to avoid the animal's hooves.

Something had gone wrong that was plain. The Anglia TV cameraman looked demented with fear and the make-up girl Daphne was attempting to calm him without much success. Without warning Bella took off at a gallop, Laura clinging to her grimly trying hard to control her. Betty was unsure which crisis to tackle first, her grand-daughter's problems with her pony or the cameraman's fear. She opted for Ransom, since she knew Laura was a skilled rider and would soon bring the horse under control.

"What's the matter?" Betty shook the man hard, "Control yourself for goodness sake."

He continued to babble on until Betty slapped him hard across the face. The shock stopped him raving. "Eh? What was that for?" He stared uncomprehendingly at Betty and Daphne. Some of the man's fear had affected the girl, she was trembling and looked pale, her lip trembling.

"There's something down there missus," Ransome was about to sound off again.

"What's down there man? Speak slowly," Betty was hard-voiced.

"A ghost, something ghastly, it turned off the lighting and ruined the cameras, like lightning, it was awful."

"Where's Holly?" Betty shook him again.

"They're unconscious down there, I was able to escape," Betty could smell the fear on him, his eyes were rolling, he was licking his lips and trembling.

She poured some tea into the cup and held it out to him. He sucked it down thirstily. It appeared to calm him.

"Now tell me what happened," said Betty, gently.

"She touched that bloody coffin missus, the next second there was a flash of lightning. Holly was on her back on the floor and the cameras were kaput when the lights went out. The blokes were all knocked out by the shock."

"Who touched the coffin?"

"That stupid cow Holly, she wanted to test it she said. I tried to talk her out of it, the stubborn bitch didn't take any notice, she put her hand on that brass plate, the next second all that lightning happened, flashing round that tomb like nothing I've ever seen before."

The two porters emerged from the van, looking uneasy.

"You OK, Carl?"

"Yeah I'm OK," Ransome seemed in control of himself again, "We gotta get Holly and Brian out of the crypt."

Betty nodded as Ransome held out the plastic cup for more tea. She filled it for him, he was eager to drink it. He gulped it down, looking round as if expecting someting to appear, "We gotta get Holly and Brian out," he repeated.

"Come on you two, give me a hand," ordered Betty to the two heavyweights.

"Oh no missus, I ain't goin' down there," said the bald one.

"No way," echoed his companion, "If that fuckin' stupid cow wants to git shot, fuck her luck!"

"Two grown men, frightened of their own shadows," sneered Betty, "I never thought I'd see the day. Get me another of those, what're they called.. Anson lamps? I'll go myself."

"You're coming with us asshole," stated Ransome, "You cop out of this and you're on SS tomorrow and if you think I'm kidding try me!" He seemed to have recovered completely.

"You can't do that agin, Union rules," said Baldie.

"You wanna bet?" snarled Ransom, "Get that Anson and let's go."

He turned to Betty, "You don't have to do this you know? We can handle it."

Baldie handed Ransome the huge light and stood back as if avoiding contamination.

"OK let's go," said Ransome.

Baldie shook his head, "You ain't the boss mush, go yourself."

"You refuse?"

"Too bloody true mate."

"We can manage," said Betty, revising her opinion of the cameraman, "If these two big men are too scared..." She put all the contempt she could muster into the words.

"Somebody's coming," said Baldie's mate, pointing.

Betty recognised Bobby's Jaguar. He braked to a stop a few yards away from the van. He and Tracy got out and hurried over. "You alright Mumsy? Laura said there was trouble down here."

"Something happened down in the crypt, two people are down there and these two brave men don't want to know," Betty pointed at the two porters sarcastically.

"Let's go Mumsy, Trace and I will help, won't we love?"

"Of course" Tracy's smooth accents, cool and un-flurried were beneficial. Her denim jeans and jacket were immaculate, obviously designed especially for her, her thick hair was shining like a TV advert.

"Got everything we need?" Bobby was in charge, "You two get lost if you refuse to help."

The two porters squared their shoulders, "You can't talk to us like that mister, you ain't our boss."

"I don't suppose your boss will be too pleased with you mister," Bobby turned his back on them, "Let's go."

The chill struck them immediately on entering the church. Making their way cautiously down the rotten stairs, Bobby leading, holding the Anson, they saw Holly Summerfield first, lying on her back near the steps. The sound man was behind the catafalque, sitting up and looking dazed.

"You OK Brian?" asked Ransome.

Molyneux scrambled to his feet looking dazed, "Yeah, where did you come from? Who are these people? Oh,yes, I know you you're Mrs Lewin, aintcha?"

"This is my son and daughter-in-law," said Betty. It sounded ludicrous in the circumstances, "You feel fit enough to make your own way out?"

Molyneux nodded, looking unsteady on his feet, "What about the gear?" he mumbled.

"Leave it, we'll pick it up later," said Ransome, looking round uneasily.

"Nobody's going to steal it," added Betty.

"This lady's unconscious," announced Bobby, bending over Summerfield, "Give me a hand someone"

"What's that burning smell?"asked Molyneux.

"It's nothing, you just make your way up the stairs Brian," said Ransome impatiently.

Betty and Tracy helped to put Summerfield over Bobby's shoulder in a fireman's lift. As they headed for the stairs, Tracy holding the Anson light for him, Betty said, "Shine the light over here a moment."

Tracy did as directed. There was no brass plaque on the coffin.

Ransome swore, "It was there when Holly touched it," he said.

"Must have dropped off some place."

"Let's go," said Bobby, "It's bloody cold down here, we've got to get this woman warm somehow and we can't do it down here."

Avoiding the power cable that snaked down the stairs they made their way into the hot sunshine.

"There's a bed in the van," Ransome opened the side door. Inside were living quarters for four people with bunks, a chemical toilet, wash basin and Calor gas stove.

Bobby eased Summerfield onto the nearest bunk, "Any blankets?" he asked Ransome.

"I'll get some," Daphne replied, opening an overhead cupboard and pulling several blankets out.

"Where're Dobie and Petherick?" demanded Ransome.

"Said they were going to the nearest pub," Daphne looked flustered.

Bobby tucked the blankets around the unconscious woman.

"What's wrong with her hand?" Daphne pointed.

"God, that's a burn," exclaimed Ransome, "Must have got it from that brass plate on the coffin."

"Let me have a look," said a voice behind them.

Funny Fanny stood beside the door to the van, clad as usual in her long skirt, blouse and shawl. The wolfhound was at her side.

"How did you get here Mrs Legge?" Betty was surprised at the sudden appearance of the mysterious Fanny Legge.

"Darren and I were looking for some herbs in the lane leading to that new housing complex," she said softly, "I felt some vibes and came over to see if I could help."

Ransome and Molyneux were both eyeing the woman and dog with apprehension. The animal was huge and looked ferocious, they thought. Her explanation didn't gel with Betty, it seemed too much of a coincidence.

"What can she do?" growled Ransome aggressively.

The wolfhound seemed to sense the cameraman's antagonism and growled deep in its throat.

"Leave Darren," said Fanny, still in her soft voice, "Go and lie down."

The dog obeyed lying down in a patch of shade, its tongue lolling.

"Let Mrs Legge have a look at Summerfield," said Betty, the experience with Wally Thompson just an hour or so away was strong. If she could perform that type of miracle, Summerfield's condition must be a pushover.

"We need a doctor, not some old harridan," snapped Ransome.

"Trust me Carl," said Betty, the use of his first name pleased the cameraman, "Let her see Holly."

Ransome motioned Fanny into the van. They all watched as she took Summerfield's hand, the hand minus the burn. She seemed to squeeze it, looking out over the fields towards the golf house, a faraway expression in her eyes. They all felt the presence of power that seemed to emanate from the tall woman. After a few moments Summerfield opened her eyes and looked up, her pupils dilating in alarm, then relaxing.

"Who are you? Where am I?" She struggled into a sitting position, "Who is this?" She nodded at Fanny.

"Mrs Legge, a neighbour of ours," said Betty quickly.

"I felt strange, like floating," said Holly, swinging her legs over the side of the bunk.

"Better thank the lady, Holly," said Ransome gruffly, "She brought you round and this chap carried you out of the crypt." He pointed to Bobby, "Better have that burn seen to."

"Burn? Where?" Summerfield looked round, puzzled.

"Your hand, dummy, where you touched that plaque," said Ransome.

"Hand? Burn?" Summerfield held up her hands, "I haven't got any burns."

Ransome goggled, "But I saw it, half your hand all scorched."

"So did I," said Daphne, "The right one."

"Yeah your right hand," Molynex agreed.

Bobby and Tracy were staring in amazement.

"No burns, look," Summerfield held up her right hand, "You were dreaming."

"Christ, I must be dreaming," said Ransome, "Your hand was all scorched, half way up your wrist, we all saw it. It must be something that old woman did, a bloody miracle. Let's have a look, I don't believe this."

Summerfield's hand was unblemished, dirty from contact with the crypt floor but smooth and soft.

"Where's she gone?" Ransome peered out of the van. They all looked, and again, no sign of Fanny.

"I'm going off my nut," Ransome shook his head, "Let's get out of this place, it's too spooky for my liking."

"Where's the gear, the cameras and mike?" Summerfield became all business like again.

"In that bloody crypt love, leave it be, we'll come back for it. I don't feel like going down there right now," Ransome looked apprehensive once more.

"We aren't leaving that footage down there mister," Summerfield was adamant, "Those cameras were on auto weren't they?"

Ransom nodded.

"That means we'll have everything on film, the plaque, the lightning, whatever, the lot, we need it."

"Well you’re on your own Madame, there's no way I'm going down that bloody crypt again."

"We'll help you Miss Summerfield," said Bobby, "Me, Tracy and Betty. Should be enough of us, shouldn't there?"

"I don't see why you should have to do it when he's perfectly capable," snapped Summerfield, pointing at her colleague.

"I'll give a hand Holly," said Molyneux.

"You up to it?"

"Sure, I feel a bit fuzzy that's all, I keep on seeing that lightning, like the aurora borealis, be great on the film though."

The four of them entered the crypt, Molyneux looked around a trifle fearfully and began dismantling the two cameras. The dismantling completed, they began to exit the crypt. Bobby was last in line, he heard it first, the eerie moaning, like a soft humming, which gradually crescendoed into full scale groans and moans.

"Fucking hell fire," he yelled, "What's that?"

The noise raised the hairs on his neck, fear almost paralysed his movement. There was a numbing quality to the sound that seemed to attack nerve endings. Bobby felt his legs begin to give way. Summerfield, the person above him, saw him hesitate and grabbed his arm, loaded as he was with the two tripods. She had to use all her strength to pull him up the last few stairs. Betty saw the problem and dumped the gear, then ran back to help Summerfield.

"Jesus," Yelled Bobby, strength returning now that he was away from the vicinity of the crypt. The noise appeared to be shaking the church to its foundations. Bobby felt his sphincter begin to lose control.

"Run!" he screamed.

Molyneux, clutching the two heavy cameras was first out, Betty, Tracy, Summerfield followed, Bobby bringing up the rear. Bobby ran for the chemical toilet, erected by Farraday's workforce, clutching his pants, downing the tripods en route. Outside the noise seemed to have ceased. The paralysing effect vanished.

****

20.

Sunday, 18th June 1995.
St Mary's Church, Babingley Marsh,
King's Lynn, Norfolk.

"Did you hear that, mush?" Molyneux demanded of Ransome.

Ransome looked blank, "Hear what?"

"That noise, the groaning."

Ransome looked derisively at his colleague, "That trip down there has blown a fuse mate, you need psychiatric help."

"I always knew there was something nasty about you Ransome. The blokes said you were a prize prick, I never believed them, I do now."

"Fuck your luck mister, if you wanna be a hero, be my guest."

"That's enough you two," snapped Summerfield, "Get this gear stowed and get back to Norwich."

"We made some food for you up at the house," said Tracy, still pale from the ordeal of the noise.

"What the devil was it?" Betty looked dazed.

"Probably just the wind being sucked through some aperture in the walls," said Tracy.

"You don't believe that do you?" Betty shuddered, "God, it was ghastly, like all the dead rising up to suck us in."

"That's what I felt," said Molyneux, "Just as if I was being drawn back down those stairs by some force. My legs were giving way, I hope your husband comes out of that toilet soon, I'm desperate."

"My son-in-law, the one who was injured down there this morning, said he heard terrible groaning noises before my husband went down to bring him out."

"This is going to earn you a bonus Mrs Lewin," said Summerfield, "I'm going to persuade My boss, Richard Cheeseman, the Director of Documentaries at Anglia that he awards you an extra payment of ten thousand for all your trouble and co-operation, how's that grab you Betty?"

Betty, still numb from the effects of the noises in the crypt for the offer to register, just nodded, "Fine thank you."

Bobby emerged from the toilet looking sheepish, a smell accompanied him, Molyneux rushed in.

"Had an accident," confessed Bobby.

"My God, you stink darling," cried Tracy, "You're not going to drive our Jaguar in that condition."

"He can come with me Tracy," said Betty.

"If you don't mind Mrs Lewin, we'll take a rain check on the refreshments, I need to get back to Norwich. I've rung our boss and told him that we have an exclusive, you only have to mention that if other media people show up. They'll try it on of course, but just be firm, they'll leave you alone and if they don't, just refer them to us. You go now, leave us to pack up here, thank you for everything."

"I'm humiliated Mumsy," said Bobby, "Better put something on this seat, I've crapped my pants."

"You can clean up at the house, nobody's going to know, or care," said Betty.

"Tracy opens her mouth too wide on occasions, it's all that play-up, play the game, tell the truth regardless syndrome she has been brought up on. It's quite wearing on occasions," said Bobby as Betty started the Landrover.

Tracy following in the Jaguar.

That awful noise," said Betty, driving faster than normal, "I'm still hearing it in my head, if Kevin heard that this morning, no wonder he felt bad."

"It did feel as if we were being drawn down again. My legs felt like water, my strength was leaving me as if I was paralysed." Bobby eased himself on his hands, "Jesus, I do stink, grown man craps his pants!"

"It's nothing, everybody feels that way under stress," Betty had to admit to herself the odour was appalling. She opened a window, "You go up to the bathroom, borrow some of your Father's gear, it should fit alright."

"Where have you been?" Jim came out of the farmhouse, "The phone's been going crazy, I've taken it off the hook. Thousands of calls asking about paranormal experiences, ghosts, spooks, gremlins and Christ knows what else.T That's all due to that bloody Summerfield woman, I knew it would end up like this."

"It wasn't her, it was Calhoun on local Radio. It seems he's on their strength as well as the 'Advertiser' He's gone to interview Murphy in hospital. I heard a bit of it in the Rover."

"We're going to have an invasion shortly, all the freaks, gawpers, curious idle onlookers..." Jim stopped, "Jesus, what's that stink? It's like shit."

"I crapped my pants Dad," said Bobby, his face red.

"Gawd, it's awful, go get yourself cleaned up. There's some spare clothes in our bedroom. What on earth happened? Where are the TV people? We've prepared all this food until young Laura came up on Bella and said there was trouble down at the church. You and Tracy took off before I could say anything."

"Is Laura OK? Bella was playing up down at the church," said Betty.

"Here I am Grandma, all in one piece. Bella calmed down after we passed the Hump."

Laura was still in jodpurs and riding boots. She sniffed, "Somebody farted?"

"Laura, where did you learn that disgusting expression?" Tracy looked horrified.

"Since I go to the best schools Mummy darling, they teach you all aspects of human life. You must admit there is a bad smell in the air."

"Your Father had an accident my girl, that's all."

"It's that junk food we eat, loosens the bowels," decided Laura. She looked past their shoulders out of the window, "Oh, Oh, we're going to get absoloution for our sins," She pointed.

"Hell's bells, the Holy Trinity," muttered Jim, genuflecting.

"Anybody home?" cooed a voice from the back door.

"I suppose it was inevitable in view of those phone calls," said Betty. She raised her voice, "Do come in Reverend."

The Reverend Charles Gates was clad in tweed sports gear, jacket and trousers. The only concession to his calling a black shirt with the collar. Betty decided that he resembled a corpse, tarted up in an American village of the dead. His body odour was worse than the smell Bobby had left behind. The Bishop wore a blue suit, which had been tailored to fit his gross frame, giving him even more of a pot-bellied pig appearance. The rings on his podgy fingers glittered like the eyes of Horus. He was puffing as if he'd attempted the ten second hundred yards, dabbing at his forehead as he had at the fete, with a starched white handkerchief. Betty saw his nose wrinkle as he entered the kitchen. She was not sure whether it was because the Reverend Gates personal problem was intensified in the enclosed space of the kitchen, or due to the residual smell of Bobby's accident.

"Expecting a lot of guests Mrs Lewin?" wheezed the Bishop de Manaury, seeing the laden table, "We won't keep you long."

Betty didn't consider the ramifications of her denial before she'd opened her mouth. 'Trust me to drop us in it', she thought. "Help yourself Bishop," She pointed to the stacked plates.

"I do feel slightly peckish, eh, Reverend? How about you?" The Bishop piled a plate with sandwiches, "My goodness, long time since I had the pleasure of smoked salmon, a special favourite of mine Mrs Lewin." A sandwich vanished into his trumpet mouth, he chomped on it like a rabbit.

"I say may I help myself Mrs Lewin?" The Reverend Gates odour now surrounding him like a miasma. His diseased gums showed in a smile.

Betty watched his spider-like fingers grasp several pieces of fruit cake and pile his plate. The resemblance to Tweety, Mrs Legge's deceased tarantula was sharp. Both priests began devouring food as if they were refugees from Biafra. Jim, Tracy and Laura watched fascinated as the smoked salmon vanished and then the pate.

"Some tea Bishop?" asked Betty, to head off the complete decimation of the food.

The Bishop nodded, his buck teeth moving rapidly like a rabbit, as sandwich after sandwich vanished into the trumpet mouth.

"If you go into the conservatory I'll bring it in to you," said Betty desperately, it was like watching two caterpillars devouring vegetation.

The Bishop piled his plate again, he then followed Tracy and Laura into the conservatory. The Reverend Gates hesitated, seeing Betty watching him, cast propriety aside and loaded his plate with the remainder of the fruit cake, following his Guv'nor into the conservatory.

"Jesus," said Jim, "I'm glad they don't come often."

"I wonder what they want?" Betty was pragmatic.

"You'd think they hadn't eaten for a bloody week," groused Jim, "I was looking forward to that fruit cake."

They heard the Bishop's fluty voice addressing Laura, asking her about her schooling and what religious instruction was offered. Betty made tea in a large pot, put mugs on a tray and arrived in time to hear her granddaughter's pithy commentary on the derth of 'pseudo religious crap' from the school curriculum. The Bishop smiled wanly at this blasphemy, unwilling to ruin the opportunities for more food.

She handed the Bishop the remaining smoked salmon sandwiches, podgy fingers relieved her of the balance. "How can we help Bishop?" she asked before Laura could deliver more succinct condemnation of RE.

"He's come to exorcise our demons Grandma," declared Laura, "He has the chicken bones under his suit."

"That's enough Laura," Tracy was horrified.

Jim smothered a grin.

The Bishop decided that discretion was the best defence, "Not exactly my child, but something along those lines I have to admit."

"I'm not sure what you mean precisely," Betty poured the tea into two mugs.

"My Reverend colleague here received a phone call from a Mr Calhoun, only gave his name after pressure from my colleague, he said that he understood there was an occult problem connected with the restoration of St Mary's, at least that's how he described what I believe he meant by paranormal activity. We came along to see if we could be of assistance, as the young lady said," he smiled benignly at Laura, "in exorcising the evil spirits."

Betty saw Tracy desperately leaning away from the Reverend Gates to avoid immolation in halitoxic vapours. Like all sufferers of this complaint, he insisted on speaking from a distance of less than six inches from his correspondent. She could smell the dead crab odour from a separation of over two yards.

"That was thoughtful of Mr Calhoun," Betty retorted, before her husband could make comments even more succinct than his granddaughter's, "What did he tell you about our problem?"

The Bishop gave a nervous smile as the final smoked salmon sandwich vanished, remains of bread stuck to the two bucked teeth, "He suggested there may well be a demon in the crypt of the church. He also made some extraordinary claim about having his hand burned by touching a catafalque." The Bishop smiled again, more confidently now, "We, the Reverend and I, are very cognisant of the fears of ordinary mortals in the presence of unidentified phenomena, prone to exaggeration of an exotic variety. Mr Calhoun seemed very eager for us to believe his story. We, my colleague and

I, since the Reverend will be intimately involved in the activities of the restored house of God, we thought we'd better come along, see for ourselves whether or not Mr Calhoun's claims were wild rumour or fact. I have to tell you that his allegation vis his burned hand, appeared to us both to be gross exaggeration, inflamed by understandable fear. If we can lay this troubled spirit to rest before any further instances of paranormal activity manifests itself, it would be beneficial."

"Mr Calhoun also made a extraordinary claim that a workman on the site had suffered a heart attack as a result of seeing this demon," Reverend Gates gave a subdued laugh and patted his mouth. It had the effect of wafting decaying crabmeat all over the conservatory.

"You have an oral hygiene problem mister," said Laura, brightly.

"Have you tried Listerine?"

The Reverend giggled nervously, adding to the toxic vapour present, "Very observant young lady," he said, "I have tried that patent remedy."

"Didn't work did it?" Laura was unrepentant, despite glares from her Mother.

"Laura, don't you think you should see to Bella?" Tracy said it through her teeth, trying to stop her from insulting the Reverend further.

"Hello, didn't realise we had visitors," Bobby appeared, clad in some of Jim's cast-offs, "Hi Bishop, Reverend, offered you some refreshment I see?"

****

21.

Sunday, June 18th 1995.
Lewin's Farm, Babingley Marsh,
King's Lynn, Norfolk.

"Laura, go see to Bella this minute, please." Tracy's fine features were red with embarrassment.

"Aye aye sir," Laura gave an American salute and stood to attention before exiting into the kitchen.

"We pay large fees every term for that educational exhibition Reverend," said Bobby, helping himself to tea.

"A sound investment I'm positive Mr Lewin," smiled the Reverend. The grimace was insincere.

"These gentlemen have come to help us with our demons," said Betty, "Mr Calhoun phoned them and gave them some sensational story about the crypt."

"You know he's a reporter for the 'Advertiser' Reverend?" asked Bobby.

The Reverend nodded, "He made his interest quite clear."

"Whilst the Advertiser is not exactly a tabloid, the main reason for all this unhealthy attention is circulation. The more lurid the story, the more copies they will sell. I'm sure you understand that?" Bobby was calm.

"Are you telling us that Calhoun's allegations are not true Mr Lewin?" Bishop deManaury pouted his rosebud mouth into a delicate trumpet, "We've neglected our Sabbath duties to come and attend to this problem."

"He's leaned towards the extravagant rather than the facts Bishop," said Betty.

"And what are the facts Mrs Lewin? Mr Calhoun had exaggerated these claims, he didn't burn his hand as a result of paranormal activity in the crypt and that Mr Murphy's heart attack was the result of natural causes?" Bishop deManuary glared at Betty suspiciously.

"Do you believe this story Bishop?" asked Bobby, sipping tea.

"I mean, you have to be rather naive to believe there are unclean spirits at work in St Mary's, or convinced there are such things as demons. I'd have thought a man of the cloth would treat such stories with reservation. Mr Calhoun is an ambitious gentleman, anxious to employ any means to enhance his reputation I'm afraid."

At that moment, the Anglia Television outside broadcast van drove past the farm en route to the main road. A dust devil trailed it. Bishop deManuary's porcine eyes gleamed triumphantly. Betty went hot with embarrassment. She also realised she was still wearing the suede jacket the young woman had lent her. She'd have to devise a way of returning the jacket without getting involved, or inviting further visits from the Anglia team.

"The TV company appear to be interested in events on your property Mr Lewin. I'm wondering what gained their attention?"

"They gained their information from the same source, Rory Calhoun, Bishop. They were largely disappointed, spent a lot of the company's money investigating rumours," Jim tried to keep a deadpan expression.

"Tell you what Mr and Mrs Lewin, permit the Reverend and I to inspect the crypt, see for ourselves that there is no substance to Mr Calhoun's claims, that way we can all be reassured?" The Bishop's little eyes were alight with triumph.

"You are welcome to inspect any time Bishop deManuary," said Jim.

"Since we've made a special journey neglectful of our Sabbath commitments, could we not visit the crypt now?"

"You're welcome to inspect it Bishop, satisfy yourself that Mr Calhoun's claims are exaggerated somewhat."

"Spendid, splendid," The Bishop arose after smiting his knees with both hands, "Come along Reverend, we'll make our way along there now."

"You realise of course there is scaffolding around the church and also inside? You'll need lighting, it's very gloomy inside the building," said Betty.

"We came prepared, just like the Boy Scouts Mrs Lewin," smiled the Bishop.

"For insurance purposes one of us will have to accompany you Bishop. If you injured yourself whilst on our property we could be sued for neglect or something of that nature."

"I can assure you Mrs Lewin, neither I nor the Reverend are in the business of invoking the law for acts of our own chosing," said the Bishop.

"Nevertheless I would feel easier if you were accompanied," said Jim.

"Oh very well Mr Lewin," The Bishop was peeved, "If you insist. We had intended to conduct our investigations without any sense of pressure, from shall we say, an interested party?"

"You won't be pressured I assure you Bishop. You will be free to go where you please, take as long as is necessary to satisfy yourself that Calhoun's claims are a trifle wild," Jim's smile was brittle, "I'll come myself, show you round."

"Can we make our way down there now?" The Bishop was anxious to go. The Reverend Gates didn't share his boss's enthusiasm, he looked a little anxious.

"I'll come along for the ride Dad," said Bobby.

Jim nodded, "Back shortly love," he said to Betty.

"The torch is on the hook in the Rover," she said, keeping her fingers crossed.

"I hope nothing happens down there," said Tracy as she and Betty watched the Landrover move off.

"We'll give them half an hour, then go see for ourselves," said Betty, "I could kill that Calhoun fellow, all the trouble he's causing."

"We'll be on Anglia TV tonight," said Tracy, dolefully, "Won't go down well with Mama and Pop. They dislike this kind of popular extravaganzas."

"I'm not exactly wild about it myself love," said Betty, tartly

"I'm sorry Mother, I didn't mean it like that, but you know what Troy is like over sensational press stories."

They both heard a car draw up at the front of the house. Voices sounded.

"Oh no, she's all we need to cap our rich experience!," moaned Betty, recognising the voice.

"Who is it?"

"Lilly Simpson would you believe?" Betty went through the house to greet Lilly.

A cream Rolls stood in the drive, a chauffeur aiding Lilly out of the rear door. Betty went to the door to greet Lilly. She mustered all the insincerity she could assemble, "How nice to see you Lilly," she enthused.

Lilly looked at her quizzically, "Why do I get the feeling that you're lying Betty Lewin?"

"Probably because I've just about had a gutful of today Lilly," Betty was relieved to tell the truth.

"I heard that item on local radio, the one about paranormal experiences down at the church, something about Paddy Murphy suffering a heart attack as a result of seeing ghosts. I was in Longley Hill, so I thought I'd come to see for myself, ask you whether they are lying, exaggerating, or just being sensational."

"Is there any difference?" asked Betty.

"Ah hello Tracy, didn't know you were here, how's your lovely Father and your beautiful daughter, Laura?"

"Very well thank you Mrs Simpson," Tracy wasn't enamoured of Lilly Simpson either.

"Do you know all about these ..er paranoraml experiences down at the church?"

"I believe they are all exaggerated, no real substance in any of it," said Tracy.

"I know Ross Lambert, the DJ on Radio Lynn, he's usually very restrained my dear. He seemed to believe that Murphy had suffered his heart attack as a result of seeing something in the crypt and that Rory Calhoun was interviewing Murphy in hospital right this minute. Funny Ross should go overboard if he was only repeating rumours. Demetrius is on the Board of Radio Lynn, he'll take a very dim view of wild rumours being peddled as fact."

"We've always had some peculiar goings on Lilly," said Betty. "My son-in-law Kevin says it's due to the fact that there two sets of ley-lines crossing our property and they contain energy of a sort. It adversely affects machinery and electrics, they cross at the Church and the Hump. It has nothing to do with paranormal experiences that your Ross what's-his-name was on about."

"Ley-lines? What are they?"

"Lilly, with the best will in the world, I couldn't even begin to explain to you what ley-lines are, you'll have to consult Kevin on that score," said Betty.

"Weird, what energy does he think causes the machinery to stop?"

"Something to do with magnetic fields Mrs Simpson," said Tracy. "Some places have strong magnetic currents flowing than others."

"Funny I never knew that," Lilly screwed her face up, "Is Mr Wilson here?"

"He suffered an accident this morning, a severe blow to the head. He's in Holdings Hill until tomorrow, under observation."

"I see, is it alright if I go down to the Church, have a look round?"

"I don't think Mr Farraday would be too delighted at people wandering around unaccompanied, the scaffolding isn't in position as yet and the fencing is locked," Betty figuratively crossed herself.

"Oh well perhaps another day, I'll call in see how Mr Wilson is, see this Murphy fellow, I'd like to understand what all the fuss Ross Lambert was talking about, paranormal activity. He'll get a rocket from Demetrius if he's spreading rumours."

Betty nearly panicked, the thought of Lilly Simpson appearing at the reception desk of Holdings Hill Hospital, one of the Trust's Board of Governors, asking questions of Paddy Murphy and Kevin, Ellen's husband, probing into just what had caused Kevin's injuries would create problems of another dimension.

"Would you like some tea before you go Lilly? I mean it is a hot day, this summer seems to be going on forever doesn't it?" Betty babbled on inconsequentially about weather, farms, golf, Mad Cow Disease.

"Are you trying to divert me Betty?" demanded Lilly shrewdly.

Betty looked all injured innocence, "Why on earth should I do that?"

"You don't particularly enjoy my company and you aren't normally this talkative. You trying to hide something from me?" She peered again at Betty as if probing into her innermost thoughts.

"You don't have to take up my invitation do you?" said Betty, realising she'd probably overdone the hospitality angle.

"No, but I will," said Lilly.

"You take Mrs Simpson through into the conservatory Mother. I'll make tea," said Tracy, cottoning on.

"Haven't seen your Father at any of the Trust's meetings lately Mrs Lewin, is he well?"

"He's been very busy settling in the new fleet," said Tracy.

"Ah, you mean the take-over of Lang's of Wisbech?"

Tracy nodded.

Betty took a deep breath, the meadow lady knew everything about everybody's business, "This way Lilly."

Lilly's piggy little eyes were everywhere en route to the conservatory. Her expression changed to one of delight on seeing the conservatory, "Well now isn't this magnificent? I'll have to try and persuade Demetrius to have one of these built. It really does look good, it would enhance the value of the property." She went on a self-guided tour of inspection, wanting to know costs, the disturbance of family life during building, the duration, everything.

Betty didn't fall into the trap of gushing, just treated the woman's curiosity with casualness. Tracy arrived with the tea tray just as Lilly had finished her inspection.

"I tried phoning you before deciding to come in person," said Lilly, "Your phone was engaged continuously."

Betty realised the phone was still off the hook to stem the flow of idle callers.

"It isn't working too well, we've asked BT to come and have a look," said Betty, as Tracy poured tea, she wondered how Jim and Bobby were getting on with the Reverend Gates and Bishop de-Manaury down at the church. If anything dramatic had occurred Jim would have contacted her via his mobile. She prayed that the two prelates and her family wouldn't arrive back before Lilly had taken off.

"Nice tea Betty," commented Lilly, sipping genteelly, her little finger extended around the cup.

"Common or garden Lilly. We use spring water, that's the only difference."

"Talking of spring water, I hear that our local witch has her own spring, she doesn't take water from the Board," said Lilly.

"That a fact?" Betty hoped this wasn't a prelude to another oblique attack.

"Must be her secret of longevity," went on Lilly, ignoring Betty, "She looks the same now as she did ten years ago. I suppose all the chemicals put in our water does have an effect on skin and looks."

Betty remained deadpan. "So someone else had noticed Fanny Legge's uncannily ageless looks, I hadn't noticed. We don't see her that often."

"Did you hear about Wally Thompson?" Lilly shot it out like a broadside.

"What about him?" Betty knew what was coming.

"Discharged himself from Longley Hill, he said he was cured of his cancer and walked out under his own steam after being in intensive care for a month, not expected to live out the week."

"How'd you know this Lilly?" Curiosity overcame Betty.

"Mrs Spragg phoned me, said she'd seen Thompson get out of your husband's Landrover at Thompson's house. She lives in Loke Road close to the Thompson's, she said he looked healthier than he has for years. He walked in without assistance, and he'd been taken to Longley Hill in an ambulance a few days ago she told me. She went across to Thompson's wife Ruth, I think her name is and asked how Wally was able to go home after being in intensive care for weeks. She said Ruth told her Fanny Legge had cured him, absolute nonsense of course, must be new treatment he's been receiving at Longley Hill I told her."

The woman had spies everywhere it seemed, feeding her gossip and news.

"Did you know about this?" Lilly fixed Betty with her piggy little eyes.

****

22.

Sunday, June 18th 1995.
Lewin's Farm, Babingley Marsh,
King's Lynn, Norfolk

How do I treat this, Betty asked herself. If I admit I know about Wally then she'll blow it to everybody in Lynn. Won't be long before paranormal activity in the church will be the cause of Wally's cure and Fanny Legge will be responsible. On the other hand if I deny it, how can I explain how Jim came to take Wally home and me not know anything about it? She knows Kevin is in Longley Hill, Moreover, she'll soon find out from her spies that we were all there when Fanny arrived.

Salvation arrived in the form of the Landrover, the Bishop and the Reverend Gates behind Bobby and Jim in the passenger seat. Lilly's eyes dilated with triumph, as if God had revealed all in the form of Bishop deManaury and the Vicar. The Bishop it seemed wasn't particularly overjoyed at seeing Lilly Simpson. His expression did not reflect his enthusiastic greeting.

"How are you Mrs Simpson?" he grasped Lilly's podgy hand in both his own, "I have been meaning to thank Demetrius for his magnificent contribution to the restoration fund. Pressure of work you know? Thank him for me will you, I'll be writing to him in due course," The effusive manner was not mirrored in his cold eyes.

"Been investigating the paranormal experiences down at the church?" Lilly battened onto what she believed was uncontroversial proof of unusual activity.

"We came, the Reverend and I to carry out exorcism of demonic presence down at the church," admitted the Bishop.

"Did you find anything?" Lilly was agog.

The Bishop shook his head, "No evidence whatsoever my dear lady, the place is calm, untroubled."

Betty caught Jim's eye, he shrugged his shoulders, his eyes looking heavenwards, Bobby was deadpan.

"I'd heard that ghosts have been seen in the crypt, Harry Farraday's site manager suffered a heart attack as a result of seeing a ghost," babbled Lilly.

The Bishop gave a wry smile, "I'm afraid that the only demon present that accounted for Mr Murphy's condition was alchohol Mrs Simpson."

Lilly was disappointed, anticipating a confession of disturbing events in the church, "I see, nobody told me Mr Murphy was drunk when he suffered his attack," She glared at Betty, accusingly.

"I don't suppose that anyone felt it was necessary to inform you my dear," The Bishop's antipathy was patent.

Lilly's mouth formed a downward crescent, her expression chilled, "You haven't heard about Wally Thompson?" she said, annoyed at being kept in the dark.

The Bishop looked blankly at Lilly. Some of her disappointment evaporated, realising she possessed seismic news of which the Bishop was unaware.

"The poor man has passed on?" The Reverend Gates assumed an expression of piety.

"He's cured," Lilly was jubilant, suddenly she was in control again.

"Cured?" The Reverend looked disoriented, "But he wasn't expected to live beyond this weekend, I visited him on Friday, in a dreadful way he was."

"The witch cured him, he got up, walked out and Mr Lewin drove him home with his wife only this morning," Lilly nodded at Jim.

"That right, Mr Lewin?"

"I did drive Wally Thompson home," said Jim.

"The witch? What witch?" The Bishop was put out that he wasn't the first to hear of the event.

"Fanny Legge Bishop," The Reverend Gates jumped in before Lilly could elaborate, "There have been rumours that she is in league with the Devil, lives with a large number of cats and other strange creatures, including a massive dog. She collects herbs from the marsh and makes balms and ointments. People, the ignorant strata in the town believe she has strange powers. I haven't had any confirmation of such gifts. Anyway, ignorant people tend to exaggerate any unusual experience."

"You say she cured a man dying of lung cancer Mrs Simpson?"

The Bishop ignored his subordinate.

"Well, I've only heard it second hand of course, but Mr Lewin can confirm that he drove Thompson home can't you Mr Lewin?"

The Bishop looked at Jim, "How did you find him, was he ill, going home to die?"

Jim saw Betty shake her head, "I drove he and Ruth home this morning, he didn't look as if he were very ill," Jim said.

"Remarkable," said the Reverend Gates, "I know they've been experimenting with a new treatment at Longley Hill. Plainly it has been a success with Thompson."

"Mrs Simpson says that this witch cured him," The Bishop was annoyed at his colleague.

The Reverend gave a nervous laugh, "Fanciful, wishful thinking Bishop," he chuckled, "People love stories of this kind, create all kinds of imagery, it satisfies ancient folklore, in-built superstition...you know how it is?"

"According to my informant Wally Thompson looked in rude health Reverend," stated Lilly.

Another nervous laugh followed, "You don't really believe such exotic rumours do you Mrs Simpson? I mean, there was no doubt that Thompson was very ill on Friday, and not expected to live beyond the weekend. It is obvious your informant got it wrong."

"You heard what he said, didn't look very ill," Lilly pointed to Jim, "What's more they wouldn't have discharged him if he was that ill would they?"

"We'll have to visit this Thompson's, see for ourselves Reverend Gates," said the Bishop. "Witches," he snorted, "Superstitious peasants, curing the sick, only our Lord was able to perform miracles, not some strange woman living an erratic lifestyle, utter rubbish"

"Have you spoken to Billy Watson recently Reverend?" demanded Lilly, angry at being dismissed.

The Reverend looked peeved at being challenged, "I haven't been to Tweedle Farm for some time, a trifle remote, it takes up valuable time that I could be spending more profitably with my more accessible parishioners."

"Why do you ask Mrs Simpson?" Bishop deManaury sensed some exotic revelation.

"Fanny cured his chronic back condition some ten years ago. Never suffered with it since," Lilly was almost dancing in her excitement, her outsize breasts wobbling dangerously.

"Watson attended that chiropractor, can't recall his name."

Reverened Gates screwed up his face so that the creases in his forehead became tramlines, "It is obvious that Watson is romancing just to make a salacious story, from my experience, I know he exaggerates."

"Billy Watson is not a liar Reverend," Lilly was cold again, "If he says Fanny Legge cured his back, I believe him."

The Bishop pulled a face, "It seems we have a Circe in our midst Reverend Gates, of whom I was not informed. We must take steps to verify this information. If this woman, Legge, is it, is peddling this dangerous nonsense, she's a menace to the spiritual well being of the diocese. It's one thing to be called a witch, quite another to practice witchcraft actively upon the ignorant amongst our flock."

"She cured my back," stated Jim, flatly. There was no way he was going to permit these two sanctimonious buzzards to lead a crusade against Fanny Legge because of some sense of injury to their standing in the community.

Betty sucked her breath in at Jim's temerity. Whilst she felt the same she wasn't sure that this declaration was going to help anyone, least of all Fanny Legge.

The two priests stared at Jim, astonished. "I beg your pardon Mr Lewin?" The Bishop hadn't heard correctly.

"I said she cured my back around the same time she cured Bill Watson's."

The Bishop was convinced that he'd heard the ultimate in blasphemy, "You mean with these ...er ..balms and ointments she prepares, they eased your condition?" he expected confirmation.

"I mean she put her hands on my back and inside a minute I felt no more pain, neither have since and that was back in '83...twelve years ago. I'd had traction at Longley Hill, manipulation by the same chiropractor as Bill Watson, nothing worked. Fanny Legge cured me in minutes, I have not suffered since. I don't very much care what you or anyone else calls her, witch, wizard, enchantress, spell-binder, she performed something miraculous for me and I won't tolerate anything said against her. She doesn't harm anybody, doesn't spread rumour, she does no harm. If she's eccentric that's her choice, if she doesn't want to conform, that's OK by me. So she makes balms and ointments, what's wrong with that? She doesn' t charge anybody or make money out of it. The NHS does out of drugs that don't do that much good..." Jim came to a stop, realising he'd probably overdone his defence of Fanny Legge.

The Bishop puffed out his plump cheeks, "It seems you are very much in favour of alternative medicine Mr Lewin," he said in a strangled voice.

"It's because she doesn't conform to your concept of what a doctor should be that it upsets your sense of orthodoxy," said Jim. "I don't care what Fanny Legge is, she saved me from years of utter misery, that puts her in a special category for me. I don't say it was a miracle, but it was the next best thing."

The Bishop gave a hurrumph, "It seems our witch has an advocate in Mr Lewin, Reverend Gates, not too sure that I approve of your defence of witchcraft Mr Lewin. Can lead to some unfortunate results when ignorant people meddle in such things."

"My brother-in-law is Chief Wizard of the Wizard Society mister. I suppose you don't approve of him either?" said Bobby.

"Wizard Society?" Bishop deManaury seemed to have difficulty in understanding Bobby's statement, "What on earth is that Mr Lewin?"

"The Ancient Order of British Wizards, they hold regular séance events, meetings to exchange ideas, promote the lost wisdom of former times that the Church attempted to stamp out because it threatened their position in society, Bishop. They're holding their Solstice Event at Bawsey Ruin on the 21st of this month, that's next Wednesday. You'd be welcome to attend sir, see what kind of magic Kevin and his Wizards perform. They might even sacrifice a virgin on the altar, hold sex orgies, all very enjoyable," Bobby was grinning", They might even find a suitable virgin for your pleasure, renew your sex-life. I'm sure it gets a little stale in your position?"

"That's enough Bobby," snapped Betty, "I'm sure the Bishop does not approve of Kevin's activities. There's no need to exaggerate what goes on."

"Just because these geriatric old farts think they know it all, dolled up in that fancy rig, dog collars and all that, makes them pillars of society, the only ones to have a direct line to God because some big-wig dog-collar incants over them, that makes it all correct?"

"Bobby!" rasped Betty, appalled at Bobby's outburst.

"I don't care Mumsy, it pisses me off that these two prigs think they can ride roughshod over everybody else's concepts of what is religious, just because it hasn't been sanctified by the Pope, or some other crettinous bastard in a funny hat. Fanny Legge does a lot of good, doesn't demand money with menaces, she just lives an unorthodox lifestyle and it offends these creeps, threatens their livelihood if someone can come up with the real McCoy without all the razzmatazz," Bobby stopped.

There was silence for at least twenty seconds. There came a slow handclap from the direction of the kitchen door.

"That was quite a speech Mr Lewin, worthy of an Oscar."

Rory Calhoun stood in the doorway, his hand bandaged, clad in jeans and denim jacket.

"I take it that isn't for publication Mr Lewin?" He entered, an aluminium camera case held by a strap over his shoulder, "Do not panic, I won't report it, I was fascinated by your defence of our local witch, commendable."

"What do want Calhoun?" Bobby was cold.

"I've just come from our dark room, back at the old fortress of public concern, you know, the 'Advertiser'." He placed the camera case on the ornamental table.

"That doesn't tell us why you're here Calhoun, or what you want?"

Calhoun ignored Bobby, "Hi there Reverend Bishop deManuary, trying to get these folks to condemn Funny Fanny are we?" He chuckled, "Wasting time I'm afraid, I've just come from Wally Thompson's place in Loke Road. I didn't believe in miracles before I paid Wally a visit. I heard whilst I was interviewing Paddy Murphy in Longley Hill that Wally had had a visit from Funny Fanny, a few minutes later, he was walking round, cured, and I've seen the evidence before my eyes. It's true alright, he looks as healthy as you do Bishop, right as rain, good for another forty years. He's given up his tailor-mades though, says it ain't worth the risks."

"There you are, I told you so," said Lilly, exultantly, "Here's proof."

"You're telling me that this..er Funny Fanny cured Walter Thompson of lung cancer?" The Bishop was unconvinced that Calhoun wasn't romancing.

Calhoun nodded, "Biggest scoop I've ever had, going to create a worldwide sensation when I syndicate the story, it'll put Lynn in the same category as Lourdes and Walsingham, only more so. Get my name in lights as big as St Paul's, ha ha, joke!" He gave the Reverend a slap on the shoulder.

"Well what do you want Calhoun, apart from boasting how smart you are? You were a nasty piece of work at St James's, nothing's changed, save perhaps you've got a bigger head and a bigger mouth," Bobby's anger showed.

"Just thought you'd like to see these old son," Calhoun didn't seem put out by Bobby's rancour. He threw some squares of celluloid onto the table from a inner pocket, "Negatives of the film I took of your church and crypt, very interesting."

"Why should we be interested?"

"Poses a lot of questions about that place that can't be answered by logic or rational thinking mister," Calhoun was unmoved by the atmosphere of hostility, "Enough material to create an even bigger sensation than Wally Thompson's cure."

"I'm not interested in your squalid games Calhoun."

The Bishop picked up one of the dark squares and held it up to the light. "There's nothing on this one Mr Calhoun," he said.

Calhoun said nothing as the Bishop picked up another, followed by the Reverend. They both went through a dozen of the negatives, Lilly following suit, squinting against the light.

"Is this a joke Mr Calhoun? There's nothing on them," The Bishop didn't bother examining any more.

****

23.

Sunday, June 18th 1995,
Lewin's Farm, Babingley Marsh,
King's Lynn, Norfolk.

Jim grasped the significance straight away, picked up the negatives discarded by the priests and held them up to the light. They were blank.

"Your camera was damaged when it fell," said Jim, dismissively.

Calhoun was grinning, "I took these a short time ago at Longley Hill with this same camera Lewin," He opened the aluminium case threw some large photos on the table.

They were of Paddy Murphy sitting up in a hospital bed looking very down in the mouth. Calhoun followed this by some of Wally Thompson and his wife Ruth in their Loke Road home. Jim was impressed by Thompson's evident good health from the images on the paper. The priests examined the photos.

Lilly then picked up the negatives and held them to the light, her little piggy eyes squinting, followed by the photos of Thompson and Murphy. "Told you so didn't I?" She was overjoyed that her evidence of Thompson's recovery was vindicated, "See, healthy as he was before he got that cancer and that witch cured him. This is proof, she does have magic powers."

Calhoun grinned at Lilly, "Can I quote you Mrs Simpson? Make good copy in Tuesday's edition, 'Wife of prominent local businessman states that we have a genuine witch in the community, who performs miracle cures?'"

Lilly nodded, "By all means Mr Calhoun," she preened herself.

"How about a photo Mrs Simpson? Always validates copy for our readers?"

Lilly nodded, delighted at the thought of some exposure in the local paper.

"How about you Bishop and you Reverend? Want to go on record along with Mrs Simpson?"

The Reverend nodded eagerly. Bishop deManaury shook his head, "I am yet to be convinced of any evidence of psychic phenomena surrounding our church Mr Calhoun. We saw nothing to convince us when we visited the crypt a short time ago with Messrs Lewin."

"You've seen Wally Thompson's photos, cured when he was just about kaput, why don't you want to confirm it?" Calhoun was blunt, "See this?" He held up his bandaged hand, "I received this burn from the plaque on the catafalque in that mausoleum. They saw it happen, they were with me. That's right Mr and Mrs Lewin, isn't it?

"We saw something Mr Calhoun, couldn't swear as to what happened precisely," said Betty.

"Wriggling out of it now are you? Don't want the publicity, is that it? Keep your cosy middle-class lifestyle all secure?" Calhoun sneered, "If those negatives don't convince you, hjow about these?" He selected more from the camera case and threw them on the table. "I took those of that area you call the Hump en route to the church. See if they're the same, go on, won't bite you. How about you Bishop, Reverend? Heard about the Hump have you? Ancient tumulus, burial chamber, Johnny Foster had trouble with the bungalow he was building on that site ten years ago. He had to abandon the work because of the weird things that happened to his machinery, men and objects. I did some boning up on these ley-lines that their son-in-law was on about, Kevin Wilson, old school mate of mine."

"Ley-lines? What are they?" The Bishop picked up the negatives Calhoun stated were of the Hump and held them up to the light. He shrugged, "Nothing on these either."

"Isn't that sufficient proof of paranormal activity around this property Bishop? The whole place is alive with energy from these crossed ley-lines."

"Come on Mr Calhoun, you are really going too far with this affair. Ley-lines, energy? What lines and what energy?"

"Energy enough to burn my hand when I touched the plaque on that catafalque down in the crypt," Calhoun's eyes were alight with zeal.

"All due to these ..er ..ley-lines. Is that your claim?" Bishop deManaury was sceptical.

"Ley-lines were suspected to exist early in the nineteenth century, a fellow named Alfred Watkins, who was a dowser, you know twisting sticks to find water. He discovered that in certain areas of the country, like Glastonbury and Stonehenge, there was a great deal of energy, magnetic or some mysterious forces not yet discovered. The energies were powerful at these points. He eventually came too the theory that ley-lines were like a printed circuit all over the face of the planet, that this energy travelled along these circuits and were most powerful where they crossed. The Chinese discovered these much earlier, they called them dragon lines. They avoided building or creating anything where dragon lines crossed. Your mates, the early missionaries, ignored warnings from the ignorant gooks. Invariably something always happened to churches built on these crossed dragon lines."

"Oh come on Mr Calhoun, surely you aren't claiming that the superstitious Chinese knew more than our technologically advanced Europeans?" Reverend Gates bulbous eyes were smoky with disdain.

Lilly was listening eagerly, her expression one of intense excitement.

"Every church in the UK is built on such sites Reverend. Your early churchmen weren't stupid, if the pagan population were aware of the power of these sites the Church wanted to eliminate any threat to their temporal power and plonked churches over these ancient tumuli, thus use any of this mysterious energy for their own use."

"What utter blasphemy my man. The Church wouldn't attempt such chicanery and certainly wouldn't countenace the existence of witchcraft," puffed the Bishop, indignantly.

"Ley-lines cross at that church Bishop, at that Hump, Bawsey Ruin, Reffley Spring, the Red Mount, to name but a few that we know about in the Lynn area. That's as far as I could learn in the short time I've spent boning it up," Calhoun was cool.

"I suspect they cross at St Margarets, St Nicholas and other sites in Lynn, but I didn't have time to research them all."

"What utter balderdash,my good man," The Reverend was contemptuous, "Mere pagan mythology, like fairies, goblins, will-o-the-wisps."

"Mrs Wilson had permission to do some research in our record department, she persuaded Ray Hammond to let her look at the old records in the central library."

"She came to me as well," said Gates, "Spent hours looking them over."

"The whole congregation of St Mary's died of bubonic plague in June 1918, at least that was the theory," Calhoun was grinning, "and the vicar and his family died also from the same complaint, that's why St Mary's was closed Bishop, no villager would go near the place. No symptoms of the plague were evidenced when the autopsies were performed on the people who died."

"Never heard such utter nonsense," spluttered Gates.

"Your records are lying then Reverend," said Calhoun, "The whole congregation died within days of that service held in St Mary's, June 21st 1918, not from the influenza epidemic that swept the globe, but bubonic plague. Have you heard of Doctor Dempsey?"

"No,I haven't."

"There was an article on him in your paper some time back. I remember reading about it involved in some scandal about choir boys?" Lilly was anxious to air her local knowledge.

Calhoun nodded, "It was never proven. Jeff ran that article to prove that child molestation isn't a modern phenomenon. He was also the medic who attended the sick congregation, he lived in a cottage in Castle Rising, with his wife and three kids."

"I suppose he left the town when the hoo-hah arose over the scandal of the boys and then the bubonic plague?"

"He was going to, but he dropped dead on June 28th, a week after the villagers of Babingley. His wife and kids were dead the next day."

"You're implying that everyone who attended that service on June 21st died?"

"Not implying Bishop, they did, every single one of them, and the people who attended them," Calhoun was confident of his facts. "There are some private papers belonging to the Reverend Fletcher Garson in the Library, he was the last vicar of St Mary's, he died along with his fifty parishioners on June 21st 1918. In his last diary entry before he died he claimed there was a flash of lightning inside the church, the lights went out, they had lanterns in those days, then there was a smell of burning cloth which last for what he estimated was twenty seconds then everybody began feeling ill. He stopped the service." Calhoun grinned, "And you aren't going to question the word of a fellow man of the cloth are you gents?"

"The poor fellow must have been confused, feeling ill," said the Reverend.

"My last revelation, ladies and gents is that a certain Myfanwy Legge was interned in that central catafalque on June 21st, 1796, according to your records Reverend and one of our earliest copies of my rag."

"Fascinating story Mr Calhoun," Lilly was avidly soaking in all the details, "What about her family? Are there any descendants in Lynn, apart from this..er witch?"

"That's the weirdest part about the whole story ladies and gents."

"Well?" demanded Lilly when Calhoun said nothing, "What's weird about it?"

"There are no records of any Legge's before that date, or after."

"You've missed the entries," puffed the Bishop, "She can't just appear and then die, and why would she be buried in St Mary's? Those crypts were normally reserved for the well-to-do local families who paid for their interment?"

"I went through all the records sir, there are no Legge's living in Babingley before or since 1796, exept for Funny Fanny, who lives in that cottage in North Wootton and performs all these miracles, raising the dead, curing backs, and what about Troy Middleton at the fete two weeks ago? Remember? Fell ill complaining about his liver. You were all there and saw it. Funny Fanny comes along whilst Barry is faffing around for his bag of tricks. Pamela Middleton is yelling blue murder and Fanny lays hands on Troy and he's cured. Lots of people saw that."

"Pure wishful thinking my dear man," said Gates, "Ignorant peasant types love all this fantasy about miracles, they thought they saw her cure Troy Middleton when all he suffered was a bout of indigestion."

"Troy has had chronic hepatitis for years Bishop," said Betty, "Would you call us ignorant peasant types? We witnessed that incident. Troy was very ill according to Barry Lassiter. Fanny comes along with that dog, puts her hands on Troy's abdomen and he gets up, all the yellowness gone. Tracy can verify that for you can't you Tracy?"

"Father has been to specialist's for years about his hepatitis, he's been living on drugs to keep it under control. Since the Fete he's off the drugs, feels better now than he has for years. He puts it all down to Funny Fanny," said Tracy.

"I was talking to Troy only last week," Lilly was anxious not to be left out. "I thought he looked well, not as yellow as he normally does. He said he felt a lot better, he didn't say anything about Funny Fanny though. I heard about his cure at the Fete."

The Bishop smiled scornfully, "I'm fully aware of your feeling for your Father Mrs Lewin, but don't you think this... er miracle is being slightly overdone? Drugs have peculiar side effects on occasions, your Father suffered from such a side-effect on that occasion. This Legge woman merely arrived in time to see the effects wear off, perfectly rational explanation."

"You can think whatever you please, I know Daddy hasn't felt better for a long time and all since Funny Fanny put her hands on him at the Fete," Tracy was indignant.

"Alright, so this area is bewitched," spat the Bishop, "Is that what you're all implying? Witchcraft, demonology, paranormal activity, psychic phenomena. My colleague and I saw nothing to support that view down at the church. I would venture to suggest that you're all slightly overwrought, imaginations playing tricks on you."

"You're at liberty to think what you like Bishop," said Jim, "We just want a peaceful life uncomplicated by any of all this hoo-hah. If you're through perhaps we can get on with our Sunday routines? I have to visit the Clubhouse, see my manager, Paul Miller, check the stables with Merry, collect the takings and do the banking."

"Well, we've outstayed our welcome Mr Lewin. We'd both like to thank you for the refreshments. I'm afraid I can't be anything else but sceptical about all this witchcraft and miracle cures. You are free to accept it or reject it. I am positive that subsequent evidence will remove all the element of sorcery. In the meantime we'll bid you farewell."

The two priests exited, Bishop deManaury waddling like a pregnant duck, the gaunt Reverend Gates like an elongated shadow.

"I must be going also Betty" said Lilly, "I've found all this so fascinating. Lynn will be the focus of world attention by the weekend. Lovely, lots of business for the shops in Lynn," she sneered. She gave Betty a wet kiss on the cheek, "You must come to my next coffee morning, tell all the girls about this magic. They'll love it, exciting." She waved a plump hand at Jim, "I hope to see you again soon Mr Lewin."

She waddled out to the cream Rolls Royce, the liveried chauffeur aided her in. She gave a regal wave as the car glided smoothly out of the drive.

"Bloody old busybody," muttered Calhoun, gathering up his negative from the table, "There is definitely something odd about that church and Hump. You'll have to anticipate a lot of visitors over the next few weeks when my article appears on Tuesday, all eager to see the site. Can't help thinking they might be right about all these miracle cures, in spite of Wally Thompson, your back and Bill Watson's. Troy Middleton could have been suffering from a remission."

"You've made your point Mr Calhoun," said Jim, shortly.

"Just thought you'd like to know about the photos. Never happened before, damn expensive camera… Japanese." He patted the aluminium case.

Jim's mobile bleeped.

"Lewin, who is it? Merry? What's the problem? Laura? How? When? We will be down there pronto."

"What is it?" Bobby was anxious.

"Laura's come off Bella, Merry's called for Lassiter."

"Is she badly hurt?" Tracy was slightly off key.

"Doesn't know until Barry gets there, she came off in the field, Bella fell on top of her."

"Oh no, that bloody horse," cursed Bobby, "Let's go love."

"If you don't mind Mr Calhoun?" said Betty, as Bobby and Tracy hurried out to Bobby's Jaguar.

"Eh? Oh yes, of course. No doubt I'll be seeing you all again."

Calhoun collected his case and moved out of the house to where his Beetle was parked, "I hope your granddaughter isn't too badly hurt."

They jumped into the Landrover and Jim drove as quickly as he could.

"I knew something like this would happen one day," Betty was agitated, "That horse is far too big for that girl to handle. Seventeen hands of stallion."

"Don't say that will you?" cautioned Jim.

"Of course not," snapped Betty, "I've said it often enough in the past though."

They passed the Hump en route to the Stable complex Jim had had built when the EEC had offered money to close down production of dairy and cereal production. The riding school had proven less of an administrative problem than dairy farming and infinitely more profitable.

Merry Springfield was an ex-Olympic show jumper with many other awards under her belt. She had been selected from a crowd of applicants to manage the riding school and stables. Not only was she an expert horsewoman, but a superlative manager into the bargain. She operated both school and stables on a strict routine, the staff she employed, she took on under a six month probationary period to study performance. Slapdash work and the employee was summarily dismissed with no redress.

****

24.

Sunday, June 18th 1995,
Stable Complex, Lewin's Farm,
Babingley Marsh, King's Lynn, Norfolk.

Merry's bungalow was located behind the stable complex. Unmarried, she lived in the four bedroom house alone, using part of the house as an office with three clerical staff to assist her administration.

The entire complex was alive with activity, Sunday being the busiest day for hiring and schooling. The client's car park was packed with expensive tin of late registrations. People clad in jodhpurs, riding hats and boots led horses or wheeled barrows of dung from the immaculate stables. The whole area was clean and tidy despite the heavy traffic in people and animals. Bobby's Jaguar was parked outside the building used as a first aid centre. Merry Springfield came out of the sandstone building as Jim drove up. Thirty-five, petite, dark narrow face, shoulder-length hair tied in a ponytail, wearing jodhpurs, boots and cowboy shirt, she looked concerned.

"How bad is she?" Betty jumped down from the Landrover.

"She came off heavily, Bella fell on top of her. Barry Lassiter should be here any sec," Merry had a Norfolk accent, "I don't know precisely how it happened, my main concern was treatment. She's on the bed in there."

A square finger indicated the First Aid Post. Bobby and Tracy were standing round the bed, Tracy looked in a bad way with worry. Laura was lying flat on the bed, no pillow, and white with pain.

"Wouldn't it have been better to get an ambulance?" asked Betty, mortified at seeing her granddaughter in obvious distress.

"No Mrs Lewin, that may have induced complications," Merry was firm, "I considered it better for Lassiter to examine her first before we attempted any more moves."

"She's right love," said Jim.

"That bloody horse, it's too big for her, always said so, a massive animal like that for a young woman," groused Bobby.

"I disagree Mr Lewin," said Merry, "Laura was a skilled horsewoman, she's been riding Bella for two years, they both got on well."

"How did this happen then?" Bobby was angry.

Merry motioned him outside, Tracy and Jim went with them.

"She was riding past the Hump Mr Lewin," stated Merry as soon as they were out of earshot, "Something spooked Bella. That animal is well-behaved and Laura has never had a problem with him before today."

"The Hump?" Jim echoed, "What was she doing riding in that area?"

"I don't know, I make it a rule that nobody rides in that part of the fields, that applied to Laura as well."

"Why?" Tracy was trembling with anxiety, "Why don't you permit riding past there? I'd have thought it was ideal riding country."

"It is."

"Then why?" Tracy was visibly upset needing to blame someone.

"Even the most stable of our animals gets nervous when in the neighbourhood of the Hump Mrs Lewin. With that in mind, I don't permit anybody to ride in that neighbourhood, it just makes good management sense. We don't need accidents, it's bad for our clients and bad for business."

"Why are they nervous Merry?" Betty was curious.

"Mrs Lewin I know all about the history of that place, Johnny Foster and your bungalow attempt. Animals are sensitive to atmospheres, especially horses, there's something about that place that upsets even the bomb-proof variety. I don't take risks, there's too much at stake. Laura knows that I don't allow riding in that section. What she was doing there I don't know. She's in too much pain to start an inquest at the moment, no doubt when she is feeling better we can find out."

"I still think it's that bloody horse," stated Bobby.

"Take it easy Bobby, Merry is no risk taker, if she thought Laura couldn't handle Bella..."said Jim.

"Bad news travels fast Mr Lewin," said Merry, "Accidents create problems, people avoid stables with a high risk factor. We have a reputation for strict control over who rides what and where, if I believed for one minute Laura was at risk I'd have stopped her from riding Bella, that you can rely on," Merry looked peeved at this question mark over her judgement.

"Here's Barry now," She pointed where Lassiter's grey BMW was approaching down the Slade Lane, a devil's tail of dust trailing it.

"Where's the patient?" Lassiter had his bag in hand. He nodded at the group collectively in greeting.

"In the Post," Merry led the way. The others followed tentatively.

Lassiter took one look at Laura and waved his hands, "Everybody outside please," he insisted.

"Oh God, I'll bet she's paralysed," moaned Tracy, shaking.

"Come and have some tea Mrs Lewin, helps settle nerves," said Merry.

She led the way into her bungalow, the vast picture window in the lounge overlooked the Hump and the escarpment that was the main Snettisham Road from Lynn. The fencing still surrounding the Hump was plainly visible over half a mile away. Merry made tea for all.

"He's taking a long time," said Tracy, "I know it's going to be bad news, I just know it."

"Do give over Trace, you're making everybody feel bad," admonished Bobby.

Lassiter entered, his face grim. "I want her moved to my clinic, I've sent for the private ambulance. We need to run more tests, a neurologist."

"Is she paralysed?" interrupted Tracy.

"She's suffered severe injuries to her back Mrs Lewin. Can anyone tell me just how it happened?" Lassiter took the tea cup from Merry.

"I don't know exactly Doctor," Merry was visibly shaken by Lassiter's news, "The first indications I had that anything was wrong was when her horse turned up at the stables without her. I went looking for her."

"How'd you know where to look?" Lassiter sipped his tea.

"The only place that Laura could have suffered an accident on that horse was in the region of the Hump."

"Hump? I seem too recall something about a place called that?"

Lassiter wrinkled his brow in recollection, "I've got it… ten or twelve years ago, Johnny Foster's men always falling ill on that building site?"

"That's the place," Merry refilled his cup, just as the sound of an ambulance sounded.

"Oh God, my poor little girl," wailed Tracy, "I know it's going to be bad news, can I go with her?"

"Can you make your own way Mrs Lewin? I don't want my paramedics disturbed attending to their patient."

"We'll tail you," said Bobby.

Lassiter hurried out as the smart ambulance arrived. Two white clad paramedics emerged carrying a stretcher. Jim and Betty watched as Laura was transported into the rear of the ambulance. The doors closed quickly before the vehicle set off again. The whole affair had lasted less than five minutes. Bobby followed in his Jaguar, Tracy still moaning to herself.

"I hope to Christ Bobby keeps her away from Laura," said Jim. "That bloody moaning will only upset the girl."

"She's worried," said Betty, "I would be if it was Bobby or Ellen."

"You wouldn't be making a song and dance routine over it like that woman," stated Jim, "She's like her Mother, remember what she was like at the Fete over Troy? Jumping around, whingeing and moaning when Fanny was attending him? Tracy's getting like her."

"Let's go home, you going to be OK Merry? It's not your fault. As you said you've made the Hump out of bounds to everybody. We'll just have to wait and see what Laura says and why she rode there despite your restrictions. She's a headstrong young girl, no blame is attached too you."

"I feel responsible," Merry looked worried.

"Merry, nobody's going to blame you, I'll see to that," said Betty, "You carry on as normal, we'll keep you posted on Laura's condition."

"She's bound to be concerned, it's the first serious accident she's ever had at the stables," said Jim as he and Betty drove to the farm.

"I'm beginning to have doubts about our choice of a home," said Betty as they passed the Hump en route.

"What's that supposed to mean? We've done alright, it was a bit of a struggle at first love I know that, but we're okay now."

"It was that place first," Betty pointed to the fenced off mound that was the Hump. The footings that Johnny Foster and his cowboys had started were still visible after ten years or so.

"Freda breaking down every time we drove her past that place, cost us a fortune bringing Wally Thompson out to tow her off and get her restarted. Now it's that damn church, the groanings and paranormal activity in the crypt. Then Kev gets injured and then Calhoun and now Laura, all because of these wretched ley-lines or whatever they are. Perhaps we should sell up, move to somewhere where we can enjoy life without all this agro?"

"You're hyper-sensitive love, we've had a long day."

"It isn't over yet, it's only seven o'clock."

Jim stopped the Landrover as the farmhouse hove into view.

"What's up now?" Betty felt irritable.

"Look at that," Jim pointed through the windshield.

A white Porsche was parked in the drive.

"Oh no, let's go over to Ellen's, I don't think I could cope with any more visitors. Those two churchmen were the last straw," Betty pleaded.

"She'll be with Kev at Longley Hill love," Jim pulled a pair of binoculars out from the glove compartment, "Oh,shit," he groaned.

"What is it?"

"It's that bloody Anglia woman... Summerfield... at least it looks like her in the driving seat. There's someone with her as well."

Betty took the glasses and trained them towards the two figures standing by the car, "Come to draw more blood," she groaned, "No good going to Bobby's either."

"I'll get rid of them love, then we'll go the Duke's Head for dinner, how's that grab you? You're too tired to make dinner."

Jim re-started the Landrover and drove the remainder of the way to the house, before parking beside the Porsche. It was Holly Summerfield, she was clad in an expensive trouser suit, an aura of perfume accompanied her as she swung her long legs from the sports car. The man with her was in a lounge suit of expensive material. He was tall, lean, with close cropped dark hair with flashes of grey at the temples. His nose drew attention to the creases either side of this organ. It was long and pointed, out of proportion to the remainder of his features.

"Sorry to bother you Mr and Mrs Lewin, I'm sure you've had a long day," said Summerfield, "I thought you should hear and see this." She held up a film canister, "Won't take long, but it is important to you both. This is my Director, Richard Cheeseman, from Anglia in Norwich," She performed introductions.

Betty thought Cheeseman's eyes were too close together to be attractive, apart from his outsize nose.

"We haven't a projector," said Jim, disliking Cheeseman at first sight, "and we have had a long day, as you said."

"I do appreciate the problems you've had to endure today Mr and Mrs Lewin, apart from the aggravation of a visit from a TV company with all the razzmatazz," said Cheeseman, "I promise we won't keep you longer than is essential. As Holly said you'll be very interested to see this."

Cheeseman's voice mitigated his unprepossessing appearance. It was a pleasant baritone, the only trouble with that feature Betty decided, was that the man realised it.

"I'll make some tea," said Betty reluctantly, moving into the house.

"You'd better come in," said Jim, with ill-grace.

"I'll bring the projector in," Summerfield opened the boot of the Porsche and removed something that looked like a squat suitcase and a mobile screen.

"Where can I set this up?" she enquired.

"The lounge Jim," said Betty, busy round the Aga. The remains of the buffet she'd prepared earlier were in evidence round the kitchen.

Summerfield had the screen and projector assembled by the time Betty entered with the refreshments.

"If we draw the curtains..." Summerfield was hesitant.

Jim obediently drew the curtains.

"We've transferred this to 8mm, make it easier to transport," explained Summerfield as the leader tape went down through the numbers.

The film flickered, it was dark, as if over-exposed.

"Not very interesting," said Jim sourly, seeing vague shadows on the screen.

The screen brightened to reveal the sequence with Betty and Summerfield outside the Hump.

"You'll recall that the cameras wouldn't work inside that area you called... The Hump...was it?" Summerfield stood beside the screen. Cheeseman operated the projector, "Turn it back to the start Dickie," she ordered.

Cheeseman reversed the film and re-started it again.

"The camera wasn't operating, yet these pictures were on the film," Summerfield used a pointed stick to indicate the shadowy images that looked like a static photo of statues in a field.

"We can't explain that, now if we go forward to the sequence in the crypt..."

Cheeseman fast-forwarded the film and stopped it at the scene in the crypt. Jim and Betty saw the camera under Ransome's direction pan round the crypt, focusing on the central catafalque and the brass plaque. The inscription was plain, 'Myfanwy Legge, June 21st, 1796'. As Ransome panned the camera round the crypt the camera focussed again on the central catafalque.

"What the devil's that?" exclaimed Jim.

"Freeze it Dickie," ordered Summerfield.

There was an image on the screen, a woman clad in a shawland long skirt, her hair done up in a bun, with clog-like shoes on her feet. Beside her was an enormous dog, a wolfhound.

"Funny Fanny!" Jim and Betty cried in unison.

"She was nowhere near the place," said Jim, staring disbelievingly.

"That was the ghost that Karl Ransome saw… and what I saw as well," said Summerfield, "before I passed out. Is that the woman who's supposed to be a witch?"

"It's her alright," declared Jim, "Once you've seen her you cannot very well forget her."

"How did she get there, into the crypt?" demanded Betty, all her irritation forgotten.

"That's the whole point of this exercise Betty," said Summerfield, "That if we are not going insane is the first genuine photograph of a ghost, and Karl wasn't off his nut."

"I thought he was when he ran out of the church screaming his head off," said Betty, "Seeing that puts a different complexion on it."

"It's the same woman who cured my hand?" said Summerfield.

"No mistaking her," said Jim.

Summerfield and Cheeseman exchanged glances. "Wind it back Dickie," said Summerfield.

Cheesemann re-wound it to the start, "Take a closer look now," invited Summerfield, pointing, "See those? look like statues don't they? Take a closer look at this one." Cheeseman enlarged the image.

"Fanny again," said Betty, awed.

The image was definitely that of Fanny Legge and beside her was the dog.

"Do you recognise these others?" Summerfield indicated the other still, statue-like figures beside Fanny.

Jim and Betty shook their heads, "Never seen them before," said Betty.

"Switch the lights on," ordered Summerfield.

Cheeseman did as he was bidden, Summerfield had some old photos in her hand, not quite Daguerreotype but almost, "Now take a look at this," She offered a photo to Jim and Betty.

It was plain that the group of people in the photo were identical in pose, dress and position as the images beside Fanny in the film.

"Turn it over," said Summerfield.

****

25.

Sunday, June 18th,
Lewin's Farm, Babingley Marsh,
King's Lynn, Norfolk.

There was an inscription in faded ink, Jim and Betty could just make out the words 'Babingley, June 17th 1918'. The figures were posed outside what appeared to be a cottage with thatched roof and a tiny porch with some creeper in flower over the roof.

"Where'd you get this?" Betty was vaguely disturbed.

"It was taken of a family who lived in a cottage in what was once called Babingley Village, I got it from the 'Advertiser', Jeff Patten, Calhoun's boss let me borrow it this afternoon after Calhoun informed him of what he thought was going on here. He opened up the office in King Street especially. There was an address on a yellowing piece of paper in the file, I found that interesting."

Betty had a premonition of what Summerfield was about to reveal, "The Hump," she said.

Summerfield nodded, "That cottage must have been located on the place called the Hump."

Jim frowned, "I don't recall seeing any evidence of another building on that site when Johnny Foster was busy with the bungalow. He didn't say anything about old foundations or anything else. Knowing him as I do, he would have moaned about it."

Summerfield shrugged, "It was the address on the paper, I just assumed it was correct."

"Weren't Elizabethan houses built without foundations?" Cheeseman threw the question into the arena, "Had oak blocks for what we'd call footings?"

Jim nodded, "But they last for centuries as in the case of some stately homes."

"What if something happened to the house? A fire or flood, would they not be destroyed, washed away?"

"Was there any record of something like that around that date?" Betty went over to the Aga to make tea as the kettle boiled.

Summerfield shook her head, "We looked through all the papers up to around 1930, couldn't find any mention of fire or flood."

"It couldn't just disappear," Jim's voice tailed away, "You suggesting that that cottage was also just an image?"

"How could it be, it's on that photo," Betty set out cups and saucers, "Perhaps Johnny Foster did find oak blocks and said nothing? All the markers were scattered whenever he tried to mark out the area?"

"Who's this Foster?" asked Cheeseman

"We got planning permission in 1983 to build a bungalow on that site, it was intended for our daughter and son-in-law, Foster was the contractor," Betty went on to describe the events that led to the abandonment of the site.

"There's enough material here for a full documentary Holly," whispered Cheeseman, "Would you be prepared to allow us access to produce such a film? We'd pay handsomely for the privelege."

He put fruity persuasion into his voice.

Betty poured the tea, "We haven't been paid for the effort earlier yet," she said.

"Five thousand pounds for exclusive rights? Is that correct?"

Cheeseman took a cheque from an inner pocket, "I've made it out to James Lewin?" He handed it to Jim.

"What do you think Jimbo?" Betty handed the cups around.

"We guarantee as little disruption as possible," said Cheeseman, "There will be some of course, but any damage would be fully compensated."

"We'll think about it," promised Jim, putting the cheque behind the clock on the mantelpiece.

"Where can we find this lady, Funny Fanny, or whatever her name is?" Summerfield sipped her tea.

"Difficult place to find and describe," said Betty, "Right on the marsh itself in North Wootton, Gatehouse Lane, off Ling Common Road. Why do you want to know?"

"It seems that since this lady is the principal figure in all this drama it would be a good idea to talk to her, perhaps she'd be willing to talk to us about these events? Cast some light on these things," said Summerfield.

"You can always try I suppose," Betty sounded dubious.

"You have some reservations about that, Mrs Lewin?" asked Cheeseman.

"I can't say I know the woman, nobody knows much about her, plenty of rumours of course and exaggerated claims about her lifestyle, but that's par for the course with an eccentric, especially one with her reputation of being a witch."

"This is the end of the twentieth century for God's Sake," burst out Cheeseman, "Surely all those myths have been exhausted?"

"You're dealing with a lot of dinky-die Norfolk people, not the outsiders who were moved up here during the fifties from London. There are a lot of legends, stories that go back centuries, 'Hereward the Wake' and others. Don't forget this part of Norfolk was cut off from the rest of England until the marsh was drained in the early part of this century. The people made their homes on the marsh, they lived and died here with very little contact with the mainstream. That kind of insularity is in-built. Witches, will-o-the-wisps, Jack-0-Lantern, ghosts, demons, phantoms, they all had a place in folk-lore," said Betty, "The genuine Norfolk people still talk about these things as if they are real."

Cheeseman raised his shoulders despairingly, "Hard to believe with TV and education, the wealth of information available."

"Could we find this lady's house?" asked Summerfield.

"I doubt it, not without guidance," said Betty.

"Would you be willing to take us?"

"Not tonight if you don't mind, we've had a long day," said Betty, "would either of you like any more tea?"

"We can take a hint," said Summerfield, refusing, "Come on Dickie we've harassed these good people enough." She began dismantling the mobile screen and rewinding the film.

"Think about my offer won't you?" was Cheeseman's farewell words as he and Summerfield left and headed towards the white Porsche, "I hope you'll agree, make a lot of money out of Anglia," he grinned. He waved as Summerfield suggested that Betty accompany her to Fanny's cottage the following morning.

Betty nodded, hoping the presenter would forget all about it when the time came.

"What do you think about all that?" asked Betty seeing the Porsche vanish in a dust cloud towards the main road.

"It's all crazy, but it fits in with everything that's happened today and other days." Jim poured the tea into a mug and sat down with a sigh, "I'm too tired to think much about it love."

"I'll ring Lassiter, find out how Laura is, that's much more important," Betty announced as she picked up the mobile.

"That you Barry?... how's the patient?... are you sure?... yes, I know all about tests... when will you know?... can't it be sooner than that?... I'm worried, that's why, she's our only grand-daughter... can't you do the tests there? ... yes of course we'll pay... better than traipsing all the way to Norwich."

Betty put down the phone, a thoughtful look on her face.

"What's up love?" Jim could read the signs after thirty years of marriage.

Tears welled into Betty's eyes, "He says he believes Laura's spine is damaged. She might not walk again, they're going to get a neurologist in to see her, to confirm his diagnosis," Betty began to sob, "That poor girl, so young, just starting life and now she's going to be crippled forever."

Jim took her into his arms, murmuring soft, nonsensical words. "Lassiter is a born pessimist love, I think we ought to wait until the specialist gives his verdict before we start talking about sackcloth and ashes. Come on now, Bobby and Tracy are going to need support, not despair."

Betty disengaged herself, she wiped her eyes, "Of course, I'm being a silly bitch, sorry Jimbo. You're right of course, It'll fall on Bobby and Tracy's shoulders more than ours. It's such a depressing prospect though."

"Like I said love, Barry is a misery guts, one case of flu and he screams epidemic of plague proportions."

Betty stared at him, horrified, "Plague?" she whispered, her face pale.

Jim caught on, "It was not plague love, the pathologist said so, didn't know the cause," He didn't feel confident.

"She was near the Hump and that caused Bella to fall Jimbo. Perhaps we should tell Lassiter? He might change his tune?"

"Create a panic love?" Jim shook his head, "Let the neurologist see her, let him make his diagnosis. Barry would go into a flap if we suggested something like that."

"We ought to go over there, support Bobby and Tracy, they'll be devastated, especially Tracy and if Pamela hears about it, God, that would be the pits, wailing and moaning, remember how she was at the fete when

Troy had that turn? If it hadn't been for Fanny curing him she'd have been in a funny farm, straight jacket, the works."Betty stopped.

They both exchanged looks.

"Impossible love," said Jim, uncertainty in his voice.

"If she cured Wally, Bill Watson and your back, especially Wally, he would have been gone this coming week if she hadn't treated him. You saw her do it, didn't you?"

"Yeah I know, I still can't believe what I saw."

"Wally walked out of Longley Hill like he'd never been ill Jimbo, it's worth a try, isn't it?"

He nodded, "Of course, I couldn't stand seeing that poor girl in a wheelchair for the rest of her natural."

"Let's go then," Betty pulled on her coat.

"It's nearly nine o'clock love, hadn't we better wait until morning? It'll be dark soon."

"Let's go now, I have a feeling about this, there's a penalty for delay, I know it."

Jim shrugged, "It's hard enough to find that bloody place in daylight," he began, "OK, OK, Let's go, better take the Landrover, the end of Gatehouse isn't what you'd call smooth."

They set off, turned down by Castle Rising into the old trunk road that formerly carried all traffic to Hunstanton, now superseded by the by-pass. They continued past the numerous small estates that cluttered what had once been North Wootton village, past Frederick Close into Gatehouse Lane. The lane terminated in a dirt track full of potholes. The marsh stretched out before them, flat as far as the eye could see, intersected by the old dykes and the disused pumping station. Flocks of sea birds wheeled over the flat land in the summer evening sunshine.

Fanny Legge's cottage was concealed behind thick hedgerows topping ten feet in height. There was no gate and the entrance was a matter of potluck rather than judgement. Jim made several false turns to find himself facing a rugged wall of further hedges before finally finding Fanny's cottage. A donkey was tethered in what could be loosely described as a front garden. He'd barely switched off the engine when the wolfhound bounded from behind the house and began barking. It's eye looked yellowish in the gathering gloom, teeth bared and jaws slavering. A flock of geese arrived, adding their cries to the cacophony. The donkey began hee-hawing throatily. Interspersed between the rest of the menagerie were hordes of cats, all adding their meowing to the curtain of noise.

"We daren't get out with that animal there," said Jim nodding towards the wolfhound.

"Try the horn," suggested Betty.

Jim gave three blasts that sent birds rising from the hedgerows in flocks, cawing, chirruping and croaking, adding to the cacophony of the dog's baying, and the noises from the geese and cats.

Fanny suddenly appeared at the side of the Landrover. Neither Betty of Jim had seen her approach.

She raised her hand, the dog ceased its barking, the birds fell silent and began settling back into the hedges once more. The donkey stopped its braying and the geese became silent. "You've come about your granddaughter I assume," Fanny greeted them, clad in her customary garb of shawl, blouse, long skirt and clogs.

It was gloomy now, the orange flame of sunset casting shadows over the garden. Jim wasn't sure at first, but when it scuttled up to Fanny's shoulder and settled down there, he knew he hadn't imagined it, an enormous hairy spider.

'This is bloody crazy', he told himself, 'and if she isn't a witch, a real,live witch, then I'm Jesus Christ Superstar'. He felt Betty recoil when she saw the arachnid, squatting on Fanny's shoulder, its eight little eyes gleamed like bright diamonds. It was like something out of a Hollywood horror movie, Jim decided. 'If Jack Nicholson appears, I won't be at all surprised', he thought.

****

26.

Sunday, June 18th.
Fanny Legge's Cottage,
Gatehouse Lane, North Wootton,
King's Lynn, Norfolk.

"Yes we have," he heard Betty acknowledge the question, "Can you do anything for her?"

"I'll see what I can do, no promises though."

Jim thought her accent was Welsh, the lilting tones and rising cadences sounded like the Celtish language.

"Would you mind Mis Legge?" said Betty nervously as Fanny made to get into the rear of the Landrover. She pointed to where the massive arachnid nestled into Fanny's long hair, "I have a real horror of spiders."

Fanny smiled, showing her perfect teeth, "I'd forgotten" she said, "Come on Tweety, down you go, you can come back soon."

She held her hand onto her shoulder as the massive creature settled on the back of her hand. She bent down, allowing the creature to run off. It vanished into the undergrowth. Betty shuddered, involuntarily.

"Is it alright if Darren accompanies me?" Fanny pointed to where the massive dog lay amongst a crowd of cats near the front door.

"Of course," Betty nodded nervously, still staring into the undergrowth where Tweety had exited, half expecting to see the creature emerge and jump onto her back again.

Jim could have sworn he heard something almost supersonic as Fanny pointed to the dog. The animal arose, shook its shaggy coat and bounded over to the Landrover, leaping into the rear behind the passenger seats and immediately settling down on the floor. Jim reversed cautiously into the lane and set off towards the main road, the Landrover lurching and swaying over the potholed track. Illogically, Jim noticed that Fanny seemed to have no difficulty in maintaining her balance. Betty was being thrown from one side to the other, holding onto the straps and yet the woman remained upright, whatever the angle the vehicle imposed on its passengers.

"Will Doctor Lassiter welcome my appearance Mr Lewin?" asked

Fanny, as they entered the metalled section of Gatehouse Lane.

That thought had occurred to Jim some time before.

"I have no wish to upset the good doctor."

"We'll cross that bridge when we come to it," Betty interposed. "He'll want the good of his patient primarily."

Jim wasn't too sure about that statement. Barry Lassiter was one of a dying breed of physician, believing that defecating every day reduced the chances of illness. Many patients had received laxatives as treatment for more problematical illnesses. Jim couldn't envisage Lassiter being ecstatic with joy at seeing Fanny Legge in his up-market establishment. He had the feeling that Fanny Legge was also aware of Lassiter's antipathy towards alternative medicine in the person of Fanny Legge, or any other practitioner of the art.

"Where did your family come from Miss Legge?" asked Betty, as Jim turned into Ling Common Road.

He nearly ran the Landrover into the rear of a parked vehicle in anxiety to hear Fanny's response. Swerving at the last moment to avoid collision, he missed Fanny's reply.

"No connection with Wales?" he heard Betty ask.

"Why do you ask these questions Mrs Lewin?" There was no reproach in Fanny's voice.

"I have to admit curiosity Miss Legge," said Betty.

"Your daughter has been to the archive department of the local newspaper and to the library in an attempt to find out more about me."

That wasn't a question either, Jim knew.

"Do you find these questions intrusive?" asked Betty.

"I would suggest that your curiosity concerns the rumours that circulate Mrs Lewin, concerning my eccentricity and lifestyle."

"Correct, Miss Legge," said Betty, "You are surrounded by an aura of mystery. We would like to distance ourselves from that kind of scenario."

"Knowing my background will assist you dispel these fears?"

She's better than any bloody politician, thought Jim, she's ducking these questions by asking another.

"I'm sorry I asked if it distresses you," Betty sounded uncomfortable.

"Knock it off love, was Jim's unspoken advice, the woman obviously has no intention of imparting this information."

Jim saw Fanny smile via the rearview, a kind of Mona Lisa smile as if she knows it all, being patronising towards ordinary mortals.

"How old is your granddaughter?" asked Fanny, as Jim entered Castle Rising Road, turning past the Castle onto the by-pass.

"Twelve" Betty replied, sounding puzzled.

"Mrs Lewin must have been pregnant when she and your son married?" said Fanny.

Jim had to grin, that was a sore point with his wife. Tracy had been five months pregnant when she and Bobby had walked up the aisle of St Margaret's Church. It had been an even sorer point with Pamela Middleton. The fuss that lady had kicked up was like the prelude to World War Three, accusing Bobby of deliberately engineering the event. Dear Pamela had been even more infuriated when Tracy had refused abortion.

"Come on love, let's see how you handle that hot potato," Jim was grinning to himself.

"Something amusing you Jimbo?" Betty was tart.

"I'm concerned about our granddaughter love, Barry isn't going to be too delighted with us."

"Hostility is bad for the curing process," said Fanny, "I have to tell you this."

"You mean if Doctor Lassiter kicks up a fuss you won't be able to do anything?" Betty sounded alarmed.

"It will be difficult Mrs Lewin."

'Now that is going to be a thorny problem', Jim decided. 'Barry is sure going to kick up hell, Fanny cries off, Barry can't do anything about Laura by orthodox medicine, we're in shit street. We remove Laura from Lassiter's Clinic and Fanny cannot do anything. The scenario was becoming complicated and if Pamela is present, oh Jesus, this wasn't a bright idea at all', he thought.

"I'm sure Doctor Lassiter would not object," Betty didn't sound convinced.

"He sees to me to be some eccentric with a penchant for witchcraft and sorcery Mrs Lewin. He's not alone, orthodox medicine views the healing process as one that can only be accomplished by drugs or the knife. He is likely to be dismissive, even refuse to treat your granddaughter if you permit me to see her."

'She's got that right as well', Jim decided. The more he experienced this woman's uncanny prescience, the more amazing she became.

As if reading his thoughts, Fanny voiced them, "I don't think, Mrs Middleton will be too delighted either, she wasn't very receptive to my treating her husband at the Fete at your farm."

"I'll deal with her," promised Betty, rashly.

"I doubt whether Mrs Middleton will have heard about Laura's condition as yet."

'Ha ha', Jim thought, 'if Bobby had his way his Mother-in-law would have nothing to do with anything concerning his wife and daughter. Pamela Middleton kicking up hell in public was not conducive to anything, save a violent reaction on Bobby's part. The lady had a prescience to equal Fanny Legge's own in the business of bad news'.

"She has heard Mrs Lewin," said Fanny quietly, as Jim turned the Landrover into Gayton Road.

As he continued left again into the long drive leading to the Lassiter Clinic, Bawsey Ruin became visible over the trees. There were Mercedes, Rolls Royce's and BMW's in the car park. With dismay Jim recognised the Simpson's cream coloured Rolls parked in a space marked for consultants only.

'She's all we need' he thought grimly, 'This is going to degenerate into farce with that lot around'. His alarm increased when he saw Troy Middleton's Jaguar parked a short distance away from the Simpson's limousine. Betty had seen it also.

"What do we do about your dog Miss Legge?" asked Jim, "He won't be allowed into the clinic."

"Darren will be fine where he is, Mr Lewin."

Jim allowed Betty and Fanny to exit from the Landrover before attempting to find a vacant space amongst all the expensive tin occupying all the nearest places to the main entrance. By the time he found a slot, the huge dog had moved forward looking staright at Jim, glowering at him as he departed, a rumbling growl coming from its throat. The dog's yellow eyes seemed to glow.

He walked back to the Reception, Lassiter, Lilly Simpson, her husband Demetrius, Pamela, Troy Middleton and Betty were already in the middle of a fire-fight over Fanny Legge's presence. It was as if his predictions had materialised into factual life. Lassiter was creating over Fanny's presence in the 'hallowed halls of medicine', let alone the proposal that she be allowed to practice her arts on Laura. Betty was also in full flood, making the point that it was up to Bobby and Tracy to decide whether or not they would permit Fanny to see Laura. Lilly Simpson was enjoying every salacious minute. Her husband, a stocky, barrel-chested man who had arrived in the UK as a DP from war-time Europe and had his Polish name changed by Deed Poll, before making a fortune out of lingerie design, was silently observing the antics of these so-called Anglo-Saxons with their reputation for bulldog characteristics with wry amusement.

"No way do I propose allowing this woman to treat any patient of mine inside my Clinic, Mrs Lewin. I have a solid reputation to maintain for sane medical practices. If any of my wealthy clients were to hear that I'd permitted some crazy woman to operate withcraft here, they'd all leave." Lassiter's face was red with indignation.

"Don't you think the reputation of your clinic would be enhanced if Miss Legge affected a cure?" Betty demanded.

"I don't believe for a moment that this lady has what some folk consider to be extraordinary powers, with the greatest respect and I certainly don't want my clinic to be used as a proving ground for alternative medicine," Lassiter was almost shouting.

"What is more, if you insist that this woman even sees your granddaughter, I wash my hands of any responsibility for her welfare. That is my last word on the subject."

"I agree with Doctor Lassiter," said Pamela Middleton, "Perfectly insane allowing this woman to practice withcraft inside a respectable medical establishment."

At this point Bobby and Tracy arrived.

"What's going on?" Bobby demanded, "What's all the noise about?"

"I brought Miss Legge along to have a look at Laura, Bobby," said Betty, "There's no harm in letting her try to cure Laura is there?"

"As much as I am inclined to agree with you Mumsy, I believe it is a trifle insensitive of you to bring her to Barry's Clinic," said Bobby, "Barry doesn't have much faith in alternative medicine, we must respect his views."

"He's just plain obstinate," declared Betty, "He doesn't want to risk being proven wrong. I'd have thought Laura's health was the prime reason for any medicine, whatever form it takes."

"Mumsy, this is not the place to argue the toss about a family matter. Don't you think it would be better to allow Barry to carry out his tests before we attempt anything exotic?"

"She cured Bill Watson, your Father and Wally Thompson and Summerfield's hand, makes sense to me if she can perform that kind of miracle to allow her to see Laura? You don't want her in a wheelchair for the remainder of her natural do you?" Betty was not to be argued with.

"If that woman sees your granddaughter, I will have to ask you to take her elsewhere for treatment. I will not permit my clinic's reputation to be sullied by this ridiculous medical concept. I am in the business of orthodox treatments, not in forms of witch doctoring," bellowed Lassiter.

"You're stuck into a rut Barry," Betty was beginning to lose her cool, Jim decided, "Just because it defies your standard medical theories and is successful, you deny its effectiveness."

"I'm not prepared to discuss the matter any further Madame," roared Lassiter, "Now do you want your daughter treated by an eminent neurological consultant Mr Lewin, or do you subscribe to the bizarre beliefs of your Mother?"

Bobby scowled, the scenario offended his sense of propriety as a lawyer, protocol should be observed even if an alternative view should be permitted.

"It's nothing but ridiculous superstition Robert," said Pamela Middleton, "Let Doctor Lassiter do his job, don't you agree, Tracy?"

"Miss Legge cured Daddy at the Fete a fortnight ago Mother." Tracy was quietly spoken, "I don't think we should neglect any possibilities. She also cured Jim's back, Daddy hasn't been in better health for as long as I can recall."

"Well Lewin?" Lassiter was furious, "Do you want your daughter treated by my consultant or don't you? If this woman..." He stopped and looked round, "Where is she?"

"She was here a minute ago," said Lilly Simpson, who'd been revelling in the spectacle of a prominent local medical practitioner arguing over the demerits of alternative medicine.

"She was standing over there," She pointed to where Jim was sure that Fanny Legge had been but a few moments before.

"She must have left," Betty was puzzled, "She wasn't too happy about coming here in the first place."

"At least the woman has some sense of protocol and decorum," snorted Lassiter, "Did anyone see her leave?"

****

27.

Sunday, 18th June 1995.
Lassiter's Clinic, Gayton Road,
King's Lynn, Norfolk

A nurse, clad in spotless uniform, came rushing into Reception, looking very distraught.

"Doctor Lassiter," She repeated his name agitatedly.

"What is it, sister?" Lassiter turned his irritation on his nurse, "Can't you see I'm engaged just now?"

"There's a huge dog in front of Miss Lewin's ward, it won't allow me or anyone else inside. It's showing its fangs if any one approaches."

"A dog?" echoed Lassiter, disbelievingly, "How did a dog get in here?"

Jim didn't offer any uncanny sixth sense to identify the dog, but he knew it was Darren, Fanny Legge's animal. "Big greyish animal with yellow eyes?" he interupted.

The Sister nodded vigorously, "Huge..about this high," She levelled a hand on her waist.

"Does it belong to you Jim?" Lassiter turned furiously on Jim.

"Hey, take it easy Barry, I'm not one of your employees you know."

"Sorry Jim, didn't mean to take it out on you," Lassiter didn't look sorry, "You know who it belongs to?"

"I've a fair idea, let's go have a look."

"Which ward is Miss Lewin in, Sister?"

"The private room off Bluebell Wing." The Sister looked fearful.

"Will you show me?"

Lassiter swung round, "Excuse me ladies and gents, we'll resume our discussion when I've sorted this animal out. Lead on Sister."

"I think Betty and I had better come with you Barry, we might be able to help."

The whole cavalcade followed the nurse down a long corridor and across several intersections.

"Round the next corner, be careful, that animal is vicious," the Sister sounded almost hysterical.

Lassiter held up his hand for everyone to stop whilst he re-considered going any further. They all heard him gasp, then go pale and stagger, clutching his heart

"You alright Doctor Lassiter?" The Sister caught his arm.

"Round there," croaked Lassiter, scarcely able to speak. There were beads of perspiration on his forehead.

Jim took a look cautiously and could hardly believe what he saw.

"It's... it's... " he stuttered, unable to articulate.

"Oh God, not you as well," snapped Betty, pulling Jim back.

"My God," was all Betty had time for as Laura appeared.

"Hello everyone," Laura was clad in a hospital night dress, "I could not find my clothes, sorry about this."

Bobby and Tracy ran forward hugging and kissing their daughter, "You should be in bed young lady," Bobby was unable to credit his eyesight.

"What on earth for? I'm fine, nothing wrong with me folks," Laura smiled, "Why all the reception comittee? You expecting royalty or something?" She greeted all in turn, "What's the matter Doctor Lassiter? You look ill, is he alright Sister?"

The Sister was gaping incredulously at her patient, her mouth opening and closing no sound emerging.

"What's the matter with you all? You look as if you're seeing a ghost."

"How were you able to get out of bed? Who helped you darling?" Tracy was crying uncontrollably.

"What on earth is the matter with everyone? All this emotion?" Laura looked puzzled, "Why should anyone want to help me out of bed? What am I doing here anyway? This is a hospital isn't it?"

"Don't you remember anything poppet?" asked Bobby.

"What am I supposed to remember? I think you should have some one look at Doctor Lassiter Nurse, he looks ill."

Lassiter shook himself free of the Sister's grasp, "Back to bed at once young woman," He was stern.

"What's he on about?" Laura looked genuinely puzzled, "Why on earth should I go to bed? What am I doing here anyway?"

"Don't you remember falling off Bella, at the Hump?" asked Bobby.

"All I remember is leading him out, tacking him up for my ride. What am I doing here? I've never fallen off Bella, he's bombproof, rock steady, nothing disturbs him. Is he alright?"

"Are you sure you're OK, poppet?" Bobby was almost in tears with emotion as well as Tracy.

"Can someone explain what all this hoo-hah is about? What are you crying for Mumsy?"

"Oh darling, I'll explain later, you feel alright?"

"I'm beginning to get a little peeved with all these silly questions, what're you doing here Mrs Simpson? And you Grandma, Grandad? I'm just fine, I want to go home, I don't like hospitals, never did."

"This is impossible," stammered Lassiter, "It's a ... " He stopped.

"Miracle, Barry?" prompted Betty mischievously.

"She must have been fooling about, deceiving us," Lassiter was still gaping, "She couldn't walk with those injuries."

"Well, you diagnosed her Barry," said Betty, "And where's this dog that was supposed to be outside the ward? I don't see any dog?"

"You must have got it wrong sunshine," said Jim, patting Lassiter on the shoulder.

"Of course I didn't get it wrong man, her spine showed signs of severe bone damage. She was paralysed from the waist down no motor reflexes whatsoever, inert indicative of neurological failure of the lower limbs."

"Well doesn't look like that now does it?" Betty was smiling.

"I wish someone would tell me what all this crap is about? Paralysis, bone damage, what's he on about?" Laura was angry.

"I think we'd better get you home poppet, before you cause anyone else a heart attack," said Bobby.

"You can't discharge her just like that Lewin. I refuse to accept any responsibility if she leaves this building, is that clear?"

"Abundantly clear Barry, old man," Bobby was calmer now, "Tracy and I hereby absolve you from any accusation of medical neglect or malpractice. You want it in writing, or is my word in front of witnesses enough?"

"That young woman should be in intensive care, not walking around like this, the danger to her will be permanent."

"I want too go home Daddy, this place is like a funny farm," stated Laura, heading off towards the Reception.

"Bye Mrs Simpson, Mr Simpson, see you again sometime," She paused, "Well Mumsy are you coming or not?"

Jim walked down to the door to what had evidently been Laura's ward and peered inside. The drip bottle was suspended on a stand, the plastic tube still dangling, the bedclothes over the cage flung back, and no sign of anything unusual. By the time he walked out, the corridor was empty. The Simpson's were in reception with Barry Lassiter.

"I hope your son knows what he's doing Jimbo," warned Lassiter, "That young woman's spine is irreparably damaged."

"Like Bobby said Barry, you're absolved from responsibility for her welfare. Gone out to the car have they?"

The Simpson's accompanied Jim out into the dark night.

"I wouldn't have believed it Mr Lewin," said Lilly, "If I hadn't seen it with my own two eyes. It is a miracle, can't be anything else."

"Have you seen Miss Legge, or her dog?" Jim tried to pierce the gloom of the car park.

"You mean Funny Fanny?" Demetrius was poker-faced, "I haven't seen anything of her since she disappeared in Reception. I thought that nurse was a bit crazy, talking about a dog outside the ward. I reckon she's in need of help."

"Did Funny Fanny have anything to do with Laura Jimbo?" Lilly was anxiously peering round the darkened car park as if expecting an apparition to appear.

"That was the intention, bringing her with us, as you know Lilly. Your guess is as good as mine. I'll be getting along if you don't mind, I still can't believe it," Jim left the Simpson's staring after him.

"No sign of Fanny?" asked Jim on reaching the Landrover.

"I've looked round, can't see any sign of her," said Betty, "It beats me how that dog got out of the vehicle, if that nurse wasn't hallucinating."

"Well neither of them are here now, I reckon we ought to go home, it's been a long and eventful day, I'm knackered. Have Bobby and the others gone?"

"Hop in, I'll drive," said Betty, "We'll have to assume Miss Legge has made her own way back."

"Funny how she just vanished into thin air in Reception," said Jim, lowering the seat back, "I'm bushed, wake me up when we get home."

"It just had to be her doing Laura's recovery," said Betty as she drove out of the car park into the long lane. Jim could see the silhouette of Bawsey Ruin on the hillside, against a background of rising moon.

"One minute Laura's sick, then she walks out of that ward cured."

Jim was vaguely aware of Betty babbling on about Funny Fanny miracles, Laura, Bella, Bobby and Lilly Simpson, but was too tired to respond.

****

28.

Monday, June 19th 1995.
Lewin's Farm, Babingley Marsh,
King's Lynn, Norfolk.

Jim awoke, vaguely aware that something had disturbed him. He lay there conscious of Betty's light breathing, hearing all the normal sounds of a summer morning beyond the window, the bird song, crow's cawing, the soft murmur of traffic along the main road a mile away. What had aroused him? He lay back, the events of the previous day crowding in on his consciousness like a series of cinematic flashbacks. Calhoun, the two priests, Summerfield, Lilly Simpson, Merry and Laura, the horse, Lassiter, the Clinic and Laura's astonishing recovery, Funny Fanny's cottage, the image of the enormous spider on Fanny Legge's shoulder. He wasn't that bothered by arachnids, but the sheer size of that creature was disturbing. Where had Fanny vanished to inside Lassiter's Reception area? Had she anything to do with Laura's recovery? He didn't remember much about events after leaving the Clinic. He remembered undressing for bed, then waking up. What had aroused him? Something unusual. Then he heard it, the front doorbell, a long insistent ring.

Betty came awake then sat up, "Laura," she said, panicky, "She's had a relapse."

"I'll see who it is," Jim arose, pulled on a dressing gown and walked over to the window, peering out to see who was outside. He noticed the white Porsche first, parked next to the Landrover, followed by the top of Summerfield's head, as she stood at the front door.

"Who is it Bobby?" asked Betty, worried.

"Your friend from Anglia," said Jim over his shoulder, "Be down in a sec!" he called.

"Oh God, I don't know whether I can handle her this morning Jimbo."

"She'll only keep coming back love," said Jim, sliding his feet into slippers, "I'll go let her in, get it over with."

"What time is it?"

"God, it's nine am," cried Jim.

"I'll be down in a few minutes, make her some tea or something," Betty said, as she went into the en suite.

"Looks like I've caught you unprepared," greeted Summerfield, "If it's inconvenient, I'll come back later."

"Won't be any different," Jim assured her, gesturing for her to enter, her perfume assailed his nostrils. The silk dress she wore flattered her slender figure, she had bare legs and was bra-less.

"Tea?" Jim filled the kettle lifted the lid of the Aga.

"That would be nice, it's hot already."

Summerfield sat in a chair at the kitchen table and crossed her long legs, "I've always wanted to own somewhere like this," Her eyes tracked round the large kitchen, "I was born in a city surrounded by pollution of all kinds. This is great, how long have you lived here?"

"Twenty-odd years. Wasn't always as fine as this though, virtually derelict when we bought it, the farm was terribly run down, we had ideas about becoming rich, creating a prize herd of Jerseys, making it organic."

"What changed?"

"The cereal mountain, milk mountain, beef mountain, the EEC wanted us out of production, gave us generous grants," Jim emptied the tea-pot, rinsed it and spooned tea into it.

"That's how you went into golf and riding stables?"

"Helps with the pocket money I suppose, "Jim fetched crockery from the dish washer and set it out.

"Id' heard about your golf course long before I knew about your farm," said Summerfield, "Well known amongst the media fraternity."

She asked more questions about their lifestyle until Betty appeared. Summerfield stood up and apologised for arriving early.

"It's alright, we had an eventful day yesterday Miss Summerfield. Our granddaughter had a riding accident and we had to take her to hospital just before you arrived last evening. We went to see her at Lassiter's Clinic."

"Sorry to hear that, you should have said before we got started on that photo session with Dickie. You must have been worried, how is she?"

"She was in a bad way, injured spine and her leg was crushed when the horse fell on top of her."

"Was... " Summerfield picked up the vibes swiftly.

"Another miracle cure," interrupted Betty, "I've just phoned her Mother, she says Laura is down at the stables, eager for another ride, absolutely fine."

"Funny Fanny?" Summerfield was alert now.

"We aren't too sure really" said Betty, "We're having breakfast, you want to join us?"

"Tell me about this Fanny Legge and your granddaughter and yes, I'd appreciate breakfast."

Over breakfast Betty related the happenings of the previous night at Lassiter's Clinic, Fanny's arrival and subsequent disappearance, followed by Laura's arrival, apparently cured.

"You say she knows nothing about Fanny? Whether she had a hand in her cure or not?"

"She was under sedation, can't remember a thing about the fall or the events following. We didn't have time to talk to her last night, we were so relieved and tired."

"So this Lassiter person, he could have misdiagnosed Laura's condition?" Summerfield had a hearty appetite.

"She looked dreadful when we saw her at the first aid post down at our stable block," Betty poured more tea, "I suppose he could have got it wrong. He's got a solid reputation for his work in Lynn, so I just don't know."

"So after Fanny disappeared, you didn't see her again?"

"Or the dog, we were going to take her back to North Wootton, she didn't turn up so we came home."

"So Laura has no idea whether it was Fanny or not?"

"As I said we haven't talked to her since so I can't comment. Toast? Marmalade?"

"Thank you, that was delicious, "Summerfield sounded genuine. "We can ask her when we see her if she was responsible for your granddaughter's cure."

"You can try," said Betty.

"You sound dubious?"

"She's a strange person. When you see her place you'll have more than an idea why I'm uncertain about her telling you anything."

"Our researchers have been busy trying to find out her background, family, parents, anything."

"They've drawn a blank?" said Jim.

Summerfield nodded, "It's just as if she just appeared out of nowhere.

That date on the brass plaque down in the crypt, June 21st 1796, people interned in crypts were usually well-to-do, rich families, able to pay for the privilege. Our girls have come up against a brick wall, there's nothing about her family, when, where she was born, how long she lived, why she was interned in that crypt, where she lived, nothing, just as if she dropped from the sky, it's the weirdest thing we've ever come across. I spoke to Dickie this morning before I left Norwich., he's dead keen on that documentary, wants to get started .a.s.a.p. Have you had time to discuss it? I don't suppose you have with everything going on, we'd make it well worth your while."

Betty looked at Jim across the table. He shrugged, "How much would it be worth?"

"We could be talking about thousands, depends on Dickie's evaluation of the importance of the programme, anything occult draws ratings and despite what you feel, it has occult connotations. Carl Ransome has told everybody about the burn on my hand, the one I got touching that plaque down in the crypt and the way Fanny cured it by simply holding it. He thinks it's a miracle and then that Wally Thompson cured of lung cancer. Could you handle it? Lot of disruption, I must warn you. The uninitiated think it's just a case of a few people with cameras and that's it. We have to plan everything before we even start, angles, shots, rails, cable, lighting and lots of people milling around. You earn your money, believe me. I don't want too put you off but you'd be well pissed-off with me if I led you up the garden path."

"What do you think Jimbo?"

"You'll be coming back here won't you?" asked Jim.

Summerfield nodded.

"Could you drop Betty Off? That will give us time to have a think about it. I have to go see Paul, he might need help. I didn't collect the banking from Merry yesterday, I'll do that whilst you're gone, we can talk about films when you get back"

Summerfield nodded, "Sounds OK to me."

"You know this might be a waste of time?" Betty began clearing the debris from the table.

"Why?"

"I have this feeling that Fanny is camera shy and she seems to have this ability to read minds. If she knows we're coming she might take off somewhere."

Summerfield smiled, "Point taken, I'm willing to risk it."

Summerfield drove the Porsche with skill, the growling power under the bonnet used with restraint. At the entrance to Gatehouse Lane, after the Porsche had rocked and bumped over potholes, Summerfield stopped the car and parked up, "I won't have any suspension left if we go further. Can we walk?"

"Not in those you won't" Betty nodded at Summerfield's high heels.

The reporter grinned, "I came prepared." Reaching over the seat, she brought out a pair of brogues. She kicked her shoes off and pulled on the other footwear. She had a portable tape recorder in her shoulder bag.

Betty had difficulty in locating Fanny's cottage despite other visits. There was always something of a puzzle about its location, as if it moved of a mysterious volition. The two women approached the gate. Darren, the wolfhound began his deep diapason barking, Geese flocked from nowhere to add to the cacophony. A donkey began braying, cats swarmed from every part of the garden. The dog would not permit them entry, its teeth bared, it kept up a threatening menace.

"God, I'm beginning to see what you mean," said Summerfield in an awed voice over the noise of dog, geese and donkey.

Fanny suddenly appeared beside the gate. Neither woman had an inkling of her approach or saw any evidence of her presence before she arrived. Fanny raised her hand, as she had done before, again the noise ceased abruptly. Dog, geese and donkey all became silent. The wolfhound, its yellowish eyes wary, regarded them from a position near the front door.

"Miss Summerfield isn't it? I know Mrs Lewin."

Betty was sure there was a Welsh twang to her voice this time.

Summerfield was impressed by this evidence of knowledge, "You've seen me on the Box, Mrs Legge?"

"Miss, please, and no, I have not seen you before. You are welcome to my home."

It was at this point that a massive arachnid emerged from Fanny's long hair, it ran down her arm and went onto the gate. Its bank of eyes gleamed in the brilliant sunlight, seeming to be studying Summerfield. Betty recoiled in horror, she almost turned and ran. From a safe distance she saw Summerfield hold out her hand whilst the huge spider ran onto her sleeve. Almost sick with loathing, Betty saw the reporter lift her arm, allowing the spider to run onto her shoulder.

"Tweety approves of you Miss Summerfield, you aren't frightened of him?"

Summerfield shook her head, "They don't worry me Miss Legge."

Betty felt faint with shock and almost ran.

"Off you go Tweety, you're frightening Mrs Lewin," said Fanny.

The spider appeared to comprehend as it ran down Summerfield's arm onto the gate and vanished into the undergrowth. "It's alright, Mrs Lewin, you can approach now."

With trepidation Betty returned to the gate, staring down at the point in the undergrowth where Tweety had gone to ground.

"How can I help you ladies?"

Fanny was clad in what seemed to be her only garb; long skirt, blouse, shawl, clogs on her feet.

"Did you help my granddaughter last night?" Betty got her question in first.

"I saw her," admitted Fanny, "She was asleep under sedation from the drugs Doctor Lassiter had administered."

"Is this something I should know about?" Summerfield was alert.

"Miss Legge cured Laura of a serious spinal injury last night at the Lassiter Clinic," Betty wondered whether passing on the good news would in some way inhibit Fanny from future miracle cures.

"That's exactly what I've come to see you about Miss Legge. We, that is Anglia TV would like to make a programme about the paranormal activity that surrounds the Lewin's farm and the church, especially the church. I was involved in some of that mysterious force, burnt my hand by touching a brass plaque on the central catafalque down in the crypt, which you cured by this marvellous power of healing you posess. How would you feel about that? It would be of abiding interest to our viewers to know that such a person as yourself lives in the Anglia area. We could also offer you a substantial sum of money for this privelege."

"Wouldn't that mean my privacy would evaporate forever Miss Summerfield? There would be hordes of idly curious people, apart from the genuinely sick all coming to disturb the tranquillity of my lifestyle, asking me to perform what you consider to be miracles to order, let alone newspapers and other television companies all demanding a circus event to satisfy their viewers."

Summerfield nodded, "That would happen I regret to have to tell you Miss Legge, would not the money compensate you for this loss of privacy?"

Betty knew Fanny's response to that offer.

"Nothing but nothing would induce me to relinquish this precious commodity Miss Summerfield. I have no use for money or riches and certainly not vulgar publicity. I am sorry, I have my animals and other creatures to consider, aside from that adverse publicity," She indicated the cats that crowded round her skirts.

"We could assist you in other less obvious ways, like providing food for your cats on a permanent basis. It must cost you a fortune to feed all those creatures."

"As attractive as your offer appears Miss Summerfield, I'm afraid my answer must be a refusal. That type of exposure would end my isolation, make a circus turn out of me, willy-nilly."

"The money does not attract you? I'm talking in terms of offering complete independence from future financial worries about food and care for your creatures."

"You are very persuasive Miss Summerfield, that is your role but no thank you."

"Aren't you worried that one day some council will wish to build great sprawling estates of council housing on this land? What will your wish for independence count for then?"

"Are you telling me you, I mean your company, could influence such a decision?"

"No,but the publicity would ensure that no council of whatever persuasion would dare intrude upon your sanctuary for the foreseeable future."

Fanny smiled, showing her perfect teeth, "You have a well deserved reputation for the persuader's art, but my answer remains, No thank you."

"We could film the surroundings of your refuge without your assent Miss Legge," said Summerfield, changing tact.

That was definitely a bad move decided Betty.

"You have my answer Miss Summerfield," Fanny's good humour vanished.

Summerfield recognised her faux pas, "I didn't mean it like that Miss Legge," she pleaded.

Fanny turned from the gate and walked back towards the cottage.

"I think we've outstayed our welcome Holly," said Betty, moving from the gate, still apprehensive about the missing spider. She was half way to the Landrover before she realised something was amiss. Summerfield was pointing to her throat, making frantic signs. Her mouth opened and closed but no sound emerged.

****

29.

Monday, June 19th 1995.
Lewin's Farm, Babingley Marsh,
King's Lynn, Norfolk.

By the time they arrived back at Babingley, Summerfield was in a desperate state. She made frantic attempts to speak, not a sound came from her mouth. Betty persuaded her to enter the house and sat her down. The woman's classical features were twisted into a torment of anguish. Lines had appeared at the side of her mouth, her eyes were wild with fear. She was a sickly grey. Betty phoned Lassiter, his first reaction was hostile, no doubt in view of Fanny's appearance and Laura's discharge from his clinic. He changed his tune when Betty mentioned Summerfield. The lure of free publicity overcame his ethical scruples, and pique over the events of the previous night. He said he would come immediately.

Betty made attempts to calm the demented TV reporter, offering her sedatives horded from the time her husband had used the drugs to ease the pain in his back, twelve years before. Nothing would soothe Summerfield's anguish. She made desperate efforts to speak, her face turning red with effort, but not a sound emerged. She asked whether she should phone Richard Cheeseman at Anglia TV. Summerfield almost went berserk in denouncing this course of action.

Into the middle of this contretemps came Ellen and Kevin. "What's the matter with her Mumsy?" Ellen looked in horrified amazement at Summerfield's frantic garglings and facial expressions.

Kevin's head was surmounted by a bandage, apart from looking pale, he was none the worse for his ordeal in the crypt the previous day. Betty held her hands up in despair and explained the circumstances that appeared to have led to the woman's condition.

"She upset Funny Fanny," asserted Ellen, "That was a daft course of action, as if Fanny would ever agree to become a TV circus act. I suppose she came the big battalions syndrome?" She mimicked a theatrical German accent, "Ve haf vays of making ze film vis-out your permission!"

"I don't think that kind of acting is appropriate Ellen, Holly was only doing her job."

"I bet she made threatening noises Mumsy, Fanny would react to threats, I'm willing to bet she put the 'curse on her."

Betty was scornful, "Oh come on love, that's taking even Fanny Legge's powers to the edge."

"How else would that come about?" Ellen was unrepentant, "She was OK before wasn't she?"

Summerfield was now in a state of collapse, her features were full of anguish. The flawless face had become a mass of twitches and tics, as if some outside power was gripping her in its tentacles.

They all saw Lassiter's BMW arrive. He hurried in, holding his bag. "God, what on earth have you done to the woman?" he cried.

"Don't expose your cretinous ignorance to all and sundry mister," said Ellen, "You don't honestly believe we were responsible for that do you?" She pointed to Summerfield, now almost in total shock.

"You've inherited some of her less attractive traits," said Lassiter, nodding at Betty.

"Charming man," jeered Ellen, "Let's see you work a miracle on her."

"What happened?" Lassiter ignored the jibe.

Betty gave her version of the events at Legge's cottage.

"That woman is a menace," Lassiter took Summerfield's pulse, as the unfortunate woman continued to attempt to speak. "I warned you last night about her activities, I knew something like this would occur, all this nonsense about miracles and cures, it has come home to roost. Come and hold her still whilst I take her temperature, for God's Sake." He shook a glass thermometer vigorously.

"You're wasting time doctor, you won't learn anything from those methods," said Ellen, coldly.

"You, I take it, are a qualified physician Madame?"

"No, neither are you by the look of it."

"Elly, that's rude," said Kevin.

"Of course it's rude, he thinks that all problems can be cured by a few drugs and what he believes is a bedside manner."

"Ellen, you are being very rude," said Betty.

"Mumsy, do you honestly believe that he can do anything for her? Only Fanny Legge can do anything. You know it, I know it, everybody here knows, except him and he's going to make a big deal out of this situation because Summerfield is a TV Personality. If it had been you, me, Dad or Kevin he wouldn't have come near us. Go on, deny it."

"I don't propose entering into a pointless discussion with you Mrs Wilson, now if you don't mind, I'll get Miss Summerfield to the clinic where I can run some tests without interference," replied Lassiter, coldly.

He pulled a mobile from his bag and dialled a number. "Eddy? I'm at the Lewin place, need the ambulance sharp... Good... How long?... I'll be waiting."

"She'll be good for a few bob mister," said Ellen, plenty of lolly in TV."

"Do I have to endure this taunting Mr Wilson? It really is quite tedious." Lassiter appealed to Kevin, eyeing the bandage around his head. He opened his mouth to enquire the reason, then thought better of it and turned back to Summerfield.

The reporter seemed to have shrivelled into a corpse-like attitude, staring with blank eyes that saw nothing, her mouth opening and closing ineffectually.

"I think we ought to inform her boss, Doctor," said Betty.

"Eh?" Lassiter looked up, puzzlement in his eyes" Oh, yes, certainly, use my mobile."

It took a good five minutes to locate Richard Cheeseman.

"Mr Cheeseman? My name is Lewin, Elizabeth Lewin. I'm ringing to tell you Miss Summerfield has had an accident... No, the nature of it is not clear. She is being taken to the Lassiter Clinic, Gayton Road, King's Lynn. The phone number is... " She read it from the back of the mobile, "I'm sorry, I can't give any other details, you'll have to speak to Doctor Lassiter at the Clinic."

She handed the phone to Lassiter just as the hee-haw of a siren sounded.

The same ambulance and paramedics as those who had helped with Laura the previous day entered the kitchen.

"Sedation Eddy please, she's in deep shock."

The instant Eddy grasped Summerfield's arm, she threw him off with surprising strength, "Leave me alone you bastard," she screamed.

There followed a tussle in which it took both paramedics all their strength to handle her. Eddy gave her a jab with a hypodermic. Summerfield subsided into limpness.

"I'll be seeing you good people," Lassiter moved out into the yard and headed for his BMW.

"Huh," scoffed Ellen.

The ambulance took off with Lassiter tailing it in his own car, "She'll be in a straight jacket the next time we see her with him treating her," declared Ellen.

"You were very rude to him my girl," scolded Betty, "And he's right in that you're not a doctor, you should be careful about comments like that."

"I agree with your Mum, love," Kevin wasn't too happy, "Let's go get some lunch, hospital breakfasts aren't very sustaining."

"I'd better ring Tracy, see how Laura is," Betty stabbed at digits on the handset

"Just as well that charlatan didn't treat Laura, she'd have been fitted up with a wheelchair by now," said Ellen. "OK.I've said my piece, my feeling is that Fanny is the one who should be treating that poor woman who probably brought that on herself by some aggression."

"She just wanted Fanny to agree to a documentary, she even offered her money."

"I bet she turned it down?"

Betty nodded, "Got up-tight, she wants her privacy sacrosanct."

There was no answer to Bobby's phone, "Must be out."

"Just imagine what would happen to her place if those media freaks moved in," Ellen tugged Kevin's sleeve, "Come on greedy, let's get you fed. I'm driving, see you all later."

Betty saw the Landrover pull up, her husband disembarked, carrying a money bag.

"What's up, Laura bad again? Lassiter's ambulance passed me like a rocket, him behind it."

Betty shook her head and told him about the visit to Fanny's cottage and subsequent events.

"That's all we bloody need," groused Jim, "Those bloody sharks will be round here trying to interview us about Summerfield. I didn't think for a minute Fanny would agree to a documentary, but I didn't want to put Summerfield off trying. How is Laura?"

"I tried phoning a minute or so ago...no reply"

"Lets drop this money into the bank and call round on the way back," said Jim, "Pay in that Anglia cheque, see if it bounces."

They drove into Lynn, parked off Broad Street and bumped into Lilly

Simpson as she exited from the bank.

"How's your granddaughter Betty? Demetrius and I were shocked by the way she'd recovered at the hands of that witch, Legge. It smacked of African witchcraft, I don't think she should be allowed to do that sort of thing. She isn't a doctor, she could do some real harm," Lilly babbled on, railing against Fanny's healing skills.

"If you'll excuse me Lilly, got a lot of money here, dangerous with witches around the place, could turn it all to lead," said Jim, irritated with Lilly's diatribe.

Lilly was too engrossed with her criticism to take the sarcasm on board. She continued with it after Jim had gone into the bank.

"I don't agree with you Lilly," said Betty, to stop the ranting.

"Eh?" Lilly's plump features went pale, "What do you mean?"

"I said I don't agree with you about Miss Legge. Laura would have been in a wheelchair for the rest of her life with orthodox medical treatment. Miss Legge cured her, you saw the results yourself."

"I saw Bishop deManaury in the Tuesday Market a little while ago. He isn't very happy letting that woman practice black magic in the town. He's going to try and get this Wizard Society banned from holding their midsummer meetings at Bawsey. Thinks its pagan, against Christian rules. He thinks there's too much of it around," Lilly was determined to have her say, "Seducing the young into blasphemy, turning them away from Christ."

Betty sighed, praying that Jim wouldn't be too long and would rescue her from this old bat.

"He's been to the police, saw the Chief Constable, he's going to see William Watson who owns the land around the Ruin and Barry Lassiter owns the right of way to the Ruin. He'll get them to stop these weirdoes practising their black arts. I think it's disgraceful, orgies, black sabbaths, demonology, intercourse with virgins."

Betty jerked into alertness at this tocsin. The old moo had enough pull, along with other prominent people to get the Police Chief Mostin to stop Kevin and his Society from holding their Summer Solstice celebrations. Lassiter would be only too delighted to pull the carpet from under Kevin's feet in view of the humiliation at the hands of his wife.

"Hi there Betty, how's it going? Any more strange happenings up at the old rancho? Hi Lilly old girl, how's Demmy? Making more money is he? Has a feel round the models does he? I'll bet he does, real randy bugger is old Demmy, all that female underwear, does he dress up on occasions?"

Johnny Foster was about to go into the bank, he looked prosperous, decided Betty. His silk shirt, grey slacks and a silk scarf tucked into his neck instead of a tie. He'd had his hair styled and had liberally dosed himself with underarm.

"I think you're being very rude Mr Foster, Demtrius wouldn't dream of doing such things," Lilly was red in the face. At least it had stopped her going on about black sabbaths, witches and demonology.

Foster grinned, showing some capped teeth, "Not what I heard, darling, some real sexy goings on in the smoke when they launch their new fashions. They tell me Demmy is one randy old fart, you'll have to watch him.

Hi Jimbo lad, how's the old EU? Still paying you not to farm are they? I hear Paddy Murphy's in dock with a bad heart working on the restoration, sounds very much like the trouble I had down at the Hump twelve years ago. Something weird about that place?

Seen Funny Fanny lately? I hear the local dog collar's got his bowels in an uproar about the Solstice Celebrations at Bawsey on Wednesday, going to get it stopped, I've heard.

Young Kevin's the boss Wizard ain't he? Personally, I don't give a damn about who does what as long as it's with consenting adults. I hear they have real orgies, copulating with virgins, boozing, I'm thinking of joining this Society myself, fancy a bit of young girl. Pity you don't qualify Lilly.

Demmy told me in the Duke the other night he fancies joining, get his end away while he can still get it up. You'll have to watch him Lilly, he's real randy, loves the young ones, makes him feel youthful. Be seeing you."

He entered the Bank, pausing in the doorway, "Oh, by the way, I thought you'd like to know I'm opening a new branch in Wisbech next month. Better business than construction, more profit in it."

"What a dreadful man," Lilly puffed, "There should be a law against such people. Slandering my poor husband in that awful fashion, as if Demetrius would ever look at another woman. He is solid, dependable, virtuous, not like some of these young ones. AIDS, drugs, don't know what the world is coming to."

"We must go Lilly," interupted Jim, "Got to organise the rave up at Bawsey on Wednesday. Midsummer Solstice you know? I'll see Demmy gets an invite, he'll enjoy himself, raping a virgin!"

Jim tugged Betty's sleeve, pulling her away from Lilly.

"You shouldn't have said that Jimbo," admonished Betty as they made their way back to the Landrover, "She told me the Bishop and Charlie Gates have seen the Chief Constable to try and get the Solstice banned on Wednesday. You'll just add fuel to the flames."

"The more I see of that meadow lady the less I like her. The Chief will never agree to banning it, he hasn't the manpower to do anything, even if he wanted to. His son is a Wizard, I remember Kev telling me. He's hardly likely to want his son exposed to media attention."

"Barry Lassiter owns the right of way to Bawsey, did you know that? That's what Lilly told me just now. He could get really nasty in view of Fanny's activities, stop Kev and his Society passing through to the Ruin."

****

30.

Monday, June 19th 1995.
Duke's Head Hotel, Tuesday Marketplace, King's Lynn, Norfolk.

"He wouldn't be that childish," said Jim as they reached the Landrover.

"I think you're wrong Jimbo, I don't approve of this Wizard business but they're harmless enough. I'd hate to see them stopped because of that Bishop and Charlie Gates invoking Blasphemy Laws to get it banned."

"I think you're being pessimistic love. That priest won't get Mostin to use precious police resources on that kind of operation."

"I'm not convinced. There are lot of busy-bodies in Lynn who'd just enjoy wrecking some innocent fun, Barry Lassiter is one of them, he'll tar Kevin with the same brush as Fanny Legge."

"We'll just have to wait and see," Jim looked over Betty's shoulder, "Oh Christ, hop in or we'll be clobbered love. I've just seen Calhoun over there by the Majestic. That Ross Lambert is with him." He snapped his fingers impatiently, "Come on love hurry it up, what're you gaping at?"

"I've just seen Lilly getting into Lane Ward's Jaguar, off to a tryst somewhere, no doubt."

"Best of luck, come on for Christ sake, that bloodsucker is looking in our direction." Jim started the Landrover just as Calhoun and the Radio Lynn DJ started walking towards them. Jim ignored Calhoun's frantic waving and drove away into Norfolk Street, then into Chapel Street and the Tuesday Market Place. He parked outside the Corn Exchange, the nearest available space to the Duke's Head.

"I'm not sure this is a great idea love," said Betty, "It's a popular lunch venue, we could meet anybody."

"I'm hungry, we'll take a chance."

They asked for a table for two in Reception. Just as they entered the restaurant they saw Harry Farraday. With him were Bill Watson and Jeff Patten of the Lynn Advertiser.

Farraday immediately rose, and walked to meet them, "Come and join us you two, we were just discussing your son-in-law with Ralph Mostin, he's just gone to the loo, he'll be back in a sec. Come on Jimbo, don't be bloody stuffy, he could do your golfing enterprise a power of good."

Watson waved, "Come on Betty, don't be so anti-social. We never see you off that farm." He held his arms wide, hands outstretched, "Brackets, paid by the EU now ain'tcha?"

"Hello Mrs Lewin," greeted Patten, "I hear Rory's been giving you a hard time? Sorry about that but the story is too good not to run. Most of the dailies are running it tomorrow since we syndicated it. Witchcraft is always a powerful draw."

Patten was tall and lean, he had a hooked nose, dark hair, greying at the temples, a wide mouth, with thick lips and deep creases either side of his nose.

"Is that the gist of your story?" Jim pulled a chair from ad adjacent table.

Patten nodded, "Ruined church, crypt, strange goings on, flashes of light, a brass plaque that burns people, all good stuff and a real live witch doctor able to cure people by holding hands. Got a photo of Wally Thompson before and after, it will create a mild sensation. I tried to get hold of your son Bobby, to get a photo of your granddaughter cured of a serious spinal injury yesterday by the same witch. He wasn't available for comment according to his secretary."

"Don't blame him," said Jim, "Going in for the sensational stuff are you? Trying to out do the News?"

"Sorry you feel that way Lewin, as Harry said, could do your golf a lot of good, free advertising and all that."

"And the horse riding," said Watson, "I met the Holy Trinity a short time ago, well,two of them anyway, deManaury and Charlie Gates. They're trying to get Ralph to ban that Summer Solstice on Wednesday, prejudicial to public order and illicit sex, drugs, etc. Want me to agree not to allow them access to the Ruin."

"Are you going to do it?" asked Betty.

Watson grinned, "Kev has always been careful not to let it get out of hand and this is the fifth year they've held it. I'm not going to turn good money away. The Bishop can go take a running jump into the font."

"What about Barry Lassiter? They have to cross his land to get to your place. He isn't very pleased with Ellen right now, she called him a charlatan this morning."

Watson and Farrady guffawed, "She got that right" roared Watson, "He couldn't cure my back or Harry's, tried for years, then our local witch comes along, cures us in minutes, and that bloody skinflint has been taking my money for yonks. If he gets stroppy I'll make sure he pays me the ten years ground rent he thinks he's been getting away with. That should change his mind, for the right of way he enjoys across a corner of my land."

"We hear Funny Fanny cured Laura last night, is that right?"

Farraday signalled for the waiter, "Fell from her horse?"

"We don't know for sure, nobody saw her do anything and Laura doesn't recall seeing her," said Betty.

"She was there though?" asked Patten.

"We took her along, over Barry's protests, I might add," said Betty.

"Then what happened?"

"She just vanished, one minute she was there, then she was gone, never saw her again last night."

"I've been going through Rory's notes about her antecedents. Your daughter was down here last week looking up old issues and I got Ray Hammond to let me have a wander down his archival section, apart from a mention of a Myfanwy Legge in June 21st 1796, nothing. Nothing in the old electoral rolls either before or since. No family by that name, nothing. That in itself is strange, when she can do what she has done for Bill, Harry, you, Jimbo and your granddaughter, just by holding hands. Makes it a marvellous mystery story, just as if she just appeared once in 1796, then vanished and appeared ten, twelve years ago in North Wootton. Then we come across the strangest piece of info of all," Patten smiled, the creases around his nose deepening, awaiting acknowledgement of the curiosity of his audience.

"Well, come on Jeff, you've built up the expense," growled Watson.

"Nobody bothered checking the present electoral roll. Rory didn't and Mrs Wilson didn't, as far as I know," said Patten.

"You saying she's not on it?" Betty was disbelieving.

Patten shook his head, "Not this year, last roll or any that I could locate."

"That's impossible, she has to be on it, Council Tax and all that, water, electricity, sewage, she has to be recorded somewhere," protested Watson.

"I checked with the Tax Department, not on their books," said Patten.

"So she's been getting away with it all these years?" said Watson as the waiter arrived.

"We better wait until Ralph comes back from the loo," said Faraday, informing the waiter. The man sighed and then departed.

"Been a long time, hasn't he?" Watson looked at his watch.

"Ten minutes," Patten looked round to where the toilets were located, "Perhaps he copped out?"

"He wouldn't just leave," said Bill, "I'll go check, see whether he's OK?"

"So Fanny pays no Council Tax or any other contribution?" demanded Jim.

"She has her own spring, no electricity and gas doesn't exist down that far in Gatehouse. Goodness knows what she does for sewage, septic tank I suppose," quipped Betty. "Now that you mention it, I didn't see any lighting of any kind, not even a paraffin lamp. I suppose she only brings it out in the darker winter nights."

"Weird isn't it?" replied Patten, "Now you can possibly understand why she's making good copy." He stopped, looking over to where Watson had emerged from the toilets. He was hurrying into Reception, "What's the matter with Bill now?"

Watson re-appeared a minute later, the manager in tow, heading for the gents. They emerged a few seconds later, the manager using his mobile phone.

"Something's wrong," said Jim, going over to Watson and the Manager. "The Chief's had a fall, hurt his back. They are calling the Ambulance," he announced.

"Good God," Patten arose, "I think we'd better call this gathering off. I can smell opportunity." He departed quickly, pulling out a mobile as he went into reception.

Betty saw Lilly Simpson and Lane Ward enter Reception. "Let's disappear," she hissed, nodding towards the arrivals, "I couldn't stand lunch with that creature, she's bound to want to join us."

Jim nodded, "Let's go then."

"Hello, we meet again," said Lilly brightly, looking guilty.

"Hello Lane," Betty smiled, "Haven't seen you since the Fete, how's business?"

Ward smiled uneasily, his face red, "Doing a bit, Betty," he said.

"Looking after Lilly, I see?"

"We bumped into one another by accident," Lilly jumped in too hastily, "Lane invited me to lunch."

They all heard the ambulance arrive, pulling up outside the hotel entrance. The two paramedics hurried in with a stretcher, and straight towards the restaurant area.

"Someone ill?" Lilly's innate curiosity was aroused.

"Ralph Mostin had a fall, hurt his back," said Betty, giving a sideways jerk of her head at Jim.

"Nice seeing you Lane, Lilly we must go," said Jim.

They hurried into the Tuesday Market Place as the two paramedics emerged from the hotel. The Police Chief was strapped into the stretcher, his face looking very pale.

"Must be fairly serious," said Betty as they hurried over to where they'd parked the Landrover, outside the Corn Exchange.

"Come on let's try The Globe," urged Jim, "We might have better luck there. We can ring Jeff Patten later, find out what was wrong with Mostin."

They saw Bobby, Tracy and Laura inside the restaurant. Bobby waved them over, signalling for a table to be added.

"We got away from the prospect of those TV people," explained Bobby, "Someone rang up early this morning, wanting to interview Laura, they said they were coming round so we got out before they arrived."

"How are you pickle?" asked Jim of Laura.

"As you can see Grandad, I'm fine now."

"You still don't remember anything about what happened in Lassiter's?"

She shook her head, "Not a thing until I came round, I wondered why I was stuck in a hospital bed."

"You didn't see anybody?" Jim persisted.

"Funny Fanny you mean?" Laura grinned, "Everybody keeps asking me that question. The answer is no, I didn't see her."

"It had to be her, Dad," said Bobby, "She was in a dreadful state when we took her in. Barry was faffing around, saying he would get the specialist in from Norwich, We could get no real answers from him as to what was wrong. Then you saw her arrive in Reception all cured. No sign of Fanny."

"We heard the ambulance just now," Tracy was clad in her designer gear, pale lemon two piece with a pearl necklace. "Has there been an accident?"

"Chief Constable Mostin hurt his back in the toilets of the Duke's Head," said Jim.

"Pissed on duty, was he?" grinned Bobby.

"That's not very nice Bobby."

"Come on Mumsy, this is the late twentieth century, I was only joking."

"He must be in a bad way if they called an ambulance," Betty ignored the jibe.

"What were you doing in the Duke?"

"About to have lunch when Lilly Simpson and Lane Ward came in. I didn't want an attack of indigestion," said Jim.

"He's having it off with Lilly," said Bobby, "I don't admire his taste, must be hard-up."

"It's his law training," said Tracy, "Sees the worst in everybody. She's probably just talking business with Mr Ward."

"Yeah, monkey business."

"Talking of monkeys," said Laura, "Look who's just come in."

"Who is it love? I don't want to turn round?" said Jim.

"That nasty type from the 'Advertiser', what's his name."

Laura snapped her fingers.

"Not Calhoun?"

Laura nodded, "He's coming this way, there's another fellow with him."

"He's all we need, "groaned Jim.

"Good-day folks," Calhoun was in his usual denim get up, his hand bandaged. "You evidently didn't see me in Broad Street a short time ago, I waved but you drove off."

"How can we help you? This is a family get-together if you don't mind Mr Calhoun."

"I thought you'd like to hear about Holly Summerfield's condition. Barry Lassiter gave me a call, apparently she suffered a slight stroke when she visited Funny Fanny's Cottage early this morning. She can't speak. I understand you went with her Mrs Lewin?"

"Is this an interview Calhoun?" Bobby was cold.

"If you want to make it one," Calhoun urged his companion forward, "This is Ross Lambert, he's a DJ on Radio Lynn."

"How do Mr Lambert and no thanks we don't want to give an interview Calhoun. How is Summerfield?"

"Can't walk either now, seems her condition is deteriorating rapidly.

Can you tell me exactly what happened at Fanny's cottage this morning Mrs Lewin? I have a tape machine here."

He pulled a dictating machine from his pocket with his left hand.

"You heard my Father, Calhoun, this is a family get-together. We don't want interruptions," said Bobby, abruptly.

Calhoun shrugged, "We'll just have to ad lib, Ross old fruit, shouldn't be too difficult, along the lines of a visit paid to the local witch in company with Mrs J Lewin resulted in a well-known TV Personality suffering a minor stroke, etc. Mrs Lewin of Lewin's Farm, Babingley Marsh, was not able to shed any light on the incident, made no comment when approached at noon today. Miss Summerfield, the TV personality in question is in a serious condition in Lassiter's Clinic, Gayton, you know the drill, Ross?"

"I can make up a few lines," said Lambert, "Should add some interest to your article in tomorrow's edition. There's going to be a lot of interest in St Mary's by tomorrow night, all the major channels will be on to it and the national dailies, real cool."

****

31.

Monday, June 19th 1995.
Globe Hotel, Tuesday Market Place,
King's Lynn, Norfolk.

"Obnoxious is the description that fits him best," said Bobby, as the two men departed for the bar and the waiter arrived to take their order.

"Were you with this woman Summerfield at Funny Fanny's cottage this morning Mother?" asked Tracy, after the man had departed.

"I went with her, Anglia TV want to do a documentary on the church, these ley-lines. Holly wanted to ask Fanny if she'd agree to the TV people filming her, they offered her money, indicating there would be a lot of it for the privilege. Fanny went all cold and walked away. The next instant Holly was clutching her throat and couldn't speak. By the time we got home she was in a dreadful state, I sent for Barry. He couldn't find anything wrong with her, but sent for an ambulance immediately."

"Sounds as if Fanny was punishing her for making what she considers to be obscene suggestions," said Tracy.

"More like a warning to others not to persist in that type of persuasion," said Bobby.

"Barry, according to that Calhoun, thinks it's a stroke," said Jim.

"I haven't much faith in Barry Lassiter Dad. I don't mean he's a bad medical man, but he is more interested in making money than curing people. If he can keep Summerfield in his clinic for a length of time," Bobby shrugged.

"That's a dreadful indictment of the man Robert," Tracy was horrified.

"How old you reckon Summerfield is Mumsy? Thirty-five, forty? I know young people do suffer from strokes, but it doesn't normally happen whilst they're walking around, more often during sleep.

"What're you getting at?" Betty was uneasy.

"I believe Fanny was responsible for Summerfield's condition and it was intended as a warning of what could happen if the media start interfering in her lifestyle."

"That's a little exotic isn't it Robert? You're assigning God like power to her."

"She cured Bill Watson's back, plus Harry Farraday, Dad and Laura last night when they'd all been suffering for years, and Troy at the Fete. He hasn't had any trouble with his hepatitis since. If that isn't God like I'd like to know what is."

"Jeff Patten was in the Duke's Head, he said he'd been doing some checking on Fanny's background. He confirmed what Ellen told us," said Jim.

"And that Fanny isn't on the current Electoral Roll, pays no Council Tax, water, sewage, electricity, gas..." added Betty, still thoughtful.

"He's just missed her that's all," said Bobby, "How could she not be on it? The Council would soon be round at her place with a demand."

Betty shrugged, "I'm only repeating what Patten said."

"And no record of any Legge's before or since 1796, the date on that plaque on the catafalque in the Crypt," said Jim, "Which was what Ellen told us last week."

"The one nobody can find?" said Bobby.

"It's odd, but she hasn't aged one bit since she came to see to Jim twelve years ago," said Betty.

"A female Dorian Gray Mumsy," mocked Bobby gently, "She must have."

"She doesn't look any different," said Jim, "and that was before Laura was born. What's more, do you recall seeing her in anything else except that long dress, that shawl and blouse and those clogs? Looks like the same one she was wearing when she fixed my back, all those years ago."

"Now we are getting into the occult," Bobby quipped.

"The way she just vanished whilst we were at Barry's clinic last night," said Betty, "and whilst we were standing at her gate this morning she seemed to just appear. One minute there were only the cats, geese, a donkey and her dog, the next minute she was there. She just waved her hand and they all stopped honking, barking, meowing, even the donkey stopped braying."

"What are we saying?" Bobby also looked uneasy now.

The arrival of the waiter, pushing a trolley with their food on board stopped all discussion whilst the man served them.

"Perhaps she is a witch, perhaps she rides on a broomstick and has a cauldron and incants over it," said Laura. She mimicked a cackling old woman.

"I think I ought to go and see Fanny," said Betty.

They all stared at her, astonished, "Why? What for?" asked Bobby.

"If she was punishing Holly for suggesting filming her cottage, I feel responsible in a way for her condition," said Betty.

"Oh come on Mumsy, you didn't suggest anything, this Summerfield did. You aren't representing Anglia TV."

"I think we ought to tell that Cheeseman that we can't accept his offer of filming the church, doing a documentary," Betty persisted.

"Why for God's Sake love?" Jim was irritated, "They'd pay a fortune for the rights, we'd be on easy street. What're you getting all weird for?"

"Well, if she did that to Holly," said Betty, lamely.

"You think she might take it out on you?" said Bobby" Christ, we really are into the esoteric, aren't we? Witches, demons, magic, disease, sounds like a third rate horror movie."

"How was she able to cure Laura, and Bill Watson, Jimbo, Troy, Harry Farraday, she must have some kind of power nobody else possesses. The moaning in that crypt, that brass plaque nobody is able to confirm the date on it. And the lightning that struck the church in 1918, again the same date and all those people die and the church falls into ruin. I think it's all connected," Betty was adamant.

"I think she's got to you love," said Jim, "You're a little uptight. Eat your food, you'll feel better after it."

"I don't feel hungry," Betty pushed her plate away, "I feel distinctly queasy, must be something I've eaten."

"You haven't eaten anything, anything since breakfast when the Summerfield woman arrived," Jim looked worried.

"It'll pass, just a slight touch of nausea. You lot carry on, I don't mind, I'll sit this one out."

"How is it connected Mumsy?" Bobby started on his soup.

"I don't know love, I just have this feeling that everything that's happened over the past few weeks all seems to have something to do with Fanny."

"You're reading things into the situation because you've become involved love," said Jim. "I think we should let Anglia do their documentary, then leave Fanny strictly alone in future."

"I just have this feeling that Summerfield's condition is the result of a...." Betty stopped.

"Spell?" said Tracy.

Jim and Bobby started to laugh, then cut it short when Betty didn't respond.

"You're serious aren't you Mumsy?" said Bobby, changing tact.

"Summerfield was perfectly OK, fit as a fiddle when she arrived this morning. Now Barry Lassiter has diagnosed a stroke, I can't believe it."

"The gypsy's warning, Grandma," intoned Laura, wringing her hands, cackling again, "Hubble bubble, toil and trouble."

She stopped when her Father gave her a stern look.

"Sounds daft doesn't it?" said Betty, "All witchcraft, spells and paranormal experiences, I think Fanny was warning Holly Summerfield not to go ahead with anything that threatens her privacy, like filming and people trampling around her cottage."

"Could be something much more pragmatic Mumsy," said Bobby.

"What, for example?"

"If she doesn't pay Council Tax, not on the Electoral Roll etcetera, if she gets a lot of unwelcome publicity the council, might decide to make her cough up, join the rest of us who have to fork out their blood money."

Betty shrugged, "Doesn't alter the fact that Summerfield's condition is connected with the visit we paid Fanny this morning."

"I'll have your soup Grandma, if you're sure you don't want it," Laura interrupted, trying to change the subject. She pulled Betty's plate toward her tentatively.

"Go ahead darling, I couldn't touch it. I think if you lot'll excuse me, I'll go and sit in the Landrover, let the seat down. The smell of food is putting me off."

She restrained Jim as he went to get up, "No you stay Jimbo, I might just go and get some magnesia from the chemist, help settle my stomach, have a lie down. The smell is really upsetting me."

They watched her walk out.

"Has she eaten anything unusual? Indian, Chinese, or something Dad?" asked Bobby, as the waiter approached with their main course.

"Not that I know of. We got back last last night and went straight to bed, only had breakfast this morning, the usuall stuff before she and Summerfield went off to see Fanny."

Jim told the waiter that Betty's order wasn't required, she felt unwell.

Bobby assured the man that it would be paid for.

"I don't recall Mumsy having a bad stomach before," said Bobby.

"Always the first time Bobby," said Tracy. "It's not always what you've eaten that causes it."

"Well I'm starving," said Jim, starting on the food.

They discussed Betty's assertion that the events over the past weeks were connected with Fanny.

"Oh Christ," said Bobby, staring at the entrance to the restaurant, "He's all we need."

"Who is it? Not Calhoun again?" Jim had his back to the door.

"Johnny millionaire Foster, Lynn's answer to Gulbenkian," said Bobby, "He's got a dolly in tow as well. Can't see any sign of Jeannie."

"That's par for the course, isn't it? Believes he's God's gift to women," Tracy sounded sour.

"He is rather good looking Mumsy," said Laura, "All that thick hair greying at the sides, those wide shoulders. The lady looks rather posh!"

"Oh my God and she's only twelve," Bobby moaned theatrically.

"What's she going to like in another four years?"

"And he's coming over here," said Tracy, glowering.

"Hi folks," Foster was all bonhomie, "Enjoying your nosh?" He saw the empty chair, "Where's the lady Jimbo?"

"Doesn't feel too well Johnny," said Jim, sourly.

Foster patted his belly, "Should get more exercise Jimbo. Never had a day's sickness mate. Down the Gym every morning, an hour's workout, then a swim in the old pool. You wanna get one Jimbo, you could probably kid the EU that it's necessary to stop BSE, eh?" He slapped Jim on the shoulder.

"This is Marie by the way, friend of mine, up to Lynn for the day, thinks we're all Swede-bashing peasants, straw in our hair. Meet the local landowner, Marie, richer than Onassis. That's Tracy Lewin, nee Middleton, this is Bobby Lewin, Jimbo's son, smart lawyer type, charges a bloody fortune for advice, and that's Laura, their gorgeous daughter."

"Aren't you the Tracy Middleton, the model?" the woman was staring at Tracy, "Model for Dior and others?"

Tracy nodded, "I do some modelling," she admitted.

"I never expected to meet someone as famous as you in a small country town like Lynn," gushed Marie, patting her coiffed blond hair. The perfume washing all over them.

"We have met haven't we?" said Tracy, "You're a model aren't you?"

Marie blossomed her face flushed prettily, "You must have a good memory Tracy, Cafe Royale last March, the Spring Collection."

"All the famous together eh,girls?" Foster resented Marie's attention being diverted, "You never can tell when you'll bump into someone in the news, or where. Come on Marie, leave these good people too finish their grub in peace. You'll have to do as I say Jimbo. Put a gymnasium in one of those old cowsheds the EU are paying for, get fit. Betty'll look better for it."

"Excuse him Mr Lewin, he's not what you call diplomatic," said Marie, "Ego-maniacal tendencies, you know?"

"Fit Jimbo, that's me, see? Flat as a pancake, hard as rock, no belly on me, the ladies go for that, don't they love?" He appealed to Marie.

"Thick as well" Marie tapped her forehead, "Nice meeting you Tracy, bump into you again sometime."

Foster almost dragged her away.

"What a creature," said Tracy, "Talk about ego!"

"You like him Mumsy, you've gone all coy," said Laura.

"Eat your food my girl and stop being smart," Tracy coloured up, guiltily.

"I believe our daughter has struck oil love," said Bobby, grinning.

The manager came into the restaurant and looked round, before coming over to their table, "Which of you is Mr Lewin?" he asked, his face anxious.

"We both are," said Bobby, "What's the problem?"

"A lady has just been taken ill in the foyer, my head waiter said she came in with your party. I wonder if..."

Jim was half way out of the restaurant before the man had finished speaking.

****

32.

Monday, June 19th 1995.
Globe Hotel, Tuesday Market Place,
King's Lynn, Norfolk.

Betty was seated in an armchair, her face a pasty grey colour. She was trembling, a sheen of perspiration on her forehead. When Jim touched her she felt hot.

"Can you phone for ambulance please?" Jim knelt beside Betty.

"Already done so sir," said the manager. "Your wife, I assume?"

Jim nodded, horrified at Betty's appearance. Wrinkles had appeared on her cheeks she normally didn't posess, her skin hung like jowls under her chin. She looked twenty years older than she had a few moments before.

"How do you feel love?" Jim was choked with emotion.

Bobby, Tracy and Laura approached. They looked in horror at Betty's appearance. Jim couldn't credit his eyesight, Betty was ageing before their gaze.

"What's wrong with her?" Bobby was incredulous.

Laura and Tracy were staring in consternation, unable to believe what they were seeing. Jim shook his head disbelievingly, holding Betty's hand, watching it wrinkling even as the seconds passed. They heard the ambulance' siren approaching, the vehicle came to a swaying halt in Ferry Street, two paramedics jumped out, one a woman. They ran into the reception.

"Stand back please," commanded the female. Jim and his family moved away whilst the two paramedics examined Betty. The woman gazed at her companion and nodded. He ran out and returned with a wheeled stretcher, blankets and breathing apparatus. In seconds Betty was being wheeled out to the ambulance.

"Where are you taking her?" asked Jim still unable to credit the evidence. His wife looked like an old woman, her pallor awful.

"Longley Hill sir," said the woman. "Who are you?"

"Her husband," said Jim.

"Can you give me a few details sir, name, age, address?"

Jim gave the detail, as best he could, his mind not with it. The female paramedic looked at Jim askance, "Sure you haven't made a mistake sir?" she asked when Jim gave her age.

"Of course not, I should know shouldn't I?"

The paramedic shrugged and looked at her male counterpart eloquently. The look said lying to make himself look good.

"Can I come with you?"

"Of course," The paramedic was over-zealously concerned, as if dealing with a mentally defective person, "You can sit in the back," She even assisted Jim up the steps into the rear of the vehicle.

"We'll follow behind Dad," said Bobby, a mobile phone in his hands, the aerial still extended.

Siren wailing,the journey to Longley Hill took less than ten minutes, traffic moving aside to permit a clear way. The medical staff moved with efficiency once Betty was inside Casualty. Jim was shunted into the reception area by an officious nurse and told to wait. Bobby, Tracy and Laura arrived a few minutes later.

"How is she Dad?"

"They've taken her into one of the cubicles, to examine her," Jim was in a state of shock.

"Want some tea Dad?" asked Bobby.

Jim shook his head, "Right as rain one minute then like that a moment later. I can't believe it!"

"Neither can I," Bobby looked round the crowded casualty area, as if seeking reassurance.

A young doctor approached, "You must be Mr Lewin, the lady's son?" He addressed Jim.

"I'm her husband," snapped Jim.

The young doctor shrugged, "Your wife is in an advanced stage of senility Mr Lewin. We can't find anything physically wrong with her save old age. We're conducting some more tests. She has an extraordinarily high temperature, we're dealing with that at present. As soon as I can tell you something positive I'll be back."

"But she's only sixty, for God's Sake," burst out Jim, "How can she be senile?"

The doctor looked at Jim pityingly, patting him on the shoulder as if reassuring a child, "Of course Mr Lewin, we understand.

"She's my Mother, Doctor," said Bobby, "Dad's right Mumsy is only sixty and only just."

The young man stared at Bobby, careful to keep a deadpan expression, "Of course sir, understandable."

"Don't patronise me you asshole," roared Bobby, "I'm telling you the truth. Tell us what's wrong with her, not give us a load of bullshit."

A senior nurse approached, "Something amiss Doctor Petit?" She was accustomed to dealing with concerned relatives.

"Mr Lewin is a trifle upset Matron. Understandable under the circumstances," said the doctor, looking apprehensively at Bobby's red face.

"Are you a relative sir?" The grey-haired, buxom Matron addressed Bobby.

"I'm her son madame. If my Mother is very ill then I'd like an experienced consultant to examine her, I'll pay for private consultation. This is my Father, the lady's husband, Mr James Lewin and please don't start handing out placebos. We'd like the truth, what's wrong with her?"

"The staff are conducting further tests Mr Lewin," soothed the Matron, "Would you mind not creating a fuss, you're upsetting other people."

"Answer the question for God's Sake," snarled Bobby, "She was perfectly fit an hour ago. People aren't taken ill without cause. Are you saying you don't bloody well know what's wrong?"

"Mr Lewin, I understand your concern but terrorising the medical staff is not an intelligent method of co-operation, I assure you. We are doing our best for your Mother. Doctor Petit is a very able practitioner. If you feel you want another opinion later that is your privelege. In the meantime we would be grateful for a little forbearance," The Matron was not intimidated by Bobby's obvious irritation.

"She's right, Bobby. Yelling isn't going to help Mother," said Tracy, "You're making it harder for Dad, as well."

"Sorry Matron, I am up-tight. This gentleman was being patron-ising, my mother is just sixty, not senile as he appears to suggest, so there must be something seriously wrong with her. If you can't handle it, I'd like another doctor to examine her."

"Something wrong Matron?"

Barry Lassiter had entered the reception area. He saw Jim and Bobby," Jimbo, are you all right? Hello Bobby, Tracy, Laura."

"It's Betty, Barry," said Bobby, assuming responsibility. Jim was too shocked to cope, "This doctor is claiming Betty is in an advanced state of senility and that nothing else wrong with her." He pointed to the young medic.

Lassiter frowned and looked over at Petit, "You sure you've examined the right patient Doctor Petit?"

"The lady was brought in a few moments ago by ambulance sir."

"Do you mind if I take a look?"

"Be my guest Doctor Lassiter. If it will assist these good people to comprehend the nature of the lady's illness. If that's the correct description, under the circumstances."

"Be back in a moment Bobby." Lassiter and Petit entered the cubicle and drew the curtain after them.

"We should get the truth now Bobby," said Tracy.

"He didn't look very pleased at seeing me Mumsy," said Laura, "I think I offended his professional judgement."

Lassiter and Petit emerged, Lassiter looked shocked and was shaking his head.

"Baffling," he said, "Doctor Petit is correct, Mrs Lewin is in an advanced state of senility."

"Oh for Christ sake Barry, you know my Mother, she's sixty. How the hell can she be senile? You saw her a few days ago. You would have noticed changes of that kind in her appearance."

Lassiter shook his head, as if to clear it of fuzziness, "I'm as baffled as you are Bobby. Come and take a look for yourself." He swept the privacy curtain aside.

Bobby stared incredulously. "That isn't my Mother Barry. That's an old woman," he spluttered, "She must be ninety plus."

Tracy and Laura stared at the inert form on the bed, horrified, "That's not Grandma," declared Laura, "Daddy's right. That's an old woman, Grandma is young, lively and still very attractive."

Jim shuffled over, staring at the form on the bed blankly. He shook his head, "Can't be Betty," he mumbled, "You've got the wrong person."

Petit took hold of the woman's left hand and raised it from the bed, "Is that your wife's wedding ring Mr Lewin?" he demanded.

"Is she wearing your wife's clothes?"

"That's her ring Bobby and she was wearing those clothes," said Tracy, examining the ring closely. "I would recognise that ring anywhere. She shuddered, "But that....!" She pointed, "Never."

"Would you excuse us just a moment Doctor Petit?" Lassiter looked shocked. He waited until the young man had departed.

"Your wife was with Miss Summerfield earlier this morning wasn't she?"

Jim nodded dully, unable to come to terms with what he saw.

"Visited that Legge woman didn't they?"

Bobby looked at Jim accusingly, who nodded, "She told you that when you attended Miss Summerfield," he said, gradually recovering from the initial shock of seeing Betty looking like a hundred year old woman.

"I have too tell you that Miss Summerfield is in a similar condition at my Clinic," said Lassiter, "I don't know what transpired at that Legge woman's cottage, but the implications aren't hard to draw."

"You telling us that Legge is responsible for this?" demanded Bobby, nodding at Betty's body on the bed.

"I don't know anything, I've never in all my years in practice, ever seen anything like this. It is horrifying and I have no idea what has caused it to happen to both women. The only thing they have in common is a visit to that Legge woman's cottage."

"You're admitting that Funny Fanny has some mysterious power to make this happen?" Bobby was cold.

Lassiter shrugged, "I tried to warn you about meddling with that woman, she treated this young lady when by all the laws of nature she should be a cripple." He nodded at Laura, "Jimbo told me she cured his back, Bill Watson said the same and she cured Wally Thompson when, again he should now be in a box, to be blunt. I don't know about powers but she has been responsible for odd happenings over the past years."

"Well, let's get her here, face her with it. See what she has to say," rasped Bobby, "If she caused this she can cure it."

"I wash my hands of any responsibility if that woman comes anywhere near. I propose acquainting Doctor Petit with my views. He must make his own decision, she's his patient."

"If Funny Fanny is responsible for this then she can reverse the process," said Jim, staring at the aged woman on the bed. "I can't believe that that is my wife."

Lassiter called out, "Doctor Petit."

The young man appeared. Lassiter explained the reasons for his call.

Petit listened, looking askance at his older colleague, "This is a joke Doctor Lassiter?" he said.

Lassiter assured him he was serious, "How long have you been here Petit?"

"A few days."

"Then you won't have heard about this Miss Legge will you?"

"I can't believe you'd joke about anything as serious as this Doctor Lassiter," protested Petit, "Let's keep it on a professional basis."

"See this young woman?" Lassiter pointed at Laura.

"Well?"

"I can assure you Petit that a mere twenty four hours ago I would have put my professional experience on the line, and predicted that the injuries she sustained as a result of a fall from a horse would have rendered her incapable of even modest movement from the waist upwards. Her lumbar vertebrae were irretrievably damaged beyond any possibility of repair. You can see for yourself she is fit and well. Funny Fanny as she is known, cured her. Wally Thompson was a patient in this hospital, terminal lung cancer, not expected to live beyond a few hours. That man is alive and walking around, doing his job once more. That was a fortnight ago, all due to this Fanny Legge."

Petit was obviously doubting Lassiter's professional competence and his mental state.

"Believe me Petit, I fully understand your response. I found it difficult to accept it, I have to face facts as I see them, unpalatable as they may appear to my medical skills. This Funny Fanny has some extraordinary powers that defy all logical explanation. They have been termed miracles. You can reject this intelligence as the ramblings of a deranged colleague. I can only assure you that I'm totally rational and in possession of all my faculties. I recommend you have this woman in, see for yourself, then judge."

Petit was silent for a moment, then "I would never have believed that I'd hear such a confession from a highly respected practitioner Doctor Lassiter. You're admitting what is tantamount to a belief in sorcery, witchcraft, faith healing, call it what you will."

"You can call it what you like Petit, I'm imparting to you events I have witnessed, that defy all known medical knowledge, skills, experience. In addition to the cases I've already quoted you, I personally was witness to a patient of mine with chronic hepatitis, necessitating the use of drugs too contain the condition. This lady's Father, this same Funny Fanny in full view of hundreds of people cured him."

"I've heard enough," interupted Bobby, "I propose bringing Mrs Legge into this scenario. If she's responsible for my Mother's condition, she can reverse it."

"I refuse to accept any further responsibility for this patient in that event Mr Lewin, "stated Petit.

"Do you know what's wrong with my Mother?"

"No I don't, we'll have to conduct some more tests."

"Can you cure her?"

Petit shrugged, "We're dealing with an unknown sets of symptoms Mr Lewin."

"In your opinion can you reverse what has happened to my Mother?"

"I can't promise anything Mr Lewin."

"I'm getting Fanny in," said Bobby, "You agree Dad?"

"I want my wife back, not that corpse," Jim pointed to Betty.

"OK, let's get over there, bring her back with us."

****

33.

Monday, June 19th 1995.
Fanny Legge's Cottage, Gatehouse Lane, North Wootton, King's Lynn, Norfolk.

Upon collecting Jim's Landrover from its parking lot in the Tuesday Market Place, a parking ticket had been affixed to the windshield. Tracy drove the Jaguar and tailed Bobby and Jim in the Landrover. The Jaguar had to be parked where the metalled road ended due to the numerous and deep potholes. Tracy and Laura then got into the Landrover. Lurching and swaying, Bobby driving, they travelled down the lane between the tall hedgerows, seeking Fanny Legge's cottage.

Despite familiarity with the locality, they had difficulty in locating the house, finally coming across it after several attempts and having to reverse long distances along the uneven surface several times. The geese immediately began creating a noise. Dozens of cats emerged from hiding places. The donkey began braying incontinently. Of the dog there was no sign. Jim braved the attacks of the geese to approach the front porch. An old brass knocker was attached to the decaying door, ivy and wisteria entwined over the roof of the wooden structure.

The door swung open on Jim's insistent knocking. "Anybody home?" called Jim, leaning in. He repeated the call several times.

The tiny lounge was deserted, old fashioned antimacassars covered the two leather-backed armchairs. A damask tablecloth concealed a rickety table surface and rag-rugs covered the floor. A vast dog basket occupied a position in the far corner of the room with blankets rumpled inside. A staircase rose from the rear of the room, the steps narrow and curving upwards. A brass table lamp gleamed on the old dresser.

Jim repeated his call," Anybody home?" His voice echoed dully.

A huge spider scuttled across the dresser and down the side, it ran across the thick carpet and climbed the leg of the rickety table, squatting on the tablecloth, observing him. The bank of eight eyes gleamed. Jim shuddered, the arachnid was at least six inches across It arched its legs, adding another dimension. The spider showed no fear, merely observing him as it sat motionless, from its position on the table top.

Jim beat a retreat, the spider turning to watch his exit. "Nobody in, save a huge spider on the table," announced Jim, "The dog's missing too. She must be out."

"Damnation!" cursed Bobby, "Now what do we do?"

"You go, I'll wait, see if she turns up," said Jim, "You have a business to run."

"How're you going to get back? It's a long leg to the village."

Bobby looked uncertain, "She might be gone for hours, looking for herbs, plants or whatever?"

"Ask Ellen or Kevin to come for me if I'm not back in a couple of hours."

"You sure you going to be OK?" Bobby looked round uncertainly.

The vast expanse of the marsh was visible at the end of the unmade road between the hedgerows. Despite the hot sunshine the place looked bleak and forbidding.

"Looks spooky," said Laura, shivering.

"Off you go, don't forget to ask Ellen to come for me in a couple of hours" Jim insisted.

Bobby turned the Landrover in the narrow lane and headed off towards the village. The instant the swaying vehicle passed round a bend in the unmade road the geese ceased their harsh cries, the donkey its braying. The sun was hot, the sky an unbroken blue from end to end of the vast horizon. Birds twittered from the tall hedges either side of the rutted pathway. Jim was reluctant to admit it to himself, but Laura's observation was valid. The place was spooky, the marsh was a forbidding environment at its best. He'd spent most of his life aware of the wide expanses of sea and sky on the marsh in all weathers. In the winter the east winds howled across the flat land, snow came down horizontally. Hawthorn hedges leaned away from the raw winds coming in from the North Sea. Sea birds haunted the sky with eerie cries. The stillness of the summer day did not diminish the feeling of implacable hostility the face of the marsh presented to all.

He wasn't conscious of time passing. The hot sun, the lack of shade seemed to be urging him to abandon his vigil, flee the unfriendly surroundings back to civilised society. He felt as if unseen eyes observed him from every angle, watching, waiting for some signal to subdue his countryman's confidence. He consulted his watch, having made up his mind to relinquish his assignation. The watch had stopped. Ridiculous he thought, the battery was virtually new. It had stopped at 3.00 pm as far as he could determine, the time Bobby and Tracy had left him to return to Lynn. He shook it and held it to his ear. No response. It wasn't as if it was a cheap instrument, it had been a birthday present from Betty only a couple of years before. From the look of the position of the sun in the sky, he'd spent over an hour already, waiting for Funny Fanny.

"Damn the thing." He gave it another shake, the second hand refused to budge.

He was about to depart when a voice, almost in his ear said "Hello Mr Lewin, what brings you to my home?"

Fanny stood behind him, the enormous wolfhound, Darren, by her side. He hadn't heard her approach, it was as if she had suddenly appeared.

She was clad as usual in long black skirt, clogs on bare feet, her usual blouse and shawl around her shoulder. Her raven dark hair parted in the middle, hanging on her shoulders. The massive wolfhound stood beside her, yellow eyes appearing malevolent hostile.

"I've come to ask your help," said Jim, avoiding looking at her.

Those black eyes seemed to be able to penetrate, like lasers.

"You mean Miss Summerfield and your wife?"

Jim tried to hide his astonishment. The woman's uncanny ability to read minds was seismic. He nodded, dumbly, "If you are concerned about Anglia TV filming yourself and your cottage, I can promise you that nothing I have done contributed to that suggestion. I don't like that kind of exposure and I can readily understand your dislike of people prying into lives."

"That is reassuring Mr Lewin."

Jim saw a flicker of movement from the direction of the gate to the cottage garden. The next instant, the massive spider had climbed up her skirt and was sitting on her shoulder. Fanny reached up and stroked the furry back gently.

"Will you help?" Jim was at a loss for words. His mind seemed to be a confused jumble of impressions, nothing logical, as if an outside agency was controlling his thoughts.

"There is a great deal of ill-will being directed at me, Mr Lewin. The more people who benefit from my skills, the greater the hostility it seems to generate. The men of God are implacable in their hatred of me because it threatens their dogma. They believe that only their God is permitted to perform so-called miracles."

"They are trying to protect their beliefs, as fragile as they might appear to non-believers. You appear to threaten their concepts of good and evil. They are frightened of you."

"The men of medicine also feel ill-will because my methods do not rely on drugs. Why should I incur more antagonism by helping people?"

"It seems I've made a wasted journey, I am sorry Miss Legge."

Jim turned away, despairing. Betty was doomed. The corpse-like figure in that cubicle in Longley Hill Casualty would gradually deteriorate into death along with Holly Summerfield in Barry Lassiter's clinic.

"A moment please, Mr Lewin."

The wolfhound bounded round Jim and stood in front of him barring his route. Its yellow eyes seemed to glow like hot cinders.

Jim turned, the spider was sitting on top of Fanny's head like some obscene headpiece. "I will come with you, see what I can do. I won't promise anything though."

She reached up, the spider scuttled down her arm onto the ground and ran for the tall hedgerow. Jim noticed she was as tall as he, slender and willowy with a grace that only wind-blown grass posesses. She matched his step too. He also noticed her clogged feet made no sound on the dusty road. His footsteps clumped at each step, sending up little clouds of dust from the dry earth. They must have walked side by side for about half a mile, when Jim saw the Landrover bouncing over potholes heading toward them.

"We can ride now Miss Legge," he said, wiping perspiration from his forehead, "It'll be more comfortable."

It was Kevin driving with Ellen beside him. The bandage around the young man's head was slightly soiled. The Landrover came to a stop beside them, sending up a dust cloud.

Ellen jumped out," You alright Dad? Helllo Miss Legge, hello Darren." She held out her hand to the dog, it came up to her nuzzle her.

Kevin slid out of the driving seat, "We heard about Mom, Bobby and the others are at the hospital with her," He nodded at Fanny.

"Can you help my Mother please Miss Legge? "asked Ellen, still fondling the dog's ears.

"I will see what I can do Mrs Wilson," Fanny seemed to glide as Ellen opened the rear door for her. Darren jumped into the rear with her and stretched out near the tailgate.

"See if I can turn this buggy round," said Kevin, "It's going to be tight, there's hardly enough room."

The vehicle seemed to have a life of its own to Jim.

"Well I'll be buggered," exclaimed Kevin, "Must have a magic set of controls, I didn't think we'd get round."

Jim cast a sly look at Fanny sitting beside him. Her eyes were closed, she seemed to be sleeping, but her lips were moving. There was something extraordinary about the way the huge car had manoeuvred in that limited area.

"Doesn't seem to be as bumpy this way," said Ellen.

"My lousy driving," said Kevin.

"Why don't you remove that bandage Mr Wilson," Fanny spoke softly. Everybody heard her over the sound of the engine.

"The wound isn't healed yet Miss Legge," said Kevin.

"It is!" She replied.

Ellen looked round, startled, "But it's all raw Miss Legge. It will start bleeding again."

Fanny shook her head, "Try it now."

Kevin braked, "Go ahead, see if the lady's right. Needs a new dressing anyway."

Ellen gently unwound the soiled bandage. There was no sign of a wound.

"But... but, it was all red this morning," stammered Ellen, as Kevin used the rear view mirror to take a look.

"Jesus, that was quick, must be those drugs the quack gave me." Kevin parted his hair to confirm his findings.

"I don't think even they could have cured that cut in the time darling," said Ellen, "I think we have Miss Legge to thank for this. Thank you Miss Legge, we do appreciate it."

"Thank you Miss Legge," Kevin echoed, "It's miraculous."

Jim was equally astonished by further evidence of Fanny's incredible powers, despite having witnessed Wally Thompson rescued from the grave in his ward at Longley Hill. It merely validated his belief that Fanny Legge could help Betty recover from whatever was ailing her.

Kevin re-started the Landrover. They emerged onto the metalled part of Gatehouse Lane and made good time to Longley Hill. Darren, the wolfhound was left in the Landrover. Jim locked the door to ensure no curious person was tempted to get at the dog. They entered Reception and asked to see Mrs Lewin. They were told that Betty was in an Intensive Care unit and they would have to gain Dr Petit's permission.

"Hi there Kev, Elly, Dad," Bobby stood behind them, looking grim. He stared at Fanny Legge incredulously. She returned his stare until he was forced to lower his gaze, "Tracy and Laura are with Betty in the IC unit."

"How is she?" asked Jim.

"I just don't believe what I'm seeing, she looks like hundred years old, like a mummy, except for no bandages. Is this your work Miss Legge? Are you punishing my mother for taking that Anglia TV woman to see you? I hope you're pleased with yourself."

"Bobby!" rasped Jim, "That's enough, Miss Legge has consented to see what she can do for Betty. We don't need recriminations."

"Mumsy was OK this morning Dad. The doctors here haven't a clue what's wrong and she's sliding fast. Someone or something is responsible for her condition and I bet it was her." He pointed an accusatory finger at Fanny.

"I'd better leave Mr Lewin," said Fanny, "Your son is antagonistic and upset. I couldn't do anything in this hateful atmosphere, I will go."

"Please Miss Legge, I beg you, my son is very fond of his Mother. He's upset at seeing her like this, he doesn't mean to be aggressive. Apologise to Miss Legge, Bobby."

"That bloody witch caused Mumsy's condition. No way am I going to apologise to her for something she brought on."

"I'm sorry Mr Lewin," Fanny began walking away.

Jim ran after her and grabbed her shawl. Even he couldn't believe the evidence of his eyes. There was nothing in his grasp. No material, no wollen fabric, nothing, save empty air.

****

34.

Monday June 19th 1995.
Reception Area, Longley Hill Hospital,
King's Lynn, Norfolk.

Everybody witnessed the incredible sight of Jim's hand travelling through empty air when he should have been grasping coarse woollen fabric. Jim made another attempt at grasping the shawl, bewildered by the result of his first try.

"Please Mr Lewin," pleaded Fanny, moving away.

"Don't go Miss Legge," cried Jim, terrified.

"What's going on here?" came a voice behind them.

Doctors Petit and Lassiter had come into Reception. Attention was diverted from Fanny to the two doctors.

"Who's that woman?" Petit pointed to where Fanny stood well back.

"That's Mrs Legge, the person I was telling you about Adam, said Lassiter.

The younger man stared at Fanny for a long moment, "What's she doing here?" he rasped

"I asked her to have a look at my wife, Doctor," Jim was still bemused at the way his hand had clutched thin air instead of Fanny's shawl.

"I forbid it!" Petit was adamant, "If that woman makes any attempt at treating my patient using any unacceptable or unorthodox methods, I refuse to accept any responsibility for your wife's condition, that's final."

"Do you know what's wrong with her yet?" demanded Jim, hurt by the aggression in Petit's manner.

"We are conducting tests, we've taken biopsy samples to the path lab, should be back soon. We can then determine the nature of this unfortunate condition," said Petit, confidently.

"For Christ sake man, my Mother's condition is deteriorating fast, can't you do something urgently?" cried Bobby, "We can't afford the time for all this medical garbage."

"If I haven't the vaguest idea what's wrong with Mrs Lewin, how can I carry out treatment? You must be patient Mr Lewin."

"What a bloody mess," snarled Bobby, "A bunch of incompetents, plus a witch, it's worse than a sit-com."

"That's not fair Bobby," protested Lassiter, "Neither myself, nor Adam here have experienced this complaint before. As far as I am aware there is no precedent for this premature ageing."

"Let Fanny have a look at Mother, Bobby," said Kevin, mildly, "See my head?" He inclined his head towards Bobby.

Bobby didn't bother to look, "I don't want that bloody witch farting around my Mother at all."

"Why don't you give your arse a chance brother?" Ellen stood in front of him, "Look at Bobby's head for Christ sake. Half an hour ago it was a raw wound, six inches long, can you see a wound now? Even his hair has been restored over the shaven bit."

Bobby deigned to glance at Kevin's head, his mouth dropping open as he did so.

"Miss Legge was responsible, she did this in the Landrover coming from her cottage," Ellen looked furious, "You take a look as well."

She directed the two medics, "She might be a witch but she has power that you'll never have."

Petit took a cursory glance, then he gaped, "Impossible," he said, stuttering. "It's an illusion, I did the stitching on that wound yesterday, put eighteen stitches into it, it's impossible."

"I've been telling you Adam, that that woman..." He pointed, then stopped in mid sentence, "Where is she?"

They all looked to where Fanny had been standing, she wasn't there.

"Did you see that woman leave?" demandeed Petit of the Receptionist.

The woman shrugged, "I didn't Doctor, I was too busy listening to you," She looked resentful.

"It's your fault you stupid man," roared Jim at his son, "You've probably condemned your Mother. If you hadn't got your bowels in an uproar she'd have cured her, I'm sure."

****

35.

Monday June 19th 1995.
Holding's Hill Hospital,
King's Lynn, Norfolk.

"She bloody well caused her condition in the first place Dad, and you know it. You want her farting around with her again?"

"This lot can't do anything for her it seems. Fanny was our best hope."

"Oh, come on Dad, you're worse than Kevin and his Wizard Society, bunch of bloody freaks all tarted up in funny gear incanting to the moon, or whatever."

"How do you account for Kevvy's wound being healed then, asshole?" screamed Ellen, "Your trouble is that you can't see farther than the end of your nose, typical bloody solicitor. A gang of bookworms, you're worse than witches."

In seconds a blazing row was in progress amongst the members of the Lewin family. The other patients in Casualty were listening to the entertainment with mixed responses. Some horrified, angry, amused and dismayed. The scenario was brought to an abrupt end by an ambulance arriving. The two paramedics who had attended Betty at the Globe hotel entered pushing a stretchered trolley.

"Doctor!" called the young paramedic, "You need to treat this one urgent, major infarction, we have him oxygen."

There was no mistaking the patient on the stretcher. The thick greying hair was a give away, Johnny Foster, one time building contractor-cum-used car dealer. His girl friend, who had been with him in the Globe was by his side, sobbing in a distraught condition.

"Is he going to die Doctor?" she moaned, between sobs.

Petit and Lassiter jerked themselves back to reality.

"Into theatre please," ordered Petit after a brief examination of Foster, "Excuse me Mr Lewin, I'm needed."

"What about my wife?" rasped Jim.

"As soon as the results of the biopsy come from the lab, I promise," Petit's attention was focussed on Foster.

Bobby's ill humour mutated to irony at the sight of Foster being rushed into the operating theatre.

"So much for his keep fit routine," he mocked.

Ellen, Tracy and Laura were attempting to comfort the distressed Marie Richards, Foster's girl friend.

"I'd keep that big mouth of yours shut sonny, you've done enough damage for one day as it is," advised Ellen.

Bobby shrugged and nettled, "The woman's gone now anyway," he muttered.

"All your damn fault mister," snorted Ellen, trying to pacify Marie.

"Shouldn't we call Jeannie?" Tracy appealed to Ellen.

"I don't want his wife here," shouted Marie, "She's a useless bitch, just wring her hands, moan, be a nuisance."

"Can you give me some details about your friend Miss… er?" asked the Receptionist.

Bobby gave the details laconically.

"I'm going to see Betty," said Jim.

"You can't go in there without permission Mr Lewin," The Receptionist was stiff, "You'll need protective clothing and a mask."

"Better not Dad, we don't want to make matters worse for Mumsy, do we?" said Ellen, leaving Marie with Tracy and Laura.

"What matters?"

Jim's mind went blank with shock. He stared doubting the evidence of his eyes. Everybody stood, frozen in stunned amazement. Betty stood at the entrance to Casualty, clad in patient's gown, trailing drip tubes, her feet bare. She looked perfectly normal, no trace of the awesome ageing that had defaced her appearance but a short time before. Jim was the first to recover, rushing to his wife, clasping her in his arms murmuring inanities of welcome. Betty seemed equally surprised by the attention she was getting as Bobby, Ellen, Tracy, Laura and Kevin all gathered round still shocked by her appearance.

"What's all the fuss, you lot?" Betty was pleased, if surprised by the attention she was receiving. Marie Richards was forgotten.

"You alright love?" gasped Jim, searching her face, unable to keep his hands off her.

"Of course I'm alright Jimbo, why shouldn't I be? There's nothing wrong with me. What am I doing in hospital? Where are my clothes?" Betty looked down at the high-necked white gown.

"But you were in an intensive care unit Mumsy," cried Bobby, shaken by his mother's return from an imaginary grave.

"Don't you remember being taken ill in the Globe, Grandma?" cried Laura.

"The last thing I remember is sitting in the restaurant with you all," said Betty.

"You were ill, we had to call an ambulance Mother," Tracy was pale with shock.

"Well, as you can see you must have all been mistaken. Fancy bringing me here, upsetting all the hospital routine over nothing."

They heard the receptionist talking agitatedly to someone on the phone, saying there was a patient in casualty just released herself from an IC Unit. Petit arrived a few seconds later, he stopped as if struck by a fist, looking dumbfounded at Betty. His mouth opened and closed soundlessly, trying to articulate something.

"It's impossible," he managed at last, "You must go back at once Mrs Lewin, you are dangerously ill."

"What on earth is he on about Jimbo? I'm just fine, I want my clothes please. I can't walk around like this forever," said Betty.

Petit felt her pulse and put his hand on her forehead, "I must be dreaming," he muttered, shaking his head, "I shall wake up in a moment."

"You really feel alright Mumsy?" Bobby was still gawping at the sight of his mother completely recovered.

"Of course I do, I don't know what all the fuss is about."

"But you looked a hundred years old only a short time ago."

"Can I have my clothes please Doctor? I want to go home."

Lassiter arrived at the scene, and stood stock still, staring incredulously.

"I don't understand it Lassiter," said Doctor Petit, "This woman was in an advanced senile state a short while ago. She's as normal as any sixty year old can be now."

"Did that Legge woman visit her?" demanded Lassiter.

Everybody had forgotten about Fanny Legge.

"She just disappeared Doctor Lassiter," said the receptionist, "One minute she standing over there, then she wasn't."

"Did Mrs Legge visit you Mrs Lewin?" demaned Lassiter.

Betty shrugged, "I've no recollection of any visitors, how long have I been in here? Hours? Days? Weeks?"

"A few hours love," Jim hugged her, "I can't believe this."

"Join the Club Lewin," said Petit, "If I wasn't witnessing it first hand I would declare it an impossibility."

"I did suggest that there was more to that woman than mere witchcraft Adam, I believe this will convince you now."

"If she has that kind of gift why haven't we made use of her? It would truly put Longley Hill on the map, we'd be famous world-wide." Petit brushed his thick hair back from his forehead.

"You don't know that it was Miss Legge's doing," said Jim, "She wasn't very keen to come and try when I approached her this morning."

"We need that woman Barry," said Petit, "She's worth a million in funding. If she can perform these miracles at will we may have a whole new ball game to contend with. We need to know how she does it, get her to train others, it could revoloutionise medicine as we know it. Where does she live? We must contact her urgently."

"Before you depart into your fantasy world Doctor, do you think we could have my wife's clothes?" Jim was pragmatic.

"Where does she live?" Petit was still in a Walter Mitty world of speculation, "I must go and talk to her, see if she would be willing to teach others her skills. The Department of Health would pay her a fortune for this knowledge, well worth it also."

"Phone call for you Doctor Lassiter, from your clinic. The lady says it's urgent."

Lassiter hurried over to the desk, "Yes sister, what is it? I pay you a handsome salary to handle emergencies… very well… tell me. If this is a joke…. I repeat, Sister if this is a joke… Put her on then. Is that really you Miss Summerfield?"

Lassiter had gone pale. The hand holding the phone shook, "You are alright? But, I don't understand, you suffered a minor stroke. It is unheard of to overcome the effects in such a short time, if ever. I would like to examine you… no not here… very well if you insist. See you shortly."

"What's the problem Barry?" Petit was anxious.

"A patient, Miss Summerfield, the Anglia TV reporter, suffered a minor stroke this morning, she was incapable of speech, a lack of motor responses and serious impairment of mobility. Anyway, that was her on the phone, says she fit and well. She's coming over here with her head of programmes for me to examine her." Lassiter shook his head, "I feel bewildered, these miracles are too much for me, I think I must be losing my reason."

The receptionist beckoned to Petit, "Sister on Agnes Ward, would like you to go there urgently Doctor, she says she can't handle it., sounds a little hysterical."

"Let me have Legge's address before you leave Mr Lewin, "Petit shouted as he hurried from Casualty.

"I want my clothes," wailed Betty, "and I want to go home."

Lassiter gave instructions to a passing nurse to locate Betty's clothes.

"Where did she go?" asked Bobby, of nobody in particular, "Did you see Jim's hand when he touched her shawl?"

"Optical illusion," said Kevin, "We thought we saw something, it happens frequently in times of stress."

"Very observant Doctor Wilson," said Ellen, "Can you explain how Mother recovered?"

Kevin looked embarrassed.

It took them a few seconds to recognise the patient, clad in hospital dressing gown who arrived at the reception desk.

"It's Mr Murphy isn't it?" Jim went up to him, "How are you?"

Then he remembered and stared again at the Irishman, "Didn't you come in here with a severe coronary?"

Murphy turned, "Sure I did, Mr Lewin isn't it? Remember you from the farm, that bloody crypt. Nobody believed me about those noises, kept on telling me it was me imagination. I know I heard them ghosts, I told that reporter when he came to see me. Says he's goin' to have it in the paper tomorrow, about the ghosts. He took some photos of me."

Jim tried to remain deadpan, "Should you be walking around like this with a heart condition Mr Murphy? Does Doctor Petit know you're up and about?"

"For God's Sake man, you're asking for trouble walking around like this," Lassiter approached, "Who gave you permission to get up?"

Murphy looked hurt, "But I'm OK now Doc, I feel fine."

"But you suffered a major infarction Mr Murphy, you could bring it in again," stuttered Lassiter, "Have you any chest pains? Or feel tight across your shoulders?"

Murphy shook his head, "Right as rain Doc. I wanna get out of this place, never did like hospitals, the wife'll be going spare."

"I think you ought to wait until Doctor Petit has seen you, examined you Mr Murphy. You don't want to be brought in here again do you?" Lassiter was only half hearted, his mind still on the subject of Summerfield's miraculous recovery.

A taxi arrived outside reception. They all saw Holly Summerfield get out. With her was Richard Cheeseman, Programme Dirctor of Anglia TV. Murphy was forgotten in the rush of excitement as patients recognised her from appearances on the television. Lassiter rushed over to her, trying hard to find some symptom that would confirm his worst fears.

****

36.

Monday January 19th 1995.
Holding's Hill Hospital,
King's Lynn, Norfolk.

"I'm fine Doctor Lassiter, completely recovered, I assure you."

She saw the Lewins and Betty, she came over, leaving Cheeseman talking to Lassiter.

"Betty, what are you doing in that garb? You alright?" Bobby explained, "My God, did Legge have anything to do with it?"

Jim could see there was nothing unusual about the woman, she looked her normal polished self.

"We don't know, my Dad went to fetch her to see to her, but we got into a hassle on arriving here with the medical staff, she just vanished and we haven't seen her since."

"This is certainly crazy, the noises, the brass plaques, the weird history and cameras that won't work, film that didn't come out, that place is a collection of paranormal activity."

"I'm sure that Funny Fanny is warning you and us not to start filming her or her cottage, or anything about her. Your collapse was a warning what will happen if you attempt it," said Bobby.

"I'm inclined to agree with you Mr Lewin. I've been trying to talk Richard, my boss over there, not to go ahead. He's convinced I'm just a little overwrought and that my stroke was brought on by overwork, nothing to do with Fanny Legge. He's determined to go ahead, he reckons it's an opportunity not to be ignored."

"Did Fanny visit you? Work your cure?" asked Jim.

Summerfield shook her head, No "I just felt fine suddenly, as if all those feelings about being old were figments of my imagination. When I looked in the mirror I looked just as I am now, I could speak normally. The sister at the clinic got quite agitated and phoned Doctor Lassiter here, then I spoke to him."

"We heard," said Bobby, "He took the call at the desk over there."

Lassiter and Cheeseman came over, "I find it difficult to come to terms with your condition Miss Summerfield. You suffered a stroke, of that I am positive, now you're cured. Have you seen anything of Mrs Legge?"

"I see what you mean Doctor, but the answer is I haven't. I just felt fine suddenly, I could speak and the ageing had all disappeared. That's when your nurse phoned you, she was most distressed. I don't believe it's necessary for you to examine me. I am very fit as you can see."

"I trust we can commence filming on your property within the next few days Mr Lewin?" Cheeseman was anxious to be gone.

Jim shook his head, "I've changed my mind, in view of what happened to my wife and Miss Summerfield, I'm sure it was a warning."

"Oh come on Mr Lewin, I didn't take you for a superstitious person. You don't believe in all this paranormal rubbish, surely? It's all in the mind."

"You didn't see Miss Summerfield earlier today did you? Unable to speak, ageing before our eyes, paralysed."

"Brought on by pressure of work I assure you Mr Lewin. No connection with paranormal acts or the work of this Funny Fanny. I'm surprised at your attitude, businessman and all that. I had you fixed as an entrepreneur, willing to earn some substantial amounts of cash for the privilege of us filming on your property and around this St Mary's Church. I made the point that any damage ensuing would be compensated. The film rights are worth substantial amounts."

"Are you married Mr Cheeseman?"

"Not exactly, divorce proceedings sadly," Cheeseman didn't look upset.

"Any children?"

"Two, why the questions?" Cheeseman was irritated.

"How'd you like to see your son or daughter ageing before your eyes, in a matter of minutes growing old?"

"I see what you're implying Mr Lewin, but aren't you making more of this incident than necessary? I mean, witchcraft, a trifle bizarre in this day and age."

"If it's that bizarre why do you want to waste money filming it?" Jim decided he wasn't keen on Cheeseman. The patronising manner, as if he were of sub-normal intelligence, had to be humoured.

"Our viewers like strange stories, fairy tales, if you like. It takes them out of their mundane lives for a brief period, Mr Lewin. Our ratings soar, it's good for our shareholders. Some of them monitor our ratings, complain to the chairman if they drop."

"So it doesn't matter a damn if people suffer as long as your ratings rise?" Cheeseman coloured slightly.

"We aren't interested Mr Cheeseman," said Bobby, "And I'm sure your ace reporter would go along with that decision, in view of her experiences this morning?"

"She's paid to do a job, well paid, I might add. That right Holly? You haven't any inhibitions about the proposed programme have you?"

"Yes I have Richard, I was frightened a short time ago, badly frightened. Made me realise there are more things to worry about than ratings, deadlines and programmes," Summerfield was cold.

"Are you telling me you don't want anything to do with this proposed film?" Cheeseman's expression was hard.

"Correct Richard and if you'd been in my shoes you would feel the same."

"My God, siding with these peasants. You know you're up for an OBE don't you. How's that going to look if you shy away from some fairy tale about ghosts and spooks?"

"Personally I don't give a damn Richard. An accolade of that kind wouldn't compensate me for spending my life in a wheelchair."

"Aren't you over-reacting? We're all under pressure in this business. Just because you suffered a minor set-back through stress, doesn't mean you have to jeopardise your career prospects."

"I don't think this is the place in which to discuss my career, do you Richard?" snapped Holly.

"Let me make it crystal clear to you madame, if you're so insecure that one incident of a bizarre nature throws you, I think it's about time we had second thoughts about your continuing with Anglia in your present elevated position. If a few peasant types cane frighten you with fanciful tales about para-normal experiences, it doesn't auger well for future assignments. There's a list of people a mile long who'd enjoy jumping into your shoes."

"I've just one thing to say to you Richard, since you're so bloody pompous and insensitive to other people feelings, which I have to say, I always suspected, but blinded myself to the evidence."

"What might that be madame?"

"Go fuck yourself" Summerfield put two fingers under his nose in a rude gesture, "The Beeb pays better." She turned to Jim, "I'm sorry that this egomaniac assigns you to the mentally defective strata. I don't share his views and my advice is don't let any of these whizz-kids persuade you to film that crypt. It's a classic case of 'Dieux et mon droit', which roughly translated means 'Fuck you Jack, I'm fireproof! 'Bye Richard, enjoy yourself in that crypt."

Summerfield exited out into the summer sunshine. Cheeseman stood there, trying to look indifferent but not succeeding.

"That's told you me fine friend," Everyone had forgotten Murphy, "That lass has got more brains than you have."

Doctor Petit entered the hospital reception. With him was a tall man with grey crew cut hair, granite-featured. He was in a police uniform, silver braid in evidence. Petit was shaking his head bewilderedly. Jim recognised Ralph Mostin, Chief Constable of the Lynn Police Force.

"I can't understand this," wailed Petit, "The Chief was in traction a short time ago, in acute pain as a result of his accident in the Duke's Head Hotel. He says all the pain has gone and his back feels fine."

"'Tis the little people sir," said Paddy, "They do some strange things in Ireland."

"Well I wouldn't have agreed with you a short time ago Mr... what's your name?"

"Murphy sir, Paddy Murphy. The little people cured me a short time ago. You're not from the Old Country are you sir?"

Mostin smiled, "I've no doubt there's some Irish blood in my veins somewhere Mr Murphy and you may well be right about your Little People. Something happened to cure my bad back a short time ago. Couldn't move earlier. Hello Mr Lewin, Mrs Lewin? How are you both?" Mostin shook hands, "You're Mr Lewin the solicitor aren't you, Jim's son? And I know you from last year, Wilson isn't it? President of the Wizard Society, hold your solstice celebrations at Bawsey in a couple of days don't you? The local Bishop is objecting, quoting Blasphemy Laws, mediaeval stuff, taking it to court to restrain you this year. You'll have to call it off if he gets an injunction. Sorry about it Wilson, I've no objections, your group are always well behaved, no nuisance problems. Nice seeing you folks, see you around, must get on, business, you know?"

He walked out into the evening sunshine, his stance upright, no sign of any distress.

"We've had a surprising day eh Doctor Petit. Not the usual traumas, most of it pleasant, like Mr Murphy here and Mrs Lewin. See if the nurse has found your clothes Mrs Lewin and yours Mr Murphy. Not a very happy one for you Mr Cheeseman, losing your star reporter. Perhaps it might not be a bad idea to call off that programme about St Mary's. There's definitely something odd about that place, tempting Providence."

"How's Johnny Foster?" asked Jim curiously.

"Coronary I'm afraid, overweight and eating too much fatty food."

"He said he works out in his gymnasium everyday keeping fit."

Lassiter shrugged, "Wasn't enough, it seems to counteract the bad eating habits." He looked over at Kevin, "By the way Wilson, the Bishop has been on at me to close off the right of way to Bawsey the day after tomorrow, prevent access to the ruin for your Solstice celebrations. I'm sure you'll be delighted to know that I won't be doing as the Bishop has been asking. You are free to use the access as usual."

"That's very generous Doctor. We could make you an honorary member of the Society, you could join us at midnight," said Kevin.

"What happened too your bandage by the way? I understand you suffered a rather nasty wound?"

Kevin looked embarrassed, "Funny Fanny cured it en route from her cottage. Just told me to remove the bandage. Ellen did so and as you can see, no sign of any wound."

"I tell you Barry, we need that woman's expertise," said Petit, examining Kevin's head. "Incredible, I put sixteen stitches in that wound only yesterday, it should have taken at least a week to heal."

"I hate to have to tell you Doctor Petit, but the chances of your recruiting Miss Legge onto your staff here is very remote I would say," said Ellen. "I'm sorry for my rude remarks yesterday Doctor Lassiter, I was rather upset."

"That's generous of you Mrs Wilson, I accept your apology. I guess we have all been under some stress this last few weeks. Ah, here's nurse Smith with your clothes Mrs Lewin. You can use my office to change in. Looks like they're still locating yours Mr Murphy. Can we do anything for you Mr Cheeseman?"

The Anglia boss was looking very disgruntled, "Unless you can persuade Holly Summerfield to reconsider her resignation. We need her at Anglia, very popular with viewers, she is, she gets substantial fan mail every week."

Betty took her clothes from the nurse and headed for Lassiter's office.

"With respect Cheeseman, you weren't very diplomatic over this St Mary's Church business," said Lassiter, "Why don't you see her, make an apology?"

"I might have to do just that I suppose. You won't change your mind over our documentary then Mr Lewin?"

Jim shook his head, "It would be tempting Fanny to take reprisals as I see it and I'm not prepared to risk it."

Cheeseman shrugged, "Pity, could have made yourself a nice nest egg. You're going to have more offers when that article of Calhoun's appears in the local rag tomorrow. I guess Jeff Patten has syndicated it. I predict that many of the nationals will take it up. You'll have to be prepared for an invasion of media people tomorrow."

"Surely they won't bother with a wild story as this must appear in such a remote location?"

Cheeseman gave a grin, "The occult has a fascination for everybody Lewin. This is rich meat for them. An exclusive with Anglia would have prevented a great deal of agro for you. However, I comprehend your reasons having seen Holly's condition earlier, I can see your worries. That lady has created quite a stir. Nothing to what it's going to be like over the next few days, I have to tell you. I'll be on my way, see if I can intercept Holly before she contacts the Beeb, see you around. If you should change your mind, here's my card. Phone me, I'll take it from there. I must stress that you'll have to make up your minds quickly."

"I'll think about it, but right now the answer is 'No.'"

Cheeseman shook hands all round and walked out of the main entrance. Jim put the card in his shirt pocket as Betty emerged from Lassiter's office fully dressed.

"Let's all go home shall we?" he said to the family.

"Sure you're feeling OK Mumsy?" asked Bobby.

"Fine," Betty assured him.

"Ring us if you need us."

Betty nodded, "Sorry to have put you to all this trouble."

"Hey, that's what families are for Mumsy," Bobby gave her a hug.

"Come on you lot, let's go home."

"Hope you get on alright with your wife Mr Murphy," said Betty

"I hope also that your experience won't put you off working on the renovations at the church?"

"I'm not superstitious ma'am," grinned Murphy, "'cept when the Little People move in! No doubt Mr Farraday will be restarting in a day or so. Mick Reilly and me need the money, not to mention Fred Boxall. He's got a whopping mortgage, can't afford to be off work too long."

They all exited together.

"You look fine love," said Jim as they reached the Landrover

"Hello, that's funny."

"What is?"

"Fanny's dog was in here when we arrived. I locked the door to be on the safe side, how did she let him out?"

"You didn't lock it love, you must have forgot in the excitement," said Betty.

"Definitely recall doing it. I didn't want some asshole opening the door and letting it out."

"If she can cure Wally Thompson and your back, Bill Watson and Holly Summerfield's hand, a mere door lock isn't going to present her with much of a problem," said Betty. "It's not here and I'm hungry, let's go home, you can worry about it later."

****

37.

Monday June 19th 1995.
Lewin's Farm, Babingley Marsh,
King's Lynn, Norfolk.

"Isn't that Harry Farraday's car?" Betty pointed to the driveway as they approached the farmhouse.

A silver Mercedes was parked in the drive. They could see the silhouettes of two people inside.

"I could do without him tonight," groused Jim.

"We can't very well avoid him, he'll have seen us by now," said Betty, as they pulled up alongside the Mercedes.

Farraday got out of the driving seat on seeing the Landrover approach, "Couldn't get you on the phone, you must have it off the hook mate," he said, "Hi Betty, heard about you being in dock, you okay now?"

"What's the problem Harry? Wouldn't it keep until tomorrow? We've had a long day."

"Sorry about that Jimbo, I just had to let you know that I'm handing over the church contract to Masons, I'm copping out. They will be coming round tomorrow to take a look and do a survey of what's needed."

"For Christ sake Harry, that means we'll have to go through all this contract work again, what's the problem?"

"You know what happened in that crypt, Paddy sick with his heart attack. Fred Boxall and the lads are refusing to work in the place because of what's been happening there."

A woman got out of the Mercedes came over. "Hello Fiona, "Betty wasn't too delighted to see Farraday's wife, "How are you?"

"How are you my dear, more to the point. Harry and I heard you'd been taken ill in the Globe, got you to Holding's Hill in an ambulance. What was wrong?"

Fiona was tall, slim, dark haired with a wide mouth and her special feature, large brown eyes. The dress must have come from an expensive boutique, Betty decided.

Fiona was examining Betty's modest clothing with disdain, "Minor tummy upset, that was all, "Betty had a job concealing her dislike.

Fiona's eyes opened wide, aware that these were her best feature, "And they took you in for that? My God, no wonder the NHS is under pressure. I don't mean that nastily Elizabeth, but I would have thought they could have sorted it out for you easily, without resorting to hospital."

"Well you know how it is, they always err on the worst side."

To have told Fiona the truth would have been worse than telling Lilly Simpson. The two women held coffee mornings for the sole purpose of disseminating gossip.

"All's well that ends well is what I say," Fiona gave a false smile.

"Stop rabbitting love," said Harry, all too aware of the antagonism between his wife and Betty.

"I saw Paddy a short time ago Harry. He's up and about, keen to get back on the job," said Jim, "So what's Fred got his bowels in an uproar about?"

"You saw him up and about?" Farraday was incredulous, "The last I heard he would be out of action for months after that major heart attack."

"Saw a ghost didn't he Harry?" Fiona hated being left out, "I heard your old church is haunted, corpses groaning, something about Dracula sucking blood."

'Pity he didn't suck you dry, thought Betty uncharitably'. "Superstitious humbug," said Betty.

"You heard it didn't you Harry? Down in that crypt on Saturday, when Paddy had his heart attack. You heard the groans and screams and you saw a plaque on the coffin, something about Funny Fanny buried in the crypt? That's what caused Paddy Murphy's heart attack. You weren't telling me a tale were you?" She glared accusingly at her husband.

'Oh Christ' Jim moaned to himself, 'if Harry told this cow, Lilly will have heard all about it. I could kill that Fred Boxall opening his big mouth in the 'Rising Sun' on Saturday, and that creep Calhoun, and when the Advertiser comes out tomorrow… God, what a mess'.

"I'm not too sure what I saw now love," said Harry.

"Changing your story are you? You told me you heard groans and saw a plaque on a coffin with Funny Fanny's name on it and then Murphy had his heart attack. Don't want to upset people is that it?"

"That's enough," snarled Farraday, becoming rattled, "It's easy to believe things in moments of stress."

"Lilly told me the Bishop and Reverend Gates came to see you about these paranormal experiences, is that right Elizabeth?

They're not too happy about your son-in-law and those weird people, wizards holding their rites up at Bawsey the day after tomorrow, midsummer day, and Dulcie Spragg said that this Funny Fanny had cured Wally Thompson by witchcraft, incanting over him, made him drink frog spawn in blood and now he's walking around cured. There should be a law against people like this Funny Fanny, as if anybody could cure lung cancer."

Fiona prattled on about the tales bandied around the table during coffee that morning at Lilly Simpson's house. She enjoyed every minute of glory. Harry was becoming increasingly agitated and angry at his wife's insensitivity.

"Let's go," he interrupted Fiona in full flood about exorcism and unclean spirits, lost souls, purgatory, frog spawn in blood.

"Eh?" Fiona stopped her rabbitting, "Go? Go where?"

"Home you silly bitch, you're upsetting Betty and Jim by all this occult crap. Now give it a rest, come on, we're going."

He pulled Fiona by her sleeve, "I'm sorry about the renovation work Jimbo, but I can't afford having my blokes hanging around whingeing about ghosts and doing no work. Masons will do a grand job for you."

"I want to tell Elizabeth about Mr Calhoun's hand, got it burnt by a demon in the crypt," protested Fiona.

"Some other time love, "Harry raised his eyes heavenwards, still pulling the protesting Fiona towards the Mercedes.

"God what a cow!" breathed Jim as Harry drove off, Fiona still trying to talk through the open passenger window.

"She might as well have a megaphone in the market tomorrow. It'll be all over Lynn by now," said Betty, as they entered the house. "Shall we put the phone back on?"

"It won't stop ringing love, leave it, I couldn't cope with that tonight. Jesus, what a day."

"And yesterday, two days of it and it'll get worse tomorrow when the Advertiser comes out. We must make sure the main gate's closed in the morning, discourage the rabble coming to gape at the ghosts and demons."

"Let's have something to eat, you must be starving," Jim went into the kitchen and put the kettle on the Aga.

"There's some steak in the fridge, if you hang about I'll do it for us with some onions."

"You sit down I'll do it love. You had me worried this morning, thought I'd lost you, you sure you didn't see Fanny?"

"The only thing I remember is feeling ill in the Globe and the ambulance, vaguely. What's Fanny got to do with anything?"

"I don't want to alarm you," Jim began preparing a meal.

"Tell me," commanded Betty.

Jim related the events that had transpired during the day, the frightening appearance of ageing. Betty listened, only half believing him, aware that her husband wouldn't exaggerate.

"You actually brought Fanny to the hospital from her cottage?"

"That young fellow, Petit got all stroppy, he said he'd refuse responsibility for you if I brought Fanny in."

"I suppose you can understand his point of view it would be like bringing in the witch doctor. Then what happened?"

"Fanny disappeared, vanished into thin air and then you walked out cured, along with Paddy Murphy and Ralph Mostin, the rest you know. It just had to be Fanny Legge's work. Petit and Barry Lassiter were running around like scalded cocks, hadn't a clue what to do, talking about biopsies, blood tests and all the other medical clap-trap. I reckon it was a warning to us on Fanny's part, not to have Anglia filming her place and inside the church. There's something definitely odd about that woman. No records of Legge's in Lynn since 1796,was it? And then all those people dying in 1918, the whole congregation inside three days. I'm beginning to wonder whether it wouldn't be a good idea to sell up, move out somewhere normal, I'm getting fed up with all this paranormal crap."

"I don't want to leave here Jimbo," Betty made tea as the kettle whistled, "Ellen and Bobby are close by, we're still a family, we'd only see them on odd occasions, Christmas and holidays."

The odour of frying onions spread through the kitchen, the steak sizzled in the pan.

"I don't mean miles away, probably Gaywood, Wootton Road, or somewhere like that. We don't need this place any longer."

"But we've lived her since we were married Jimbo, I love this place. I don't want to move to some suburb with all the neighbours having coffee mornings, like Lilly Simpson and Harry's wife Dulcie Spragg, it would be awful."

"But you'd have more free time not all the mess we have to put up with, the animals, chickens, geese, mud all the time over the carpets."

"I like it Jimbo, please no more talk of moving. All this will blow over and we'll be back to normal again," Betty poured two mugs of tea and handed one to Jim.

"It won't blow over love. The minute the Advertiser appears tomorrow we'll be inundated with freaks, newspaper reporters and as soon as the old church has been renovated there'll be people coming all the time, apart from the freak value it will gain as a result of these weird goings on. And you have to admit they are weird, the cold inside that place, the plaque that keeps on appearing on that catafalque, the ley-lines and all that razzamatazz. It certainly won't go away."

"Let's encourage it Jimbo, charge five quid to enter the crypt, five quid a car to park in the field," Betty warmed to her idea of a tourist attraction. "We could make a fortune out of ghosts, demons and crypts, all good stuff for the unwashed."

"You kidding?" Jim was astounded at Betty's enterprising ideas.

Betty sat at the kitchen table and watched Jim cooking the food, while sipping her tea. "We advertise in the nationals, make this place a tourist mecca, real live ghosts. We could even apply for permission to build a hotel."

"On the Hump of course?" Jim was caustic, he switched the light on. Dusk was advancing, exposing one of Norfolk's spectacular sunsets, the red sky giving an unnatural glow over the fields.

"That could be an additional attraction, get them to enter the Hump so their cameras don't work, like those Anglia ones yesterday, remember Freda? Having to bring Wally out every time she wouldn't start. We could even run a competition, a thousand pounds to run their cars over the Hump without stopping."

"You're serious, love?"

Jim sliced the steaks from the pan and arranged them on plates, with onions and vegetables.

"Of course, why not? Lots of hotels advertise their ghosts with far less validity than ours, we could make a feature of it. Ladies in diaphanous nightdresses wandering around the corridor in the middle of the night."

"Eat that, you'll feel better love," said Jim, sitting down. "Your imagination's overheating."

"Could rival Beulieu, Alton Towers, Chessington."

"Alright Mrs Gulbenkian, let's not get carried away with pipe dreams, huh?

Without warning the lights went out. "This is all we need a bloody power cut. Christ will it never end?" moaned Jim.

"Put the generator on love, I'm sure it won't last long."

Jim went cautiously to the welsh dresser to retrieve the torch, "Back in a mo, shove the food in the oven, keep it warm."

Betty slid the two plates into the Aga oven, feeling her way cautiously around the kitchen. A brilliant flash lit the sky suddenly, followed by others in quick succession.

'Lightning', was Betty's first thought. She fumbled her way to the back door and stared outside. Stars glittered in the sky and a half moon hung like a cheese in the eastern sky. Not the slightest evidence of a breeze. The flashes occurred again, stabbing forks of electric energy, there was something odd about them. She was puzzled, no thunder followed the flashes, the sky was cloudless. The blue pulses lit up the countryside, highlghting trees and buildings. She could even see the outlines of the Estate on Slade. The suddenly it struck her, the flashes were horizontal, not vertical as lightning should be. Darkness followed, blacker for the lack of illumination. She moved cautiously further out from the doorway to widen her vision. The next series lit up the church tower and the shattered roof with Farraday's scaffolding plainly visible.

"Did you see that?" Jim came out of the house, a large torch in his hand, "It's affecting Slade as well. No lights on over there. It's coming from the direction of the church."

"What's the matter with the generator? Didn't you switch it on?"

"Bloody thing won't work, must need a service or something."

"Damn, could be hours before the electricity people fix it."

They waited, the darkness palpable, save for the yellow light from the waning moon. The flashes re-commenced, forked lightning travelling over the ground. It was from the direction of the church. Again, it was horizontal and faintly blue-ish in colour.

"It is coming from the church," stated Jim, excitement in his voice, "Can't be normal lightning, there's no thunder, no clouds, no breeze."

The church was illuminated again, the outline of nave and tower plain in the vivid streaks of light.

"Let's go see what's causing it," said Jim, walking towards the Landrover.

They both climbed in, Jim turned the ignition key to start the car. Nothing happened. "Oh!Shit, this is all we need, the fucking battery flat."

"Try it again," Betty ignored Jim's bad language.

There wasn't even a groan from the direction of the battery.

"No bloody electricity, car won't start, the end of a perfect day,"cursed Jim.

****

38.

Monday, June 19th 1995.
Lewin's Farm, Babingley Marsh,
King's Lynn, Norfolk.

"And lightning from the church," added Betty, a sudden desire to giggle bubbling up, "Let's try the other one, they can't both be flat."

They both made their way to the double garage, the torch beam cutting a lane though the dark. They reached the up and over just as another display of energy occurred.

"Definitely coming from the church," said Betty, seeing Jim's features lucent in the blue-ish incandescence. "Hurry up, I't'll be over before we get there."

"Bloody door won't operate, I'll have to do it manually, stand back."

He heaved at the massive door pulling the handle up, "Jesus, what the hell's wrong with this bleeding thing? I can't move it."

"Let me give you a hand, you pull, I'll try and get my hands under the bottom."

It took all their strength to raise the door, as if some force were preventing the port to rise.

"It's usually light as a feather," snarled Jim, breathing hard. "Everything's gone wrong today."

"Keep cool Jimbo, nothing to get yourself in a tizz-wazz about." Betty was breathing just as hard from the exertion.

"The raising gear is normally operated by electricity, we do not normally notice it."

"Get in," groused Jim, opening the door of the Nissan 'Bluebird'.

Another bout of flashes illuminated the interior of the garage and the inside of the Nissan. The car wouldn't start.

"I don't bloodywell believe this. They can both be fucking flat," Jim beat the steering wheel in frustration.

"Let's use the bikes, long time since we had a ride," said Betty, worried at Jim's unnatural display of irritability.

They wheeled the two mountain bikes out and began peddling along the track towards the church, the pulses of energy coming every few seconds. They almost came to grief in potholes but managed the half mile track just as another display of the ethereal light emanated from the church and travelled over the countryside.

"It's going towards the Hump," said Betty, dismounting and leaning her bike against Farraday's perimeter fence.

"You're imagining it," scoffed Jim, "It seems to be coming from the inside."

As they both moved towards the mesh gate the whole fence became alive with worms of shimmering electrical discharges, every diamond of wire blue with energy.

"Christ, don't touch it," gasped Jim, starting back as the whole fencing became active with dancing eels of blue energy writhing, incandescent, seeming to travel upwards and zig zag-ging from diamond to diamond. There was a smell of burning in the air. Another burst of lightning emanated from the interior of the church. This time there was no doubt about the fact, it was travelling towards the unseen Hump, the tongues of blue energy jagged, crackling with power.

"What on earth can be causing it?" Jim was staring, his face silhouetted by the lightning.

"I know this sounds daft," said Betty, "But it's coming from the direction of the crypt."

"Rubbish love, there's nothing down there that could cause this."

The lightning died again, the fencing assumed a normal mien.

"Holly and Calhoun both got burns from that plaque," said Betty.

"I know, but this is something different again, as if there was a pylon down there, leaching out electricity."

"After today I can believe anything," stated Betty, waiting for the next flashes.

Jim turned the torch on when no more flashes occurred and trained it on the building through the mass of scaffolding.

"There's somebody in there," cried Betty, "I saw someone pass that window," she pointed.

Jim directed the torch beam at the window in question. It outlined the interior scaffolding and the opposite walls, there was no sign of human form.

"You imagined it love," he said.

"He, or she, or whatever it was, was heading towards the font," said Betty.

Jim played the powerful torch beam over the entire area, there was no sign of human form. After several minutes, there were no more electrical discharges.

"Let's go and have a look inside!" urged Betty, "If there is someone in there, they could be injured, possibly even electrocuted."

Jim wasn't too sure about entering the building with the possibility of another storm occurring whilst they were inside.

Betty sensed his unease, "I'll go, you stay here,"she offered.

"No way, I'll come with you."

The mesh gate was open, they had a job entering the main door because of the tree sprouting. From the balmy air of a June night the instant they entered the nave the temperature dropped alarmingly. The burning smell was strong inside.

"Smells as if some clothes are on fire," muttered Betty.

Jim directed the torch around the walls, silhouetting the scaffolding. They passed the font to the tower aperture. The stairs had long since gone, leaving only the dark square of the trapdoor. Jim shone the torch upwards, the beams that had once supported a peal of eight bells were visible, but nothing more. They moved back down towards the entrance to the crypt adjacent to where the altar had once graced the building. The chill was enervating. Betty shivered. The torch beam illuminated the crumbling stone steps leading down into the crypt.

"Let's leave it" said Jim, nervously, "There's nobody here and I don't fancy going down there tonight, or at any other time after what's happened," his voice echoed.

"Windy Jim Lewin?" Betty mocked gently, "Frightened of ghostie demons, hobgoblins?"

"Too true love, there's been plenty of evidence of those over the last few days. If that lightning starts up again and it is coming from down there…" Jim couldn't rid himself of the feeling once again that they were under observation. It suddenly commenced as a low moaning, like wind, mutating to a soft groaning as if from a body in agony. Within a minute the noise was as if a horde of djinns were screaming imprecations of doom. It came from the direction of the crypt. They both started back, terrified by the sound, they hurried from that arched aperture back through the body of the church. Jim banged his head on some low scaffolding that nearly dazed him, then they were outside into the warm night, where no sound could be heard. Jim rubbed his forehead, trembling with fear.

"God, that was dreadful," cried Betty.

"Funny we can't hear anything now," said Jim. A trickle of something warm and sticky come down over the bridge of his nose down his cheek. He dabbed at it with his handkerchief and shone the torch on it, it was blood.

"You've cut your forehead," said Betty, "Give me that." She cleaned his forehead, "You've got a small cut and a bump."

"What in hell causes that screaming, I wonder?" Jim shivered. "Frightened six colours out of me, I don't know about you?"

"It was terrifying, yet there's nothing out here. We couldn't both have imagined it."

"Let's get out of here love, I still feel as if someone's watching us." Jim moved towards the mesh gate.

Betty followed. The gate was closed!

"How did that happen?" Jim pulled the steel piping that formed the frame to open it.

It refused to budge.

"What's the matter?" Betty came up.

"Gate's shut, I can't open it."

"Come on love, don't start that spooky stuff, I'm not in the mood," said Betty irritably.

"You try," Jim offered.

It refused to budge.

"This is silly, there's no wind, nobody around," said Betty, shaking the gate vigorously.

They could see their bikes resting against the fence further along.

"We can't climb eight feet of fencing without doing ourselves injury," said Jim, looking round, training the torch back into the church.

"It isn't locked either," said Betty, peering at the latch. She didn't sound too sure, "It must have been that person I saw in there, locked us in."

"It isn't locked," Jim shone the torch on the latch, "It must be jammed somehow."

"This weird Jimbo, "A tinge of nervousness coloured her voice. "How can the thing not open without being locked?"

"Let's go round the other side, there might be some loose wire we can pull aside."

They covered the circumference, the mesh wire guard was impenetrable.

"We can't stay here all night," said Betty, knowing how illogical it sounded.

Jim shone the torch on the scaffolding nearest the gate. "If we put a couple of those planks from that scaffold to the top of the gate, we could climb down."

"That's a bit risky isn't it?" Betty looked dubiously at the six feet of space that separated the nearest scaffold from thhe top of the steel poles of the mesh gate.

"As you said, we can't stay here all night love," said Jim. "You shine the torch, I'll climb up and bring a couple of planks from the side there."

He assembled two long planks from a pile and leaned them against the scaffolding. He then climbed up with difficulty to where the horizontal joints braced the uprights and sat on the level section.

"Lift the end up, I haven't any leverage balanced like this, he directed. Betty obeyed, careful not to fall. Jim tossed the heavy plank to the top of the gate, it connected with a metallic bang.

"Now the other one," he was sweating with the effort.

The second was easier, since he had only to slide it along the first.

"OK, here goes."

"For God's Sake be careful Jimbo. I don't want your back all bad again or you to fall off."

Jim straddled the planks and began jockeying his way over the gap. The plank bent alarmingly, but held. He reached the gate and swung his leg over, dropping down on the outside. The eight feet seemed enormous. He landed with a thump that knocked the wind out of him.

"Your turn love."

Betty made several attempts to climb the scaffolding, unable to grasp the horizontal beams because of her height, she tried to lever herself up.

"Come on love, you have to try," he urged her.

She made several attempts, but failed miserably.

"You go, get some help, a ladder or something, bolt cutters, anything," said Betty, a note of desperation in her voice.

"I can't leave you here," said Jim.

"Go on, I have the torch, I'll be okay, you have to do it, there's no other way."

Jim was reluctant, all kinds of scenarios flashing across his brain. More electrical discharges, that mysterious something Betty claimed to have seen inside the church, and the Stygian darkness, despite the rising moon, Betty insisted.

He set off, promising to return urgently. He was some way off when he saw the street lights were back on. Looking out over the fields beyond the Hump, the lights in the estate had come back on too. He was rummaging in the tool room, trying to locate the bolt cutters, when he heard a motor vehicle arrive.

"You there Dad?" It was Bobby's voice.

"In here," he called.

"What're you looking for? Where's Mumsy?" Bobby looked anxious.

"I came over when we had the power cut, thought you might need help."

"Did you see the lightning?" Jim pulled open drawers, boxes, tool chests, unbable to locate the bolt cutters.

"What lightning?" Bobby looked puzzled.

"Lit the whole sky up a short time ago," said Jim.

"You okay Dad? How'd you get that cut on your forehead? I haven't seen any lightning, are you sure you saw it? There isn't a cloud in the sky. Where is Mumsy?"

"Down at the church."

Bobby echoed it, incredulously, "What in hell is she doing down there on her own?"

"It will take time to explain son, help me find these bloody bolt cutters."

"What do you need bolt cutters for?"

"To get your mother out of the fenced-in section, I had to climb out, she couldn't make it. She was too short to reach the bar. No more questions until we get her out please son. She must be getting desperate by now."

"Sounds crazy to me," Bobby aided his father search for the elusive bolt cutters.

After a few minutes of searching they found them under a pile of old sacking.

"Let's get down there at the double," urged Jim, "She'll be going frantic."

"I'm not surprised, leaving her there on her own," His voice was cold.

"You don't honestly think I'd have left her there without good cause do you?" Jim was irritated, anxious for Betty's welfare.

"I don't understand any of it," groused Bobby, "Lightning, Mumsy down at the church in the middle of the night alone, Christ, knowing what's been going on in that place recently."

"Don't rub it in, for fuck's sake son," roared Jim, exasperated.

"I'm just as anxious as you are. Better go in your car, ours wouldn't start."

Bobby said nothing, his look eloquently reflecting his opinion.

"Doubt whether my Jag'll make it down there with those potholes, it'll bang the silencer or the underside, let's try the Landrover."

"I told you it wouldn't start," Jim was impatient to be off.

"The alternative is a walk," snapped Bobby.

He ran over to the vehicle, the key still in the ignition. It started first time. "Come on, let's go."

Bobby drove like a madman, throwing the vehicle from side to side to avoid the deeper holes. The headlights illuminated the wire mesh surrounding the church, the skeletal scaffolding and the gate. When they got there, there was no sign of Betty.

****

39.

Monday June 19th 1995.
St Mary's Church, Babingley Marsh,
King's Lynn, Norfolk.

They both rushed to the fence and peered in, the headlights of the Landrover casting gigantic shadows of themselves over the wall of the ruined building.

"Betty, Mumsy," they both yelled.

"Let's get that lock cut," said Jim,when Betty did not reply.

Fear was tearing him apart. What if something dreadfull had befallen Betty whilst he'd been gone? He'd never forgive himself.

"There's no lock on this gate," said Bobby, in a hard voice, "And the bloody thing opens."

"Watch those planks son," yelled Jim, hurrying over.

"You sure you're alright Dad? There's no planks."

There wasn't a sign of the two planks Jim had used to bridge the gap from the scaffolding to the gate. They both rushed in, calling Betty. Bobby ran back for the torch kept in the Landrover. They entered the main door, sque-zing past the tree, the chill struck them immeadiately. The headlight beams threw fantastic shadows over the interior scaffolding and walls, but there was no sign of Betty in the main church.

"Perhaps she got free and walked out," offered Bobby.

"We'd have seen her," Jim had a gut feeling, something nasty and chilling had happened as he said it.

"Let's have a butcher's," He pointed to the dark aperture of the crypt door. "She'd need her head read going down there," choked Bobby.

"She isn't here is she?" Jim made for the door, "Give me the torch."

"I'm coming."

They walked cautiously down the crumbling stone stairs. Any second, Jim expected a re-run of the savage moaning he and Betty had heard earlier. He found it hard to think of any reason why his wife should want to enter this creepy place at this time of night, under the circumstances they'd experienced. Then suddenly, they saw Betty, she was lying in a crumpled heap beside the central catafalque.

"God!"Gasped Jim, rushing over to her.

She felt ice-cold. For a single horrible second he believed the worst, he felt her carotid, there was a pulse.

"Give me a hand up," said Bobby, his hands under his mother's armpits.

It was no easy task. The inert form of his wife seemed to weigh a ton. Bobby fireman's lifted her up the stairs out into the warm June night and laid her down on the grass. He began rubbing her wrists and patting her face. Jim despaired of any response and fetched a blanket from the Landrover, covering her up. Without warning Betty stirred, she opened her eyes. Jim offered a prayer to a Deity he did not believe in.

He cradled her head, "You alright love, what happened?"

Betty stared up at him, her features in shadow cast by the headlights, "Of course I'm alright, you were a long time, Jimbo."

"Sorry, I couldn't find the bolt cutters."

Betty recognised Bobby and sat up, "How'd you get here, son? What's the blanket for? Why am I lying out here?"

"Hey, one thing at a time love," Jim was inordinately thankful.

"Let's get you back home, can you walk?"

"Why shouldn't I walk, of course I can." She arose, picking up the blanket, "Come on then, let's go!, you got the buggy to start at last?"

Bobby looked at them both, puzzlement in his eyes. He said nothing, just aided his mother into the passenger seat.

"I'm not an invalid you know Bobby. I don't need help."

Betty shrugged him off. They made it back to the farmhouse, Bobby taking it cautiously.

"I'd like some tea love," said Betty.

"What the devil's going on? Perhaps somebody can explain to me now," said Bobby, as they sat around the kitchen table, sipping tea.

Jim and Betty took it in turns.

"You sure you're both not overwrought, seeing things?" Bobby was sceptical, "I mean lightning flashing, why didn't we see it? It's only a stone's throw to Slade. We had a powercut, it's true, but that's par for the course."

"I know it sounds ridiculous son, but a lot of things have happened over the past weeks or so that defy explanation. Wally, for example, dying of lung cancer, only expected to live to the week-end, then he gets up and walks out of the hospital. Your Mother, Ralph Mostin, Paddy Murphy, Holly Summerfield and your own Father-in-law the day of the Fete."

"I know all about that Pop, Fanny Legge was responsible for those things, but lightning and a locked gate, takes some swallowing, especially when it opened when you and I got there, and what happened to the planks you say you walked on?"

Jim shrugged, "I don't know the answers son. I don't know how your Mother came to be in the crypt, neither does she."

"Well, all's well that ends well. I heard that Bishop deManaury is going to get an injunction stopping Kev and his pals holding their summer solstice at Bawsey, just a rumour, invoking Blasphemy Laws."

"Ralph Mostin said he had no objections and Barry Lassiter has given them right of way. Bill would give them access if Barry got stroppy, but he isn't."

"It'll be the first time Kev and his wizards have been prevented from holding their vigil at Bawsey day after tomorrow."

"I didn't like the man the minute I clapped eyes on him," said Betty, pouring more tea for them, "Pompous, sanctimonious…"

"He can hold it at the Hump," interrupted Jim, "Keep quiet about it, then that interfering nutter will be too late to do anything."

"It's only a rumour," said Bobby, "I'll pass your invite on to Kev, he'll be delighted." He rose from his seat, "Must go, got a long day tomorrow. You'll be subjected to some scrutiny when people read the 'Advertiser', there'll be hordes of newshounds all trying to pump you for a story."

"You could be mistaken son, it's not that important."

Bobby shrugged, "I'll keep my fingers crossed and in the meantime don't look out for lightning, huh?"

They heard him drive off.

"I'm knackered love," announced Jim.

"Well let's go, nothing stopping us now."

****

40.

Tuesday, June 20th 1995.
Lewin's Farm, Babingley Marsh,
King's Lynn, Norfolk.

Jim awoke to a thunderous knocking at the door. He looked at his watch, Six am, ho the hell…? He climbed out of bed, Betty was still asleep, snoring faintly. He opened the bedroom window. A man was at the front door in the act of knocking again.

"What the devil do you want mister, it's six a.m." roared Jim.

"My name's Rayner, I'm from the Daily News. Are you Mr Lewin, the ghost man?"

He was clad in smart suit. A late regtistration BMW was parked in the drive.

"Best of luck sunshine, that's your problem."

"Hey, don't close up on me, there's a bus load of colleagues en route, they'll make your life a misery, I promise you."

"What do you want?"

"See this?" Rayner waved a piece of paper. Even at that distance Jim could see that it was a cheque, "Write your own figures for an exclusive, save you a load of agro shortly."

"Exclusive on what?"

Rayney held up a copy of the Lynn Advertiser. The headlines were an inch high, easily visible. ***'GHOSTS ON RAMPAGE'***

Jim saw another car enter the drive from the main road, just as another man holding an expensive looking camera came out of Rayner's car. He took a series of photos of Jim leaning out of the window.

"You've got around two minutes Mr Lewin, he circus has just started," called Rayner. His photographer was busy taking shots of the house, the buildings and then a telephoto of St Mary's.

"Well?" Rayner saw the other vehicle, "You're going to be hassled any second now."

"It's a load of extravagant crap," said Jim, "There's no ghost."

"Not what this says Mr Lewin," Rayner stabbed a finger at the headline.

Jim could see the second vehicle, a Renault Espace full of people. The occupants had been drinking and were singing in inebriated tones about ghosts and vampires. It came to a shuddering halt a yard from Rayner's BMW. Several men and women piled out, cameras and camcorders in evidence.

"Hi Jolly old man." A portly man, sporting a bushy moustache and clad in loud check tweeds slapped Rayner on the back, "Stealing a march, huh, you snide bastard? That the Ghost fellow? Hi there Mr Lewin, don't do anything until you've spoken to me. He's a crook, promise you anything, until it's paytime."

The man had been drinking and could hardly stand upright," Get some pictures you lot. Where's this bloody church where it's all happening Lewin? It is Lewin, isn't it?"

Jim saw a minibus turn into the drive from the main drag.

"I've nothing to say," he yelled over the drunken bedlam.

"What is it Jim?" Betty was sitting up in bed, bewildered.

"The media have arrived and I didn't shut that bloody gate last night. There's a dozen of them out here already."

There was a thunderous knocking at the door once more, "Come on out Ghost Man, give us an interview." There was more drunken chanting of, "Why are we waiting?"

Jim heard another vehicle arrive, more voices added to the cacophony and yet another.

"We better phone the police," Betty took a brief glance out of the window at the crowded drive, "There's a TV van out here with a platform on the top."

Jim took a look as the platform telescoped. A man wielding a camera was soom directing the camera on a level with the bedroom window.

Betty, still in her nightdress, jerked the curtains across. "This is that Calhoun's doing," she said, "What're we going to do?"

Jim took a peep from behind the curtain, some of the newcomers had erected a collapsible table on the lawn and were sitting round drinking from bottles and flasks. Jim stabbed at the phone digits, "Police? My name's Lewin, Lewin Farm Babingley. I have a crowd of drunks trespassing on my property, threatening my wife and I. Can you help us?"

The weary voice wasn't particularly vibrant but promised a patrol would visit to investigate. A radio was blaring pop music somewhere, adding to the noise. People were hammering at the door and windows, demanding interviews. More vehicles arrived, the clink of bottles and glasses could be heard over the inebriated singing and chanting.

Betty came from the en suite, "What on earth can the police do if they do come? Two officers aren't going to dent that lot." She looked harassed already.

More vehicles were arriving every minute, the clamour was awful. Jim and Betty were dressing when two men holding cameras entered their bedroom and began taking flash photos.

"Out," roared Jim, "You're trespassing, I've called the police."

The stout man in the tweed suit appeared, "We want an interview, Lewin, we'll pay you for an exclusive on this ghost story." He held up a copy of the Advertiser, "Where are these demons, spouting fire, sucking blood and raping virgins?"

"Get out of my house," roared Jim, "Nobody invited you in."

He made a threatening move toward the three men. They stood their ground, taking photos of him, clad in shirt and underpants.

"An exclusive, Lewin.We want to see these ghosts, tell us your story," said the tweedy man, "Here's a cheque for five thousand on account. More if we get the genuine article." He threw a signed cheque on the dressing table.

Jim took a.16 bore shotgun from the corner of the room, "Get lost or I swear I'll let you have it," he roared, aiming the gun at the men.

The three men stampeded down the stairs. "He's a fucking madman," Jim heard them shout on exiting, "The idiot's got a submachinegun."

Jim took another peep from behind the curtains, the cameraman perched on a cradle atop the TV van swung the boom round and zommed in to within three feet of the window.

"The sooner you come out Lewin, give us an interview, the sooner we leave," chanted the crowd outside.

There were several collapsible tables on the lawn now, decked round with chairs. Groups of men and women were eating and drinking. Close by the ornamental pool another group had erected a barbecue and were frying bacon and eggs. The noise was horrendous. Jim and Betty finished dressing just as the police patrol arrived. Two young officers in uniform got out and were greeted by some good humoured ribaldry and offers of breakfast and drink. Jim let them in, slamming the door, locking it after them.

"They're all trespassing, making a public nuisance. We want them off our property officer," Jim was stuttering in his excitement.

The eldest was scarcely out of his twenties and looked bewildered, "We can ask them to leave sir," he offered.

"Ask them?"Echoed Jim, "They're creating a nuisance, damaging our property, is that all you can do?"

"They claim you threatened them with a gun sir," said the youngest, a mere stripling of twenty.

"They invaded our bedroom, what else did you expect me to do? They were breaking and entering," Jim choked.

"We can ask them to leave sir," repeated the older man.

"You honestly believe they're going to leave officer?" rasped Jim, "Just by asking them? Can't you order them off?"

"Not without a warrant sir, or if they were using threatening behaviour."

"What the devil do you call that activity out there? Camped out on our lawn, ruining our garden, surely you can order them to leave?"

"We can ask them sir."

"Do you know Chief Mostin?"

"Yes sir, our boss."

"I'm going to phone him, tell him you're refusing to act, how does that grab you?"

"Your privelege sir," said the older constable, stiffly.

"You refuse to remove these people?"

"I did explain sir."

"That's it, I'm going to phone the Chief," Jim made for the phone.

"Hang about Jimbo," Betty stopped him. Jim glared at her, "These officers are only doing their job according to the rules."

Jim opened his mouth to argue, but stopped when he saw the look in his wife's eyes.

"If you are unable to remove these people officers, there's no need for us to hold you up, we'll handle it ourselves," she said, sweetly.

"Not with a gun I hope Mrs Lewin?" The two young men looked relieved.

Betty shook her head, "Goodness me no, perish the thought."

"Very well, we'll be on our way." The two cops exited to some ironic cheers and ribald remarks from the crowd of reporters.

Betty waited until the police car had vanished from view.

"I hope you know what you're doing love."

"They want an interview, let's give them one."

"Are you crazy? They'll mince us."

Betty shook her head, "I don't think soJimbo."

"You mean tell 'em all about it?"

"Of course, not here though."

"You mean?"

Betty grinned and nodded.

Jim grinned in his turn, "That's a brilliant idea love, should sort them out."

"You agree?"

Jim nodded.

Betty unlocked the door and waved to the nearest reporters. Rayner and the tweedy individual hurried up, eager to be first to get the story. Cameras flashed everywhere.

"We'll give a statement gentlemen," announced Betty.

"Exclusive?" Rayner was smoking a cheroot.

"No a public interview," corrected Betty.

"Well that's a step in the right direction," Rayner was almost shouting over the noise, "We're ready when you are. Right Arthur?"

"Better than nothing I suppose," groused the other, his rheumy eyes baleful, "An exclusive would be better for me." He was perspiring and smelled of BO.

The others crowded round, mikes thrust forward, cameras held high. There were two ITV companies now, one from Anglia, the other from Central and the BBC made a third. All had roof mounted cameras and boom mikes and all were clamouring for exclusives, asking questions continuously.

Betty held up her hand.

"Not here, ladies and gents."

"Where?" Rayner and his colleague looked suspicious.

"In the church of course gentlemen, and in the crypt. I think you'll then be convinced there is no story."

There was a concerted rush for transport, Betty winked at Jim as he drove the Landrover along the potholed track. The ordinary vehicles were soon in strife and fell behind, unable to negotiate the pitted track. The three TV vehicles, their cameramen hurled from side to side, soon had to stop, their crews hastily changing to shoulder held cameras and trying to keep up on foot. By the time they reached the church only a handful remained. The others were strewn along half a mile of rough road, all trying to make the church, wielding heavy equipment.

Arthur had arrived in a Mitsubishi Shogun with his crew. Rayner was left behind with dozens of others, his BMW failing to handle the road. He breathed alchohol over Betty and Jim, along with halitosis.

"Exclusive, Lewin. Ten grand if you agree," He was breathing stertoriously, mopping his forehead with a handkerchief.

"How are you going to handle all those?" Jim pointed to what resembled a kind of bizarre marathon, men and women struggling along the road as far as they could see.

"You leave that to me Lewin," panted Arthur, "I'm from the Journal."

"If you can handle those, then OK," said Betty, "Ten thousand pounds."

Arthur nodded eagerly, sweat dripping from end of his veined nose. "You blokes stop them when they get here," he instructed his denim clad team, "Tell'em we've signed up."

"You'll need lights," Betty warned them.

Jim and Betty led the way into the fenced-off area, beneath the scaffolding into the church.

****

41.

Monday June 20th 1995.
St Mary's Church, Babingley
King's Lynn, Norfolk.

"Christ, it's cold in here," said Arthur's cameraman, "You got the fridge door open?"

Arthur was looking apprehensive, "What causes this Lewin?" From sweating profusely he'd begun shivering, "Must be well below freezing."

"Haven't the vaguest idea why," said Jim.

"Shit, I'm going back for a jacket Arthur, you carry on," said one of the denim clad young men, his thick hair carefully coiffed, smelling of underarm.

Arthur hesitated when they reached the doorway to the crypt. "What's down there?" He pointed a wrinkled finger.

"The crypt, where it all happened," Betty smiled.

"Looks bloody dangerous to me, are those stairs safe?"

"You wanted the exclusive?" Betty let it hang.

Arthur switched on a powerful torch. Jim entered, he went first. Arthur and his three colleagues followed, Betty bringing up the rear.

"Well, what now?" Arthur played the torch around the crypt. He looked uneasy.

"Fuck-all here Arthur mate," said one of his crew, "Bloody freezing."

"As you can all see now, no ghosts, demons, spooks, anything like that," said Betty.

"Who's buried in that?" Arthur swung the torch onto the central catafalque.

"No idea, the church was last occupied in 1918. It was closed due to a lack of people. We aren't too clear why the church was built here in the first place, in the middle of nowhere."

"We're wasting our time Arthur. That creep Calhoun was giving us a load of shit, I told you he was a twenty-four carat wanker, trying to make the big time," said the burly young man.

"You want to cancel that ten K?" demanded Jim.

"There's no story here, just a load of old stone coffins like he said," Arthur was miffed.

"We did explain to you," said Betty, shivering.

The other team members arrived, "I've told'em we got the contract Arthur, they've all pissed-off, especially your mate Jolly. He was calling you all kinds of names and ng aspersions on your parentage. Where's the ghosts?"

"There aren't any fucking ghosts mate, just a load of stone boxes," complained the burly young man, "I'm getting out of here before I catch pneumonia. Never been so cold since our Lapland trip."

"Where's this witch live?" demanded Arthur, "The one that's being doing all the miracles?"

"What witch is that?" Betty sounded surprised.

"I'll kill that bastard Calhounn when I get hold of him. He told me that some woman was performing miracles," Arthur was shivering now, "You telling me there's no such woman?"

"I don't know of any witch," Betty was economical with the truth.

"Who's this Legge woman Calhoun was telling us about, then?"

"She's an eccentric, lives with a load of cats, geese and other animals. You know what people are like, exaggerate just because she is eccentric," Betty kept a straight face. There was no way she was going to invite further disasters by revealing Fanny's location. If someone else gave out the information it would be down to them.

"Calhoun was definite about her, he said she cured the sick and some bloke dying of bowel cancer. He wouldn't be that stupid, he'd know we'd check it out." The burly young man was suspicious, staring at Betty coldly.

"You'd better take that up with this Calhoun then hadn't you?"

"We will, no worries on that score lady. It's cost us a bloody fortune to come up to this one-horse shitheap, we'll get it out of Calhoun alright. He also told us there was paranormal goings on down here, he said he heard moans, groaning and ghosts. He put it in his this article," He brandished a copy of the'Advertiser. "He'd have to be a complete asshole to print this without facts to back it up. I reckon these two are covering up Arthur. We want our ten K for fuck-all."

"That's your prerogorative isn't it mister? We told you you were wasting time," said Jim, "You wanted an interview. Think we enjoy a load of pricks camping out on our lawn, making a nuisance of themselves, disturbing the peace. You wanted an interview, we couldn't care less. You take all that fairy tale crap up with Calhoun, like your mate here said, he's an eighteen carat wanker with a yen for the lights."

"Where's all these ghosts?" came a voice from the direction of the stairs. Jolyon Rayner came clattering down followed by a horde of other bedraggled reporters, all with cameras.

"There aren't any sunshine," said Harris' assistant, "That twat Calhoun has been giving us a loada rubbish just to git his name in lights. No witch, no miracles, no ghosts, just a freezing tomb with stone coffins. Be our guest mate, there's no way the 'Journal'is going to pay out ten K for a lousy crypt. Come on Arthur, let's get the fuck out of this bleeding cold."

"You heard Lewin, no ghosts, no bread," Harris gave Betty and Jim the evil eye.

"You believed all that shit pal. We told you that you were out of order. Stuff your ten K up your arse, shut the gate when you come out. We're leaving you to it," said Jim,angrily.

More of the latecomers crowded into the crypt, all demanding to see the ghosts and demons. Betty and Jim pushed through the crowd to the church to find more reporters all wandering around, looking bewildered. They battened onto Betty and Jim, demanding to know where the ghosts were kept.

Jim gave them all the same story, "If you see any let us know, we'll make a fortune sonny."

Harris and his sidekick emerged from the crypt with Rayner, "We've been had you blokes, Calhoun made it all up," said Harris' assistant, "If you wanna freeze in that snake pit be our guest."

Jim and Betty returned to the house, the place was deserted now, save for the littered lawn and parking area, abandoned chairs and tables and numorous parked vehicles.

"Christ, what a mess," Jim surveyed the scene, "They've ruined the lawn."

"We got rid of them didn't we?" Betty was philosophic, "They'll all leave now."

"I wouldn't bet on that love, look who's turned up."

Calhoun's yellow Beetle with its oversize tyres approached up the drive. Calhoun looked exited, his lank greasy hair had been pony-tailed, his jeans all starched and tight. He carried the usual plethora of cameras, lenses and arc lights. He walked with a swagger towards the house, Jim met him half way.

"Got the full treatment I see Lewin," He was chewing spearmint gum, the odour spreading before him. He waved a hand to indicate the parked vehicles.

"I wouldn't hang around if I were you tosh, they're after your blood," said Jim.

"Who is? What're you on about?"

"Your pals from Fleet Street. Very upset at not seeing any ghosts, demons or paranormal experiences. They think you've lied to get notoriety."

"I supppose you encouraged them to think that?" Calhoun's brash manner subsided, he looked wary.

"We didn't have to sunshine. We just took them down the crypt and there was nothing down there, exept the cold. They're really pissed-off."

They both heard the engine sounds simultaneously. Harris' Shogun wobbled and lurched over the potholes approaching the farmhouse.

"That's Harris of the 'Journal' and his mate, tough-looking fellow with a crew-cut, said he was going to remove your balls. If you want to go before they arrive…"

Calhoun shrugged, some of his confidence subsiding, "I've nothing to hide," he said, nervously.

"Well bully for you pal, I'll leave you to it. They haven't buried anyone in the churchyard there since 1918, no doubt your other pal, the Bishop would be prepared to make an exeption for you."

"Fuck you Lewin, you'll be sorry for this."

The Shogun lurched to a halt, the healthy young man jumped out, "Just the man Calhoun, we've been dying to meet you."

Calhoun wasn't too sure about him and gave a sickly grin. Harris came from the passenger seat along with his other staff.

"This is Calhoun Arthur, Lynn's aspiring reporter of the year," said the assistant. Meet Arthur Harris of the Sunday Journal, he's been dying to meet you, haven't you Arthur?"

"What've you been giving us all this shit about paranormal experiences, ghosts and demons Calhoun?" Harris looked pissed-off.

"Trying to make a name for yourself, get into the Guiness?"

"I've reported things as they happened Mr Harris," Calhoun

interrupted, developing a stutter.

"These good folk took us down into that ice-box called a crypt. No ghosts, no demons, no paranormal gear, nothing, save my knackers got frozen. So where did you get all this shit from?"

Harris waved a copy of the Advertiser in front of Calhoun's nose. The inch high headlines of 'Ghosts on Rampage' were uppermost. "Where's this witch woman? Where're these miracle cures and what's more I want to see these ghosts you've splashed over the front page of this rag and syndicated it all over. I know Jeff Patten, ex-Sunday Observer man, he wouldn't allow you to print this crap without good reason, so where are they?"

"It's all fact Harris. Look!" He held his bandaged hand up, "I got this down in the crypt, touching that brass plaque on the catafalque."

"I didn't see any brass plaque, did you Arthur?" The healthy type looked menacing, "I reckon he's been manufacturing some little porkies to get into the big time."

"I can take you to the Legge woman, see for yourselves and you can talk to Wally Thompson, she cured his back twelve years ago." He pointed to Jim, "Tell them Lewin."

"I haven't the vaguest idea what you're on about Calhoun," said Jim.

"You saw my photos, the one's in here." Calhoun pointed to the newspaper in Harris' hand.

"Anyone could've faked those sonny," Harris was unrelanting.

"Alright, did any of you take any photos of the Hump?" Calhoun was getting desperate.

"We read about that in this pack of lies, where is it, what is it?"

"That's where all those things happened ten years ago, blood in the tap, bags of concrete hard as nails overnight and the blokes refusing to work because of the paranormal events. The contractor who worked the site is still in Lynn, he can vouch for it all. He pulled out because of all the agro, the machinery and so on wouldn't operate."

"OK, take us to this Hump, let's have a butcher's," Harris didn't believe a word of it.

"It's on his land, in that direction!" Calhoun pointed back in the direction of the church, "He'll have to give permission."

Harris looked at Jim, "That OK Lewin? We won't make a mess, just want to justify the expense of coming down here checking out this garbage."

"OK by me," Jim shrugged, "You'll need your Shogun though."

"Let's go, you come with us Calhoun. God help you if this is a hoax as well." The crew all moved back to the Shogun.

Some of the other reporters were showing up in the distance, walking wearily back to the house, Rayner in the lead.

"I wonder if we're doing the right thing Jimbo," Betty came out into the yard.

"We've done our bit love if they don't find anything we'll be left alone."

"What happens if that Shogun stops on the Hump and their cameras don't work?"

"We'll have to chance it, love," Jim saw the Shogun stop beside Rayner, they seemed to hold a conversation with the reporter, then Rayner got into the Shogun. The vehicle then set off back the way it had come. The line of weary journalists all stopped as the Shogun passed them, ome backtracked after it. The majority resumed their trek back to the farmhouse.

"You realise it's only eight am? Seems like we've been up all night," Betty mused, "I'd better put the kettle on, those people will be dying of thirst." She saw Jim look askance, "If we're going in for tourism we'll have too put up with this Jimbo."

"Funny nothing happened to that lot isn't it, after what happened to you down there and all the other things. The lightning last night, the Landrover not starting, or the Nissan, that mesh gate stuck fast so we have to climb over it and yet it was open when Bobby gets there."

"It's just as if somebody doesn't want all the publicity and turns it all off at will."

They saw the Shogun arrive at the fenced off Hump, the occupants jumped out. Rayner and Harris were easily recognisable, Calhoun was boxed in by the four healthy types. The first of the weary journalists reached the house, all were perspiring, tired out, cursing the heat of the morning and blaming Calhoun, the Church, the lack of anything newsworthy to justify their time and expense.

"Sit down, I'm making tea," offered Betty, "We're sorry you've had a wasted journey."

"That's very generous of you Mrs Lewin, in view of the agro we've caused you. We appreciate it, don't we fellers?"

There was a chorus of approval, more of the weary men and women arrived. There were requests to use the toilets and soon there were a score of men and women drinking tea on at the tables still assembled on the lawn.

"Any chance of some breakfast Mrs Lewin? We'll pay you for the trouble?" asked one young man, black patches of sweat showing under his armpits and on his back.

"Egg and bacon for everybody?"

There was an approving chorus.

Half an hour later all were busy enjoying a farmhouse breakfast. Two of the female journalists offered to wash up, the men mucking in.

"Sorry you've had a wasted journey ladies and gents," said Betty, "We did warn your friends Harris and Rayner earlier."

"We've enjoyed a day in the country Mrs Lewin, and a damn good nosh, it was very generous of you. Here, we've made a collection," He handed Betty his hat. It was piled high with notes and coins. "We won't take a refusal, you've both been more than understanding, we don't often get this treatment, we're social pariahs most places."

The ice broken, professionalism took over, questions by the dozen on how, where, why the farm, and how Calhoun had come to print the article in the 'Advertiser' without proof. The name of Wally Thompson came up and that of Funny Fanny who was able to cure him of lung cancer when within an ace of death.

"Perhaps we haven't a wasted journey after all. If we could interview this Funny Fanny, she's evidently a faith healer of some distinction. Where do we find her?"

"I'm not prepared to give you her address ladies and gents. She's a very private lady and resents publicity of any sort. We have to respect that privacy."

"OK Mrs Lewin, that's fair enough isn't it you lot?" The red-haired correspondent who had made his peace with Betty first addressed his colleagues.

There was a chorus of approval.

"Give our love to Harris and Jolly Rayner when they come back Mrs Lewin and thanks again for the nosh."

There was a great deal of manoevering, several of the journalists had collected the litter into refuse sacks, the chairs and tables removed. By the time the cavalcade had departed, save for the wheel marks in the lawn, the patio and farm looked much the same as it had before their arrival.

"They'll try and locate Fanny," said Jim, "They won't come all this way for nothing. A story like that will make good news."

"Ring Wally, warn him," said Betty.

Jim immediately went to the phone. "Wally? Jim Lewin here, you aren't going to believe this but a gang of reporters are heading your way. They want your story how you came to be cured by Funny Fanny. I'm not handing out advice but Fanny got really upset when we didn't respect her privacy. I'd hate something unpleasant to happen to you after what she did for you mate."

"What am I supposed to do Jimbo, I feel great. It's a good story, there could be some money in it for me," Thompson sounded as he always had.

"Up to you pal, you didn't see what happened to Betty and the bird from Anglia as a result of us not doing that. It wasn't pretty, I can assure you of that. I wouldn't like anything to happen to you."

"You're being bloody mysterious Jimbo. What did happen to Betty and the Anglia woman?"

"Take too long to tell you now, I'm warning you, don't talk to that lot, get lost somewhere, take Ruth to Hunston for the day and on no account tell them where Fanny lives. You've got around fifteen minutes pal, it's up to you."

"I know you wouldn't have me on Jimbo, and I certainly don't want anything happening to me again, I'm on my way. Ruthie," Jim heard him yell, "We're going to the beach for the day, get yourself tarted up. See you Jimbo and thanks for the advice."

Jim had time to put down the phone before Bobby arrived in his Jaguar. Tracy and Laura with him. "We past a convoy en route, what was that all about Dad?"

Betty gave him the facts. "They're down at the Hump?"

Bobby was surprised.

"Calhoun is with them. They aren't too pleased with him since they've seen nothing, no ghosts or paranormal stuff. They think he's been having them on to get notoriety. What brings you here at nine-thirty on a Tuesday morning anyway?"

"I've heard on the grapevine that those two dog collars have got their injunction, stopping Kev and his wizards holding their solstice celebrations tomorrow night at Bawsey."

****

42.

Tuesday June 20th 1995.
Lewin's Farm, Babingley Marsh,
King's Lynn, Norfolk.

"Does Kev know yet?"

"We've just been round to his place, they aren't in, thought they might be here with you?"

"Haven't seen them since last night at Holding's Hill"

"He'll need to use the Hump in view of the injunction. What he won't need is a gang of media freaks interfering," Bobby helped himself to tea from the pot. "In view of all this publicity that lot might just pay a visit to make up for lack of paranormal experiences."

"They were whingeing about the expense of coming all this way for no result. I doubt whether they'd want to stay for a pantomime like a summer solstice do by a load of Swedes," Jim followed Bobby's example. "They'll be busy at Stonehenge, more visibility at that location!"

"I wouldn't bet on that. If deManuary opens his big mouth about sex orgies, fertility rites and virgins being raped on the altar, all rich material for the gutter press, especially the Sunday Journal. That gentleman is not known for reticence with the Press. He's after the Archbishops number, the better the profile the more chances he has."

A Fiat Punta drew up in the driveway.

"We're going to hear all about it now," grinned Bobby, as Ellen got out hurrying over, an official-looking document in her hand.

"Look at this," She greeted them without preamble, "That bloody priest has gone and done it. He's stopped our solstice celebrations at Bawsey tomorrow night, just served it on me."

Bobby took it from her glanced at it, "Well you can't use Bawsey tomorrow night love, that'as for sure. Barry wouldn't let you use his right of way and Bill Watson would be in the khazi if he did."

"But it's not fair, we've been using it for yonks, we do no harm. What's he got his bowels in an uproar about?" Ellen burst out.

"He's going to get some exposure love, and he wants it. He's ambitious," said Bobby.

"But he's quoting laws that haven't been excercised for centuries. How can he do that?"Ellen was angry.

"Unless it is repealed by Parliament it's still on the Statute Book and he can do just that love."

"Can't we appeal, you're a lawyer, do something, get it removed."

Bobby shook his head, "I know Sir William Cranford, the Magistrate, deManaury will have asked him to procrastinate any appeal, and Sir Willy is a geriatric who believes in original sin, the Bible, blasphemy, the lot. A pagan festival is calculated to rouse his religious fervour, an offence against God and all that jazz."

"You're telling me we wouldn't get it heard it time?"

"Fraid not love," Bobby handed the document back.

"We've told everybody, they'll all be turning up in the gear," wailed Ellen.

"You could use the Hump love," said Jim, "Same kind of location, ancient burial site, ley-lines cross there you said some time ago. Phone round your members, tell 'em the venue has been changed, come here instead. Caution them not to say anything in public about it. If deManaury thinks he's being out-manoevered he'll put pressure on this magistrate to get it through, is that correct?" Jim appealed to Bobby.

"It's the easiest soloution Sis" said Bobby, "Dad's right.deManaury would get it stopped if he heard about the change and whilst you're phoning them, warn them on no account to talk to Lilly Simpson. That woman is better than a megaphone in the Tuesday Market Place, or a full page advert in the 'Sun.'"

"I can verify that," said Betty.

"Get on to it as soon as you can love," advised Bobby, "Where's Kevin?"

"At work, couldn't afford any more time off. Old Marshall gets stroppy about time wasters and Kev is key personnel in the organisation."

"Paul wouldn't mind you doing it if you explained to him the reasons, would he?" asked Betty.

"He's a Wizard," said Ellen.

"Do it love," replied Bobby, "He'll be sympathetic, I'm sure Dad won't mind you using work time to do it for once?"

"If it's alright by Paul it's okay by me love," said Jim.

"Phone bill will go up," she warned.

"We don't mind, it's only a one off," said Betty.

"Better do it soon," said Bobby.

"I could kill that bloody dog-collar, we'll have to alter the ritual. Everybody knew what to do at Bawsey."

Ellen made for the door, just as Calhoun came running up the track from the Hump. He was sweating profusely, face red, breathing hard, he looked exhausted.

"Phone for ambulance," he gasped, trying hard to draw breath, "Quickly," he collapsed into a chair.

"What do you want an ambulance for?" Betty was cold, despite Calhoun's obviously distressed state.

"Rayner and Harris have both had heart attacks, they're in a bad way," His message was jerky between gulps of air, "Phones wouldn't work, cameras, nothing. Hurry please or we're going to have a fatality on our hands."

"Both had heart attacks?" Jim was dubious, despite his gut-feelings, "You sure about it? Not just indigestion?"

"For God's sake don't argue, I've seen enough to know a coronary when I see one," Calhoun wiped his forehead with a hankerchief.

Bobby poured him a cup of tea, sugared it and handed it to him. Betty dialled 999 and asked for Ambulance. She and Jim exchanged glances as Calhoun sucked at the hot tea gratefully.

"What happened?" Betty offered the reporter a handtowel.

Calhoun wiped his face and neck. "We all got down there to this Hump, opened the gate, walked in and looked at those old footings at the site hut. We were just standing around, then the cameras wouldn't work, not one of them.The girl was poking around in amongst those old foundations, she said there was a skeleton sticking out of the earth. Everybody laughed, they thought she was joking. She got all excited and up-tight, she invited us all over to see for ourselves."

"You're making this up Calhoun," said Bobby, sourly.

"You can please yourself what you make of it Lewin, I'm just telling you what happened," his breathing was still ragged.

"Let him finish Bobby," said Betty, quietly, "Go on Mr Calhoun."

"There was a skull and part of the ribcage showing, it looked intact like one of those you see in training rooms at hospital. Harris and Rayner bent down to examine it and I know you're going to tell me I was hallucinating, but I swear it happened." Calhoun pasued to draw breath and took another drag at the tea.

"Well, what?" Bobby was caustic.

"Both that skeleton's hands moved."

Bobby gave a guffaw, "Should take more water with it Calhoun," he jeered.

Calhoun ignored Bobby's jibe, "It touched Harris and Rayner, since they were closest. The next minute both Harris and Rayner was jerking around holding their chests, having difficulty breathing, trying to suck air, then they collapsed. I tried my mobile," Calhoun patted his belt where the mobile reposed in a plastic holster, "Wouldn't work. Neither would any of the others, I ran up here to get help. They're both in a bad way, they looked awful."

"That should make Patten a very happy man Calhoun," jeered Bobby, "A skeleton come to life. Make the journey for those newshounds well worthwhile. You'll be able to print another fairy story next week."

Calhoun glared at Bobby, "I know you don't like me Lewin, even at school you were always taking the piss, but my story will be verified by the others, they all saw it happen."

"I can just see the headlines," scoffed Bobby, "Skeleton jumps up and bites well-known journalist."

"Bobby, if you don't mind," warned Betty in a hard voice.

"Mumsy, you know what this creep is like, a bloody sensation monger, trying to make to the big time. You believe all this shit? He's romancing to make it sound good."

"You can accuse me of what you like Lewin, I saw it happen.so did the others, especially Robinson, that healthy type who thinks he knows it all. He was all macho, then just flaked out when he saw that thing move. A real toughie, made of paper. That's why I had to run up here, none of them could make it."

"I'll bet Patten has a hard job swallowing it. Need more proof than your word, sunshine."

"He'll have the word of half a dozen national journalists," flared Calhoun, "Not that he'd doubt mine anyway."

"We'd better go and see if we can render any assistance at the Hump," said Ellen, practically.

They all heard the ambulance siren approaching rapidly, it arrived outside the house, one of the paramedics jumped out and Betty met them at the door. One of them was the female who had taken her from the 'Globe' the previous day.

"I'll take you," she offered before the man could say anything.

"Let's go then lady. Can't afford to waste time."

"I'll tail you in the Landrover love," said Jim, "You'll need a ride back. You coming Calhoun?"

The young man shook his head, "I'll stay here if that's OK?"

The ambulance had a hard time over the potholes, but finally reached the Hump with difficulty. They could see the recumbent forms of Harris and Rayner. The other journalists seemed lethargic, none of them coming to meet the ambulance, as if in shock. The paramedics examined Harris and Rayner and quickly put them on stretchers and into the ambulance inside five minutes.

"Those people are in shock," said the paramedic, the woman who had treated Betty in the Globe barely twenty-four hours before. "Getting to be a habit coming here, isn't it? We haven't room to take them in and these two gents need urgent treatment."

"How about us bringing them in? We have enough room in the Landrover," asked Betty.

The woman was staring at Betty curiously, "Aren't you the Mrs Lewin we picked up yesterday from the 'Globe'?"

"That's me!"

The paramedic shrugged as if to clear her head of false images, as he assisted her male counterpart with the two journalists. They got into the rear of the ambulance with the patient and, closed the doors. The vehicle set off, swaying violently over potholes. Betty and Jim urged the four journalists to get into the Landrover. All four looked dazed, shocked and they were all shivering. They didn't object as Betty urged them in, offering no resistance. She covered them with blankets as Jim drove off in the wake of the ambulance. Harris and Rayner were already being attended to when they arrived. The woman paramedic took charge, ushering the four men into Casualty.

Doctor Petit emerged from one of the examination cubicles, he saw Betty and Jim, "My God, not you again. Don't tell me, you've brought that witch with you?"

Betty shook her head, "Not this time, how are those two?"

"They'll be going into IC immeadiately. Can you tell me what happened?"

Betty looked at Jim, "I don't think you'd believe us if we told you Doctor. If you consider Fanny Legge to be a witch, then what happened to those two gentlemen would sound like something out of a horror movie."

"After yesterday, seeing you looking like Tutenkhamun Mrs Lewin, and Mr Murphy and Chief Mostin walking out of here cured when all medical experience told me they couldn't, I'm ready to believe anything."

Betty told him what she knew. Petit's reaction was predictable, "A skeleton that moved?" he echoed, his look was eloquent.

"I warned you Doctor," said Betty, "That's what we were told by Calhoun, the'Advertiser' reporter, when he arrived at our farm.

"Not Rory Calhoun?" Petit looked dubious.

"You know him?"

"If it's the same one, he belongs to the Conservative Club, he and I don't hit it off. If I see him first I avoid him, ambitious type, wants to achieve national notoriety via a scoop."

"That's him"

"My God!" muttered Petit again, "If he's involved I can believe anything. I have to admit that Calhoun has really taken first prize this time. I read his article in the rag this morning. That was hardly credible, but skeletons that move," Petit shook his head sadly," It's worse than Frankenstein, Dracula, Moriarty, Strangelove, all rolled into one."

"He was in a state," admitted Betty, "I can hardly imagine he'd make up that story in view of those two patients you've just admitted, they're both Fleet Street men. When they're able to tell you what happened, I'd imagine they'll tell you the same story."

"And I thought being a doctor was a noble profession, full of human interest. I've had my psyche badly shaken this last forty-eight hours, I don't know what to believe any more."

"Join the club," said Jim, piously.

"I can't ever say that my experience in Lynn has been anything but apocryphal. Should stand me in good stead when I get to Harley Street, that's if they don't certify me first. Skeletons that move, oh God, whatever next."

****

43.

Tuesday June 20th 1995.
Tuesday Market Place.
King's Lynn, Norfolk.

"It's still only lunchtime love," said Jim, morosely. "We've had a jolly time today, awakened at dawn by some bloody journalist, invaded by a mob of reporters, including our very own bete noir, Calhoun, served breakfast for twenty people, had two men suffer heart attacks at the Hump, four others in shock. Plus, Ellen had an injunction served on her regarding Kevin's wizard society and their solstice celebrations. What else could possibly happen?"

"We may as well have lunch in Lynn since we're here," Betty ignored Jim's recitation of disasters.

"Think that's wise love? This town is full of people with hang-ups. Lilly Simpson, Calhoun, Patten, Fiona Farraday, just to mention but a few. If we bump into any of those our lunch would be ruined."

"I don't feel like cooking again after running an impromptu restaurant at breakfast-time."

"I did warn you," said Jim, "We didn't ask that doctor how John Foster is doing."

"Talk of the devil," said Betty, nodding towards the door of casualty reception.

Marie Richards, the blond model, Foster's paramour entered. She paused in the doorway to allow people full value for money in exposure terms. She saw Betty and Jim and walked towards them, hips rolling seductively. She wore a pale pink lipstick that glistened and a pastel green two piece that fitted her as if she'd been poured into it. Eyes of every male supplicant in casualty devoured this spectacle of sexual attraction from her gleaming shoulder-length blond hair to her green high heeled shoes. The woman absorbed this energy as her right, revelling in the sensation she caused.

"Hello," she cried, as if Betty and Jim were Royals, "You're Tracy Middelton's in-laws aren't you? We met in that crumby hotel in the town square yesterday? How are you both?" She made sure everybody could hear her. "How is Tracy? I envy you, having her as an daughter-in-law, quite famous you know, makes us ordinary girls sick with envy. Dior, Cardin, marvellous girl. I've come to see Johnny, got to take care of my old-age pension, you know?" She giggled. "The charms are only temporary, Johnny is a sweetie though, he gives me everything I ask for. Pity he lives in this dreadful place, so provincial. I want him to move to London when he recovers from this set-back," she gushed on, oblivious to Betty and Jim, using them as a foil.

"I hope he makes provision for Jeanne before he leaves," Betty wasn't impressed by the miasma of perfume and expensive clothes.

"His little mousey wife, you mean?" Marie wasn't put out, "I expect he'll give her an allowance of some sort to keep her happy. Not much help to him you know, thinks that pipe and slippers and an evening meal is all he needs, and a little bit of the slap and tickle on Saturday nights. Keep his libido under control, he needs promoting, make him famous."

"I hope you're able to do the washing-up Miss Richards. Johnny isn't that well-heeled," said Betty sourly.

"He's rolling in it, just taken on that new agency in Wisbech, another poxy little one-horse town. He's going to open two more this year, on a high is Johnny. Must dash, make the most of my visiting time you know. Got a show this evening in London, winter collection."

"Nice meeting you Miss Richards. Give our regards to Johnny won't you?" Betty made for the door.

Marie held her hand out to Jim, "Don't let her take over old boy, pushy type, isn't she? You're very sexy you know that? I could fancy you myself if I wasn't involved with Johnny. You are sweet," She patted Jim's cheek, then minced off, her buttocks swaying.

"God, what a creature," Betty stared after the model as she made for reception, all male eyes followed her.

"I don't know, she is rather exuberant, nice figure though," said Jim, admiringly.

"You men," scoffed Betty, "She hasn't any tits and she resembles a beanpole, must be at least six feet, too big for you Jimbo. Let's go and eat somewhere," She dragged Jim by the sleeve.

"Oh God no," Jim groaned, as they reached the Landrover, "Let's get out of here."

"Coo-ee!" Lilly Simpson was adjuring her chauffeur, waving at them frantically. Demetrius was with her, looking bored out of his skull.

"Too bloody late," moaned Jim, "Two of 'em in less than five minutes."

Lilly hurried over, dragging her husband with her. "Have you heard about the injunction Betty my dear? I'm sure you have. The Bishop wants to put a stop to all these orgies going on, nip it in the bud before all these New-Age people start getting into the act, be awful wouldn't it? Caravans and old bangers parked in every spare ground, rubbish all over the place, dreadful children with running noses, dressed in cast-offs. Those wizards and this solstice nonsense, just the type of activity to attract these gypsy types, come to Lynn instead of going to Stonehenge. I mean the dreadful things these weirdies get up to, I've heard some awful stories, too lewd to mention in decent company. I only heard yesterday that that young manager of the Babingley Golf Club is one of them, been asking a lot of young girls to come to the orgies with him. What's his name Demmy? I forget. Mark, Matthew, Luke, John, can't just recall it, dreadful people. He was a well-brought up young man never thought he would entertain such awful goings-on. Well, what is his name Demmy? You're always on that course, you should know it." She shook her husband.

"You mean our manager Lilly, Paul Miller?" Betty was cold.

"Should always think before you open that big mouth of yours darling," growled Demetrius, "Jim here owns the Golf Club and that young man manages it for him."

Jim had never seen the stocky Demetrius clad in anything by a lounge suit, he looked uncomfortable with a tie round his neck.

"Oh, I didn't realise that," Lilly didn't look put out by her gaffe.

"I'm thinking of joining this wizard society Lilly, sounds like a lot of fun," grinned Demtrius. "I fancy a little young female flesh at midnight on a marbel slab."

"Demmy, what a disgusting thing to say," exploded Lilly, "What will Elizabeth and James think of you?"

"I reckon Jimbo could manage a bit of fresh gear, eh Jimbo?"

Demtrius nudged Jim theatrically, "Should get a flood of new members on account of that injunction Jimbo. Young Kevin Wilson is Chief Wizard,isn't he? You can tell him I want to enroll. If they need a contribution to tart that Bawsey Ruin up, I'd be delighted. I hear Troy

Middleton's going to removate the Priory, make himself a palace like royalty. Living next door to the Ruin, should have a grandstand view of the orgies, lucky bastard."

"Demmy, stop this disgusting talk at once, you're shocking Elizabeth and James. Anyway, I'm sorry I slandered your manager James, didn't realise who he was. The Bishop is determined to put a stop to all these pagan rites, blasphemous and shocking, using young girls for orgies, it's awful. Don't know what things are coming to nowadays."

"Better than when I was a lad darling," grinned Demetrius, "No orgies in those days, tough if you got'em in the club. You had to marry 'em, don't think anything of it now with the pill, condoms, vasectomies, lucky sods."

"Come on we'll be late. Got to do our volounary bit for the poorer folk you know. Make them tea and serve sandwiches for them, let them see we better off people aren't all stuck-up." Lilly dragged Demtrius away.

"Tell Kevin I'll be joining his Society, put some money into it for him," called Demetrius, "Organise a nice piece of crumpet for me."

"Poor bastard," muttered Jim, unlocking the Landrover.

"We all get what we deserve," said Betty, "She does her bit as a volountary worker, organises the friends very well."

"If that injunction was in doubt she'll have convinced Sir William that he's doing the right thing," said Jim. "You sure you want to go into Lynn? Risk meeting more of the scandal mongers?"

The Simpson's liveried chauffeur was busy polishing their cream Rolls. He had a cigarette concealed in his cupped hand.

"Have a look round the Market maybe? It's been a long time since I had the chance," said Betty.

"If we can find anywhere to park."

"Let's go before we see someone else," urged Betty. "Lilly hates people smoking," the chauffeur was sucking hard on his cigarette, his cheeks hollow.

Jim tried several parking areas before finding a vacant slot in Baker Lane. They entered Queen Street to bump into the Bishop deManaury and the Reverend Gates. The Laurel and Hardy syndrome was hard to miss. The Bishop was wheezing from the unaccustomed excercise, the Reverend breathing a contribution to polloution. Both were perspiring, using handkerchiefs to stem the trickles coursing down plump and gaunt cheeks.

"How nice," breathed the Bishop, his pig's eyes not reflecting any pleasure, "I haven't had an opportunity of thanking you for reaching the target set for the restoration of St Mary's my dear," A well-fed hand, clammy and cold clasped Betty's.

"A truly splendid effort, we are very grateful aren't we Charles?"

"Indubitably Bishop." The Reverend nodded his turkey head, his Adam's apple bobbing. The dead crab odour infected a wide area, "I understand there has been a problem with the restoration work. Mr Farraday has relinquished the contract to Mason's, do you happen to know the reason Mr Lewin?"

"You'll have to ask Harry, Reverend, I'm not at all sure why. Mason's are a reputable company, I'm sure they'll do a good job," Jim ducked that one, imagining the interrogation that would ensue if the truth were known.

"I'll do that of course," The Reverend nodded, his goggly eyes appeared red-rimmed. "Very unusual in this day and age for a building contractor to turn down steady work isn't it?"

"No doubt Harry has good reasons," said Jim.

"I have managed to persuade the Court to put an injunction on that pagan busines at Bawsey tomorrow night Mr Lewin. I'm sure you approve, appalling blasphemy, an insult to our Lord, especially on consecrated ground," The Bishop's look asked for signals of approval.

"It's up to everybody to make up their own minds on that score Bishop," said Jim.

"Surely you don't approve of pagan rites being enacted on consecrated ground Mr Lewin?" The Bishop bent forward fixing Jim with his stare.

"We're not regular church goers Bishop," Betty interjected, "All matters of religious protocol we leave to the appropriate authorities such as you. If you feel that harmless celebrations of the Solstice are blasphemous, you must act accordingly. That's your duty, I'm sure."

"Harmless?" The Bishop echoed, "Disgusting sexual orgies involving innocent young women. Surely as a mother, you can't approve of that scenario?" The Bishop fanned himself with his scented handkerchief.

"I believe all these tales of impropiety are what people would like to think goes on Bishop. I can't imagine my son-in-law approving such activities either. He and Ellen are model husband and wife and since she would have been present, neither would she permit it."

The Bishop's trumpet mouth formed a large 'O', his piggy eyes bulged with indignation, "But it is a well known fact that these people indulge in orgies Mrs Lewin. Not only is it blasphemous to use consecrated ground for such licentious behaviour, but I'd have thought that all decent citizens would approve of my action?"

"I feel you've been sadly misled Bishop. This is just wishful thinking on the part of a salacious minority who, as usual, are vociferous and articulate. The reality is much more mundane."

"Well," gasped His Excellency, "I never believed a civilised citizen of this town would defend such Pagan rites."

"You've got it wrong Bishop, and you've acted on prejudice, not on facts. That's your prerogorative of course. I can't be expected to agree with the exotic imagery conjured up by a few ill-informed people in the community."

"I see we've made some basic errors of judgement Reverend Gates. I'd have thought that wealthy citizens, highly respected would have been on the side of common decency, it seems we were wrong."

"Sorry you feel that way Bishop, I still insist that you listened to some inflammatory propaganda by prejudiced people, didn't give Mr Wilson an opportunity to putting his own case before you. I'd have thought that being a man of God you'd have sought guidance and full information before plunging in with drastic court action."

The Reverend Gates looked appalled at this challenge of ecclesiastical authority, the odour of decaying crabs spread over the area in his agitation.

"His Excellency was acting in the best interests of all God fearing citizens Mrs Lewin," he gabbled, "We can't permit acts of blasphemy to be enacted on consecrated ground. Surely you aren't denying that this Summer Solstice ceremony is basically profane, an affront to God?"

"I deny your premise Reverend. You listened to your own prejudices, and didn't enquire more into the nature of these celebrations," Betty wasn't moved.

"I believe we're amongst heathens Reverend," puffed the Bishop. "It seems I acted with commendable alacrity to get this pagan rite suspended. If mature citizens are prepared to defend such sacriligious activity, then I fear my action has the approval of him, and I didn't act a moment too soon."

"Well we'll leave you with the thought Bishop, that a little careful investigation would have been enlightening and democratic, assuaging your nightmares of rites and blasphemous acts. We wish you good day," Betty moved off.

"Your wife is a forthright woman Mr Lewin, even if she is misguided," The Bishop's puffy face was contorted in anguish.

"That's also a prejudiced opinion Bishop. Good day to you, have a nice one," Jim joined Betty.

"Pompous old goat," Betty was indignant.

"I suppose he's acting within his own terms of reference love," said Jim, as they walked down King Street. "If he ignored what he sees as blasphemy he'd be neglecting his duty as a church man."

"Don't make excuses for the stupid man Jimbo. He acted without consulting anybody, just on the basis of some busybodies accusing Kevin of obscene acts."

"You wouldn't have taken that view before Kev and Ellen were married love. You half believed it yourself"

****

44.

Tuesday June 20th 1995.
Globe Hotel, Tuesday Market Place,
King's Lynn, Norfolk.

"That was then, we're talking about now."

They passed the entrance to Bobby's office just as he emerged.

"How're those two journalists doing Mumsy?"

"They were being treated when we left the hospital. I don't know any more than that."

"They'll be well looked after," grinned Bobby, "Trouble is they will be convinced there's paranormal activities going on now."

"Might put the others off when they see what happened to those two," said Betty. "We just bumped into the Bishop and the Reverend.getting all up-tight about rave-ups, orgies etc."

"He got that old bastard Crawford to agree to an Injunction. Didn't take much persuading either, he half believes all the rumours as well. You going someplace?"

"Thought we'd have lunch at the Globe," said Betty.

"You aren't put off by what happened yesterday Mumsy?"

"So many weird things have happened over the past few weeks, I'm sort of getting used to it. The answer is no, I refuse to be put off like this."

"Well have lunch on me. Meeting Tracy in the Globe."

Tracy was waiting in the reception. Troy and Pamela Middleton were with her.

"Oh God," muttered Jim"The Angel of Doom!"

"You're insulting my dear Mother-in-law Dad," grinned Bobby.

"Hi love, hi Pam, Troy, come to sponge on the in-laws have you?"

"Pity you don't use that wit in the courtroom," said Pamela in an acid tone.

"You're looking well Troy," Bobby ignored her, "The treatment Funny Fanny gave you at the fete did you wonders."

"I certainly feel better than I have for years," Troy was conscious of

Pam's disapproval of him mentioning Fanny, "I don't know what she did but it was beneficial. I've booked a table, no doubt they can organise a double. How are you James? We've heard some weird stories about goings on up at your place, read the article in the Advertiser this morning."

"The least said about that disgusting rag the better," said Pamela, "'Ghost on the Rampage, our neighbours phoned us up asking questions about it. I think you should move out of that farm Elizabeth, it's giving you a bad name."

"We can't afford to renovate a priory Pamela," said Betty, "And we like it there despite the publicity."

Jim walked in with Troy and Bobby. The three women were gossiping away.

"How's the renovation work going?" asked Jim.

"Should be ready for us to move in before Christmas. Masons are doing a good job for us. Harry Farraday couldn't cope with it, along with the work on the Church, otherwise we'd have stuck with a local firm." I don't know why Pamela gets so up-tight about Mrs Legge, I'm very grateful to her for what she did, I haven't felt so good in years."

"I supose she feels that you should have stuck with orthodox medicine not dabbled with what she sees as witchcraft," said Jim.

"Barry admitted he couldn't do anything for me, only contain it. I always felt off, never as good as I have since she treated me at the Fete. I suppose they'll be hounding her since that article appeared in the 'Advertiser' unfair, really."

"She'll cope with it in her own way," said Jim, "You heard about what happened to Betty yesterday?"

Two tables had been joined, additional places set as they arrived in the restaurant.

"I heard all abbout it from Lilly Simpson," said Pamela, tartly. "She should have been in the KGB."

Betty met Jim's gaze as she raised her eyes heavenwards.

They talked about Farraddy's wife Fiona, Lilly and Lane Ward and their affair, John Foster and Marie Richards. Pam was bitter about Jeannie Foster being cuckolded by Foster's affair with Richards. Then the talk moved to Wally Thompson and his miraculous recovery from lung cancer. Pam, true to form was contemptuous of the events surrounding Thompson's recovery, dismissive of Fanny Legge's role. Betty defended Fanny vigorously, giving details of what had transpired the day before and the cure attributed to Fanny. Pamela refused to acknowledge any debt to Fanny Legge became heated when Betty persisted. Jim, seeing the discussion getting out of hand, intervened with a description of the scene at their house earlier that morning. Harris and Rayner being taken to Longley Hill suffering from heart attacks as a result of visiting the Hump. Pamela was equally vitriolic about the publicity engendered by the article in the Advertiser, claiming that such exposure was lowering the tone of the whole town. Jim kicked Betty under the table when he saw her about to reposte, shook his head.

Pamela then transferred her spleen to the Wizards and the Solstice celebrations at Bawsey the following night, voicing all the prejudices and rumours surrounding the event, including orgies, drugs and pagan rites. She didn't mention Kevin or Ellen but the inference was plain that she considered them worse than New Age travellers. Jim jumped in again, diverting Betty from a hot response to this criticism by talking about the success of the golf club under Paul Miller's management, which was a mistake.

Pamela jumped in, "That man is vice-President of these Wizard people, he'll be corrupting all the young women who use your course."

"He'd have a hard job corrupting some of them," said Betty, "I hear that the goings on at Blanche's are not what our Bishop would term the activities of well-brought-up young ladies."

"Tracy went to Blanche's, she never mentioned any problems like that, did you Tracy darling?"

"I didn't want to frighten you Mother," said Tracy.

Pamela's eyes opened wide, "You mean to tell me there were things going on?" she looked shocked.

"The Boys from King Edward VII used to climb in at night, we had a great time. That's how I met Bobby," Tracy grinned.

"You mean…?" Pamela stuttered.

"My God Mother, what century are you living in? Haven't you h eard of the Pill? The contraceptive one, we all used them."

"Were you aware of these things Troy?" Pamela looke accusingly at her husband.

"Of course he wasn't. Don't blame Daddy Mother."

"And did you…?" Pamela stopped, horrified.

"Five nights a week Mother," said Bobby, "Great time was had by all."

"Good God," Pamela lapsed into silence.

"We enjoyed our time at Blanche's Mother," said Tracy, "Learned about the birds and the bees the best way, practical experience."

"Mason's are taking over from Farraday at the Church," said Jim to divert attention. Harry says his men won't work with ghosts present."

"That man used to be alright until he married that awful woman," said Pamela, "When Charlotte was alive he was a gentleman."

"I wouldn't have thought grown men would have subscribed to those kind of fairy tales, especially unimaginative types like workmen," said Troy, alert to his wife's predilection for scandal. "You won't get that problem with Mason's, very large and professional group, used to handling large contracts."

"Their surveyor is coming round in the morning to do the necessary," Jim saw Pamela winding herself up again for another onslaught. Simultaneously he, facing the entrance to the restaurant, saw Arthur Harris' young assistant enter, accompanied by a young woman.

The opporjunity to divert Pamela from more acrimonious commentary was ideal.

"How's Harris?" He stopped the young man as they passed the table.

"You're Lewin aren't you?" The man's muscular frame was plain even under the denim jacket.

Jim nodded acknowledgement.

"He and Jolly are in a bad way," The cockiness of the earlier meeting had gone. The man looked stressed, there were dark rings under his eyes.

"We arrived at that... what did you call it, the Mound?"

"Hump,"said Jim.

"The mesh gate was open so we went in and saw the old workings of a building site, footings I believe you call them. We took a look in the site hut when Kerry here called us, said she'd found a skeleton in the ground." Robinson looked embarrassed.

"There was one." Kerry was dark slimly built, dressed in a linen frock with a wide white collar. Her fine features were pale. "I tried to take photos of it but my camera wouldn't work, so I called Arthur and Robbie, they both came out of the hut. Arthur's not what you call an easy person, gets stroppy if he suspects inefficiency."

"He started to give Kerry a bollock..., sorry a telling off. Said she should have checked her equipment before she came out. Jolly had his camera, he tried but his wouldn't work either. Arthur was in a right paddy by this time, he started bawling Kerry out. I went out to the Shogun to get Arthur's gear." Robinson looked ill-at-ease.

"Jolly and Arthur bent down to examine this skeleton, it seemed to be intact, all the bones present, arms, legs, skull, ribs, even teeth." Kerry paused, "I know this sounds like something out of a crummy movie, I'm not even sure what I did see now. Jolly and Arthur both reached out to touch it," The young woman looked flustered, unsure.

"Go on love, finish it," urged Robinson.

"It seems idiotic now."

"Tell them exactly what you saw," insisted Robinson.

"This thing, a skeleton reached up, both hands grabbed Arthur and Jolly by the wrist. Maybe I'm imagining all this."

"You weren't love, I arrived back with Arthur's camera gear, I saw that skeleton grab their wrists. Both Arthur and Jolly jumped back. There was a blue flash, like an electric shock, it jumped from that thing to both of them. They were flung back, both complaining about pains in their arms and shoulders, they had difficulty breathing, Jolly was gasping. That local jerk, the one who started all this off, Calhoun, tried to call emergency on his mobile. It wouldn't work, neither would mine or Robbie's. The next thing this Calhoun ran off towards your place, yelling that he'd get help."

"We dragged Jolly and Arthur outside the fence, kept them warm as we could. They were both complaining they felt ill."

"Some of the other blokes with us used their phones, they worked fine, they called Emergency 999. Some of them went inside the fenced-off part and tried taking photos of this skeleton. They came back saying there was nothing there and that we'd made it all up, so I went back in. We couldn't do much for Jolly or Arthur, those blokes were right, no sign of any skeleton in that place. I thought perhaps I'd got the wrong location, but I searched all over that compound, nothing! I thought I was going off my nut, seeing things, hallucinating. Nobody's camera would work inside that compound. Then there was the Shogun, when I got around to thinking the obvious, that wouldn't start either, it refused to budge." Robinson was obviously distressed by the recollection.

"Sounds stupid doesn't it?"

"It sounds it, but it isn't," Betty assured the two of them.

"You mean you don't think we're crazy, mixed up?" Kerry looked startled.

"We believe you," added Jim.

"What utter nonsense," burst out Pamela, "Ghosts, skeletons that move, cameras that don't work, blue flashes, I reckon you've been victims of hallucinations, it happens under stress, you imagine all sorts of things. Just take an aspirin and have a cup of tea, you'll feel better."

"Who're you madame? A Psychiatarist, a shrink, a medic?" demanded Robinson, angrily, "I wasn't hallucinating. If I was half the correspondents of Fleet Street were as well."

"They said they didn't see any skeleton," said Pamela, primly.

"I don't think you're in any position to make judgements of that kind my dear," said Troy, mildly, "You weren't there, these people were."

"They're from newspapers aren't they? They're all sensation mongers, specialise in disaster and weird stories, just to titillate their moronic readership."

"There was nothing weird about Mrs Legge curing my hepatitis was there?" Troy was nettled. Robinson and Kerry looked angry.

****

45.

Tuesday June 20th 1995.
Globe Hotel, Tuesday Market Place,
King's Lynn, Norfolk.

"You always were a hypochondriac Troy Middleton," said Pamela. "You're being very aggravating my dear."

"You believe all this rubbish about crypts, groaning, ghosts and all that, do you?" Pamela was red-faced, "And now a skeleton that moves, can't you see through this nonsense for goodness sake? They want to make a sensation out of nothing just to tease their readers with para-normal experiences."

"We've heard of this Mrs Legge, read about her in Calhoun's article in the local rag," Robinson was alert suddenly, his news instincts rising, "You say she cured your hepatitis sir?"

"And cured that man Thompson of his lung cancer, according to Calhoun," added Kerry.

"Could I have your name sir?" Robinson was all business like.

"No you can't young man, we don't want our names associated with all this sensationalist nonsense."

"We respect your privacy madame, but we'd like to talk to this Mrs Legge. Do you know where we can locate her?" Robinson seemed to have miraculously recovered from his travail.

"No I don't and what's more we don't need you scandal-mongering round our town. That Calhoun creature is quite enough, thank you.

"She lives in North Wootton," said Troy, "Not sure where precisely."

"Where's that sir?" Robinson had produced a notebook and pen.

"Miles away from here," snapped Pamela, "It's only a rumour that she lives here."

"Do you mind woman?" Kerry was curt, "We're talking to this gentleman," She nodded at Troy.

"You've said enough Troy Middleton, off you go you two, peddle your scandal somewhere else, we don't need your sort in Lynn."

"Can you tell us where this Wooden is madame?" Robinson addressed Betty.

"Wouldn't help you if I did Mr Robinson. Nobody knows for sure where Mrs Legge lives."

"Come on Larne, we can get it from the Electoral Roll. These people don't want to tell us, frightened of us."

"You've certainly got that right young woman. We don't need your type in Lynn upsetting people, writing scandal, sensatalist rubbish."

"You're being very rude my dear. These young people are only doing their jobs."

"You want your hypochondriacal rubbish in print do you? Think they'll stick to fact, they'll be making this Legge woman into a Saint, a Saint Bernadette, or Mother Teresa, in their filthy paper. Off you go, we don't need you in Lynn."

"Thanks for your co-operation sir," Robinson was coldly angry.

"Pity your wife isn't a lady."

"Don't you dare be rude to me young man, I'll call the manager, have you thrown out."

The other diners were becoming irritated by this altercation. Someone had sent for the manager. He bustled in, full of self importance.

"If you don't mind please, you're upsetting the guests."

"We're leaving sunshine," said Robinson, "Don't get your knickers in a twist."

"Now, if you don't mind sir," insisted the manager.

"I said we were leaving, tosh. Take your hand off my sleeve."

Robinson looked capable of lifting the manager off the floor.

"Disagreeable young people," spat Pamela as they were escorted from the restaurant, "Typical of people from the big cities, think we're all simple peasants."

"You were acting like one my dear," said Troy, "There was no need to be rude to them, they eere doing what they're paid to do."

"You're far too soft with the hooligan element, you surprised me talking about this Legge creature, it made them think she's something extraordinary instead of some charlatan, confusing every guillible person with these ridiculous mystic powers. You should be more circumspect, Troy Middleton."

"I think you were rude also,Mother," said Tracy.

"You're always taking his side Tracy, you know very well how naive he is. He'd give our money away to anyone."

"Oh for God's sake, shut up all of you," rasped Bobby, "You're like a bunch of bloody fish-wives. Let's hear no more about it, they'll never find Funny Fanny's cottage anyway, and according to Ellen she's not in the Electoral Roll, so let's enjoy what's left of our lunch, huh?"

"I'm don't intend to be spoken to in this fashion by you or anyone else, Robert Lewin. I'm leaving, are you coming Troy?"

Pamela stood up and grabbed her handbag.

Troy stood up, looking sheepish, "I'm sorry James, if we've ruined your lunch."

"Don't worry about it, see you around," Jim waved a dismissive hand.

"Stupid old moo," growled Bobby, watching Pamela and Troy exit.

"That big mouth of hers will get into deep shit one of these days."

"Bobby!" Tracy was frowning.

"Well, she's a pain in the arse your Mother, all that artificial snobbery makes me puke."

"You've made your point Bobby," said Betty, "Leave it at that."

"Women sticking together eh Mumsy?" Bobby was himself again.

"We have to in view of male chauvinists like you Bobby Lewin," snapped Tracy, "Mother was right, we don't need those scandal mongers in Lynn, upsetting the place."

Bobby held up his hand, "OK, OK, I'll shut up, I hear enough of this feminist crap as it is."

"Go on, say it," said Tracy.

"Say what?"

"Should never have let'em out of the kitchen."

"Most blokes would go along with that. Give us a kiss, let's make up."

"He really is one, love," said Betty, "He was such a sweet child as well, can't understand it."

"We'll have to be going love, I have to see Paul this afternoon."

"What's Kevin going to do about tomorrow night in view of the injunction?" asked Bobby.

"We've offered him the Hump."

"Keep quiet about that if I were you, that dog collar has a lot of pull. He could get Sir William to set another injunction."

The manager stopped Jim as he was about to depart, "Sorry to trouble you sir," He didn't look sorry.

"What is it?"

"There's the matter of the bill for yesterday sir, when this lady was taken ill, I know how it looks, but I do have to make a profit."

"How much?"

The manager handed him the bill, "I don't want to buy the place mister," Jim was surprised on seeing the amount.

"Just pay him Jimbo," said Betty.

"Have you seen the amount?"

"I'll go halves Dad," said Bobby. He took a glance at the amount. "Hell's bells, you sure you've got this right mister?"

"Fraid so sir," The manager was firm.

"Just pay it," insisted Betty.

Jim handed the manager a bundle of notes. The tarted-up manager took the money into his office and came back a few moments later with a receipted invoice, "Much appreciated sir, I trust you're feeling better now madame?"

"She might be but I'm not," said Jim.

"That was a bit saucy," said Bobby, handing Jim some tens. "I insist," he said, when Jim refused.

"Let's have a look round the market," said Betty, "It's a long time since I've been round it."

"Must get back," said Bobby, "See you later."

The entire square was filled with stalls, selling everything from fruit and veg to crockery, tools, meat, clothing. It was crowded, mainly with women.

"Isn't that...?" began Betty staring.

"It is," said Jim, "There can't be two dogs that size."

"Hello Miss Legge," Betty greeted her. The dog growled in its throat.

"Hello Mr and Mrs Lewin." Fanny was clad in her usual apparallel, long black skirt, a maroon blouse, lace shawl and wooden clogs. "I understand the Bishop has been obstructive over your son-in-law's Solstice Ceremonies at Bawsey tomorrow night?"

"How did you learn that?" Jim was surprised.

Fanny merely smiled and twisted her wrist. The dog continued to growl, a faint rumbling noise in its throat.

"It's alright Darren, friend" Fanny spoke quietly, "Sit!"

Most people gave the dog a wide berth, accompanied by curious look at Fanny's outlandish dress. Jim stroken the dog's head, the fur was smooth, not slightly rough as with most Wolfhounds. The animal's head was on a level with Jim's chest.

"He's invoking ancient blasphemy laws that are still on the statute book," said Betty.

"We've told him he can use the Hump," said Fanny.

Betty couldn't understand the gasp of surprise.

"Something wrong Mrs Lewin?" Fanny's accent was faintly Welsh.

Betty shook her head, "I haven't thanked you for your help yesterday, at the hospital," she said when Fanny looked blank.

"It must have been your help Miss Legge," said Jim, "Remember I went to your cottage to ask for your help?"

"Oh yes, I recall," Fanny seemed preoccupied, "It was nothing."

"We couldn't find you to take you home and Darren here was missing out of my Landrover."

"You cured my son-in-law's head wound as well," said Betty, "We would like too thank you."

"The media have been looking for you Miss Legge, we thought we'd better warn you. We don't care for their attentions and we're positive you don't want it either. They wanted us to give them your address."

"You are very kind," Fanny smiled, showing her model dentifrice. "I don't want to be interviewed by anyone, least of all people like that, rough, brash and insensitive. Before I forget, I would like to thank you for your gift of hay for my animals, every week for the past ten years. You don't have to do it."

"You cured my back Miss Legge. I'm very grateful, saved me from years of acute discomfort."

Jim was still fondling Darren's massive head. People passed by, staring curiously at the strange figure of Fanny and the dog.

"Oh God, look," Betty pointed.

The Anglia TV outside broadcast van had appeared at the edge of King Street. There was a camera mounted on the roof with an operative panning the camera to take in the market scene. A smartly clad woman wielding a bulbous microphone appeared. It took Betty only a few seconds to identify the woman as Daphne Charlesworth, the make-up girl. Accompanying her were the cameramen Carl Ransome, Gary Smith and Brian Molyneux. The group were making for Fanny with determined steps.

"The cameraman on the roof of the van must have seen us," said Betty, "If you don't want their attentions..." She stopped, looked round bewilderedly. Fanny had gone.

Charlesworth and her group reached them. There was a newer assurance to the young woman that hadn't been present at the church on Sunday.

"Where did she go?"

Charlesworth looked puzzled. Ransom was swinging his shoulder-held camera round in futile sweeps. Smith and Molyneux were asking people if they'd seen Fanny. The recipients of this attention shook their heads, puzzled.

"Where did she go?" repeated Charlesworth, "Did you say anything to her?" She was accusing.

"She didn't want anything to do with cameras Miss," said Jim.

"Or interviews," added Betty.

"These two were bolshie with Holly, Daph," said Ransome, "Obstructing her over that bloody church and the crypt. They probably told her to get lost." The cameraman's craggy face was hostile.

"You probably recall Mr Ransome's eagerness to go down into the crypt Miss Charlesworth, a really macho-type, until it comes to the crunch."

Ransome scowled, still panning the camera in a vain hope of picking out Fanny from the crowded market. Several boys were staring curiously at the TV crew, waving, sticking two fingers up in rude gestures.

"Go away you little sods," roared the burly cameraman.

"Watch it Carl, they're the future for us," said Molyneux.

"Christ help us," muttered Ransome.

"How's Holly?" asked Betty, sweetly, "You stepped into her shoes?"

"She's more co-operative than that stuck-up bitch," stated Ransome.

"She's going over to the Beeb Mrs Lewin," Charlesworth wasn't too self-assured as yet. "Are you telling us that you didn't tell the witch to get lost?"

"We did, she doesn't care for publicity," said Betty. "Where she went, we don't know. She has this ability to vanish, like all witches," added Betty.

"Got her broomstick parked near the Corn Exchange," said Jim.

That didn't go down too well with Charlesworth. "I hear the Bishop of Lynn is trying to secure an injunction against the local solstice freaks for tomorrow night? I understand the chief rabbi of the odd-bods is your son-in-law, a Mr Kevin Wilson?"

"We can screw that lot up Daph," said Ransome, holding the camera by its hand-strap, "A full-blooded orgy will go down well on the box. Raping virgins, blood sacrifices and all these swedes tarted up in their funny gear, incanting. Bawsey isn't it? Along the Gayton Road, the old ruin on the hill? I fancy filming a load of swedes screwing young girls in their smocks, straw sticking out of their pants!"

"That's just about your mark, paedophile, is he?" said Betty.

"Saucy cow" growled Ransome.

"We'll leave you to it Miss Charlesworth. I wish you every success in your new role as TV reporter. You've had a good role model in Holly Summerfield," Betty linked Jim, "Let's go love."

She urged him in the direction of the High Street. "Don't you want to go round the market?"

"That lot's put me off, I wonder how she found out about that injunction? If that lot turn up tomorrow night it would ruin it for Kevin and Ellen."

"He thinks it's being held at Bawsey and she evidently does not know that that injunction has been served and is in place. So they'll turn up at Bawsey, find the cops in situ," grinned Jim.

"If they bump into Lilly Simpson though, she'll put them straight," said Betty, as they passed the Marks & Spencer store.

****

46.

Tuesday June 20th 1995.
King's Lynn, Norfolk.

"Let's go in here," hissed Jim, pushing Betty into the store hastily.

"I don't particularly want to come in here Jimbo," protested Betty.

"You will when I tell you I've just seen Lilly with Fiona Farraday just up the street," said Jim.

They hurried to the back of the store, hoping to remain concealed and that the objects of their flight would pass by. To their consternation, Lilly and Fiona appeared in the High Street entrance and sauntered inside, inspecting the female clothing.

"Let's go," urged Jim, heading for the Norfolk Street entrance.

"Coo-eee," They heard the dreaded summons, "Over here Elizabeth." Lilly was waving frantically from the women's wear department.

"Oh, God, I don't think I can stand any more of her, love" said Jim.

"We can't ignore her, in view of Demetrius' contribution to the restoration fund, besides, Demetrius is a golf freak."

Betty waved at Lilly, a false smile on her face. Lilly and Fiona hurried over.

"I've just been telling Fiona about the Injunction," Babbled Lilly, smelling of some new perfume and garlic, "I said that this sort of thing should be nipped in the bud didn't I Fiona? We don't want hordes of New Age travellers camping on the verges round the town dumping rubbish, lots of half naked children, dogs, horses and broken down vans and lorries, it would be awful. Once these things arre allowed to happen it escalates, worse than Stonehenge, the cost to the police is awesome."

Lilly paused for approval, Betty and Jim said nothing. Fiona was staring at Betty, dislike patent, "Any more groans from your crypt Elizabeth? I read the Advertiser this morning, very entertaining. Ghosts on the Rampage, sounds very dramatic, like one of those horror movies, 'Gremlins' or 'Alien'. Lots of slimy monsters all roaring and eating people. There was a special train in this morning, a load of people from the Paranormal Society, or something. There were buses laid on to take them to the Church."

"You're joking?" Jim couldn't help it.

"Oh no, we saw it, didn't we Lilly? Must have been over a hundred in the party, with cameras and funny apparatus, all laughing and singing. We thought you knew all about it?"

"Christ," said Jim, "Let's go love, they'll be wrecking the place, breaking into the house."

"Excuse us won't you, you do understand?" Betty was appalled, wondering whether Fiona and Lilly were exaggerating.

"What's the matter?" Lilly looked all innocent.

"How'd you like gangs of freaks camped on your lawn?" snarled Jim, "I'll bet you'd love that."

"See you sometime," Betty waved as she and Jim hurried out.

"This way," Jim indicated the crowded High Street.

"You reckon she was lying?" Betty had a job keeping up.

"Daren't take the risk, dare we?" Jim headed down Purfleet Street.

"God, I hope she's wrong, I don't think I could cope with a crowd of freaks after that lot this morning."

The parking ticket had run out, there was another summons attached to the windshield, it was fixed hard. Jim had a job removing it, leaving a residue of paste on the windscreen.

"That's all we need, two bloody tickets," groused Jim.

They made it to the farm in under ten minutes. Their worst nightmare was reality. There were five coaches all parked on the lawn, hordes of men, women and children all milling riound the house, peering in. The potholed road to the church was filled with a host of straggling people, all walking happily towards the distant edifice. Jim had difficulty finding a space to park, the tourists reluctant to move aside for him, glaring resentfully at the Landrover.

Jim stopped once group as they de-bussed, "Who's the organiser of this jamboree?" He was so angry he could barely be civil.

"Mr Richardson, the tall chap over there," A languid hand indicated a geriatric teenager in khaki shorts, knee-high stockings and epaulettes on his shirt, who was ushering even more people from the last bus to arrive.

"You the boss of this lot?"Demanded Jim, indicating with his thumb the crowds of people.

"I am the official organiser my man", haw-hawed Richardson, his sloping forehead gleaming with perspiration, "Who might you be?"

"I'm the owner of this farm, tosh, and I want this lot off my property toute suite. I haven't give permission for anybody to visit my farm and you're trespassing. I want you and this transport off my land in fifteen mionutes or I get the police, is that clear enough for you?"

"Now look here my man, we are a legitimate accredited organisation with over two thousand members. We were given permision to come officially," Richardson was six feet plus and towered over Jim.

"I never gave permission for an invasion of this kind. I can't carry on my business with this invasion of private property," snarled Jim. "Those buses are parked on my lawn and those hooligans are damaging my home."

"I have a letter from the owner," Richardson wasn't dismayed by Jim's obvious anger.

"I am the owner mister. I never gave permission to any group or organisation."

"What's your name my man?" Richardson extracted an envelope from his pocket.

"Lewin, and this is Lewin's Farm, Babingley."

"This letter is signed by a Mr Calhoun who claims to have access to this church. I assume he is the rightful owner?"

]"Let me see it," Jim snapped his fingers.

Richardson extracted the letter from the envelope and opened it, handing it to Jim, whilst he ushered more people from the interior of the bus onto the lawn. People were staring at Jim and Betty as if they were aliens. It was on official Parker Press stationery, proprietors of the 'Advertiser'. It had been signed by Rory Calhoun. The body of the letter stated that there was evidence of paranormal activity at Lewin's Farm, Babingley and that he, Calhoun, would welcome the intervention of the Paranormal Research Society to establish the presence of such a body to investigate the phenomena.

Jim was speechless for a long minute, in the meantime the occupants of the bus had disembarked and were milling around in bewildered fashion, all had holdalls of food, cameras and other impedimenta. The driver of the coach was unloading some folding tables from the luggage bays. Others were busy erecting them, spreading table cloths and laying out plates from hampers between the parked coaches.

"This is not permission and this man has nothing at all to do with my property. He is a local journalist, as is obvious from this headed paper. He has invited you to trespass on private land, now I want you off my property or I call the police to have you moved."

"Wait a moment Jim," Betty intervened. She faced Richardson calmly, "We are prepared to tolerate your society on our land on payment of fifty pounds per coach and an entry fee of two pounds per head for each visitor. Half price for children under sixteen. There will be an additional fee of one hundred pounds for the use of facilities on our property, those picnic tables, etc. You pay immeadiately or you vacate our property at once."

"What's the problem Rex?" A stocky man in a suit, jacket draped over his arm, red braces holding up his trousers arrived.

He was perspiring in the heat, sweat patches under his arms and across his back. He carried a leather briefcase.

"This, er... gentleman claims he is the owner of this property and didn't give us permission to enter his land. He also claims that Calhoun is just a local journalist who has not even any jurisdiction over this land," Richardson nodded at Betty and Jim.

Deep-set eyes glared at Jim from under bushy eyebrows, "You got ID mister?" he demanded.

"I don't need to identify myself pal. That's my house and you are on my land. My wife says she's prepared to tolerate this invasion of privacy on payment of an entry fee. You pay now or I call the police and I am not joking."

The newcomer exchanged glances with Richardson, "Looks like we jumped the gun Dickie. I was a bit dubious about this letter when I received it. I think we've been had." He turned to Jim and Betty, "It seems we owe you good people an apology. We assumed that this Calhoun was the rightful owner of Lewin's Farm. I'm sure you will agree the content would imply this," He pointed to the letter in Jim's hand. "It would be extremely difficult to extract our members at short notice, as I think it is fairly obvious. Can we come to a mutual arrangement Mr Lewin? We can pay for the inconvenience inflicted if that would be satisfactory. You agree Dickie? Richardson is President of our Society and my name is Howard, John Howard, I'm Secretary and Treasurer."

"A thousand pounds Mr Howard and you have permission to remain on our property for twentyfour hours," said Betty.

"Reasonable, Dickie?" said Howard without hesitation. "We could not move all our members without a lot of trouble, as I'm positive Mr Lewin appreciates." He opened his briefcase and took out a chequebook, "A thousand pounds, made out to…?"

"Lewins Farms Ltd," said Betty, without hesitation.

Howard wrote the cheque and handed it to Betty, "Once again, our apologies Mr and Mrs Lewin, I shall be taking this matter up with Mr Rory Calhoun."

"Join the club Mr Howard," added Jim, grimly.

"Better lock the gate before any more arrive Jim," said Betty sotto voce.

"Any chance of tea, coffee, or some other beverage Mrs Lewin?" asked Howard.

"I'll get it organised, fifty pence a cup," said Betty.

"And we have your permission to investigate that church?" Howard pointed to where St Mary's stood out in the clear sunshine.

Betty nodded, "I'll get tea organised," she said.

"I'll ring Paul, see if he can send some help over," Jim picked up the mobile from the Landrover.

By ten o'clock, most of the society members had departed in their coaches for various destinations. Betty and her helpers from the golf club had been consistently busy making tea, coffee and in the end sandwiches for the hundreds of PNRS members who had flocked to the temporary refreshment point outside the kitchen door. Jim had made a trip to the local supermarket and bought in bread, milk, tea, coffee and snacks. The visitors had not quibbled over the prices charged for the service. By six o'clock Jim made another trip to buy in fresh supplies. Ellen and Kevin turned up at six thirty helping Betty with the catering. At eight Bobby, Tracy and Laura arrived, attracted by the noise heard clearly by residents on the Slade Estate. They all assisted. John Howard and Richardson were among the last to depart, the two men profuse in their appreciation of Betty's efforts on the catering front.

"Was it worth it?" asked Jim, curiously.

"Definite signs of paranormal activity in that church building," declared Howard, "The low temperature for starters indicates the presence of extra-normal forces operating. We didn't see anything paranormal, but we've taken readings of vibrations and other psychic phenomena, very rewarding experience. That old building site is also very powerfully affected. The

Hump, I believe you call it. Were you aware of the fact that ley-lines cross at both locations? You are aware of ley-lines, I assume?"

Kevin, Ellen and the two visitors were soon into deep discussion on the presence of such phenomena on the site of the Hump and Church, and into a history of the discovery of the existence of such abstract concepts. William of Malmesbury, Alfred Watkins, Druids, Glastonbury, Stonehenge, The Great Pyramid, tumuli, Old Straight Tracks, St Elmo's Fire, dowsing, Pythagoras, magnetic centres and dragon paths.

Jim and Betty began the business of clearing up the detritus created by their amateur catering efforts, leaving the four people deep into their world of magic, geomancy and the sacred numbers.

Just after eleven pm, Paul Miller arrived followed in swift succession by members of the Wizard Society, to prepare for the Solstice Celebrations. Miller was an athleticly built young man of thirty-five, good looking, an accountant by profession. He had been a rare find as manager of the Golf Club created five years before by EEC funding to curtail milk and farm production. He was efficient, careful, honest and had increased memebership a hundred fold by his astute marketing and salesmanship. Howard and Richardson and several members of the PRN Society asked if they could be present at the ceremony as guests.

Betty and Jim retired at Eleven-thirty pm, dog tired, leaving the hundred or so wizards to complete their arrangements, dress up in their druid robes and depart for the ceremony at the Hump. Jim was soon in a deep sleep, tired out from the sustained effort of catering for hundreds of visitors. Betty, as was her custom, sat up in bed reading. Just before midnight, Betty heard a car arrive, followed by a thunderous knocking the front door. Betty had to shake Jim to awaken him.

"What in hell's that?" groused Jim, looking at the bedside clock, "It's midnight for Christ's Sake, Bloody sauce!" He climbed wearily out of bed and went over to the window.

He discerned the outlines of two policemen, illuminated by the oscillating blue light from their car. Another car arrived on the heels of the police vehicle.

"What's the problem officer?" called Jim from the bedroom window, "You know what time it is?"

"Sorry Mr Lewin, we have to serve this injunction on you?"

The policeman's features looked bizarre in the blue light as he gazed upwards.

"This is a joke, isn't it?" Jim was irritable at being awakened from deep sleep.

"Fraid not Mr Lewin," called the Constable.

"This is no joke Lewin," came a voice from the second vehicle "This is perfectly legal under the Blasphemy Act of 1796. I am serving you this injunction to prevent you using your premises as a vehicle for devil worship. You know full well those Blasphemers are using your land to perform sacriligious rites. Come down at once."

There was no mistaking the voice, Bishop de Manaury!

****

47.

Wednesday June 21st 1995.
Lewin's Farm, Babingley Marsh,
King's Lynn, Norfolk.

"Come back in the morning, I'm too tired to bother with that rubbish at this time of night," roared Jim, angrily.

"I have to warn you Lewin, you are breaking the law." The Bishop was evidently in a highly excited state.

The security light went on suddenly, illuminating the two young policemen and the Bishop and the Reverend Charles Gates.

"Go away mister, I'm too tired to bother with that crap. Serve it on me in the morning."

The Bishop started to threaten all kinds of legal action if Jim didn't come down to accept and sign for the injunction. One of the constables attempted to quieten the prelate, to allow the police to conduct their business.

"I'm afraid there's a timescale on this document Mr Lewin."

It was obvious that the policeman considered the whole business bizarre and unnecessary, "We have to get your signature before midnight I'm afraid, I'm sorry about this."

The Bishop started up again, accusing the police officers of partiality, dereliction of duty, disobeying Magistrate's instructions, indiscipline and ignorance of the importance of the Prevention of Blasphemy Act of 1796. The young policeman attempted again to quieten the Bishop who refused to cease his rambling, claiming that his church rank gave him the authority of a magistrate.

"I don't propose signing anything mister, so on your way. See you in the morning, good night!" Jim shut the window.

The knocking re-commenced.

"I'll go," said Betty, getting out of bed. "He's going to keep that up all night if we don't."

"No, let him sweat it out, he'll tire of it before we will. You know what it is don't you?"

"Yes, somehow they've heard about the new venue, someone's opened their mouth out of turn. We can't just leave it like that."

"You sign it and you drop Kevin and Ellen in it, it's almost midnight. If there's a timescale on it and we delay doing anything about it, it will be invalid." Jim sat the edge of the bed, irritable at being roused and furious that the priest should want to pursue the vendetta so single-mindedly over such an innocent celebration.

"I've an idea," said Betty, pulling on her dressing gown.

"Don't go down, you'll be required to sign it," cried Jim.

"I'm not sighing anything love," Betty exited from the room.

"Jesus Christ," snarled Jim, snatching his own dressing gown before following Betty downstairs.

By the time he arrived into the kitchen, Betty had opened the door to the two priests and constables. Bishop deManaury bustled in uninvited, an official looking document in his hand. The Reverend Gates followed him, but with more uncertainly. The Bishop was in his purple shirt and white collar and was also wearing a jacket, he was sweating profusely. The Reverend Gates looked apprehensive, his turkey crop prominent.

The Bishop plonked the document on the table and held out a pen to Jim, "Sign it!" he ordered.

"He's lost his spectacles, can't see as thing without them," said Betty.

Jim mimed myopic searching.

"You're obstructing the law Lewin," screeched the Bishop, furiously.

"He can't sign if he can't see sir," said one of the young constables.

"You condoning this charade constable?" demanded deManuary, "He can see to sign his name, he doesn't need spectacles for that."

He indicated the place on the document with a plump and sweaty forefinger, "Sign there."

Jim continued to myopically search amongst the piles of magazines and newspapers on the sideboard, on the dresser and on the table. "Can't see a thing without them," he muttered, "Now where did I put them? Do you rememberlove?"

"Don't recall seeing you with them since this morning," said Betty, performing a similar routine, "I'll have a look in the car." She went out to the Landrover.

"You're obstructing the law Lewin, that's a serious offence. Warn him Constable," raved the Bishop.

"He can't carry out the law's requirements if he's unable to see sir," said the Constable, a faint grin on his face, "That doesn't constitute an offence, it's unreasonable pressure and that's also illegal."

"I'm going to report your dereliction of duty to Chief Mostin, he will take a very serious view of your behaviour my man."

"You can check with the duty officer sir, he'll clarify the position for you," said the constable. "Can His Excellency use your phone sir?" Both policemen wore grins.

"Be my guest, officer," said Jim, "Can you see the phone anywhere? Dreadful affliction when you can't see you know?"

"You're delaying deliberately Lewin," screamed the Bishop, almost incoherent with fury. Sweat dripped from the end of his pug nose, he mopped his forehead with a handkerchief.

Betty returned, smiling faintly, "Would you mind telling us what this is all about Bishop? Why are you harrassing law-abiding citizens in this fashion? I'm surprised that a man of your standing should stoop to this kind of harassment in the middle of the night."

"You know very well what it's all about madame. That son-in-law of yours, Kevin Wilson, has organised a sacreligious pagan festival on these premises, contravening the Blasphemy Act of 1796. He's carrying out demon worship and public indecency on this land."

"Where is this law breaking supposed to be carried on?"

"On your property madame," choked the Bishop looking at his watch.

"We've no knowledge of such law breaking Bishop," said Betty, "How can you expect us to be responsible for such activity without proof of your accusation?"

"It's taking place this minute, down at that place called the Hump madame!" roared the Bishop, "You are well aware of it."

"Do you know anything about it Jimbo?" Betty appealed innocently to her husband, winking theatrically.

Jim caught on, "Ridiculous nonsense," he said.

Betty turned to the Bishop, "If you could prove that such acts are being perpetrated on our property Bishop deManuary, we'd be only too happy to co-operate, naturally."

"You're prevaricating madame, obstructing the process of law."

Betty shook her head, "Prove it then we'll sign."

"Sounds reasonable to me sir," said the young officer, "Let's go take a look at this… er Hump, see if blasphemous acts are taking place."

"It's half a mile officer, the road is impassable to ordinary vehicles, the night is humid and it will make it difficult to walk."

"Well sir, it seems prefectly reasonable to me, the provision of proof is incumbent on you sir. These good people are within their rights to refuse to sign if your accusation is unfounded." The officer was grinning openly.

"Come on then, let's go, you can drive us there in your high vehicle Lewin," puffed the Bishop.

"Not possible sir," said Jim.

"Oh? Why not? The vehicle is out there."

"Sadly the keys are with my specs, wherever they might be. You can't expect me to drive without my spectacles, that would be breaking the law," said Jim. "Just let us get dressed, you make your way down to the Hump, we'll join you shortly."

The Bishop looked as if he were about to decline, but changed his mind, "Come on Reverend Gates, let's prove to these people that indecent acts are being performed on their property. You will accompany us officer to verify the evidence."

"Certainly sir, delighted," The officer gave Betty a wink behind the Bishop's back.

"I phoned Kevin on the mobile," said Betty, "They're going to the church for awhile until these two busybodies have gone."

"Great stuff love," grinned Jim, "By the time they get there it will be past the deadline anyway. Let's have a cuppa whilst they sweat it out, we can always find the keys when we're ready."

Half an hour later Jim and Betty arrived at the Hump, the headlights showed the two constables and the Reverend Gates standing round a recumbent Bishop.

"He's had a heart attack sir," said the young officer, "That's what it looks like to me." He was agitated, panicking. The joke had misfired, the Reverend Gates was flapping, wringing his hands and moaning about demons and devil worshippers and God punishing them all.

"Have you phoned for an ambulance?" asked Jim.

"My phone's out of order sir," said the young man, "It was working perfectly earlier."

Betty and Jim exchanged glances, "Let's get him up to the house officer. Even the ambulance has difficulty in traversing this road."

It took all four of them to lift the unconscious Bishop into the Landrover. Jim drove the overloaded vehicle back to the farmhouse and Betty phoned for an ambulance en route. The Reverend Gates kept up a whining monologue all the way about the state of his superior's health, and the scandal if the media got hold of the story.

Two hundred yards from the house, Jim saw the unmistakeable outlines of the Anglia Outside Broadcasts van parked in the driveway.

"Oh no, that's all we need." The whole area was floodlit suddenly by arc lights from the TV crew.

Holly Summerfield arrived at the Landrover, Ransome, the cameraman at her heels, his camera held on his shoulder.

"What's the problem?" Holly held out a microphone to Betty.

"The Bishop's had a heart attack. down at the Hump, give us a hand to get him indoors can you?"

The TV crew aided Jim and the two policemen to carry the overweight Bishop into the lounge.

"God, there's some beef there," gasped Ransome.

"I thought you were off to the BBC Holly?" asked Betty.

"Richard made me an offer I couldn't refuse, as long as I rescinded my resignation. Daphne's a mite miffed, understandably, had her nose put out of joint."

"What're you doing here at this time of night?" asked Jim as the ambulance siren could be heard approaching.

"Friend of yours told us that the local wizards were celebrating the Solstice here. Thought it might be a good follow up on the para normal stuff," Holly grinned. "We won't get in your way. I heard all about Rayner and Harris this morning, yesterday now isn't it? Seems that everybody visiting that Hump suffers heart attacks, although after lifting that fat bastard, it's obvious he's been a prime candidate for some time."

The ambulance came to a standstill outside the door. The two paramedics who had attended Harris and Rayner entered the lounge, "You're getting to be our best customers Mrs Lewin," said the young woman. She recognised Holly and was all self-conscious as Ransome took film of them attending to the Bishop.

"Good fill-in footage," said Ransome to Holly.

The TV crew assisted the medics to carry the Bishop out to the ambulance. The two young constables waited until the ambulance had departed.

"No need for this now Mr and Mrs Lewin, the time limit has passed. We'll be on our way, sorry about all the agro," The taller policeman said, looking down at the injunction in his hand.

"You were only doing your job officer. Want some refreshment before you leave, cold drink, tea, coffee?"

"That's very kind of you Mrs Lewin, coffee would go down nicely, you reckon Mal?"

His companion nodded, "We don't need to report in for a while."

It was plain both young men were in awe of the great TV personality, Holly Summerfield, they even asked for her autograph. They both sat down looking curiously at the TV equipment and the team members.

"Is it true that Rayner and Harris were bitten by a skeleton at this Hump this morning?" asked Holly.

"How'd you hear about that?" Betty was curious.

"Some blue rinse lady volounteer lady at Holding's Hill told us and Calhoun of course, the local Robin Day!"

"At long length," added Ransome.

"Any idea of her name?"

Holly consulted a notebook, "A Mrs Simpson, she also told us about the injunction the Bishop took out to stop the local wizards holding their Summer Solstice at... " She consulted her notebook again, "Bawsey Ruin. I interviewed the magistrate who issued the injunction..." she leafed through her notes again, "A Sir William Crawford, who told us the Bishop had taken out another one against them holding it on your farm, providing the document was served before midnight on the 20th June."

"There was that young feller as well as Calhoun," said Ransome, "Gave us the whole story about Rayner and Harris at this Hump. Wasn't that the place where our gear wouldn't work on Sunday?"

Betty nodded, "Who was this young man you spoke to about the two newspapermen?"

"A Larne Robinson, one of these excercise freaks, all muscle and sinew," said Holly, "He didn't look too healthy at the hospital though, must have frightened him shitless, and Calhoun wasn't too kosher either"

The two young policemen were listening fascinated to the great TV personality and her cohorts.

"The Bishop having a coronary should make good news as well. We heard that a special train had arrived in Lynn with members of the Paranormal Research Society on board. They were headed in your direction, did they come?"

"The two officials are down at the Hump now, going to observe the Solstice with the wizards," said Betty, "The rest went back home."

"Did they see anything?"

"I don't think so, their cameras wouldn't work at the Hump, neither would the phones."

"Have you any objections to our filming the wizards and their Solstice Celebrations?" asked Summerfield.

"You'll have to ask Mr Wilson, he's the Grand Wizard. If he doesn't object then it's OK by us," said Betty.

"Where is he now?"

"They went down to the Church to avoid the Bishop," said Jim.

Summerfield grinned, "Very astute, I suppose his Lorship was too exhausted to make the extra journey?"

"He didn't know."

"We'll get down there, find this Mr Wilson, see what his reaction is to our filming the ceremony. Should be a rival to Stonehenge with all the national publicity yesterday." Summerfield signalled to the driver of the van to start off.

Jim and Betty watched the huge vehicle swaying and lurching on the rough track, heading towards the Hump.

"Perhaps we can get to bed now love," said Jim.

"What's that?" Betty was pointing towards the main road.

A long caterpillar of headlights was moving at a snail's pace towards the entrance to the farm. The sound of many engines washed over the night air. The two policemen came out of the house.staring at the chain of lights.

"Oh God, no!" groaned Jim, running for the Landrover.

"Where're you going?" cried Betty.

"I'll bet they're New Age people, come to celebrate the Solstice," yelled Jim, "If I don't close that gate we'll be swamped."

"We'll come with you Mr Lewin," offered the policemen, running for their own vehicle, "You might need some help."

By the time they'd arrived at the main entrance on the A149, the first of the vast convoy had halted, evidently attempting to locate the entrance. There were old buses, mobile homes, caravans, lorries with makeshift shelters erected, converted furniture vans and even a steamroller. The tail of the convoy was out of sight towards Lynn. Close up the noise was unbelievable, the voices, the sound of heavy diesel engines and radios blaring.

A long haired man jumped from the driving seat of the bus in the lead and approached Jim and the policemen.

"Where's this Hump mate?" he enquired, the rank smell of unwashed body assailed Jim's nostrils. He was joined by several other men all dressed in outlandish fashion.

"It's on private property mister," said Jim, "Nobody's allowed entry."

"You kidding pal?" demanded the spokesman, "We've come a long way to join in the Solstice. The pigs are out in force at the Stone. We want to gain access."

"You heard the gentleman sir," said the young cop, "He's the owner of the land, he has a right to refuse you entry."

"You on his side?" sneered the spokesman.

"We're her to uphold the law sir, that's all," said the officer.

At that moment the familiar motorbike sound of a Volkswagen engine could be heard approaching over the roar of many static vehicles. The yellow Volkswagen with its balloon tyres betrayed ownership. It skidded to a halt at the head of the convoy. Calhoun, clad in his usual washed denim, jumped out.

****

48.

Wednesday June 21st 1995.
Lewin's Farm, Babingley Marsh,
King's Lynn, Norfolk.

"What's the hold-up? "He demanded of the spokesman, ignoring Jim and the police.

"This joker's proving difficult mate," growled the man, accompanied by muttering from the men round him, "Coming the old capitalist crap about private land and all that."

"You refusing to let these people entry to the Hump Lewin?"

Calhoun was all bouncy, cocky with confidence.

"If you believe for one minute I'm going to let this lot onto my property Calhoun, forget it," said Jim.

"Let's open that bloody gate, drive in, see if this joker can stop us," yelled one of the men around Calhoun, "Fucking landowners, all the same, the land belongs to the people, not to rich bloody capitalist pigs."

Several of the men rushed to the gate.

"Bring the bolt-cutters, Tom, the fucker's locked it."

"I must ask you not to do anything of the sort sir," protested the young policemen, shakily, "That's trespass." He and his companion stood between the ragged-looking men and the gate.

"Move sonny, or we'll throw you in that river," threatened the lanky leader.

The young policeman's colleague was speaking into his mobile radio, in an urgent voice. The sound of a patrol car's siren was heard rapidly approaching. It arrived with a squeal of rubber on the road, the siren switched off. Four policemen jumped out.

"That was quick," exclaimed one of the young cops, gratified.

"We were on our way," said the newcomer, a sergeant. "What's the problem?"

"These people want access to Mr Lewin's land. Plainly, he doesn't need this invasion of privacy, Sarge. These men propose breaking into Mr Lewin's property, using bolt cutters," explained the young policemen.

"You know you'll be breaking the law sir?" The sergeant addressed the crowd of New Age Travellers that had swelled into dozens as others came to the head of the convoy to investigate the hold-up.

"Move aside pig, nobody owns the land, it belongs to everybody."

"I must warn you sir," insisted the Sergeant, a tinge of hysteria in his voice.

"Yeah yeah, we heard all your capitalist bullshit, pig, now move before we throw you into that fucking river."

Two more patrol cars arrived with police to capacity, they joined their colleagues at the gate. There was a uniformed Inspector with the latest arrivals.

"Move back please," he yelled, "Disperse at once."

The number of New Age Travellers had swelled to a crowd of men and women all milling round the gate. Calhoun, Jim noticed, was busy taking flash photos of the throng. He was also quietly inciting the travellers to cut the chain on the gate. Scuffles broke out between police and New Age people, just as a minibus of police reinforcements arrived. The newcomers all clad in riot gear.

"Kill the pigs," yelled a voice. Fighting started between the riot police and travellers. Jim saw Calhoun talking to some late arrivals. Crowds of the travellers swarmed over the fences and began pulling at the chain link fencing. A bearded individual brandishing bolt cutters jumped the gate and tried to apply the tool to the padlock. He was prevented by two police. The fencing was giving way under the violent treatment applied by the travellers. More men joined the fighting around the gate and more bolt cutters appeared. The police were unable to cope with the sheer numbers. Several more minivans arrived, followed by a larger vehicle. Jim, trying to avoid the fighting, recognised Chief Constable Mostin in full uniform. He used a bullhorn to address the screaming, elling mob. By this time the fencing had almost been torn up. Others were attempting to sever the padlock on the gate, prevented from doing so by the efforts of the police.

"Ladies and Gents, please listen to me," intoned the Chief, his voice echoing, "You are breaking the law. Unless you desist I shall be compelled to use other means to restrain your unlawful acts. I am reluctant to resort to this, but unless I get some response from you I shall be obliged to do so."

"Hello Chief," Jim made his way to Mostin's side.

"Hello Lewin, we'll do our best to stop them, but they've heard that crettin Lambert on Radio Lynn informing them of the Solstice being held on your land. We can't hold them for long. I've asked for help but it's going to take some time before they arrive."

"I believe Calhoun is stirring them up," said Jim, "He arrived some time ago, urging them to chop the locks." They both had to yell over the bedlam that surrounded them.

Mostin spoke to one of his Inspectors who moved over to where Calhoun was making hay with his camera, taking shots of police and travellers fighting. The Inspector spoke to him, the content plain from gestures. Calhoun was angrily refuting the Inspector's claims, waving his arms and shouting. Two constables seized him and frog-marched him to the large police vehicle.

"Gate's open," came a yell from exultant travellers, "Let's go."

The lead vehicle began moving towards the gate, it entered as police had to give way before others trailed them in. Chief Mostin signalled to the driver of the large police vehicle, who began edging his way towards the gate to block entry. Crowds of travellers swarmed round it, trying to up-turn it. Police rushed to prevent them, exposing the entrance to other traveller's vehicles. Soon the whole convoy was heading down the lane towards the farmhouse.

"Sorry Jim," said Mostin, "I haven't enough bodies to contain them."

Jim watched with dismay as the convoy began moving towards the house. Without warning there was a sudden gout of flame from the proximity of the house, the whole area was soon illuminated by a wall of fire. Jim knew instinctively the cause. Betty had blocked the road with hay bales and poured petrol over them, making an impenetrable barrier and preventing their ingress. The convoy halted, men began milling around. Soon enterprising travellers had formed a human chain from the Babingley River, passing buckets of water to people close to the fire wall. The police watched helplessly as the human swarm flooded over the land towards the house. More vehicles joined the convoy, jammed close together. Soon the fire was extinguished, the travellers began removing the scarred bales. The lead vehicle, a converted double decker bus began moving toward the house. The remainder followed closely. Jim's Landrover was hoplessly isolated by the throng. When he was able to get anywhere near it, he found it had been vandalised. The seats, radio, rope and most of the controls had all been ripped out.

He was standing contemplating this disaster when he heard a corporate groan coming from the mob near the farmhouse. The news was passed along the mob like bush telegraph, the lead bus had come to a halt in a ditch. Jim was puzzled for a moment, there was no ditch on the route to the farm. Then he had it, Betty and the others had removed the cattle grid. The double decker had plunged into the pit, effectively stopping all ingress to the farm. The succeeding vehicles had attempted to by pass the double decker, only to come to grief in the marshy ground either side of the road.

"What's happened Jimbo?" asked Mostin, as the police caught up with him.

He explained.

"That'll stop them getting any further," The Chief approved grimly.

"Looks as if they're abandoning their transport sir," said one of his Lieutenants.

Even in the darkness of the countryside away from the main road, it was plain that hundreds of travellers were leaving their vehicles, making their way on foot past the farmhouse.

"They'll be vandalising my house," Jim hurried forward, mixing with the throngs of men, women and children, all surging along the track.

Mostin and a platoon of police accompanied him. They were still a good four hundred yards from the farmhouse when they heard shotguns being fired. The reports were muted by the noise of the mob. The security lights were blazing from the house walls, illuminating the milling crowds. Jim saw Betty, Bobby, Tracy and Laura, standing like the thin red line in front of the house. They all held shotguns, levelled at the yelling, screaming mob.

As soon as Jim and the police appeared, the mob scattered. Jim saw several windows had been smashed but none had dared approach nearer the house. Mostin ignored the letter of the law at the use of firearms and spread his men in a cordon around the buildings. Most of the crowd were surging past, ignoring the police presence and the grim-faced guardians of the house. Those that had intended malicious damage or theft were arrested by the police.

"Thank God you arrived Mr Mostin," Betty was a bundle of nerves, her hands shaking, "They were going to break in, we had to stop them."

Betty and the others surrendered their guns to the police. She ran to Jim, who clasped her in his arms, soothing her.

"You did a cracking job stopping them Mrs Lewin," said Mostin, "That firewall and the cattlegrid has stopped any more vehicles attempting to come this way, the road is blocked."

"They'll be tearing the church apart," wailed Betty, anguished.

"They're more interested in the Hump love, it's Kevin, Ellen and the wizards we have to worry about. This lot will swamp them."

"Two of my officers served an injunction on them, how come they're still there?" demanded Mostin.

"They attempted to serve it on us, being the owners of the land," said Jim.

"Why didn't they?" Mostin was piqued.

]"The Bishop accompanied them, he was yelling, complaining, making a great deal of noise. We suggested he go to the Hump, see for himself they weren't holdings orgies, drugs, sex, etc. That's when he suffered his heart attack."

"Heart attack?" echoed the Chief, incredulously.

"We went down to the Hump to see how he was getting on. That is when we found out about the Bishop. No phones worked so we had to transport him here, phone from here for an ambulance. He's in Holding's Hill now."

"That's when the time limit ran out for serving the injunction. By that time this mob had begun to arrive," said Betty.

"I warned the man not to interfere," muttered Mostin, "Anyway we have more pressing problems on our hands. I'll deal with those two officers later."

"They did their job, Ralph, if that old goat hadn't been so brash, bullying us, we'd probably have signed it. Don't know what we could have done about it though, the wizards were already at the Hump."

"Forget it for now, how far is it to this Hump?" Mostin was perspiring himself now.

"Half a mile, give or take abit." Jim saw the police milling around outside on the patio, "None of your vehicles could get down there even if you had them available. The road's too bad, save for high vehicles, Landrovers, Jeeps, four-wheel drives, that sort of thing."

"My men will be exhausted after that fracas at the gate," The Chief was half talking to himself.

"What can you do if you go there?" asked Betty, "You won't be able to control them. The place is barricaded with mesh fencing. I know they could rip it down, but would you be able to prevent it, realistically?"

"I'm thinking of the damage they could inflict on your property Jimbo."

"There's nothing down there they can do much damage to, they could to he church though, the scaffolding and the mesh fencing. Mason's won't be too happy if they have to erect new scaffolding."

"I thought Harry Farraday was carrying out the work?"

"He copped out, his men refused to work there because of the experiences they've had. Masons have agreed to take over," said Jim.

"Is that what that article in the Advertiser was all about yesterday morning, Ghosts on the Rampage and all this paranormal activity?" Mostin looked sceptical.

"There have been peculiar things happening that can't be explained by normal factors," said Jim.

"I can't believe civilised people can swallow all that nonsence, ghosts, crypts, lightning, groaning noises…" began Mostin.

The whole room was suddenly illuminated by a blue flash.

****

49.

Wednesday June 21st 1995
Lewin's Farm, Babingley Marsh,
King's Lynn, Norfolk.

"What the devil's that? A storm?" Mostin rushed outside just as another series of blue flashes lit the sky.

"Must be a storm coming sir," said one of his officers.

"Seems to be coming from the direction of that old church."

The officer pointed to where the silhouette of St Mary's was just visible.

"No thunder," said another, "Peculiar!"

The whole sky was suddenly illuminated by violent flashes of electric blue light. Betty looked at Jim, he shrugged.

"Good morning," said a voice from the perimeter of the patio

Everybody turned.

Fanny Legge stood in the shadows, the huge wolfhound was by her side. Its eyes seemed to glow with a yellow light.

"Miss Legge, what are you doing here?" cried Betty.

The policemen were all staring at Fanny, their attention diverted for the time being from the blue lightning that was illuminating the whole sky.

"It seems that people are profaning the sacred sites," said Fanny.

"Funny old cow," muttered one of the policemen.

"Looks like something out of a horror movie," said another.

They fell silent when they saw their chief glaring at them. "Excuse me madame, what sacred sites?" asked Mostin.

"The church and the place you call the Hump sir," said Fanny.

"Look at the size of that fucking dog," said one of the policemen to his companion.

"Its eyes," said another, "Real Hammer House of Horror stuff."

"Quiet," snapped Mostin, "Why are those places sacred madame?"

"The ancient pathways cross at both places, the power is at its strongest during the night of the solstice."

"Pathways? What pathways?" Mostin was becoming irritated.

"Ley-lines, Chief" said Jim.

"What the devil are ley-lines?"

"Take too long to explain," said Jim, "Is that what's causing the lightning, Miss Legge?"

"Those people are in acute danger," Fanny didn't seem to have heard. She was staring over the heads of the assembled officers towards the church.

"Danger? What danger madame? Explain please."

"I must go, warn them," said Fanny.

A flash of extraordinary brilliance suddenly lit up the countryside, highlghting trees, fencing, houses and hedges. Everybody turned to see the flash, ducking involountarily.

"She's gone," said one of the policemen.

"Where is she? Can't be far," rasped Mostin, "She can explain all about this phenomena. Find her, get her back."

"You're wasting your time Ralph," said Jim, "She has this ability to disappear at will. Remember your back on Monday? She cured it for you along with Paddy Murphy and Holly Summerfield, the TV lady from Anglia, and Betty here. She has some power that defies any explanation."

"I read all that guff Calhoun printed in the Advertiser yesterday, pure sensationalist journalism, fabrication, I would imagine," scoffed Mostin. "Find that woman you men, be quick about it, she can't have got far."

The policemen dispersed at the irritation in their Chief's voice.

"They won't find her, chief, you're merely wasting time, she's gone."

"My God, you don't subscribe to all that rubbish Calhoun printed do you Jimbo?" Mostin was peeved.

"We told you, there have been some peculiar things happening over the past few days, Ralph, in the crypt at the church and at the Hump. We've always had problems comnnected with the Hump, machinery won't operate, cars won't start, that's why Johnny Foster pulled out of the bungalow building a couple of years ago. The footings were always ruined as soon as they put them in, the cement hardened in the sacks and there was even blood in the tap water, his men felt ill."

"Oh come on Jimbo, you can't be serious."

"Foster will confirm it, if he ever gets over his coronary."

Jim was nettled by the obvious scorn in Mostin's voice.

The lightning continued its spectacular display, illuminating the entire countryside. They became aware of voices, gradually becoming louder.

"The men must have found that weird lady," said Mostin, looking at his watch. His radio crackled, "Yes... you've found her?"

"No sir, but that mob is heading this way, they sound panicky to me."

"You haven't located this Legge woman?"

"Difficult sir, in the dark, despite all this lightning. The road isn't what you'd call smooth highway, just potholes. Christ, look at that Ray. There must be hundreds of 'em."

They could hear the screaming and shouting now, via the Chief's radio.

"Watch it sir, this bloody lot are panic-strick-en, heading your way."

The sound of voices, men yelling, women screaming, could be heard above the radio background. Jimbo, Mostin and Betty heard the officer via his radio attempting to find out the cause of the panic. A babel of voices filled the radio, then suddenly the radio went silent. Mostin tried several times to recall his officer without success.

"The fool has dropped it," he cursed, savagely.

The sound of fear-filled men and women rapidly approaching was plain now. The flashes of lightning showed a panic-stricken mob running stumbling, hastening towards the farmhouse. The more athletic members reached the house first, their faces showed badly frightened people. Mostin attempted to stop them to ask what was wrong. They shrugged him off and continued on towards the main road. The next arrivals were near-exhausted people, barely able to keep going.

"What's the matter?" demanded Mostin, stopping a youngish man and woman, "What's the rush?"

"Them skeletons!" babbled the man, his eyes stark with fear.

Mostin could get nothing more from him. The man shrugged him off and ran on, dragging the exhausted woman with him.

"What on earth is the man on about?" Mostin attempted to stop others, they brushed him aside and ran on towards the main road.

Jim estimated at least a hundred people must have passed the house, all showing fear, panting with weariness. The older people appeared, trying desperately to keep going.

Mostin stopped one couple, "What's wrong sir? Why are you running like this?"

"Skeletons!" cried the man, face contorted in fright, "Burning people, dozens of 'em, out of the ground."

He shrugged Mostin's hand off his sleeve and hurried on, dragging a woman with him.

"They're crazy," Mostin shrugged, looking in vain for sight of his officers.

At last two of them arrived, looking shaken, perspiration gleaming on their faces.

"What's the matter, Smith? Get a grip on yourself man. Calm down, tell me the problem."

"Skeletons sir, ghosts, don't know how you'd describe them. They're running amok amongst these people." He had to shout above the fearful yelling and screaming of the crowd.

"For God's sake Smith, have you gone completely mad? Cool it, tell me rationally what the problem is."

Smith calmed down somewhat, his companion was shivering with fright, unable to speak. "I know it sounds daft sir," gabbled Smith, "If I hadn't seen them myself, I wouldn't have believed it either."

"Believed what, for Christ's sake man?" Mostin shook Smith's shoulders, "You aren't making any sense."

Two more policemen arrived amongst the crowd, an Inspector amongst them.

"You tell me what's causing this panic, Fraser, I can't seem to get sense from these two."

Fraser was a burly man, craggy-faced, obviously fearful, "I know how you're going to react sir, I swear it's fact."

"What man, come on now, get hold of yourself." Mostin shook him gently, "Take your time, there's nothing to be scared of."

"There is down there at that Hump sir, dozens of skeletons coming out of the ground, running amok, attacking people, they're getting fearsome burns." Fraser was stuttering with fear.

"Fraser, you're not making any sense, skeletons don't do anything exept lie there." Mostin was literally dancing with irritation.

"The skeletons are coming," screamed passing travellers, "Run, or they'll get you."

"Thousands of them, grabbing people, killing them," yelled another hoarase voice hurrying past.

Jim heard engines being revved on the distant main road, headlights were being switched on, silhouetting people hurrying for their own transport. Several other policemen arrived, all looked paralysed with fear.

Mostin addressed a Superintendant, "What is it Fletcher? What's causing all this? What's this nonsense about skeletons?"

Fletcher's eyes were wild, "It's true sir, I can only describe them as skeletons, you know, bones, skulls, ribs, all running amok. When they grab people they get burned. I know you think I've gone mad, I didn't want to believe it either. I thought I was seeing things at first, hallucinating, but it's true, it's crazy, that place is a charnel house of burned people."

"What about the wizards, officer?" cried Betty, "Are they being attacked as well?" Fear larded her voice.

"I didn't stop to look madame, I was shitting my pants in fright," said Fletcher.

The mob had thinned to a trickle now, of the older and those less able to walk. They were yelling fearfully about skeletons.

"Let's go Jimbo, Kevin and Ellen are down there. We better phone for an ambulance if there are injured people down there at the Hump."

"I wouldn't go down there missus," cried Fletcher, "Those... er... things are killers."

"Get a grip on yourself, Fletcher," rasped Mostin, "Organise medical help, tell those comedians I told you to. Get them here at the double, tell them they're burn cases. Did you find the woman, this Funny Fanny?"

Fletcher shook his head, his lip trembling, "No sign of her or the dog sir."

"You're in charge here man, get things organised, I'm going down there with Mr and Mrs Lewin, see for myself. Skeletons, never heard such rubbish in my life."

Jim took a powerful torch from the kitchen and joined Mostin and Betty. They passed scattered groups of travellers and the remaining police officers. All gave the same story of skeletons running amok, burning people. Stumbling over the uneven track, Jim, Mostin and Betty hurried towards the Hump, ignoring the warnings of the few remaining travellers that they were heading for danger from the skeletons. The lightning had increased in intensity until the night was almost totally luminescent with continuous blue flashes. They were two hundred yards from the site of the Hump when the white cloaks of the wizards became visible, tinged violet by the unearthly illumination of the lightning. They were all bunched together in the centre of the fenced off area, facing outwards. Jim estimated there were twenty of them. Kevin was recognisable due to the archbishop-type hat he wore. The blue flashes gave the whole group a surrealistic effect.

"Don't come in Mumsy," he yelled, recognising his mother, "Some odd goings on."

"Are you alright son?" yelled Jim, a nameless fear gripping him.

"Perfectly OK Dad, we just daren't move off the site."

"You alright Ellen, Paul?" called Betty.

"OK, don't come in, like Kevin says," called Ellen.

"What's the problem, Wilson?" yelled Mostin, "What's all this nonsense about skeletons running amok?"

"It's true sir," said Kevin, "Come from the centre there," They saw him nod towards the disturbed earth mound. "We haven't been affected, but a lot of those travellers were seriously injured by burns."

"Where are they?" called Mostin.

"Ran off screaming, sir."

"Where're the TV people?" asked Jim.

"Went on down to the church," said Kevin.

"What about Fanny Legge? Have you seen her?" Betty was anxious.

They all denied having seen any sign of her.

"She came to the house, said that the spirits were angry, I don't know whether she meant angry at you or the travellers."

"You saw these skeletons Mr Lewin?" asked Mostin, "Running around burning people?"

There was a muttered consultation amongst the assembled wizards, "We saw them," announced Kevin.

"All those people were screaming about skeletons running amok and burning people," said Mostin, "How come you aren't affected?"

"I think it's because we know about the forces that travel along the ley-lines sir," said Kevin.

"I don't know how I'm going to report all this to my boss," muttered Mostin, "Ley-lines, lightning, skeletons running around burning people. He's just going to think I've flipped."

"I think it would be a good idea if you found Fanny Legge Mumsy. I've got an idea she could help us off this site. This lightning only started up when we arrived here. If she's around it would help."

"I'll go down to the church, see if she's there," offered Jim.

"I'll come with you Lewin," said Mostin.

"You be alright love?" asked Jim.

"I think Fanny is the key to all this Jimbo, you go, I'm OK."

Jim and the Chief set off, the church was garishly silhouetted against the blue flashed of lightning.

"I've seen some weird things in my career, but his take first prize without any doubt," groused Mostin as they walked down the rutted track. "Nobody's going to believe me, the Chief Constable will have me certified."

****

50.

Wednesday June 21st 1995.
St Mary's Church, Babingley,
King's Lynn, Norfolk.

They saw the ATV van when they were two hundred yards from the church, illuminated by the violent blue flashes of lightning that seemed to be emanating from the church itself and travelling in the direction of the Hump, there was no sign of any Anglia personnel. On arrival, Jim peered into the driving cab and into the interior, it was devoid of life. His torch showed the technical equipment, but there was no sign of the crew.

"Must be in the church."

Jim led the way towards the mesh gate. It was locked tight, the padlock secured.

"Got to be someplace else," said Mostin, as Jim directed the torch beam over the scaffolding and walls of the ruined church.

The lightning, close as they were now, seemed to be originating from the where Jim knew the entrance to the crypt was located. They made a complete circuit of the church, but saw no evidence of the presence of the Anglia crew.

"Must've gone off somewhere," mumbled Mostin.

"They'd hardly leave their valuable equipment and that van without someone remaining behind."

Jim directed the torch beam into the body of the church. Apart from the shadows cast by both the blue light and the torchlight, they could see nothing.

"Can't we get into that place Jimbo? Seems that that lightning, whatever it is, is coming from inside the building. Most peculiar, they could have gone inside," the Chief was examining the padlock.

"It's locked," Jim reminded him, remembering his and Betty's experience on Monday night.

He had the uneasy feeling that that was precisely what had happened to the Anglia people. They were inside the church unable to get out.

"Don't touch it Ralph," warned Jim as the Chief reached out for it.

"Why not for God's sake, I'm just about up to here with all this paranormal crap. They could well be inside that place where we can't see them," Mostin touched the padlock.

The next instant he was on his back, stunned by a shock. He arose shakily, rubbing his hand, "This place is bloody weird, outside my experience completely, I'm just a copper trying to do a job."

"Can I help?"

Both men whirled. Funny Fanny stood behind them, the massive dog by her side. Its eyes glowed with that yellow inner light. Neither man had heard her approach.

"Miss Legge!" cried Jim, "We were looking for you."

Mostin was staring at the woman, still rubbing his injured hand.

"Why?" She spoke softly, yet every syllable was distinct.

"This activity, the lightning, the things those travellers saw, skeletons running around, I'm sure you can explain all this."

"Those people were going to disturb the dead, buried under the Hump, vandalising their resting place. It is the night of the solstice, two hundred years to the day when this church was built. They are very unhappy at being disturbed by such sacriligious acts."

"Two hundred years." Jim recalled the date on the mysterious plaque - June 21st 1796 and the name, Myfanwy Legge, affixed to the side of the catafalque, the plaque that appeared, then vanished.

"You mean the wizards at the Hump?" Jim was still pondering on the significance of the dates, times.

"No, they are sympathetic to the forces that travel the lines. I mean those crude people, vulgarly trying to grab unusual experiences, crude, rough, brash. They were going to vandalise the sacred site."

"Did you send those skeletons Miss?" demanded Mostin, looking askance at the huge dog.

"Skeletons, Mr Mostin?" Fanny's voice held humour, Jim was sure.

"They were screaming about skeletons running amok and burning people." Jim could tell Mostin could hardly bring himself to admit the validity of the phenomena.

"When the power flows Mr Mostin, people see what they believe they're seeing, a kind of corporate holograph, transmitted from one person to the next."

"So they didn't see anything of the sort?" Mostin sounded relieved. He was careful to avoid going near the wolfhound.

"Oh they saw them inside their own heads, that is what they believed they were going to see, therefore they saw it."

"Miss Legge, we believe the TV people might be inside the church. We can't open the lock, it is charged with electricity, can you help us?"

"You believe it is charged Mr Lewin, therefore it is. It is not terrestrial energy that travels along the lines, but power from the ancient sites the Church has abused over the centuries, trying to deny the existence of such energy that has no origin with the Christian Church. They are the vandals destroying the ancient knowledge, in their eagerness to crush any semblance of power save their own."

"Can you open that lock Miss Legge?" pleaded Jim, all this was over his head.

"It is open Mr Lewin, you believed it was locked."

"I got a shock from it," said Mostin, aggrieved.

"You received the thoughts that emanated from Mr Lewin sir, thus the actuality was realised."

"Oh Christ," muttered Mostin.

Jim went over to the gate and touched it gingerly. There was no shock, the padlock was undone.

"I will come with you Mr Lewin," said Fanny, "Stay, Darren, wait."

The huge dog lay down, its glowing eyes regarding the two men with what seemed to Jim to be malevolence. She seemed to brush past Mostin, part of her passing through him as if he was a ghost. Jim didn't see Fanny touch the gate, it swung open.

"Hells bells, it's bloody chilly in here," said Mostin as they sqeezed past the tree growing in the middle of the doorway.

Jim shivered uncontrollably as the chill struck him. Inside, they could see that the lightning was coming from entrance to the crypt. The whole arched aperture was incandescent with energy. There was no sign of the Anglia crew inside the main body of the church.

"Can you do anything about the lightning, Miss Legge? They must have gone into the crypt," said Jim, rubbing his arms to keep warm.

Without warning the flashes ceased. There was a smell of burning, the gloom inside the nave without the lightning was intense.

"You wish to go into the crypt?" Fanny seemed to glide, her clogs making no sound on the littered stone floor. She appeared unaffected by the chill.

"You reckon it's safe to go in there with all that electricity present?" Mostin was dubious.

"It is safe Mr Mostin," said Fanny in that same calm voice that was characteristic of her, "Now" she added.

"Anybody down there?" Jim shone his torch down the flaking stone stairs.

There came a moan from the dark opening. Not the inhuman groaning Jim had experienced on previous visits, this was wholly human and in distress. Jim sensed that Mostin looked unhappy about entering the crypt.

"Stay here Ralph, Miss Legge and I will go down?"

"It's OK" Mostin assured them.

"Watch your footing, the stone on these stairs isn't too good."

Jim led the way, Fanny following and Mostin in the rear, stepping gingerly over the crumbling stairs. Jim's torch revealed the Anglia team all lying on the floor.

"Thank God you've come," cried Summerfield, attempting to rise, "I can't get up, can you help?"

There were cameras, mikes and cables littering the floor around the members of the Anglie team.

"You can now Miss Summerfield," said Fanny.

Summerfield sat up cautiously, "Jesus, I couldn't do that a minute ago when the lightning stopped." She felt over her body as if parts were missing.

Jim saw an Anson lamp on the floor the large lense smashed. It worked when he switched it on, casting a fuller light over the scene. Ransom and Molyneux were prone behind the central catafalque, attempting to rise. Fanny seemed to wave her hand over them. Instantly both men sat up.

"Where's Gary?" Summerfield was upright now, brushing down her clothes.

"Over here Holly," came a weak voice from the far corner.

"You can get up now Mr Smith," said Fanny.

"Who's she?" Ransome pointed at Fanny.

"This is Miss Legge," said Jim.

"That bloody witch creature," snapped Ransome,"I'll bet she had a hand in this business."

"Watch your mouth mister, without her you'd have been down here for good," rasped Jim.

"It's alright Mr Lewin, Mr Ransome is justifiably upset." Fanny went behind the catafalque to Smith, the Sound man.

"How'd you know my name missus?" demanded Ransome, "I ain't ever seen you before, and you're damn right I'm uptight. If you were the cause of this, you want prosecuting!"

"Shut up Carl," said Summerfield, "You don't have to talk to Miss Legge in that manner."

"It's alright for you Miss Glory Seeker, you get all the kudos, Gary, Brian and me just get the shit, like being down here with these bloody corpses." He was flexing his arms and legs, "Look at our gear, it's all broken because of her." He pointed at Fanny as he came from behind thhe catafalque.

"It had nothing to do with Miss Legge Carl, so button your big mouth for Christ sake," snapped Summerfield.

"Who are you mister?" She saw Mostin standing at the foot of the stairs.

"This is Chief Constable Mostin of King's Lynn Constabulary," said Jim.

"You wanna put that cow away for good Chief," Ransome was angry, "She's a menace too society."

"It strikes me that most would call you media people the principal menace, Mr Ransome," said Mostin. "If you had been more circumspect and not after some cheap sensationalist rubbish with which to regale your viewers, you wouldn't be in this situation," Mostin was tart. "I could claim that you have been responsible in a way for my having to bring half my officers on special duty to control all these New Age Travellers, who arrived her as a result of things seen on their screens."

"That's a little unfair Mr Mostin," Summerfield was still brushing herself down, "There was only a fifteen second item on the screen about the Solstice at Babingley."

"Enough to trigger off a virtual invasion of Mr Lewin's land, causing a great deal of damage to his property, Miss Summerfield," Mostin's voice was cold.

"Told you, didn't I? The pigs are on the side of these Swedes, fuck the media," snarled Ransome.

"I believe we should have left these people down here Jimbo," said Mostin, "Our community would have been better served."

"Can I quote you Chief?" asked Summerfield.

"I believe I'm reflecting the views of most of our citizens, Miss Summerfield. By all means quote me if you feel it is relevant. I think it would be a good idea to thank Miss Legge for her help in getting you out of here."

"I still think the woman should be put a..." Ransome seemed to stop in mid-sentence, only cobbled sound came from his mouth. Unintelligible noises as if he were a crettin came from his mouth.

He gave a hoarse scream, pointing to his mouth, his eyes wild with fear. The Anglia teamm all stared at their stricken colleague in horror. Saliva was dripping from Ransome's mouth, his lips all twisted in a rictus of awesome shape.

"She's done that to him," cried Molyneux, "She is a fucking witch. Casting spells, she's made him dumb."

Ransome was making horrible gargling sounds, looking terrified.

"That should warn you to keep your mouth shut," said Jim, unmoved.

"It's the same thing that happened to me on Monday, outside her cottage," cried Summerfield. "Can't you release him Miss Legge? I will vouch for his silence in future, he will apologise for his rudeness."

"Where is she?" Molyneux was looking round, wildly.

"She was here a second ago," Smith walked round the catafalque.

"She's vanished."

"That brass plaque has gone as well," said Molyneux. He was pointing to the catafalque, "How the hell did she get out of here without us seeing her? One second she was here, then she wasn't. She is a bloody witch, I'm going nuts."

Ransome was still gargling frantically, turning round and round in his distress, trying to manipulate his mouth.

"What's wrong with him?" Smith was horrified.

Mostin was awestruck, staring at the cameraman with dismay. "She must have caused that," he said, half to himself.

"Too bloody true she did, Chief. Like Carl said, she's a fucking menace, should be put away," said Smith

"Let's get out of here, I'm freezing," said Summerfield, "The sooner we get him medical help the better."

"What about the equipment?"

"Leave it, we can pick it up later. Come on Carl, let's get you to a quack." Summerfield took Ransome's arm. He shook her off, pointing to his mouth, making the meaningless noises.

"OK, if you don't want help."

Summerfield made for the stairs, the others followed her.

"You staying mister?" demanded Jim, finding it hard to feel sympathy for the man, in view of his attitude toward Fanny.

Ransome stumbled up the stairs in the wake of his colleagues.

"Let's get out of here Jimbo, it gives me the willies," said Mostin. He shuddered, "This cold is frightening!"

****

51.

Wednesday June 21st 1995.
The Hump, Babingley Marsh,
King's Lynn, Norfolk.

They were both at the foot of the stairs leading to the nave when they heard the groaning behind them.It started as a low moaning.In seconds it was a ferocious snarling.

"Jesus, what's that?" Mostin was paralysed with fear, looking fearfully behind him. The Anson lamp the Anglia people had left behind was still blazing highlighting the crypt and the central catafalque. The entire crypt seemed to pulse with an energy, invisible, yet palpable. Mostin gave a hoarse scream of fear, he stumbled frantically up the stone stairs into the church. Jim was transfixed in a nameless terror. The walls seemed to be pulsing, as if part of some living creature, breathing in some nameless power source. The demonic groaning rose to a crescendo of hideous shrieking as if in pain, trying to disgorge the suffering into the crypt. The central catafalque was glowing with an ochre light, pulsing like a heart beat. Jim willed himself to flee, but his feet seemed encased in concrete, glued to the stone floor. His brain was numb with fear, the desire to run from the maelstrom of the pit overwhelming reason. His will powerless in the energy that pulsed from wall to wall, involving the stone coffin, as if his inner being was gradually sucked into the coffin. He knew he was screaming in terror, the animal desire to flee the raw energy that filled the crypt, overpowering all other emotion. He felt himself remorselessly being drawn towards that glowing catafalque. His terror-crazed mind saw something like a skeletal hand rise from the lid of the coffin, glowing as if filled with liquid fire, beckoning him. A brazen skull clawed upwards, appearing over the rim, the twin eye sockets filled with piercing laser light that seemed to be drawing the brains from his own head. The bony fingers of the other hand appeared followed by the ribcage until the thing was upright in the coffin. The fingers curled beckoning him, the light from those laser-like sockets hypnotising, destroying his will. He knew he was being drawn towards that awesome apparition to be held in an embrace of death.

"Dad!"

The voice boomed round the crypt, bouncing off the pulsing walls, echoing, re-echoing into infinity.

He knew that it was the voice of his son, Bobby. Hope flared. He had but to resist for a few second longer and the spell would be shattered, the grisly spectre would vanish, evaporate into the stone. He was within a yard of the coffin, he could see dervishes of fire in the centre of those horrid sockets. The skeletal fingers of the hand were reaching out to embrace him. He would be drawn into a vortex of doom.

"Dad!"

It seemed Bobby's voice was a mammoth gong that filled his whole brain with sound. He was aware of another presence behind him. The bony fingers, glowing with that orange light, were an inch from him. The ribs seemed to be beating to a rythym of a pulsing heart, the teeth in a ghastly rictus of welcoming smile.

Without warning the hideous scenario vanished. The shrieking ceased, the stone cataflaque was just that, the crypt its normal deadly chilling entity, gloomy, shadowed from the light of the Anson.

"You OK Dad?" He felt Bobby's hand on his shoulder.

Weakness filled him. He would have collapsed but for Bobby's hands under his armpits. He didn't same able to control his legs, they felt rubbery without substance, unable to support his body.

Then he was over Bobby's shoulder in a fireman's lift and they were going up the crumbling stairs to the nave. He knew he was shivering violently. A terrifying chill seemed to be penetrating to his innermost being. He was vaguely aware of passing beneath the interior scaffolding in the church and then blessed warmth of the summer night enveloped him.

"He alright?" Mostin's voice, calm, normal, reassuring.

"Frightened shitless" came Bobby's voice, "Give me a hand will you?"

Then he felt soft earth under his shoulders, the scent of grass in his nostrils. It was as if he'd been on a long journey into space, where all norms were invalidated, but now, he was back.

"You lie there Dad, we'll get help."

"I'm OK," he croaked, "Just give me time to come round."

He could see the vast silhouette of the church tower looming over him. He didn't want to be left alone, he needed the reassurance of warm humanity to restore his traumatised brain. The images of the scene inside the crypt filled his mind, the glowing light the dread apparition rising from the catafalque, beckoning him towards it, wanting to embrace him.

"Take your time."

They were both leaning over him, their faces pale in the moonlight, anxious. He struggled to a sitting posture, gazed round him. The exterior scaffolding, the tree growing in the centre of the main entrance. The walls of the church, with the glassless window apertures like openings into darkness.

"Take your time Dad," Bobby repeated, his son's hand was rubbing his shoulder massaging life back into it.

"Give me a hand up," Strength seemed to be returning to his limbs.

Upright, with their assistance, he swayed but remained stable, he took a few faltering steps, aided by Bobby and Mostin. After a few yards he was able to walk unaided. They were heading towards the Hump. He could vaguely make out a kind of procession of shrouded figures, circling the mound, chanting as they went. He recognised the bishop-like headdress of his son-in-law Kevin, leading the column of chanting figures.

"Dawn's is only a few minutes away," Jim heard Mostin mutter.

"I'll be damn glad to see daylight on this night, I was shit-scared in that bloody crypt, that groaning and screaming. If I hadn't heard it myself I would have considered anybody a raving nutter."

"Did you see the light Bobby?" he asked, longing for a drink. His mouth felt like old leather. "Or the skeleton?"

"Leave it Dad, you were upset, it'll be OK shortly."

"But… but it was awful, a skeleton was in that stone coffin, sucking me into it," Jim wanted Bobby to believe what he'd seen.

"Save it for later Dad, you're OK now. It must have been a dreadful experience, we all believe we see things under duress."

"But I did see it, all lit up, the skull, hands, chest, fingers, the walls pulsing like a heart beating."

Jim was aware that Mostin was staring at him strangely.

"Alright Dad, later you can tell us," Bobby was trying to soothe him.

Betty came rushing up to him as they reached the Hump. The circle of cloaked Wizards chanting as they encompassed the mound was louder now.

"You alright Jimbo?" Betty was anxious.

"He's okay Mumsy, he was in the crypt, had a bit of an experience, he'll tell us about it later, when things calm down."

"Those Anglia people drove past us, didn't stop," said Betty, "I don't know whether they'll be able to get out onto the road with that bus stuck in the grid."

"I'll be getting back to my men, if that's OK by you Jimbo? I have had a gutful of paranormal experiences for one lifetime. You going to be OK now?"

"Certain, thanks for your help earlier. Don't know what we'd have done about those travellers if you hadn't come along with your men."

Mostin departed. Tracy and Laura were observing the Wizards.

Laura came up to Jim, "You OK Grandad?"

"Fine love," Jim assured her. The sight of youth and health was restorative.

"Dawn's only minutes away," said Betty, trying to see her watch.

"Have you seen Fanny and her dog?" asked Jim.

"I'm here Mr Lewin."

They all turned. Fanny and the wolfhound were standing a few yards away, staring at the Wizard procession.

"Have you recovered from your experience in the crypt?" asked Fanny.

"How did you…?" began Jim.

"Two hundred years ago tonight," intoned Fanny, "June 21st 1796, since the church was founded. The spirits want to be released."

Bobby was trying hard to wipe the grin from his face, "It's 1995, only 199 years, Miss Legge," he said, "How do you make it two hundred?"

"Terrestrial years, Mr Lewin," said Fanny. "In a few moments I shall be gone, joining my forebears, the instant the sun rises over the marsh. My journey will be ended."

"But you haven't any forbears, Miss Legge, we checked," said Bobby, brashly. "No mention of any Legges before 1796 or after. You are the only one. You don't exist on the electoral rolls or in any of the old records, parish or official."

"Terrestrial ancestors Mr Lewin, you are correct."

"Are you telling us that you are an alien, from another world?" Bobby was scornful.

"You are all aliens on this world Mr Lewin. We colonised this planet aeons ago. One of our exploration vessells became lost due to navigational breakdown. They were here for several of your years."

"Oh come on Miss Legge, we all know about sciencce fiction," said

Bobby.

"Up to you of course Mr Lewin, you may believe what you wish. Who do you think created the ley lines? Even your technology couldn't cope with engineering on that scale. You have some primitive space vehicles after fifty centuries of development. It's going to take you a lot longer before you free yourselves of this yoke restricting you to this speck of dust in what you term the cosmos, on the assumption you don't commit mass suicide by foolish overpopulation."

"You serious?" scoffed Bobby, "You expect us to swallow all this sci-fi nonsense?"

Fanny shook her head, "I expect very little from near primitives. From what I have observed over the past two centuries, we made a grave error in allowing you complete freedom to develope unchecked. You have polluted, destroyed, ruined what was once a pristine planetary system, due to incredible acts of folly. I shall reccomend that we terminate all responsibilty for this colony, allow it to wither. It is close to becoming utterly unviable as an experiment. It has gone badly wrong."

"This is a joke, isn't it? Even Wells in his most fevered ramblings never implied that kind of scenario, van Voigt, Alldiss and all the others, they all have Earth as the starting point, the home base."

"That is why you will never be free. You will be incarcerated in your tiny prison until you suffocate and perish in your own excreta. There have been some amongst you who have seen the way ahead clearly, but your religious myths and social shibboleths will be your ruin. Humanity has become verminous. You have succeeded in destroying all the original life on this tiny planet. Retribution is now but a few years away.

"She thinks she's God," Bobby scoffed.

"I want to hear what she has to say Bobby," said Betty.

"Surely you aren't going to swallow all this sci-fi crap Mumsy?"

"You dismiss it Bobby, you aren't very imaginative, too pragmatic."

Jim was still vividly recalling the events in the crypt. Nothing Fanny had said up to now disposessed any of the nightmare.

"Why do you suppose your... er Council has no record of my ancestry, Mr Lewin? Why am I not paying the dues you and all you other terrestrial beings surrender to spurious self-imposed authority?"

"They'll catch up with you sooner or later."

"I'd like to demonstrate the fallaciousness of that viewpoint Mr Lewin.

It might convince you that my story has some truthful base?"

"At least I won't need to disabuse my guillible parents that all this paranormal activity is just pure imagination inflamed by stress. Be my guest, Miss Legge."

"That primitive electro contraption in your hand Mr Lewin, Strike me with it."

"I might be a primitive, Miss Legge, but I'm not vicious."

"I assure you it won't have the effect you believe it will have, Mr Lewin. Darren will not intervene in any way, I promise you. Come on, Allow your primitive savagery free rein for a few seconds. Or is it you have not the strength of your convictions?"

"On your head be it madame." Bobby strode forward, the heavy torch raised to strike.

"Bobby," cried Betty, "You mustn't."

He ignored her and jabbed at Fanny as he would prod a wall. Jim couldn't believe what he saw, Betty and the others gasped. The torch went through Fanny Legge as if she wasn't there.

"Try again, Mr Lewin?" mocked Fanny, "That was pathetic. Muster up some of your base savagery."

"No Bobby, you mustn't," Betty cried.

Bobby, nonplussed by the prod, raised the torch and struck Fanny on her head.

It met no resistance, describing a parabola until he struck his own leg. He recoiled in horror and amazement, massaging his bruised knee. Then he went berserk, lashing out with uninhibited violence. It had no effect, other than slicing through the entity that was Fanny Legge with no result, other than an expenditure of useless energy. She remained standing, smiling, observing his demonstration unflinching.

"You're a ghost," he gasped.

"No Mr Lewin, I am merely what you would describe as an holistic emanation of what you want to see, a medaeival witch, I believe your description would be. Weaving spells and potions, cacklking over a cauldron of unspeakable horrors. Sadly, I am not one of those benighted creatures."

"But… but how..?" cried Betty.

"My time here is up, I have now to report what I have found on this remote planet. The Council, I suppose you'd call it, our controlling body, will then have to decide whether it is worthwhile allowing this cruel experiment to continue with all its disgusting facets, or terminate it before irreparable damage is inflicted on this system as a result of crude attempts at space flight. We have monitored those clumsy, ill-designed space vehicles you have despatched to various destinations in your own system. Polloution of this kind cannot be tolerated. Your own tiny planet is littered with defunct hardware of other rough attempts at space travel, making it hazardous for visiting observers to navigate through this litterbin of metal."

"Hang about Miss Legge, let me understand what you are telling us. Our crude brains permit only limited grasp of startling events. You're suggesting you come from somewhere beyond our Solar System, an explorer in disguise to examine what you call an experiment instituted by some other agency beyond our star some time in the past?"

****

52.

Wednesday June 21st 1995.
The Hump, Lewin's Farm, Babingley Marsh,
King's Lynn, Norfolk.

Fanny smiled, "Correct Mrs Lewin, I come from a planetary system in what you have called the Constellation of Andromeda. Without being patronising, we started this experiment some ten millenia ago, with some very basic life forms, to see how they would prosper in this environment. Many were disastrous failures, unable to cope with the vagaries of climate and conditions, the first serious efforts were what you call dinosaurs."

"See what I mean?" cried Bobby, "This is just an elaborate hoax. Someone somewhere is manipulating this image. Dinosaurs existed millions of years ago. You're fabricating all these fairy tales, Andromeda, space flight, experiments. You'll be telling us next you arrived on a flying saucer."

"We have an elaborate system of observation platforms that circle this planet from time to time. You call them flying saucers, at least some of your more astute fellow humans call them by that name, dismissed as fantasies by your orthodox establishment, cranks, nutters, madmen. We try to be discreet so as not to alarm your basic concepts of what is feasible, scientifically. They've been visiting this system for more than twenty thousand of your years to monitor the experimental life forms."

"You'll be telling us that we are just another experiment set up by this Council of yours next," jeered Bobby.

"That is true Mr Lewin. As I said earlier, it has gone badly wrong. It is now but a disgusting mess of creatures devouring other creatures, depositing unmanageable amounts of excreta on the environment, pollouting everything, making it impossible for other life forms to prosper. You are like a plague swamping everything, destroying, killing. It is a ghastly mess. I am positive the Council will decide that it has gone far enough and should be aborted before you damage other experiments being conducted on other planets in this system by crude interference."

"You're going to kill us all off?" mocked Bobby, "Send a bomb to wreck Earth?"

"That won't be necessary Mr Lewin, your own inability to control the homanid population growth will take care of that conundrum for us. It is a pity, for this was such a fair example of planetary development, one that could have provided an idyllic living space if the population could have been self-regulated with strict rules governing spawning. We didn't endow you with the specific intellectual ruthlessness to enable that to happen. Who you term your liberals, do-gooders and opponents of control will ensure your own early termination. I, and my colleagues, I think you'd call us, will reccomend we withdraw from this ugly mess, allow it to wither under its own volition. The power system, what you call ley lines, will remain intact. It will only need some basic restoration work on the central generator, and some minimal work on the circuitry, to restore things as they were when we commenced the experiment."

"Atomic power, I suppose you mean?"

"That was your most revolting experiment in energy creation. If your population problems did not solve the decision-making for ourselves, then this dreadful leap into ignorance and cruelty will confirm it inexorably. You have already amassed an unmanageable mess of pollutants that we shall have to dispose of in the future. Persistence in this field of science will ultimately result in total extinction of humanity, without mountains of your own excreta solving the problem for us. It is incredibly sad. We have watched the antics of crude homanid life forms on other planets, but have yet to witness such wanton disregard for basic self-preservation."

"Where is this central generator then madame?"

"What you call the Great Pyramid of Gizeh. You humans have nearly ruined its capacity for re-generative power, by stripping away its protective insulation, what you call marble, to build those minescule temples to vanity."

"The Pryamids were built by the Ancient Egyptians as tombs for the Pharoahs madame, which if nothing else, exposes your hoax. Powerhouse indeed."

"Your son is just another example of misguided intellectual aberration Mrs Lewin, a misfit of which there are multitudes upon this planet."

"Watch it madame, you might be a hologram but you can still be destroyed."

"Luckily for me Mr Lewin, you haven't that capability, and your basic inability to come to terms with unlikely concepts is another unattractive example of how our experiment has gone wrong."

"The Pyramid a powerhouse, tell us another tale Miss Legge. When is your personal flying saucer due to arrive?"

"Don't you think it would be wise to listen Bobby?" said Betty, mildly.

"Mumsy, this is all a big con. Ley lines, Pyramids, flying saucers, experiments, Andromeda, doesn't even sound convincing. It is all a load of cobblers."

"I cured your head wound for you Mr Lewin. I used my powers on your Mother, on Wally Thompson, Mr Mostin, Mr Murphy and on your Father's back. Do you deny that? You tried striking me, and that failed to produce the result you believed. Your scepticism is profound, amounting to ignorance. As soon as the star you call the sun comes over the horizon, you will have all your worst nightmares realized, I promise you."

"Can you elaborate Miss Legge?" Betty interjected before Bobby could say anything.

"What you call 'The Solstice' is the moment when energy flows most actively along the ley lines, it is a re-generative force. In earlier centuries of terrestrial time, when the Great Pyramid was operating fully, these forces of renewal enabled the land to become more productive, enriching the soil. The areas you now call deserts were only created as a result of the wanton destruction of the Pyramid. Bereft of the central power source, the various arteries tended to wither, become less effective. The time-span you know as spring will eventually disappear due to the ruthless exploitation of this planet. It is becoming less effective every century as the circuitry you call ley lines are obliterated by de-forestation and development, mining and road building. The time is not far distant when this time period you know as spring will not arrive. The oxygen created by the plant life will be drastically reduced and will ultimately fail. I hardly need elaborate the result of that disaster. It is a very tenous and delicate envelope surrounding this planet. You have already made deep inroads into its capacity for re-generation by destruction of the ley system, de-forestation, pollution of the oceans destroying the phyto-plankton that create seven tenths of the oxygen needed for the spawning mass of homanid life forms. Need I go further?"

"And what's is the catalyctic event due to take place when the sun rises?" Bobby could not keep the scorn from his voice.

"In a few moments Mr Lewin, you will witness the event. Your sister, her husband and those others presently celebrating the solstice on the

Hump are nearest to understanding the portent of midsummer, primitive and misguided though their activities may be. Your ancestors, the Druids and other early people, understood the importance of the solstice, erecting the diffusing centres you know as Stonehenge, Glastonbury, Woodhenge and other stone circles all over the planet. These, what you would term substations, enabled the energy to multiply at the time of the Solstice, enriching the spring and renewal of the earth."

The grey of dawn was apparent now. The shape of plants, trees and buildings on the Slade Estate were visible. They all felt it, each with a differing response. A feeling of well-being, almost intoxication as the dawn broke more fully. Betty felt a sense of euphoria, every moleulce in her body seemed to be imbued with new life, dancing with effervescent energy. The edge of the sun's disk pierced the sea over the marsh. A shaft of intense lights prang from the tower of the old church. The brightness forced everybody too turn away. The Hump was enveloped in a dazzling aura of dancing effulgence that shimmered and boiled in a circular area of energy. The Wizards were bathed in the light, every person becoming a vivid torch of light, haloed by the vigour of the force that swept from the sun's rays as the star rose over the horizons rim. Jim saw it first, like a shooting star that merged with the sun, separated until a mass of light hovered over the Hump in a ball of fearsome energy.

"Farewell everybody."

They all turned on hearing Fanny's voice, clear and sharp over the vibrant hum emanating from the incandescent shape hovering over the Hump. The entity they had come to know as Fanny Legge dissolved in front of them, fading rapidly until a mere outline remained. And finally, this shape vanished. They saw the dog shape also gradually fade, until a mere outline remained, until this also evaporated. The shaft of energy suddenly vanished, the ball of what seemed to be fire hovering over the Hump, moved slowly, gathering speed rapidly, until only a blur of light could be seen in the distant sky.

Jim came back to awareness of himself and his companions with a jerk. There was no Fanny, no dog or energy shafts. The Hump appeared as it always had been. The church was sharply outlined against the rays of the sun. Everything was normal again, save for the feeling that they had witnessed something singularly unique. Something never to be seen again.

****

53.

December 24th 1996.

The whole family were gathered in the lounge of the farmhouse on Christmas Eve.

"Seems strange knowing that Funny Fanny is not around anymore, doesn't it?" said Jim, a glass of port in his hand, his back to the log fire in the vast hearth.

"Mass hypnosis," said Bobby, a paper hat on his head, "No other explanation."

"Funny that nothing has happened in the crypt lately. The restoration work will be finished in the spring. No noise, no chill, no groans, no electric shocks," said Jim

"And you can travel over the Hump without machinery stopping dead," said Kevin.

"All in the skull," said Bobby, "We imagined it all."

"Difficult to imagine all that that happened," said Betty, a plastic apron around her waist. "Wally Thompson is still around, looking healthier than he did two years ago. Billy Watson, your father's back, Troy's hepatitis. We can't deny that, and all that isn't inside our skull's Bobby."

"Well, we can say that that was the end of an era," said Pamela.

"We couldn't believe all those stories of healing, of flying saucers and noises from the crypt down at the church. They're just flights of fancy, if you ask me."

"How do you account for the fact that Fanny's cottage is not there any more? No animals, no spider, no cats, geese, ducks, nothing, just pristine marsh, Pamela? Just as if nothing had been there in the first place. No hay needed, I had to bring the normal load back. I thought I'd got lost as first, her place was always hard to find.I walked the length of Gatehouse Lane thinking I'd overshot, but there was nothing."

Pamela shrugged, sipping her Baccardi, looking slightly uneasy.

"Well, she isn't around any more and we all saw that flying saucer arrive and she disappeared before our eyes," said Laura. "I think it's all very sad. I liked her, if you could call an insubstantial being a her. When you hit her with that torch Daddy, I thought you were going to be charged with murder. I couldn't believe it went right through empty air. That wasn't mass hypnosis, we all saw it happen."

"I met the Bishop in Lynn last week. He's withdrawing his injunction about the Wizards holding the Solstice at Bawsey next summer," said Ellen. "He's been converted on the road to Damascus, seen the light, the error of his ways. He looked almost human as well, he's lost a lot of weight. Must be down to Fanny."

"Well, let's have a toast to 1997. The Bishop and Charlie Gates will be pleased when the church is re-consecrated and he holds his first service in there for nearly eighty years."

Jim held his glass up. "Everythhing's prospering, the golf, the stables, the farm, and the new road down to the church will soon be full of traffic. The holy going to receive absoloution from sin. It'll be exciting. Even Lilly says she'll attend instead of St Margaret's. You have to admit that's a turn-up for the book."

"You've gained a lot of money from members of the PNS coming to see the crypt where all the strange events occurred," said Troy, "That was a shrewd move Betty. Five pounds a vehicle and a two pound entrance fee."

"The East Anglian Bus Company isn't doing too badly since you took over Lang's, Troy," said Jim, "You aren't as big as Stagecoach yet, but soon will be when you take over the Midlands Group."

Troy nodded, "Very satisfactory arrangement, Moss Vallour is a member of the PNRS. Helped after that Dickie Richardson came here a couple of years ago. The Secretary of the PNS, John Howards is Personnel Director of Midlands, they all know one another."

"Small world," said Pamela, helping herself to another Baccardi.

"You can all enjoy Christmas in the Priory next year. Our renovation work is just about complete. We'll be moving in at the end of March. No ghosts there thank goodness. I like that man Richardson, but wouldn't enjoy his society trampling all over the place looking for ghosts."

"Well, Merry Christmas everyone," said Jim, raising a glass, "Let's hope that Fanny's prophecies never come to pass."

****

****

**

THE END.